THE EVERYMAN
LIBRARY

*The Everyman Library was founded by J. M. Dent
in 1906. He chose the name Everyman because he wanted
to make available the best books ever written in every
field to the greatest number of people at the cheapest possible
price. He began with Boswell's 'Life of Johnson';
his one-thousandth title was Aristotle's 'Metaphysics',
by which time sales exceeded forty million.*

*Today Everyman paperbacks remain true to
J. M. Dent's aims and high standards, with a wide range
of titles at affordable prices in editions which address
the needs of today's readers. Each new text is reset to give
a clear, elegant page and to incorporate the latest thinking
and scholarship. Each book carries the pilgrim logo,
the character in 'Everyman', a medieval mystery play,
a proud link between Everyman
past and present.*

L. P. Hartley

NIGHT FEARS AND OTHER SUPERNATURAL TALES

Introduction by
SIR PETER QUENNELL

EVERYMAN
J. M. DENT · LONDON
CHARLES E. TUTTLE
VERMONT

First published in Great Britain 1951
First published as an Everyman Classic 1984
as *The Travelling Grave*
Reissued and updated 1993

© The Executors of the Estate of the late L. P. Hartley
Introduction © J. M. Dent & Sons Ltd, 1984

All rights reserved

J. M. Dent
Orion Publishing Group
Orion House, 5 Upper St Martin's Lane,
London WC2H 9EA
and
Charles E. Tuttle Co. Inc.
28 South Main Street,
Rutland, Vermont 05701, USA

Photoset in Sabon by Deltatype Ltd, Ellesmere Port, Cheshire
Printed in Great Britain by
The Guernsey Press Co. Ltd, Guernsey, C.I.

This book if bound as a paperback is subject to the condition
that it may not be issued on loan or otherwise except in its
original binding.

British Library Cataloguing-in-Publication Data is available
upon request.

ISBN 0 460 87360 1

CONTENTS

Note on the Author and Editor vii
Introduction ix

A Visitor from Down Under 3
Podolo 19
Three, or Four, for Dinner 28
The Travelling Grave 44
Feet Foremost 64
The Cotillon 94
A Change of Ownership 112
The Thought 125
Conrad and the Dragon 137
The Island 162
Night Fears 176
The Killing Bottle 182

NOTE ON THE AUTHOR AND EDITOR

LESLIE POLES HARTLEY was born on 30 December 1895 in Whittlesea, near Peterborough, the son of a solicitor. He was educated at Harrow and Balliol College, Oxford and served as an officer in the First World War. After the war he spent part of each year in Venice, until the outbreak of the Second World War in 1939. He reviewed extensively for a wide variety of journals – *Saturday Review*, the *Observer*, *Time and Tide* – in the twenties and thirties, and was first published as a writer of stories, with *Night Fears* in 1925. This was followed by the novella *Simonetta Perkins* (1925) and a second volume of stories, *The Killing Bottle*, in 1932. *Simonetta Perkins* was received as 'Jamesian' in tone, but this, together with the macabre stories, hardly hinted at what was to follow.

In 1944, at the age of forty-eight, Hartley published a novel, *The Shrimp and the Anemone*, the first part of a trilogy hailed as 'one of the finest and most accurate evocations of boyhood and young manhood in our fiction' (*The Times*) – *Sixth Heaven* in 1946 and *Eustace and Hilda* in 1947 completed the series. Thereafter Hartley wrote and published with remarkable regularity until his death in 1972. *The Boat* (1951) was acclaimed as a major achievement, but has long been eclipsed by his finest novel *The Go-Between* (1953), a powerful story of a young boy's emotional and sexual life warped by premature involvement in the secret affair of an Edwardian lady with a Norfolk farmer. Following these successes Hartley was awarded the C.B.E. in 1955. But it was the Joseph Losey/Harold Pinter film of the *The Go-Between* in 1970, closely followed by a film of *The Hireling* (1957), that rescued Hartley from the obscurity that might otherwise have followed upon his death. These novels and the trilogy have stayed in print and more than twenty years later form the body of work upon which his reputation rests. The critical 'norm' has been that Hartley's range was 'narrow', that his experiments away from the subtleties of Jamesian fiction – for example his venture into the territory of *Brave New World* with *Facial Justice* (1960) – were unfortunate lapses. Yet it is undeniable that Hartley's skill at the grisly short story in volumes such as this one has long won him a following.

SIR PETER QUENNELL was educated at Balliol College, Oxford and became editor of *History To-Day* (1951–79) and *The Cornhill Magazine* (1944–51) as well as the author of numerous books including *Shakespeare: the poet and his background*, (1964); *Romantic England* (1970); and *A History of English Literature*, (1973). He received the C.B.E. in 1973 and was knighted in 1992.

INTRODUCTION

Not far from Stratford-upon-Avon lies a quiet Warwickshire village that, even thirty years ago, was still notorious as a centre of the witch-cult – and the scene of at least two ritual murders, the victim in each case having been skewered with a pitch-fork to the earth. But I have always doubted if Shakespeare himself, despite his affection for the legends of his own country, was a strong believer in the supernatural. The ghost of Hamlet's father is a majestic rather than a horrific apparition; and by the time he has delivered over sixty lines of blank verse, he ceases to alarm the audience; while Macbeth's witches, compounding their nasty potion, whatever ingenious devices a producer may employ, have at times a slightly comic air. They were inserted, one cannot help suspecting, to attract the attention of the new king, James I, who was deeply interested in the Black Arts and had already, as Shakespeare, of course, knew, published a learned book on demonology.

Yet, at every period, nearly every good writer's imagination has had a certain superstitious edge – a sense of fear, a feeling of the essential strangeness of life, a glimpse of the darkened realms of the mind into which reason fails to penetrate. There have been periods of literary history, indeed, when the ability to arouse such feelings was regarded as a virtue. The 'Gothick Novel', launched in 1764 by Horace Walpole, whose *Castle of Otranto* was derived, he said, from his recollections of a particularly terrifying dream, and triumphantly carried on towards the end of the century by Anne Radcliffe's bestselling *Mysteries of Udolpho*, excited a nationwide cult of the mysterious and the 'horrid'. Readers of *Northanger Abbey* will recall the impassioned dialogue of Catherine and Isabella about the new books a young girl, a keen frequenter of the local circulating library, is most likely to admire. 'Are they all horrid? Are you sure they are all horrid?' Catherine eagerly demands.

Today, the supernatural, though not completely banished from literature, is represented by the imaginative novelist in a somewhat subtler form; and among those who have treated it with the greatest skill was the author of 'The Travelling Grave'. His fourfold novel, *Eustace and Hilda*, notwithstanding its realistic background, has itself a ghostly central theme. Eustace, its hero, a nervous, self-effacing, hypersensitive youth, spends his whole existence rather uneasily poised between the actual world and the world of dreams and visions, between the demands of the present and the obsessions of the past. Behind what he sees rises the ghost of what he remembers; and often they are difficult to disengage. Here, for example, in the final section of the book, he is contemplating the familiar landscape of an English seaside town:

> Sliding back into his former self was a sensation as grateful as putting on an old suit of clothes . . . It seemed to him that the slate pinnacles of Palmerston Parade now climbed into the sky with something of their ancient majesty, and there was mystery again among the black-boughed laburnums and wind-shredded lilacs . . . He felt the old contraction of the heart that the strangeness in the outward form of things once gave him; the tingling sense of fear, the nimbus of danger surrounding the unknown which had harassed his imagination but enriched his life . . .

At an earlier stage of the narrative, however, Eustace's fears have reached a traumatic crisis when he meets a real ghost – in as much as any ghost can be called 'real' – amid the rubbish and tangled foliage of a derelict Venetian garden. This is the black-shawled *'larva'* known to haunt the ancient palazzo where he has passed a carefree holiday, and from which he has just been recalled by the news that his beloved elder sister Hilda, whose devotion has obsessed him since childhood, protecting yet also crippling and thwarting him, has suffered a paralytic stroke and is now dangerously ill.

This episode, which follows a vivid description of the scenic splendours of Venice and of the picturesque gaiety of its citizens, strikes an especially affective note – the note of impending doom and irretrievable disaster that runs through so many of L. P. Hartley's stories. I had the privilege of knowing him, and it would never have occurred to me at a first glance that his was a gloomy, apprehensive spirit. He had a rounded, well-balanced look, usually a gentle smile, a broad, lofty forehead and a small moustache. He was unmarried; and, according to a dictionary of modern authors, 'his private life, at least as far as the public knows, was almost entirely absorbed by his literary life'. Certainly he worked hard. His *Eustace and Hilda* series was concluded in 1947, twenty years after he had begun writing fiction. But I cannot believe that, meanwhile, his personal existence had been completely untroubled. 'Imaginative literature', he once agreed, when he was kind enough to congratulate me on the publication of a new book, 'takes its raw material from private life'; and I feel sure he must have very often drawn his themes from his own experiences. Henry James was a master he always revered; and, like James, he was frequently possessed by ideas of guilt and solitude and evil. As a contemporary reviewer remarked, beneath a surface that seems 'almost over-civilized' a 'hollow of horror' sometimes lay hidden.

Both aspects of his talent are fully illustrated by the tales collected here. Not only does he portray the exterior of social life with a novelist's sharp eye for detail; but he also explores the underworld of fears and fantasies through which we wander in our ugliest dreams. It is the combination of these two aspects that gives his stories their strength and their peculiar diversity. Subjects range from human crimes to supernatural visitations, or to any event that shakes our reliance on the explicability of an inexplicable universe. L. P. Hartley was a highly skilled narrator; and all his tales are admirably told. What is more, to answer Catherine Morland's question, almost all are eminently 'horrid'.

SIR PETER QUENNELL

NIGHT FEARS
AND OTHER SUPERNATURAL TALES

A VISITOR FROM DOWN UNDER

'And who will you send to fetch him away?'

After a promising start, the March day had ended in a wet evening. It was hard to tell whether rain or fog predominated. The loquacious bus conductor said, 'A foggy evening', to those who rode inside, and 'A wet evening', to such as were obliged to ride outside. But in or on the buses, cheerfulness held the field, for their patrons, inured to discomfort, made light of climatic inclemency. All the same, the weather was worth remarking on: the most scrupulous conversationalist could refer to it without feeling self convicted of banality. How much more the conductor who, in common with most of his kind, had a considerable conversational gift.

The bus was making its last journey through the heart of London before turning in for the night. Inside it was only half full. Outside, as the conductor was aware by virtue of his sixth sense, there still remained a passenger too hardy or too lazy to seek shelter. And now, as the bus rattled rapidly down the Strand, the footsteps of this person could be heard shuffling and creaking upon the metal shod steps.

'Anyone on top?' asked the conductor, addressing an errant umbrella-point and the hem of a mackintosh.

'I didn't notice anyone,' the man replied.

'It's not that I don't trust you,' remarked the conductor pleasantly, giving a hand to his alighting fare, 'but I think I'll go up and make sure.'

Moments like these, moments of mistrust in the infallibility of his observation, occasionally visited the conductor. They came at the end of a tiring day, and if he could he withstood them. They were signs of weakness, he thought; and to give way to them matter for self-reproach. 'Going barmy, that's what you are,' he told himself, and he casually took a fare inside to prevent his mind dwelling on the unvisited outside. But his unreasoning disquietude survived this distraction, and murmuring against himself he started to climb the steps.

To his surprise, almost stupefaction, he found that his misgivings were justified. Breasting the ascent, he saw a passenger sitting on the right-hand front seat; and the passenger, in spite of his hat turned down, his collar turned up, and the creased white muffler that showed between the two, must have heard him coming; for though the man was looking straight ahead, in his outstretched left hand, wedged between the first and second fingers, he held a coin.

'Jolly evening, don't you think?' asked the conductor, who wanted to say something. The passenger made no reply, but the penny, for such it was, slipped the fraction of an inch lower in the groove between the pale freckled fingers.

'I said it was a damn wet night,' the conductor persisted irritably, annoyed by the man's reserve.

Still no reply.

'Where you for?' asked the conductor, in a tone suggesting that wherever it was, it must be a discreditable destination.

'Carrick Street.'

'Where?' the conductor demanded. He had heard all right, but a slight peculiarity in the passenger's pronunciation made it appear reasonable to him, and possibly humiliating to the passenger, that he should not have heard.

'Carrick Street.'

'Then why don't you say Carrick Street?' the conductor grumbled as he punched the ticket.

There was a moment's pause, then:

'Carrick Street,' the passenger repeated.

'Yes, I know, I know, you needn't go on telling me,' fumed the conductor, fumbling with the passenger's penny. He couldn't get hold of it from above; it had slipped too far, so he passed his hand underneath the other's and drew the coin from between his fingers.

It was cold, even where it had been held. 'Know?' said the stranger suddenly. 'What do you know?'

The conductor was trying to draw his fare's attention to the ticket, but could not make him look round.

'I suppose I know you are a clever chap,' he remarked. 'Look here, now. Where do you want this ticket? In your button-hole?'

'Put it here,' said the passenger.

'Where?' asked the conductor. 'You aren't a blooming letter-rack.'

'Where the penny was,' replied the passenger. 'Between my fingers.'

The conductor, reluctant, he did not know why, to oblige the passenger, the rigidity of the hand disconcerted him: it was stiff, hard and perhaps paralysed. And since he had been standing on top his own hands were none too warm. The ticket doubled up and grew limp under his repeated efforts to push it in. He bent lower, for he was a good-hearted fellow, and using both hands, one above and one below, he slid the ticket into its bony slot.

'Right you are, Kaiser Bill.'

Perhaps the passenger resented this jocular allusion to his physical infirmity; perhaps he merely wanted to be quiet. All he said was:

'Don't speak to me again.'

'Speak to you!' shouted the conductor, losing all self-control. 'Catch me speaking to a stuffed dummy!'

Muttering to himself he withdrew into the bowels of the bus.

At the corner of Carrick Street quite a number of people got on board. All wanted to be first, but pride of place was shared by three women who all tried to enter simultaneously. The conductor's voice made itself audible over the din: 'Now then, now then, look where you're shoving! This isn't a bargain sale. Gently, *please*, lady; he's only a poor old man.' In a moment or two the confusion abated, and the conductor, his hand on the cord of the bell, bethought himself of the passenger on top whose destination Carrick Street was. He had forgotten to get down. Yielding to his good nature, for the conductor was averse from further conversation with his uncommunicative fare, he mounted the steps, put his head over the top and shouted 'Carrick Street! Carrick Street!' That was the utmost he could bring himself to do. But his admonition was without effect; his summons remained unanswered; nobody came. 'Well, if he wants to stay up there he can,' muttered the conductor, still aggrieved. 'I won't fetch him down, cripple or no cripple.' The bus moved on. He slipped by me, thought the conductor, while all that Cup-tie crowd was getting in.

The same evening, some five hours earlier, a taxi turned into

Carrick Street and pulled up at the door of a small hotel. The street was empty. It looked like a cul-de-sac, but in reality it was pierced at the far end by an alley, like a thin sleeve, which wound its way into Soho.

'That the last, sir?' inquired the driver, after several transits between the cab and the hotel.

'How many does that make?'

'Nine packages in all, sir.'

'Could you get all your worldly goods into nine packages, driver?'

'That I could; into two.'

'Well, have a look inside and see if I have left anything.' The cabman felt about among the cushions. 'Can't find nothing sir.'

'What do you do with anything you find?' asked the stranger.

'Take it to New Scotland Yard, sir,' the driver promptly answered.

'Scotland Yard?' said the stranger. 'Strike a match, will you, and let me have a look.'

But he, too, found nothing, and reassured, followed his luggage into the hotel.

A chorus of welcome and congratulation greeted him. The manager, the manager's wife, the Ministers without portfolio of whom all hotels are full, the porters, the lift-man, all clustered around him.

'Well, Mr Rumbold, after all these years! We thought you'd forgotten us! And wasn't it odd, the very night your telegram came from Australia we'd been talking about you! And my husband said, "Don't you worry abour Mr Rumbold. He'll fall on his feet all right. Some fine day he'll walk in here a rich man." Not that you weren't always well off, but my husband meant a millionaire.'

'He was quite right,' said Mr Rumbold slowly, savouring his words. 'I am.'

'There, what did I tell you?' the manager exclaimed, as though one recital of his prophecy was not enough. 'But I wonder you're not too grand to come to Rossall's Hotel.'

'I've nowhere else to go,' said the millionaire shortly. 'And if I had, I wouldn't. This place is like home to me.'

His eyes softened as they scanned the familiar surroundings. They were light grey eyes, very pale, and seeming paler from their setting in his tanned face. His cheeks were slightly sunken and very deeply lined; his blunt-ended nose was straight. He had a thin, straggling moustache, straw-coloured which made his age difficult to guess. Perhaps he was nearly fifty, so wasted was the skin on his neck, but his movements, unexpectedly agile and decided, were those of a younger man.

'I won't go up to my room now,' he said, in response to the manageress's question. 'Ask Clutsam – he's still with you? – good – to unpack my things. He'll find all I want for the night in the green suitcase. I'll take my despatch-box with me. And tell them to bring me a sherry and bitters in the lounge.'

As the crow flies it was not far to the lounge. But by the way of the tortuous, ill-lit passages, doubling on themselves, yawning with dark entries, plunging into kitchen stairs – the catacombs so dear to *habitués* of Rossall's Hotel – it was a considerable distance. Anyone posted in the shadows of these alcoves, or arriving at the head of the basement staircase, could not have failed to notice the air of utter content which marked Mr Rumbold's leisurely progress: the droop of his shoulders, acquiescing in weariness; the hands turned inwards and swaying slightly, but quite forgotten by their owner; the chin, always prominent, now pushed forward so far that it looked relaxed and helpless, not at all defiant. The unseen witness would have envied Mr Rumbold, perhaps even grudged him his holiday air, his untroubled acceptance of the present and the future.

A waiter whose face he did not remember brought him the *apéritif,* which he drank slowly, his feet propped unconventionally upon a ledge of the chimneypiece; a pardonable relaxation, for the room was empty. Judge therefore of his surprise when, out of a fire-engendered drowsiness, he heard a voice which seemed to come from the wall above his head. A cultivated voice, perhaps too cultivated, slightly husky, yet careful and precise in its enunciation. Even while his eyes searched the room to make sure that no one had come in, he could not help hearing everything the voice said. It seemed to be talking to him, and yet the rather oracular utterance implied a less restricted audience. It was the utterance of a man who was aware that, though it was a duty for him to speak, for Mr Rumbold to listen would be both a pleasure and a profit.

'... A Children's Party,' the voice announced in an even, neutral tone, nicely balanced between approval and distaste, between enthusiasm and boredom; 'six little girls and six little' (a faint lift in the voice, expressive of tolerant surprise) 'boys. The Broadcasting Company has invited them to tea, and they are anxious that you should share some of their fun.' (At the last word the voice became completely colourless.) 'I must tell you that they have had tea, and enjoyed it, didn't you, children?' (A cry of 'Yes', muffled and timid, greeted this leading question.) 'We should have liked you to hear our table-talk, but there wasn't much of it, we were so busy eating.' For a moment the voice indentified itself with the children. 'But we can tell you what we ate. Now, Percy, tell us what you had.'

A piping little voice recited a long list of comestibles; like the children in the treacle-well, thought Rumbold, Percy must have been, or soon would be, very ill. A few others volunteered the items of their repast. 'So you see,' said the voice, 'we have not done so badly. And now we are going to have crackers, and afterwards' (the voice hesitated and seemed to dissociate itself from the words) 'Children's Games.' There was an impressive pause, broken by the muttered exhortation of a little girl. 'Don't cry, Philip, it won't hurt you.' Fugitive sparks and snaps of sound followed; more like a fire being kindled, thought Rumbold, than crackers. A murmur of voices pierced the fusillade. 'What have you got, Alec, what have you *got*'? 'I've got a cannon.' 'Give it to me.' 'No.' 'Well, lend it to me.' 'What do you want it for?' 'I want to shoot Jimmy.'

Mr Rumbold started. Something had disturbed him. Was it imagination, or did he hear, above the confused medley of sound, a tiny click? The voice was speaking again. 'And now we're going to begin the Games.' As though to make amends for past lukewarmness a faint flush of anticipation gave colour to the decorous voice. 'We will commence with that old favourite, Ring-a-Ring of Roses.'

The children were clearly shy, and left each other to do the singing. Their courage lasted for a line or two and then gave out. But fortified by the speaker's baritone, powerful though subdued, they took heart, and soon were singing without assistance or direction. Their light wavering voices had a charming effect. Tears stood in Mr Rumbold's eyes. 'Oranges and Lemons' came next. A more difficult game, it yielded several unrehearsed effects before it finally got under way. One could almost see the children being marshalled into their places, as though for a figure in the Lancers. Some of them no doubt had wanted to play another game; children are contrary; and the dramatic side of 'Oranges and Lemons', though it appeals to many, always affrightens a few. The disinclination of these last would account for the pauses and hesitations which irritated Mr Rumbold, who, as a child, had always had a strong fancy for this particular game. When, to the tramping and stamping of many small feet, the droning chant began, he leaned back and closed his eyes in ecstasy. He listened intently for the final accelerando which leads up to the catastrophe. Still the prologue maundered on, as though the children were anxious to extend the period of security, the joyous carefree promenade which the great Bell of Bow, by his inconsiderate profession of ignorance, was so rudely to curtail. The Bells of Old Bailey pressed their usurer's question; the Bells of Shoreditch answered with becoming flippancy; the Bells of Stepney posed their ironical query, when suddenly, before the great Bell of Bow had time to get his word in, Mr Rumbold's feelings underwent a strange revolution. Why couldn't the game continue, all sweetness and sunshine? Why drag in the fatal issue? Let payment be deferred; let the bells go on chiming and never strike the hour. But heedless of Mr Rumbold's squeamishness, the game went its way.

After the eating comes the reckoning.

> Here is a candle to light you to bed,
> And here comes a chopper to chop off your head!
> Chop – chop – chop.

A child screamed, and there was silence.

Mr Rumbold felt quite upset, and great was his relief when, after a few more half-hearted rounds of 'Oranges and Lemons', the Voice announced, 'Here We Come Gathering Nuts and May'. At least there was nothing sinister in that. Delicious sylvan scene, comprising in one splendid botanical inexactitude all the charms of winter, spring, and autumn. What superiority to circumstances was implied in the conjunction of nuts and May! What defiance of cause and effect! What a testimony to coincidence! For cause and effect is against us, as witness the fate of Old Bailey's debtor; but coincidence is always on our side, teaching us how to eat our cake and have it! The long arm of coincidence! Mr Rumbold would have liked to clasp it by the hand.

Meanwhile his own hand conducted the music of the revels and his foot kept time. Their pulses quickened by enjoyment, the children put more heart into their singing; the game went with a swing; the ardour and rhythm of it invaded the little room where Mr Rumbold sat. Like heavy fumes the waves of sound poured in, so penetrating, they ravished the sense; so sweet, they intoxicated it; so light, they fanned it into a flame. Mr Rumbold was transported. His hearing, sharpened by the subjugation and quiescence of his other faculties, began to take in new sounds; the names, for instance, of the players who were 'wanted' to make up each side and of the champions who were to pull them over. For the listeners-in, the issues of the struggles remained in doubt. Did Nancy Price succeed in detaching Percy Kingham from his allegiance? Probably. Did Alex Wharton prevail against Maisie Drew? It was certainly an easy win for someone: the contest lasted only a second, and a ripple of laughter greeted it. Did Violet Kingham make good against Horace Gold? This was a dire encounter, punctuated by deep irregular panting. Mr Rumbold could see, in his mind's eye, the two champions straining backwards and forwards across the white, motionless handkerchief, their faces red and puckered with exertion. Violet or Horace, one of them had to go: Violet might be bigger than Horace, but then Horace was a boy: they were evenly matched: they had their pride to maintain. The moment when the will was broken and the body went limp in surrender would be like a moment of dissolution. Yes, even this game had its stark, uncomfortable side. Violet or Horace, one of them was smarting now: crying perhaps under the humiliation of being fetched away.

The game began afresh. This time there was an eager ring in the children's voices: two tried antagonists were going to meet: it would be a battle of giants. The chant throbbed into a way-cry.

> Who will you have for your Nuts and May,
>   Nuts and May, Nuts and May;
> Who will you have for your Nuts and May
>   On a cold and frosty morning?

They would have Victor Rumbold for Nuts and May, Victor Rumbold, Victor Rumbold: and from the vindictiveness in their voices they might have meant to have had his blood, too.

> And who will you send to fetch him away,
>   Fetch him away, fetch him away;

> Who will you send to fetch him away
> On a cold and frosty morning?

Like a clarion call, a shout of defiance, came the reply:

> We'll send Jimmy Hagberd to fetch him away,
>   Fetch him away, fetch him away;
> We'll send Jimmy Hagberd to fetch him away
>   On a wet and foggy evening.

This variation, it might be supposed, was intended to promote the contest from the realms of pretence into the world of reality. But Mr Rumbold probably did not hear that his abduction had been antedated. He had turned quite green, and his head was lolling against the back of the chair.

'Any wine, sir?'

'Yes, Clutsam, a bottle of champagne.'

'Very good, sir.'

Mr Rumbold drained the first glass at one go.

'Anyone coming in to dinner besides me, Clutsam?' he presently inquired. 'Not now, sir, it's nine o'clock,' replied the waiter, his voice edged with reproach.

'Sorry, Clutsam, I didn't feel up to the mark before dinner, so I went and lay down.'

The waiter was mollified.

'Thought you weren't looking quite yourself, sir. No bad news, I hope.'

'No, nothing. Just a bit tired after the journey.'

'And how did you leave Australia, sir?' inquired the waiter, to accommodate Mr Rumbold, who seemed anxious to talk.

'In better weather than you have here,' Mr Rumbold replied, finishing his second glass, and measuring with his eye the depleted contents of the bottle.

The rain kept up a steady patter on the glass roof of the coffee-room.

'Still, a good climate isn't everything. It isn't like home, for instance,' the waiter remarked.

'No, indeed.'

'There's many parts of the world as would be glad of a good day's rain,' affirmed the waiter.

'There certainly are,' said Mr Rumbold, who found the conversation sedative.

'Did you do much fishing when you were abroad, sir?' the waiter pursued.

'A little.'

'Well, you want rain for that,' declared the waiter, as one who scores a point. 'The fishing isn't preserved in Australia, like what it is here?'

'No.'

'Then there ain't no poaching,' concluded the waiter philosophically. 'It's every man for himself.'

'Yes, that's the rule in Australia.'

'Not much of a rule, is it?' the waiter took him up. 'Not much like law, I mean.'

'It depends what you mean by law.'

'Oh, Mr Rumbold, sir, you know very well what I mean. I mean the police. Now if you was to have done a man in out in Australia – murdered him, I mean – they'd hang you for it if they caught you, wouldn't they?'

Mr Rumbold teased the champagne with the butt-end of his fork and drank again.

'Probably they would, unless there were special circumstances.'

'In which case you might get off?'

'I might.'

'That's what I mean by law,' pronounced the waiter. 'You know what the law is: you go against it, and you're punished. Of course I don't mean you, sir; I only say "you" as – as an illustration to make my meaning clear.'

'Quite, quite.'

'Whereas if there was only what you call a rule,' the waiter pursued, deftly removing the remains of Mr Rumbold's chicken, 'it might fall to the lot of any man to round you up. Might be anybody; might be me.'

'Why should you or they,' asked Mr Rumbold, 'want to round me up? I haven't done you any harm, or them.'

'Oh, but we should have to, sir.'

'Why?'

'We couldn't rest in our beds, sir, knowing you was at large. You might do it again. Somebody'd have to see to it.'

'But supposing there was nobody?'

'Sir?'

'Supposing the murdered man hadn't any relatives or friends: supposing he just disappeared, and no one ever knew that he was dead?'

'Well, sir,' said the waiter, winking portentously, 'in that case he'd have to get on your track himself. He wouldn't rest in his grave, sir, no, not he, and knowing what he did.'

'Clutsam,' said Mr Rumbold suddenly, 'bring me another bottle of wine, and don't trouble to ice it.'

The waiter took the bottle from the table and held it to the light.

'Yes, it's dead, sir.'

'Dead?'

'Yes, sir; finished; empty; dead.'

'You're right,' Mr Rumbold agreed. 'It's quite dead.'

It was nearly eleven o'clock. Mr Rumbold again had the lounge to himself. Clutsam would be bringing his coffee presently. Too bad of Fate to have him haunted by these casual reminders; too bad, his first day at home. 'Too bad, too bad,' he muttered, while the fire warmed the soles of his slippers. But it was excellent champagne; he would take no harm from it: the brandy Clutsam was bringing him would do the rest. Clutsam was a good sort, nice old-fashioned servant ... nice old-fashioned house ... Warmed by the wine, his thoughts began to pass out of his control.

'Your coffee, sir,' said a voice at his elbow.

'Thank you, Clutsam, I'm very much obliged to you,' said Mr Rumbold, with the exaggerated civility of slight intoxication. 'You're an excellent fellow. I wish there were more like you.'

'I hope so, too, I'm sure,' said Clutsam, trying in his muddle-headed way to deal with both observations at once.

'Don't seem many people about,' Mr Rumbold remarked. 'Hotel pretty full?'

'Oh, yes, sir, all the suites are let, and the other rooms, too. We're turning people away every day. Why, only tonight a gentleman rang up. Said he would come round late, on the off-chance. But, bless me, he'll find the birds have flown.'

'Birds?' echoed Mr Rumbold.

'I mean there ain't any more rooms, not for love nor money.'

'Well, I'm sorry for him,' said Mr Rumbold, with ponderous sincerity. 'I'm sorry for any man, friend or foe, who has to go tramping about London on a night like this. If I had an extra bed in my room, I'd put it at his disposal.'

'You have, sir,' the waiter said.

'Why, of course I have. Well, well. I'm sorry for the poor chap. I'm sorry for all homeless ones, Clutsam, wandering on the face of the earth.'

'Amen to that,' said the waiter devoutly.

'And doctors and such, pulled out of their beds at midnight. It's a hard life. Ever thought about a doctor's life, Clutsam?'

'Can't say I have, sir.'

'Well, well, but it's hard; you can take that from me.'

'What time shall I call you in the morning, sir?' the waiter asked, seeing no reason why the conversation should ever stop.

'You needn't call me Clutsam,' replied Mr Rumbold, in a sing-song voice, and rushing the words together as though he were excusing the waiter from addressing him by the waiter's own name. 'I'll get up when I'm ready. And that may be pretty late, pretty late.' He smacked his lips over the words.

'Nothing like a good lie, eh, Clutsam?'

'That's right, sir, you have your sleep out,' the waiter encouraged him. 'You won't be disturbed.'

'Good-night, Clutsam. You're an excellent fellow, and I don't care who hears me say so.'

'Good-night, sir.'

Mr Rumbold returned to his chair. It lapped him round, it ministered to his comfort: he felt at one with it. At one with the fire, the clock, the tables, all the furniture. Their usefulness, their goodness, went out to meet his usefulness, his goodness, met, and were friends. Who could bind their sweet influences or restrain them in the exercise of their kind offices? No one: certainly not a shadow from the past. The room was perfectly quiet. Street sounds reached it only as a low continuous hum, infinitely reassuring. Mr Rumbold fell asleep.

He dreamed that he was a boy again, living in his old home in the country. He was possessed, in the dream, by a master-passion; he must collect firewood, whenever and wherever he saw it. He found himself one autumn afternoon in the wood-house; that was how the dream began. The door was partly open, admitting a little light, but he could not recall how he got in. The floor of the shed was littered with bits of bark and thin twigs; but, with the exception of the chopping-block which he knew could not be used, there was nowhere a log of sufficient size to make a fire. Though he did not like being in the wood-house alone he stayed long enough to make a thorough search. But he could find nothing. The compulsion he knew so well descended on him, and he left the wood-house and went into the garden. His steps took him to the foot of a high tree, standing by itself in a tangle of long grass at some distance from the house. The tree had been lopped; for half its height it had no branches, only leafy tufts, sticking out at irregular intervals. He knew what he would see when he looked up into the dark foliage. And there, sure enough, it was: a long dead bough, bare in patches where the bark had peeled off, and crooked in the middle like an elbow.

He began to climb the tree. The ascent proved easier than he expected, his body seemed no weight at all. But he was visited by a terrible oppression, which increased as he mounted. The bough did not want him; it was projecting its hostility down the trunk of the tree. And every second brought him nearer to an object which he had always dreaded; a growth, people called it. It stuck out from the trunk of the tree, a huge circular swelling thickly matted with twigs. Victor would have rather died than hit his head against it.

By the time he reached the bough twilight had deepened into night. He knew what he had to do: sit astride the bough, since there was none near by from which he could reach it, and press with his hands until it broke. Using his legs to get what purchase he could, he set his back against the tree and pushed with all his might downwards. To do this he was obliged to look beneath him, and he saw, far below him on the ground, a white sheet spread out as though to catch him; and he knew at once that it was a shroud.

Frantically he pulled and pushed at the stiff, brittle bough; a lust to break it took hold of him; leaning forward his whole length he seized the bough at the elbow joint and strained it away from him. As it cracked he toppled over and the shroud came rushing upwards . . .

Mr Rumbold waked in a cold sweat to find himself clutching the curved arm of the chair on which the waiter had set his brandy. The glass had fallen over and the spirit lay in a little pool on the leather seat. 'I can't let it go like that,' he thought. 'I must get some more.' A man he did not know answered the bell. 'Waiter,' he said, 'bring me a brandy and soda in my room in a quarter of an hour's time. Rumbold, the name is.' He followed the waiter out of the room. The passage was completely dark except for a small blue gas-jet, beneath which was huddled a cluster of candlesticks. The hotel, he remembered, maintained an old-time habit of deference towards darkness. As he held the wick to the gas-jet, he heard himself mutter, 'Here is a candle to light you to bed.' But he recollected the ominous conclusion of the distich, and fuddled though he was he left it unspoken.

Shortly after Mr Rumbold's retirement the door-bell of the hotel rang. Three sharp peals, and no pause between them. 'Someone in a hurry to get in,' the night porter grumbled to himself. 'Expect he's forgotten his key.' He made no haste to answer the summons; it would do the forgetful fellow good to wait: teach him a lesson. So dilatory was he that by the time he reached the hall door the bell was tinkling again. Irritated by such importunity, he deliberately went back to set straight a pile of newspapers before letting this impatient devil in. To mark his indifference he even kept behind the door while he opened it, so that his first sight of the visitor only took in his back; but this limited inspection sufficed to show that the man was a stranger and not a visitor at the hotel.

In the long black cape which fell almost sheer on one side, and on the other stuck out as though he had a basket under his arm, he looked like a crow with a broken wing. A bald-headed crow, thought the porter, for there's a patch of bare skin between that white linen thing and his hat.

'Good evening, sir,' he said. 'What can I do for you?'

The stranger made no answer, but glided to a side-table and began turning over some letters with his right hand.

'Are you expecting a message?' asked the porter.

'No,' the stranger replied. 'I want a room for the night.'

'Was you the gentleman who telephoned for a room this evening?'

'Yes.'

'In that case, I was to tell you we're afraid you can't have one; the hotel's booked right up.'

'Are you quite sure?' asked the stranger. 'Think again.'

'Them's my orders, sir. It don't do me no good to think.'

At this moment the porter had a curious sensation as though some important part of him, his life maybe, had gone adrift inside him and was spinning round and round. The sensation ceased when he began to speak.

'I'll call the waiter, sir,' he said.

But before he called the waiter appeared, intent on an errand of his own. 'I say, Bill,' he began, 'what's the number of Mr Rumbold's room? He wants a drink taken up, and I forgot to ask him.'

'It's thirty-three,' said the porter unsteadily. 'The double room.'

'Why, Bill, what's up?' the waiter exclaimed. 'You look as if you'd seen a ghost.'

Both men stared round the hall, and then back at each other. The room was empty.

'God!' said the porter. 'I must have had the horrors. But he was here a moment ago. Look at this.'

On the stone flags lay an icicle, an inch or two long, around which a little pool was fast collecting.

'Why, Bill,' cried the waiter, 'how did that get here? It's not freezing.'

'*He* must have brought it,' the porter said.

They looked at each other in consternation, which changed into terror as the sound of a bell made itself heard, coming from the depths of the hotel.

'Clutsam's there,' whispered the porter. 'He'll have to answer it, whoever it is.'

Clutsam had taken off his tie and was getting ready for bed. He slept in the basement. What on earth could anyone want in the smoking-room at this hour? He pulled on his coat and went upstairs.

Standing by the fire he saw the same figure whose appearance and disappearance had so disturbed the porter.

'Yes, sir?' he said.

'I want you to go to Mr Rumbold,' said the stranger, 'and ask him if he is prepared to put the other bed in his room at the disposal of a friend.'

In a few moments Clutsam returned.

'Mr Rumbold's compliments, sir, and he wants to know who it is.'

The stranger went to the table in the centre of the room. An Australian newspaper was lying there which Clutsam had not noticed before. The aspirant ot Mr Rumbold's hospitality turned over the pages. Then with his finger, which appeared even to Clutsam standing by the door unusually pointed, he cut out a rectangular slip, about the size of a visiting card, and, moving away, motioned the waiter to take it.

By the light of the gas-jet in the passage Clutsam read the clipping. It seemed to be a kind of obituary notice; but of what possible interest could it be to Mr Rumbold to know that the body of Mr James Hagberd had been discovered in circumstances which suggested that he had met his death by violence?

After a longer interval Clutsam returned, looking puzzled and a little frightened.

'Mr Rumbold's compliments, sir, but he knows no one of that name.'

'Then take this message to Mr Rumbold,' said the stranger. 'Say, "Would he rather that I went up to him, or that he came down to me?"'

For the third time Clutsam went to do the stranger's bidding. He did not, however, upon his return open the door of the smoking-room, but shouted through it:

'Mr Rumbold wishes you to Hell, sir, where you belong, and says, "Come up if you dare!"'

Then he bolted.

A minute later, from his retreat in an underground coal-cellar, he heard a shot fired. Some old instinct, danger-loving or danger-disregarding, stirred in him, and he ran up the stairs quicker than he had ever run up them in his life. In the passage he stumbled over Mr Rumbold's boots. The bedroom door was ajar. Putting his head down he rushed in. The brightly lit room was empty. But almost all the movables in it were overturned and the bed was in a frightful mess. The pillow with its five-fold perforation was the first object on which Clutsam noticed bloodstains. Thenceforward he seemed to see them everywhere. But what sickened him and kept him so long from going down to rouse the others was the sight of an icicle on the window-sill, a thin claw of ice curved like a Chinaman's nail, with a bit of flesh sticking to it.

That was the last he saw of Mr Rumbold. But a policeman patrolling Carrick Street noticed a man in a long black cape, who seemed, by the position of his arm, to be carrying something heavy. He called out to the man and ran after him; but though he did not seem to be moving very fast, the policeman could not overtake him.

PODOLO

The evening before we made the expedition to Podolo we talked it over, and I agreed there was nothing against it really.

'But why did you say you'd feel safer if Walter was going too?' Angela asked me. And Walter said, 'What good should I be? I can't help to row the gondola, you know.'

Then I felt rather silly, for everything I had said about Podolo was merely conversational exaggeration, meant to whet their curiosity, like a newspaper headline: and I knew that when Angela actually saw the dull little island, its stony and inhospitable shore littered with broken bottles and empty tins, she would think what a fool I was, with my romancing. So I took back everything I said, called my own bluff, as it were, and explained that I avoided Podolo only because of its exposed position: it was four miles from Venice, and if a boisterous bora got up (as it sometimes did, without warning) we should find getting back hard work, and might be late home. 'And what will Walter say,' I wound up, 'if he comes back from Trieste' (he was going there for the day on business) 'and finds no wife to welcome him?' Walter said, on the contrary, he had often wished such a thing might happen. And so, after some playful recriminations between this lately married, charming, devoted couple we agreed that Podolo should be the goal for tomorrow's picnic. 'You must curb my wife's generous impulses,' Walter warned me; 'she always wants to do something for somebody. It's an expensive habit.' I assured him that at Podolo she would find no calls on her heart or her purse. Except perhaps for a rat or two it was quite uninhabited. Next morning in brilliant sunshine Walter gulped down his breakfast and started for the station. It seemed hard that he should have to spend six hours of this divine day in a stuffy train. I stood on the balcony watching his departure.

The sunlight sparkled on the water; the gondola, in its best array, glowed and glittered. 'Say good-bye to Angela for me,' cried Walter as the gondolier braced himself for the first stroke.

'And what is your postal address at Podolo?' 'Full fathom five,' I called out, but I don't think my reply reached him.

Until you get right up to Podolo you can form no estimate of its size. There is nothing near by to compare it with. On the horizon it looks like a foot-rule. Even now, though I have been there many times, I cannot say whether it is a hundred yards long or two hundred. But I have no wish to go back and make certain.

We cast anchor a few feet from the stony shore. Podolo, I must say, was looking its best, green, flowery, almost welcoming. One side is rounded to form the shallow arc of a circle: the other is straight. Seen from above, it must look like the moon in its first quarter. Seen as we saw it from the water-line with the grassy rampart behind, it forms a kind of natural amphitheatre. The slim withy-like acacia trees give a certain charm to the foreground, and to the background where they grow in clumps, and cast darker shadows, an air of mystery. As we sat in the gondola we were like theatre-goers in the stalls, staring at an empty stage.

It was nearly two o'clock when we began lunch. I was very hungry, and, charmed by my companion and occupied by my food, I did not let my eyes stray out of the boat. To Angela belonged the honour of discovering the first denizen of Podolo.

'Why,' she exclaimed, 'there's a cat.' Sure enough there was: a little cat, hardly more than a kitten, very thin and scraggy, and mewing with automatic regularity every two or three seconds. Standing on the weedy stones at the water's edge it was a pitiful sight. 'It's smelt the food,' said Angela. 'It's hungry. Probably it's starving.'

Mario, the gondolier, had also made the discovery, but he received it in a different spirit. '*Povera bestia*,' he cried in sympathetic accents, but his eyes brightened. 'Its owners did not want it. It has been put here on purpose, one sees.' The idea that the cat had been left to starve caused him no great concern, but it shocked Angela profoundly.

'How abominable!' she exclaimed. 'We must take it something to eat at once.'

The suggestion did not recommend itself to Mario, who had to haul up the anchor and see the prospect of his own lunch growing more remote: I too thought we might wait till the meal was over. The cat would not die before our eyes. But Angela could brook no delay. So to the accompaniment of a good deal of stamping and heavy breathing the prow of the gondola was turned to land.

Meanwhile the cat continued to miaow, though it had retreated a little and was almost invisible, a thin wisp of tabby fur, against the parched stems of the outermost grasses.

Angela filled her hand with chicken bones.

'I shall try to win its confidence with these,' she said, 'and then if I can I shall catch it and put it in the boat and we'll take it to Venice. If it's left here it'll certainly starve.'

She climbed along the knife-like gunwale of the gondola and stepped delicately on to the slippery boulders.

Continuing to eat the chicken in comfort, I watched her approach the cat. It ran away, but only a few yards: its hunger was obviously keeping its fear at bay. She threw a bit of food and it came nearer: another, and it came nearer still. Its demeanour grew less suspicious; its tail rose into the air; it came right up to Angela's feet. She pounced. But the cat was too quick for her; it slipped through her hands like water. Again hunger overpowered mistrust. Back it came. Once more Angela made a grab at it; once more it eluded her. But the third time she was successful. She got hold of its leg.

I shall never forget seeing it dangle from Angela's (fortunately) gloved hand. It wriggled and squirmed and fought, and in spite of its tiny size the violence of its struggle made Angela quiver like a twig in a gale. And all the while it made the most extraordinary noise, the angriest, wickedest sound I ever heard. Instead of growing louder as its fury mounted, the sound actually decreased in volume, as though the creature was being choked by its own rage. The spitting died away into the thin ghost of a snarl, infinitely malevolent, but hardly more audible from where I was than the hiss of air from a punctured tyre.

Mario was distressed by what he felt to be Angela's brutality. 'Poor beast!' he exclaimed with pitying looks. 'She ought not to treat it like that.' And his face gleamed with satisfaction when, intimidated by the whirling claws, she let the cat drop. It streaked away into the grass, its belly to the ground.

Angela climbed back into the boat. 'I nearly had it,' she said, her voice still unsteady from the encounter. 'I think I shall get it next time. I shall throw a coat over it.' She ate her asparagus in silence, throwing the stalks over the side. I saw that she was preoccupied and couldn't get the cat out of her mind. Any form of suffering in others affected her almost like an illness. I began to wish we hadn't come to Podolo; it was not the first time a picnic there had gone badly.

'I tell you what,' Angela said suddenly, 'if I can't catch it I'll kill it. It's only a question of dropping one of these boulders on it. I could do it quite easily.' She disclosed her plan to Mario, who was horror-struck. His code was different from hers. He did not mind the animal dying of slow starvation; that was in the course of nature. But deliberately to kill it! *'Poveretto!* It has done no one any harm,' he exclaimed with indignation. But there was another reason, I suspected, for his attitude. Venice is overrun with cats, chiefly because it is considered unlucky to kill them. If they fall into the water and are drowned, so much the better, but woe betide whoever pushes them in.

I expounded the gondolier's point of view to Angela, but she was not impressed. 'Of course I don't expect him to do it,' she said, 'nor you either, if you'd rather not. It may be a messy business but it will soon be over. Poor little brute, it's in a horrible state. Its life can't be any pleasure to it.'

'But we don't know that,' I urged, still cravenly averse from the deed of blood. 'If it could speak, it might say it preferred to live at all costs.' But I couldn't move Angela from her purpose.

'Let's go and explore the island,' she said, 'until it's time to bathe. The cat will have got over its fright and be hungry again by then, and I'm sure I shall be able to catch it. I promise I won't murder it except as a last resource.'

The word 'murder' lingered unpleasantly in my mind as we made our survey of the island. You couldn't imagine a better place for one. During the war a battery had been mounted there. The concrete emplacement, about as long as a tennis court, remained: but nature and the weather had conspired to break it up, leaving black holes large enough to admit a man. These holes were like crevasses in a glacier, but masked by vegetation instead of snow. Even in the brilliant afternoon sunlight one had to tread cautiously. 'Perhaps the cat has its lair down there,' I said, indicating a gloomy cavern with a jagged edge. 'I suppose its eyes would shine in the dark.' Angela lay down on the pavement and peered in. 'I thought I heard something move,' she said, 'but it might be anywhere in this rabbit-warren.'

Our bathe was a great success. The water was so warm one hardly felt the shock of going in. The only drawback was the mud, which clung to Angela's white bathing shoes, nasty sticky stuff. A little wind had got up. But the grassy rampart sheltered us; we leaned against it and smoked. Suddenly I noticed it was past five.

'We ought to go soon,' I said. 'We promised, do you remember, to send the gondola to meet Walter's train.'

'All right,' said Angela, 'just let me have a go at the cat first. Let's put the food' (we had brought some remnants of lunch with us) 'here where we last saw it, and watch.'

There was no need to watch, for the cat appeared at once and made for the food. Angela and I stole up behind it, but I inadvertently kicked a stone and the cat was off like a flash. Angela looked at me reproachfully. 'Perhaps you could manage better alone', I said. Angela seemed to think she could. I retreated a few yards, but the cat, no doubt scenting a trap, refused to come out.

Angela threw herself on the pavement. 'I can see it,' she muttered. 'I must win its confidence again. Give me three minutes and I'll catch it'.

Three minutes passed. I felt concerned for Angela, her lovely hair floating over the dark hole, her face as much as one could see of it, a little red. The air was getting chilly.

'Look here,' I said, 'I'll wait for you in the gondola. When you've caught it, give a shout and I'll have the boat brought to land.' Angela nodded; she dare not speak for fear of scaring her prey.

So I returned to the gondola. I could just see the line of Angela's shoulders; her face, of course, was hidden. Mario stood up, eagerly watching the chase. 'She loves it so much,' he said, 'that she wants to kill it.' I remembered Oscar Wilde's epigram, rather uncomfortably; still, nothing could be more disinterested than Angela's attitude to the cat. 'We ought to start,' the gondolier warned me. 'The signore will be waiting at the station and wonder what has happened.'

'What about Walter?' I called across the water. 'He won't know what to do.'

Her mind was clearly on something else as she said: 'Oh, he'll find his own way home.'

More minutes passed. The gondolier smiled. 'One must have patience with ladies,' he said; 'always patience.'

I tried a last appeal. 'If we started at once we could just do it.'

She didn't answer. Presently I called out again. 'What luck, Angela? Any hope of catching him?'

There was a pause: then I heard her say, in a curiously tense voice. 'I'm not trying to *catch* him now.'

The need for immediate hurry had passed, since we were irrevocably late for Walter. A sense of relaxation stole over me; I wrapped the rug round me to keep off the treacherous cold sirocco and I fell asleep. Almost at once, it seemed, I began to dream. In my dream it was night; we were hurrying across the lagoon trying to be in time for Walter's train. It was so dark I could see nothing but the dim blur of Venice ahead, and the little splash of whitish water where the oar dipped. Suddenly I stopped rowing and looked round. The seat behind me seemed to be empty. 'Angela!' I cried; but there was no answer. I grew frightened. 'Mario!' I shouted. 'Where's the signora? We have left her behind! We must go back at once!' The gondolier, too, stopped rowing and came towards me; I could just distinguish his face; it had a wild look. 'She's there, signore,' he said. 'But where? She's not on the seat.' 'She wouldn't stay on it,' said the gondolier. And then, as is the way in dreams, I knew what his next words would be. 'We loved her and so we had to kill her.'

An uprush of panic woke me. The feeling of relief at getting back to actuality was piercingly sweet. I was restored to the sunshine. At least I thought so, in the ecstasy of returning consciousness. The next moment I began to doubt, and an uneasiness, not unlike the beginning of nightmare, stirred in me again. I opened my eyes to the daylight but they didn't receive it. I looked out on to darkness. At first I couldn't believe my eyes: I wondered if I was fainting. But a glance at my watch explained everything. It was past seven o'clock. I had slept the brief twilight through and now it was night, though a few gleams lingered in the sky over Fusina.

Mario was not to be seen. I stood up and looked round. There he was on the poop, his knees drawn up, asleep. Before I had time to speak he opened his eyes, like a dog.

'Signore,' he said, 'you went to sleep, so I did too.' To sleep out of hours is considered a joke all the world over; we both laughed. 'But the signora,' he said. 'Is *she* asleep? Or is she still trying to catch the cat?'

We strained our eyes towards the island which was much darker than the surrounding sky.

'That's where she was,' said Mario, pointing, 'but I can't see her now.'

'Angela!' I called.

There was no answer, indeed no sound at all but the noise of the waves slapping against the gondola.

We stared at each other.

'Let us hope she has taken no harm,' said Mario, a note of anxiety in his voice. 'The cat was very fierce, but it wasn't big enough to hurt her, was it?'

'No, no,' I said. 'It might have scratched her when she was putting her face – you know – into one of those holes.'

'She was trying to kill it, wasn't she?' asked Mario.

I nodded.

'*Ha fatto male,*' said Mario. 'In this country we are not accustomed to kill cats.'

'*You* call, Mario,' I said impatiently. 'Your voice is stronger than mine.'

Mario obeyed with a shout that might have raised the dead. But no answer came.

'Well,' I said briskly, trying to conceal my agitation, 'we must go and look for her or else we shall be late for dinner, and the signore will be getting worried. She must be a – a heavy sleeper.'

Mario didn't answer.

'*Avanti!*' I said. '*Andiamo! Coraggio!*' I could not understand why Mario, usually so quick to execute an order, did not move. He was staring straight in front of him.

'There *is* someone on the island,' he said at last, 'but it's not the signora.'

I must say, to do us justice, that within a couple of minutes we had beached the boat and landed. To my surprise Mario kept the oar in his hand. 'I have a pocket-knife,' he remarked, 'but the blade is only so long,' indicating the third joint of a stalwart little finger.

'It was a man, then?' said I.

'It looked like a man's head.'

'But you're not sure?'

'No, because it didn't walk like a man.'

'How then?'

Mario bent forward and touched the ground with his free hand. I couldn't imagine why a man should go on all fours, unless he didn't want to be seen.

'He must have come while we were asleep,' I said. 'There'll be a boat round the other side. But let's look here first.'

We were standing by the place where we had last seen Angela.

The grass was broken and bent; she had left a handkerchief as though to mark the spot. Otherwise there was no trace of her.

'Now let's find his boat,' I said.

We climbed the grassy rampart and began to walk round the shallow curve, stumbling over concealed brambles.

'Not here, not here,' muttered Mario.

From our little eminence we could see clusters of lights twinkling across the lagoon; Fusina three or four miles away on the left, Malamocco the same distance on the right. And straight ahead Venice, floating on the water like a swarm of fire-flies. But no boat. We stared at each other bewildered.

'So he didn't come by water,' said Mario at last. 'He must have been here all the time.'

'But are you quite certain it wasn't the signora you saw?' I asked. 'How could you tell in the darkness?'

'Because the signora was wearing a white dress,' said Mario. 'And this one is all in black – unless he is a negro.'

'That's why it's so difficult to see him.'

'Yes, we can't see him, but he can see us all right.'

I felt a curious sensation in my spine.

'Mario,' I said, 'he must have seen her, you know. Do you think he's got anything to do with her not being here?'

Mario didn't answer.

'I don't understand why he doesn't speak to us.'

'Perhaps he can't speak.'

'But you thought he was a man . . . Anyhow, we are two against one. Come on. You take the right. I'll go to the left.'

We soon lost sight of each other in the darkness, but once or twice I heard Mario swearing as he scratched himself on the thorny acacias. My search was more successful than I expected. Right at the corner of the island, close to the water's edge, I found one of Angela's bathing shoes: she must have taken it off in a hurry for the button was torn away. A little later I made a rather grisly discovery. It was the cat, dead, with its head crushed. The pathetic little heap of fur would never suffer the pangs of hunger again. Angela had been as good as her word.

I was just going to call Mario when the bushes parted and something hurled itself upon me. I was swept off my feet. Alternately dragging and carrying me my captor continued his head-long course. The next thing I knew I was pitched pell-mell into the gondola and felt the boat move under me.

'Mario!' I gasped. And then – absurd question – 'What have you done with the oar?'

The gondolier's white face stared down at me.

'The oar? I left it – it wasn't any use, signore. I tried . . . What it wants is a machine gun.'

He was rowing frantically with my oar: the island began to recede.

'But we can't go away!' I cried.

The gondolier said nothing, but rowed with all his strength. Then he began to talk under his breath. 'It was a good oar, too,' I heard him mutter. Suddenly he left the poop, climbed over the cushions and sat down beside me.

'When I found her,' he whispered, 'she wasn't quite dead.'

I began to speak but he held up his hand.

'She asked me to kill her.'

'But, Mario!'

' "Before it comes back," she said. And then she said, *"It's* starving, too, and it won't wait . . ." ' Mario bent his head nearer but his voice was almost inaudible.

'Speak up,' I cried. The next moment I implored him to stop.

Mario clambered on to the poop.

'You don't want to go to the island now, signore?'

'No, no. Straight home.'

I looked back. Transparent darkness covered the lagoon save for one shadow that stained the horizon black. Podolo . . .

THREE, OR FOUR, FOR DINNER

It was late July in Venice, suffocatingly hot. The windows of the bar in the Hotel San Giorgio stood open to the Canal. But no air came through. At six o'clock a little breeze had sprung up, a feebler repetition of the mid-day sirocco, but in an hour it had blown itself out.

One of the men got off his high stool and walked somewhat unsteadily to the window.

'It's going to be calm all right,' he said. 'I think we'll go in the gondola. I see it's there, tied up at the usual post.'

'As you please, Dickie,' said his friend from the other stool.

Their voices proclaimed them Englishmen; proclaimed also the fact that they were good clients of the barman.

'Giuseppe!' called the man at the window, turning his eyes from the Salute with its broad steps, its mighty portal and its soaring dome back to the counter with the multi-coloured bottles behind it. 'How long does it take to row to the Lido?'

'Sir?'

'Didn't you say you'd lived in England, Giuseppe?'

'Yes, sir, eight years at the Hôtel Métropole.'

'Then why—'

His friend intervened, pacifically, in Italian.

'He wants to know how long it takes to row to the Lido.'

Relief in his voice, the barman answered, 'That depends if you've got one oar or two.'

'Two.'

'If you ask me,' said Dickie, returning to his stool, 'I don't think Angelino, or whatever his damned name is, counts for much. It's the chap in front who does the work.'

'Yes, sir,' said the barman, solicitously. 'But the man at the back he guide the boat, he give the direction.'

'Well,' said Dickie, 'as long as he manages to hit the Lido . . . We want to be at the Splendide by eight. Can we do it?'

'Easily, sir, you have got an hour.'

'Barring accidents.'

'We never have accidents in Venice,' said the barman, with true Italian optimism.

'Time for another, Phil?'

'Three's my limit, Dickie.'

'Oh, come on, be a man.'

They drank.

'You seem to know a lot,' said Dickie more amiably to the barman. 'Can you tell us anything about this chap who's dining with us – Joe O'Kelly, or whatever his name is?'

The barman pondered. He did not want to be called over the coals a second time. 'That would be an English name, sir?'

'English! Good Lord!' exploded Dickie. 'Does it sound like English?'

'Well, now, as you say it, it does,' remonstrated his companion. 'Or rather Irish. But wait – here's his card. Does that convey anything to you, Giuseppe?'

The barman turned the card over in his fingers. 'Oh, now I see, sir – Giacomelli – il Conte Giacomelli.'

'Well, do you know him?'

'Oh yes, sir. I know him very well.'

'What's he like?'

'He's a nice gentleman, sir, very rich . . .'

'Then he must be different from the rest of your aristocracy,' said Dickie, rather rudely. 'I hear they haven't two penny pieces to rub together.'

'Perhaps he's not so rich now,' the barman admitted, mournfully. 'None of us are. Business is bad. He is *grand azionista* – how do you say?' he stopped, distressed.

'Shareholder?' suggested Philip.

'Good Lord!' exclaimed Dickie, 'I didn't know you were so well up in this infernal language. You're a regular Wop!'

The barman did not notice the interruption.

'Yes, shareholder, that's it,' he was saying delightedly. 'He is a great shareholder in a *fabbrica di zucchero*—'

'Sugar-factory,' explained Philip, not without complacence.

The barman lowered his voice. 'But I hear they are . . . ' He made a curious rocking movement with his hand.

'Not very flourishing?' said Philip.

The barman shrugged his shoulders. 'That's what they say.'

'So we mustn't mention sugar,' said Dickie, with a yawn.

'Come on, Phil, you're always so damned abstemious. Have another.'

'No, no, really not.'

'Then I will.'

Philip and even the barman watched him drink with awe on their faces.

'But,' said Philip as Dickie set down his glass, 'Count Giacomelli lives in Venice, doesn't he?'

'Oh yes, sir. Usually he comes in here every night. But it's four – five days now I do not see him.'

'Pity,' said Philip, 'we might have given him a lift. But perhaps he has a launch?'

'I don't think he's using his launch now, sir.'

'Oh well, he'll find some way of getting there, you may be sure,' said Dickie. 'How shall we know him, Giuseppe?'

'I expect you'll see him double, my poor Dickie,' remarked his friend.

The barman, with his usual courtesy, began replying to Dickie's question.

'Oh, he's a common-looking gentleman like yourself, sir . . . '

'I, common?'

'No,' said the barman, confused. 'I mean *grande come lei* – as tall as you.'

'That's nothing to go by. Has he a beard and whiskers and a moustache?'

'No, he's clean-shaven.'

'Come on, come on,' said Philip. 'We shall be late, and perhaps he won't wait for us.'

But his friend was in combative mood. 'Damn it! how are we to dine with the chap if we don't recognize him? Now, Giuseppe, hurry up; think of the Duce and set your great Italian mind working. Isn't there anything odd about him? Is he cross-eyed?'

'No, sir.'

'Does he wear spectacles?'

'Oh no, sir.'

'Is he minus an arm?'

'*Nossignore*,' cried the barman, more and more agitated.

'Can't you tell us anything about him, except that he's common-looking, like me?'

The barman glanced helplessly round the room. Suddenly his face brightened. 'Ah, *ecco*! He limps a little.'

'That's better,' said Dickie. 'Come on, Philip, you lazy hound, you always keep me waiting.' He got down from the stool. 'See you later,' he said over his shoulder to the barman. 'Mind you have the whisky pronto. I shall need it after this trip.'

The barman, gradually recovering his composure, gazed after Dickie's receding, slightly lurching figure with intense respect.

The gondola glided smoothly over the water towards the island of San Giorgio Maggiore, the slender campanile of which was orange with the light of the setting sun. On the left lay the Piazzetta, the two columns, the rich intricate stonework of St Mark's, the immense façade of the Ducal Palace, still perfectly distinct for all the pearly pallor in the air about them. But, as San Giorgio began to slide past them on the right, it was the view at the back of the gondola which engrossed Philip's attention. There, in the entrance of the Grand Canal, the atmosphere was deepening into violet while the sky around the dome of the Salute was of that clear deep blue which, one knows instinctively, may at any moment be pierced by the first star. Philip, who was sitting on his companion's left, kept twisting round to see the view, and the gondolier, whose figure blocked it to some extent, smiled each time he did so, saying '*Bello, non è vero?*' almost as though from habit. Dickie, however, was less tolerant of his friend's aesthetic preoccupations.

'I wish to goodness you wouldn't keep wriggling about,' he muttered, sprawling laxly in the depths of the more comfortable seat. 'You make me feel seasick.'

'All right, old chap,' said Philip, soothingly. 'You go to sleep.'

Dickie hauled himself up by the silk rope which was supported by the brass silhouette of a horse at one end and by a small but solid brass lion at the other.

He said combatively: 'I don't want to go to sleep. I want to know what we're to say to this sugar-refining friend of yours. Supposing he doesn't talk English? Shall we sit silent through the meal?'

'Oh, I think all foreigners do.' Philip spoke lightly; his reply was directed to the first of Dickie's questions; it would have been obviously untrue as an answer to the second. 'Jackson didn't tell me; he only gave me that letter and said he was a nice fellow and could get us into palaces and so on that ordinary people don't see.'

'There are too many that ordinary people do see, as it is, if you ask me,' groaned Dickie. 'For God's sake don't let him show us any more sights.'

'He seems to be a well-known character,' said Philip. 'He'll count as a sight himself.'

'If you call a limping dago a sight, I'm inclined to agree with you,' Dickie took him up crossly.

But Philip was unruffled.

'I'm sorry, Dickie, but I had to do it – couldn't ignore the letter, you know. We shall get through the evening somehow. Now, sit up and look at the lovely scenery. *Cosa è questa isola?*' he asked the gondolier, indicating an island to the right that looked if it might be a monastery.

'*Il manicomio,*' said the gondolier, with a grin. Then, as Philip looked uncomprehending, he tapped his forehead and smiled still more broadly.

'Oh,' said Philip, 'it's the lunatic asylum.'

'I do wish,' said Dickie, plaintively, 'if you must show me things, you'd direct my attention to something more cheerful.'

'Well, then,' said Philip, 'look at these jolly old boats. They're more in your line.'

A couple of tramp-steamers, moored stern to stern, and, even in the fading twilight, visibly out of repair – great gangrenous patches of rust extending over their flanks – hove up on the left. Under the shadow of their steep sides the water looked oily and almost black.

Dickie suddenly became animated. 'This reminds me of Hull,' he exclaimed. 'Good old Hull! Civilization at last! Nothing picturesque and old-world. Two ugly useful old ships, nice oily water and lots of foreign bodies floating about in it. At least,' he said, rising unsteadily to his feet, 'I take that to be a foreign body.'

'*Signore, signore!*' cried the first gondolier, warningly.

A slight swell, caused perhaps by some distant motor-boat, made the gondola rock alarmingly. Dickie subsided – fortunately, into his seat; but his hand was still stretched out, pointing, and as the water was suddenly scooped into a hollow, they all saw what he meant: a dark object showed up for an instant in the trough of the wave.

'Looks like an old boot,' said Philip, straining his eyes. '*Cosa è, Angelino?*'

The gondolier shrugged his shoulders.

'*Io non so. Forsè qualche gatto,*' he said, with the lightheartedness with which Italians are wont to treat the death of animals.

'Good God, does the fellow think I don't know a cat when I see one?' cried Dickie, who had tumbled to the gondolier's meaning. 'Unless it's a cat that has been in the water a damned long time. No, it's – it's . . . '

The gondoliers exchanged glances and, as though by mutual consent, straightened themselves to row. '*E meglio andare, signori*', said Angelino firmly.

'What does he say?'

'He says we'd better be going.'

'I'm not going till I've found out what that is,' said Dickie obstinately. 'Tell him to row up to it, Phil.'

Philip gave the order, but Angelino seemed not to understand.

'*Non è niente interessante, niente interessante*,' he kept repeating stubbornly.

'But it is interesting to me,' said Dickie, who like many people could understand a foreign language directly his own wishes were involved. 'Go to it! There!' he commanded.

Reluctantly the men set themselves to row. As the boat drew up alongside, the black patch slid under the water and there appeared in its place a gleam of whiteness, then features – a forehead, a nose, a mouth . . . they constituted a face, but not a recognizable one.

'Ah, *povero annegato*,' murmured Angelino, and crossed himself.

The two friends looked at each other blankly.

'Well, this has torn it,' said Dickie, at last. 'What are we going to do now?'

The gondoliers had already decided. They were moving on.

'Stop! Stop!' cried Philip. 'We can't leave him like this.' He appealed to the men. '*Non si puo lasciarlo cosi.*'

Angelino spread his hands in protest. The drowned man would be found by those whose business it was to patrol the waters. Who knew what he had died of? Perhaps some dreadful disease which the signori would catch. There would be difficulties with the police; official visits. Finally, as the Englishmen still seemed unconvinced, he added, '*Anche fa sporca la gondola. Questo tappeto, signori, m'ha costato più che mille duecento lire.*'

Somewhat grimly Philip explained to Dickie this last, unanswerable reason for not taking the drowned man on board. 'He will dirty the gondola and spoil the carpet, which cost twelve hundred lire.'

'Carpet be damned!' exclaimed Dickie. 'I always told you dagoes were no good. Here, catch hold of him.'

Together they pulled the dead man into the boat, though not before Angelino had rolled back his precious carpet. And when the dead man was lying in the bottom of the boat, decently covered with a piece of brown water-proof sheeting, he went round with sponge and wash-leather and carefully wiped away every drop of water from the gunwale and its brass fittings.

Ten minutes sufficed to take them to the Lido. The little *passeggiata* that had started so pleasantly had become a funeral cortege. The friends hardly spoke. Then, when they were nearing the landing-stage and the ugly white hotel, an eyesore all the way across the lagoon, impended over them with its blazing lights and its distressing symmetry, Dickie said:

'By Jove, we shall be late for that fellow.'

'He'll understand,' said Philip. 'It'll be something to talk to him about.'

He regretted the words the moment they were out of his mouth: they sounded so heartless.

The landing-stage was almost deserted when the gondola drew up at the steps, but the aged, tottering and dirty *rampino* who hooked it in and held out his skinny hand for *soldi*, soon spread the news. While Philip was conferring with the gondoliers upon the proper course to be taken, a small crowd collected and gazed, expressionlessly but persistently, at the shapeless mound in the gondola. The *rampino* professed himself capable of keeping watch; the gondoliers declared they could not find a *vigile* unless they went together; they hinted that it might take some time. At last Dickie and Philip were free. They walked along the avenue under acacia trees stridently lighted by arc-lamps, towards the sea and the Hotel Splendide. As they looked back they saw that the little knot of spectators was already dispersing.

No, they were told: Count Giacomelli had not yet arrived. But that is nothing, smiled the *maître d'hôtel*; the Signore Conte is often late. Would the gentlemen take a cocktail while they waited?

Dickie agreed with enthusiasm. 'I think we've earned it,' he said. 'Think of it, but for us that poor chap would be floating about the lagoons till Doomsday and none of his dusky offspring know what had happened to him.'

'Do you think they will now?' asked Philip.

'You mean . . . ? Oh, I think anyone who really knew him could tell.'

They were sitting at a table under the trees. The air was fresh and pleasant; the absence of mosquitoes almost miraculous. Dickie's spirits began to rise.

'I say,' he said. 'It's damned dull waiting. He's twenty minutes late. Where's that boy?'

When a second round had been served, Dickie motioned the page to stay. Philip looked at him in surprise.

'Listen,' said Dickie, in a thick, excited undertone. 'Wouldn't it be a lark if we sent this lad down to the gondola and told him to ask the chap that's resting inside to come and dine with us?'

'A charming idea, Dickie, but I doubt whether they understand practical jokes in this country.'

'Nonsense, Phil, that's a joke that anyone could understand. Now, put on your thinking-cap and find the appropriate words. I'm no good; you must do it.'

Philip smiled.

'We don't want to be four at dinner, do we? I'm sure the Count wouldn't like having to sit down with a – a drowned rat.'

'That's absurd; he may be a man of excellent family; it's generally the rich who commit suicide.'

'We don't know that he did.'

'No, but all that's beside the point. Now just tell this boy to run down to the jetty, or whatever it is called, give our message and bring us back the answer. It won't take him ten minutes. I'll give him five lire to soothe his shattered nerves.'

Philip appeared to be considering it. 'Dick, I really don't think – a foreign country and all, you know . . .'

The boy looked interrogatively from one to the other.

'It's a good idea,' repeated Philip, 'and I don't want to be a spoil-sport. But really, Dickie, I should give it up. The boy would be very scared, perhaps tell his parents, and then we might be mobbed and thrown into the Canal. It's the kind of thing that gives us a bad name abroad,' he concluded, somewhat pompously.

Dickie rose unsteadily to his feet.

'Bad name be hanged!' he said. 'What does it matter what we do in this tuppeny ha'penny hole? If you won't tell the boy I'll arrange it with the concierge. He understands English.'

'All right,' agreed Philip, for Dickie was already lurching away, the light of battle in his eye. 'I don't expect it'd do any harm, really. *Senta piccolo!*' He began to explain the errand.

'Don't forget,' admonished Dickie, 'we expect the gentleman *subito*. He needn't bother to dress or wash or brush up or anything.

Philip smiled in spite of himself.

'*Dica al signore*,' he said, '*di non vestirsi nero*.'

'Not "smoking"?' said the boy, pertly, delighted to display his English.

'No, not "smoking".'

The boy was off like a streak.

It must be boring waiting for a bomb to go off; it is almost equally tedious waiting for a practical joke to take effect. Dickie and Philip found the minutes drag interminably and they could think of nothing to say.

'He must be there now,' said Dickie, at last, taking out his watch.

'What's the time?'

'Half-past eight. He's been gone seven minutes.'

'How dark it is,' said Philip. 'Partly the trees, I suppose. But it wouldn't be dark in England now.'

'I've told you, much better stick to the Old Country. More daylight, fewer corpses, guests turn up to dinner at the proper time . . . '

'Giacomelli's certainly very late. Over half an hour.'

'I wonder if he ever got your message.'

'Oh yes, he answered it.'

'You never told me. How long ago was that?'

'Last Wednesday. I wanted to give him plenty of time.'

'Did he write?'

'No, he telephoned. I couldn't understand very well. The servant said the Count was away but he would be delighted to dine with us. He was sorry he couldn't write, but he had been called away on business.'

'The sugar factory, perhaps?'

'Very likely.'

'It's bloody quiet, as the navvy said,' remarked Dickie.

'Yes, they are all dining in that glass place. You can see it through the leaves.'

'I suppose they'll know to bring him here.'

'Oh, yes.'

Silence fell, broken a moment later by Philip's exclamation, 'Ah, here's the boy!'

With no little excitement they watched his small figure approaching over the wilderness of small grey pebbles which serve the Venetians in lieu of gravel. They noticed at once that his bearing was erect and important; if he had had a shock he bore no traces of it. He stopped by them, smiling and breathing hard.

'*Ho fatto un corso*,' he said, swelling with pride.

'What's that?'

'He says he ran.'

'I expect he did.'

The friends exchanged amused glances.

'I must say he's got a good pluck,' remarked Dickie, ruefully admiring. Their joke had fallen flat. 'But I expect these Italian kids see corpses every day. Anyhow, ask him what the gentleman said.'

'*Che cosa ha detto il signore?*' asked Philip.

Still panting, the boy replied:

'*Accetta con molto piacere. Fra pochi minuti sarà qui.*'

Philip stared at the page in amazement.

'*Si, si, signore*,' repeated the boy. '*Cosi ha detto, "vengo con molto piacere".*'

'What does he say?' asked Dickie irritably.

'He says that the gentleman accepts our invitation with great pleasure and will be here in a few minutes.'

'Of course,' said Dickie, when the boy had gone off with his *mancia*, whistling, 'he's having us on. But he's a tough youngster. Can't be more than twelve years old.'

Philip was looking all round him, clenching and unclenching his fingers.

'I don't believe he invented that.'

'But if he didn't?'

Philip did not answer.

'How like a cemetery the place looks,' he said, suddenly, 'with all the cypresses and this horrible monumental mason's road-repairing stuff all round.'

'The scene would look better for a few fairy-lights,' rejoined

Dickie. 'But your morbid fancies don't help us to solve the problem of our friend in the boat. Are we being made fools of by this whippersnapper, or are we not?'

'Time will show,' said Philip. 'He said a few minutes.'

They both sat listening.

'This waiting gives me the jim-jams,' said Dickie at last. 'Let's call the little rascal back and make him tell us what really did happen.'

'No, no, Dickie, that would be too mortifying. Let's try to think it out; let's proceed from the known to the unknown, as they do in detective stories. The boy goes off. He arrives at the landing stage. He finds some ghoulish loafers hanging about . . .'

'He might not,' said Dickie. 'There were only two or three corpse-gazers when we left.'

'Anyhow, he finds the *rampino* who swore to mount guard.'

'He might have slipped in for a drink,' said Dickie. 'You gave him the wherewithal, and he has to live like others.'

'Well, in that case, the boy would see – what?'

'Just that bit of tarpaulin stuff, humped up in the middle.'

'What would he do, then? Put yourself in his place, Dickie.'

Dickie grimaced slightly.

'I suppose he'd think the man was resting under the waterproof and he'd say, "Hullo, there!" in that ear-splitting voice Italians have, fit to wake . . .'

'Yes, yes. And then?'

'Then perhaps, as he seems an enterprising child, he'd descend into the hold and give the tarpaulin a tweak and – well, I suppose he'd stop shouting,' concluded Dickie lamely. 'He'd see it was no good. You must own,' he added, 'it's simpler to assume that half-way down the street he met a pal who told him he was being ragged: then he hung about and smoked a cigarette and returned puffing with this cock-and-bull story – simply to get his own back on us.'

'That is the most rational explanation,' said Philip. 'But just for fun, let's suppose that when he called, the tarpaulin began to move and rear itself up and a hand came round the edge, and—'

There was a sound of feet scrunching on the stones, and the friends heard a respectful voice saying, '*Per qui, signor Conte.*'

At first they could only see the robust, white-waistcoated figure of the concierge advancing with a large air and steam-roller tread; behind him they presently descried another figure, a tall man dressed in dark clothes, who walked with a limp. After the concierge's glorious effulgence, he seemed almost invisible.

'Il Conte Giacomelli,' announced the concierge, impressively.

The two Englishmen advanced with outstretched hands, but their guests fell back half a pace and raised his arm in the Roman salute.

'How do you do?' he said. His English accent was excellent. 'I'm afraid I am a little late, no?'

'Just a minute or two, perhaps,' said Philip. 'Nothing to speak of.' Furtively, he stared at the Count. A branch of the overhanging ilex tree nearly touched his hat; he stood so straight and still in the darkness that one could fancy he was suspended from the tree.

'To tell you the truth,' said Dickie bluntly, 'we had almost given you up.'

'Given me up?' The Count seemed mystified. 'How do you mean, given me up?'

'Don't be alarmed,' Philip laughingly reassured him. 'He didn't mean give you up to the police. To give up, you know, can mean so many things. That's the worst of our language.'

'You can give up hope, isn't it?' inquired the Count.

'Yes,' replied Philip cheerfully. 'You can certainly give up hope. That's what my friend meant: we'd almost given up hope of seeing you. We couldn't give *you* up – that's only an idiom – because, you see, we hadn't got you.'

'I see,' said the Count. 'You hadn't got me.' He pondered.

The silence was broken by Dickie.

'You may be a good grammarian, Phil,' he said, 'but you're a damned bad host. The Count must be famished. Let's have some cocktails here and then go in to dinner.'

'All right, you order them. I hope you don't mind,' he went on when Dickie had gone, 'but we may be four at dinner.'

'Four?' echoed the Count.

'I mean,' said Philip, finding it absurdly difficult to explain, 'we asked someone else as well. I – I think he's coming.'

'But that will be delightful,' the Count said, raising his eyebrows slightly. 'Why should I mind? Perhaps he is a friend of mine, too – your – your other guest?'

'I don't think he would be,' said Philip, feeling more than ever at a loss. 'He – he . . .'

'He is not *de notre monde*, perhaps?' the Count suggested, indulgently. Philip knew that foreigners refer to distinctions of class more openly than we do, but all the same, he found it very difficult to reply.

'I don't know whether he belongs to our world or not,' he began, and realizing the ludicrous appropriateness of the words, stopped suddenly. 'Look here,' he said, 'I can't imagine why my friend is staying so long. Shall we sit down? Take care!' he cried as the Count was moving towards a chair. 'It's got a game leg – it won't hold you.'

He spoke too late; the Count had already seated himself. Smiling, he said: 'You see, she carries me all right.'

Philip marvelled.

'You must be a magician.'

The Count shook his head. 'No, not a magician, a – a . . . ' he searched for the word. 'I cannot explain myself in English. Your friend who is coming – does he speak Italian?'

Inwardly Philip groaned.

'I – I really don't know.'

The Count tilted his chair back.

'I don't want to be curious, but is he an Englishman, your friend?'

Oh God, thought Philip. Why on earth did I start this subject? Aloud he said: 'To tell you the truth I don't know much about him. That's what I wanted to explain to you. We only saw him once and we invited him through a third person.'

'As you did me?' said the Count, smiling.

'Yes, yes, but the circumstances were different. We came on him by accident and gave him a lift.'

'A lift?' queried the Count. 'You were in a hotel, perhaps?'

'No,' said Philip, laughing awkwardly. 'We gave him a lift – a ride – in the gondola. How did you come?' he added, thankful at last to have changed the subject.

'I was given a lift, too,' said the Count.

'In a gondola?'

'Yes, in a gondola.'

'What an odd coincidence,' said Philip.

'So, you see,' said the Count, 'your friend and I will have a good deal in common.'

There was a pause. Philip felt a growing uneasiness which he couldn't define or account for. He wished Dickie would come back: he would be able to divert the conversation into pleasanter channels. He heard the Count's voice saying:

'I'm glad you told me about your friend. I always like to know something about a person before I make his acquaintance.'

Philip felt he must make an end of all this. 'Oh, but I don't think you will make his acquaintance,' he cried. 'You see, I don't think he exists. It's all a silly joke.'

'A joke?' asked the Count.

'Yes, a practical joke. Don't you in Italy have a game on the first of April making people believe or do silly things? April Fools, we call them.'

'Yes, we have that custom,' said the Count, gravely, 'only we call them *pesci d'Aprile* – April Fish.'

'Ah,' said Philip, 'that's because you are a nation of fishermen. An April fish is a kind of fish you don't expect – something you pull out of the water and—'

'What's that?' said the Count. 'I heard a voice.'

Philip listened.

'Perhaps it's your other guest.'

'It can't be him. It can't be!'

The sound was repeated: it was only just audible, but it was Philip's name. But why did Dickie call so softly?

'Will you excuse me?' said Philip. 'I think I'm wanted.'

The Count inclined his head.

'But it's the most amazing thing,' Dickie was saying, 'I think I must have got it all wrong. But here they are and perhaps you will be able to convince them. I think they're mad myself – I told them so.'

He led Philip into the hall of the hotel. The concierge was there and two *vigili*. They were talking in whispers.

'*Ma è scritto sul fazzoletto*,' one of them was saying.

'What's that?' asked Dickie.

'He says it's written on his handkerchief,' said Philip.

'Besides, we both know him,' chimed in the other policeman.

'What *is* this all about?' cried Philip. 'Know whom?'

'Il Conte Giacomelli,' chanted the *vigili* in chorus.

'Well, do you want him?' asked Philip.

'We *did* want him three days ago,' said one of the men. 'But now it's too late.'

'Too late? But he's . . . ' Philip stopped suddenly and looked across at Dickie.

'I tell them so,' shouted the concierge, who seemed in no way disposed to save Count Giacomelli from the hands of justice.

'Many times, many times, I say: "The Count is in the garden with the English gentlemen." But they do not believe me.'

'But it's true!' cried Philip. 'I've only just left him. What do the *vigili* say?'

'They say that he is dead,' said the concierge. 'They say he is dead and his body is in your boat.'

There was a moment of silence. The *vigili*, like men exhausted by argument, stood apart, moody and indifferent. At last one of them spoke.

'It is true, *signori*. *Si è suicidato*. His affairs went badly. He was a great swindler – and knew he would be arrested and condemned. *Cosi si è salvato*.'

'He may be a swindler,' said Philip, 'but I'm certain he's alive. Come into the garden and see.'

Shaking their heads and shrugging their shoulders, the *vigili* followed him out of the hotel. In a small group they trooped across the stony waste towards the tree. There was no one there.

'You see, *signori*,' said one of the *vigili*, with an air of subdued triumph, 'it's as we said.'

'Well, he must have gone away,' said Philip, obstinately. 'He was sitting on this chair – so . . . ' But his effort to give point to his contention failed. The chair gave way under him and he sprawled rather ludicrously and painfully on the stony floor. When he had picked himself up one of the policemen took the chair, ran his hand over it, and remarked:

'It's damp.'

'Is it?' said Philip expressionlessly.

'I don't think anyone could have sat on this chair,' pursued the policeman.

He is telling me I am a liar, thought Philip, and blushed. But the other *vigile*, anxious to spare his feelings, said:

'Perhaps it was an impostor whom you saw – a confidence man. There are many such, even in Italy. He hoped to get money out of the *signori*.' He looked for confirmation; the concierge nodded.

'Yes,' said Philip, wearily. 'No doubt that explains it. Will you want us again?' he asked the *vigili*. 'Have you a card, Dickie?'

The *vigili*, having collected the information they required, saluted and walked off.

Dickie turned to the concierge.

'Where's that young whippersnapper who took a message for us?'

'Whippersnapper?' repeated the concierge.
'Well, page-boy?'
'Oh, the *piccolo*? He's gone off duty, sir, for the night.'
'Good thing for him,' said Dickie. 'Hullo, who's this? My poor nerves won't stand any more of this Maskelyne and Devant business.'

It was the *maître d'hôtel*, towing obsequiously.

'Will there be three gentlemen, or four, for dinner?' he asked.

Philip and Dickie exchanged glances and Dickie lit a cigarette.

'Only two gentlemen,' he said.

THE TRAVELLING GRAVE

Hugh Curtis was in two minds about accepting Dick Munt's invitation to spend Sunday at Lowlands. He knew little of Munt, who was supposed to be rich and eccentric and, like many people of that kind, a collector. Hugh dimly remembered having asked his friend Valentine Ostrop what it was that Munt collected, but he could not recall Valentine's answer. Hugh Curtis was a vague man with an unretentive mind, and the mere thought of a collection, with its many separate challenges to the memory, fatigued him. What he required of a week-end party was to be left alone as much as possible, and to spend the remainder of his time in the society of agreeable women. Searching his mind, though with distaste, for he hated to disturb it, he remembered Ostrop telling him that parties at Lowlands were generally composed entirely of men and rarely exceeded four in number. Valentine didn't know who the fourth was to be, but he begged Hugh to come.

'You will enjoy Munt,' he said. 'He really doesn't pose at all. It's his nature to be like that.'

'Like what?' his friend had inquired.

'Oh, original and — and strange, if you like,' answered Valentine. 'He's one of the exceptions — he's much odder than he seems, whereas most people are more ordinary than they seem.'

Hugh Curtis agreed. 'But I like ordinary people,' he added. 'So how shall I get on with Munt?'

'Oh,' said his friend, 'but you're just the type he likes. He prefers ordinary — it's a stupid word — I mean normal, people, because their reactions are more valuable.'

'Shall I be expected to react?' asked Hugh, with nervous facetiousness.

'Ha! Ha!' laughed Valentine, poking him gently — 'we never quite know what he'll be up to. But you will come, won't you?'

Hugh Curtis had said he would.

All the same, when Saturday morning came he began to regret

his decision and to wonder whether it might not honourably be reversed. He was a man in early middle life, rather set in his ideas, and, though not specially a snob, unable to help testing a new acquaintance by the standards of the circle to which be belonged. This circle had never warmly welcomed Valentine Ostrop; he was the most unconventional of Hugh's friends. Hugh liked him when they were alone together, but directly Valentine fell in with kindred spirits he developed a kind of foppishness of manner that Hugh instinctively disliked. He had no curiosity about his friends, and thought it out of place in personal relationships, so he had never troubled to ask himself what this altered demeanour of Valentine's when surrounded by his cronies, might denote. But he had a shrewd idea that Munt would bring out Valentine's less sympathetic side. Could he send a telegram saying he had been unexpectedly detained? Hugh turned the idea over; but partly from principle, partly from laziness (he hated the mental effort of inventing false circumstances to justify change of plans), he decided he couldn't. His letter of acceptance had been so unconditional. He also had the fleeting notion (a totally unreasonable one) that Munt would somehow find out and be nasty about it.

So he did the best he could for himself; looked out the latest train that would get him to Lowlands in decent time for dinner, and telegraphed that he would come by that. He would arrive at the house, he calculated, soon after seven. 'Even if dinner is as late as half-past-eight,' he thought to himself, 'they won't be able to do me much harm in an hour and a quarter.' This habit of mentally assuring to himself periods of comparative immunity from unknown perils had begun at school. 'Whatever I've done,' he used to say to himself, 'they can't kill me.' With the war, this saving reservation had to be dropped: they could kill him, that was what they were there for. But now that peace was here the little mental amulet once more diffused its healing properties; Hugh had recourse to it more often than he would have admitted. Absurdly enough he invoked it now. But it annoyed him that he would arrive in the dusk of the September evening. He liked to get his first impression of a new place by daylight.

Hugh Curtis's anxiety to come late had not been shared by the other two guests. They arrived at Lowlands in time for tea. Though they had not travelled together, Ostrop motoring down, they met practically on the doorstep, and each privately suspected the other of wanting to have his host for a few moments to himself.

But it seemed unlikely that their wish would have been gratified even if they had not both been struck by the same idea. Tea came in, the water bubbled in the urn, but still Munt did not present himself, and at last Ostrop asked his fellow-guest to make tea.

'You must be deputy-host,' he said; 'you know Dick so well, better than I do.'

This was true. Ostrop had long wanted to meet Tony Bettisher who, after the death of someone vaguely known to Valentine as Squarchy, ranked as Munt's oldest and closest friend. He was a short, dark, thick-set man, whose appearance gave no clue to his character or pursuits. He had, Valentine knew, a job at the British Museum, but, to look at, he might easily have been a stockbroker.

'I suppose you know this place at every season of the year,' Valentine said. 'This is the first time I've been here in the autumn. How lovely everything looks.'

He gazed out at the wooded valley and the horizon fringed with trees. The scent of burning garden-refuse drifted in through the windows.

'Yes, I'm a pretty frequent visitor,' answered Bettisher, busy with the teapot.

'I gather from his letter that Dick has just returned from abroad,' said Valentine. 'Why does he leave England on the rare occasions when it's tolerable? Does he do it for fun, or does he have to?' He put his head on one side and contemplated Bettisher with a look of mock despair.

Bettisher handed him a cup of tea.

'I think he goes when the spirit moves him.'

'Yes, but *what* spirit?' cried Valentine with an affected petulance of manner. 'Of course, our Richard is a law unto himself: we all know that. But he must have some motive. I don't suppose he's *fond* of travelling. It's *so* uncomfortable. Now Dick cares for his comforts. That's why he travels with so much luggage.'

'Oh does he?' inquired Bettisher. 'Have you been with him?'

'No, but the Sherlock Holmes in me discovered that,' declared Valentine triumphantly. 'The trusty Franklin hadn't time to put it away. Two large crates. Now would you call that *personal* luggage?' His voice was for ever underlining: it pounced upon 'personal' like a hawk on a dove.

'Perambulators, perhaps,' suggested Bettisher laconically.

'Oh, do you think so? Do you think he collects perambulators? That would explain everything!'

'What would it explain?' asked Bettisher, stirring in his chair.

'Why, his collection, of course!' exclaimed Valentine, jumping up and bending on Bettisher an intensely serious gaze. 'It would explain why he doesn't invite us to see it, and why he's so shy of talking about it. Don't you see? An unmarried man, a bachelor, *sine prole* as far as we know, with whole *attics-full* of perambulators! It would be *too* fantastic. The world would laugh, and Richard, much as we love him, is terribly serious. Do you imagine it's a kind of vice?'

'All collecting is a form of vice.'

'Oh no, Bettisher, don't be hard, don't be cynical – a *substitute* for vice. But tell me before he comes – he *must* come soon, the laws of hospitality demand it – am I right in my surmise?'

'Which? You have made so many.'

'I mean that what he goes abroad for, what he fills his house with, what he thinks about when we're not with him – in a word, what he collects, is perambulators?'

Valentine paused dramatically.

Bettisher did not speak. His eyelids flickered and the skin about his eyes made a sharp movement inwards. He was beginning to open his mouth when Valentine broke in:

'Oh no, of course, you're in his confidence, your lips are sealed. Don't tell me, you mustn't, I forbid you to!'

'What's that he's not to tell you?' said a voice from the other end of the room.

'Oh, Dick!' cried Valentine, 'what a start you gave me! You must learn to move a little less like a dome of silence, mustn't he, Bettisher?'

Their host came forward to meet them, on silent feet and laughing soundlessly. He was a small, thin, slightly built man, very well turned out and with a conscious elegance of carriage.

'But I thought you didn't know Bettisher?' he said, when their greetings had been accomplished. 'Yet when I come in I find you with difficulty stemming the flood of confidences pouring from his lips.'

His voice was slightly ironical, it seemed at the same moment to ask a question and to make a statement.

'Oh, we've been together for *hours*,' said Valentine airily, 'and had the most enchanting conversation. Guess what we talked about.'

'Not about me, I hope?'

'Well, about something very dear to you.'

'About you, then?'

'Don't make fun of me. The objects I speak of are both solid and useful.'

'That does rather rule you out,' said Munt meditatively. 'What are they useful for?'

'Carrying bodies.'

Munt glanced across at Bettisher, who was staring into the grate.

'And what are they made of?'

Valentine tittered, pulled a face, answered, 'I've had little experience of them, but I should think chiefly of wood.'

Munt got up and looked hard at Bettisher, who raised his eyebrows and said nothing.

'They perform at one time or another,' said Valentine, enjoying himself enormously, 'an essential service for us all.'

There was a pause. Then Munt asked—

'Where do you generally come across them?'

'Personally I always try to avoid them,' said Valentine. 'But one meets them every day in the street and – and here, of course.'

'Why do you try to avoid them?' Munt asked rather grimly.

'Since you think about them, and dote upon them, and collect them from all the corners of the earth, it pains me to have to say it,' said Valentine with relish, 'but I do not care to contemplate lumps of human flesh lacking the spirit that makes flesh tolerable.'

He struck an oratorical attitude and breathed audibly through his nose. There was a prolonged silence. The dusk began to make itself felt in the room.

'Well,' said Munt, at last, in a hard voice, 'you are the first person to guess my little secret, if I can give it so grandiose a name. I congratulate you.'

Valentine bowed.

'May I ask how you discovered it? While I was detained upstairs, I suppose you – you – poked about?' His voice had a disagreeable ring; but Valentine, unaware of this, said loftily:

'It was unnecessary. They were in the hall, plain to be seen by anyone. My Sherlock Holmes sense (I have eight or nine) recognized them immediately.'

Munt shrugged his shoulders, then said in a less constrained tone: 'At this stage of our acquaintance I did not really intend to enlighten you. But since you know already, tell me, as a matter of curiosity, were you horrified?'

'Horrified?' cried Valentine. 'I think it a charming taste, *so* original, so – so human. It ravishes my aesthetic sense; it slightly offends my moral principles.'

'I was afraid it might,' said Munt.

'I am a believer in Birth Control,' Valentine prattled on. 'Every night I burn a candle to Stopes.'

Munt looked puzzled. 'But then, how can you object?' he began.

Valentine went on without heeding him.

'But of course by making a corner in the things, you *do* discourage the whole business. Being exhibits they have to stand idle, don't they? You keep them empty?'

Bettisher started up in his chair, but Munt held out a pallid hand and murmured in a stifled voice:

'Yes, that is, most of them are.'

Valentine clapped his hands in ecstasy.

'But some are not? Oh, but that's too ingenious of you. To think of the darlings lying there quite still, not able to lift a finger, much less scream! A sort of mannequin parade!'

'They certainly seem more complete with an occupant,' Munt observed.

'But who's to push them? They can't go of themselves.'

'Listen,' said Munt slowly. 'I've just come back from abroad, and I've brought with me a specimen that does go by itself, or nearly. It's outside there where you saw, waiting to be unpacked.'

Valentine Ostrop had been the life and soul of many a party. No one knew better than he how to breathe new life into a flagging joke. Privately he felt that this one was played out; but he had a social conscience; he realized his responsibility towards conversation, and summoning all the galvanic enthusiasm at his command he cried out:

'Do you mean to say that it looks after itself, it doesn't need a helping hand, and that a fond mother can entrust her precious charge to it without a nursemaid and without a tremor?'

'She can,' said Munt, 'and without an undertaker and without a sexton.'

'Undertaker . . . ? Sexton . . . ?' echoed Valentine. 'What have they to do with perambulators?'

There was a pause, during which the three figures, struck in their respective attitudes, seemed to have lost relationship with each other.

'So you didn't know,' said Munt at length, 'that it was coffins I collected.'

An hour later the three men were standing in an upper room, looking down at a large oblong object that lay in the middle of a heap of shavings and seemed, to Valentine's sick fancy, to be burying its head among them. Munt had been giving a demonstration.

'Doesn't it look funny now it's still?' he remarked. 'Almost as though it had been killed.' He touched it pensively with his foot and it slid towards Valentine, who edged away. You couldn't quite tell where it was coming; it seemed to have no settled direction, and to move all ways at once, like a crab. 'Of course the chances are really against it,' sighed Munt. 'But it's very quick, and it has that funny gift of anticipation. If it got a fellow up against a wall, I don't think he'd stand much chance. I didn't show you here, because I value my floors, but it can bury itself in wood in three minutes and in newly turned earth, say a flower-bed, in one. It has to be this squarish shape, or it couldn't dig. It just doubles the man up, you see, directly it catches him – backwards, so as to break the spine. The top of his head fits in just below the heels. The soles of the feet come uppermost. The spring sticks a bit.' He bent down to adjust something. 'Isn't it a charming toy?'

'Looking at it from the criminal's standpoint, not the engineer's,' said Bettisher, 'I can't see that it would be much use in a house. Have you tried it on a stone floor?'

'Yes, it screams in agony and blunts the blades.'

'Exactly. Like a mole on paving-stones. And even on an ordinary carpeted floor it could cut its way in, but there would be a nice hole left in the carpet to show where it had gone.'

Munt conceded this point, also. 'But it's an odd thing,' he added, 'that in several of the rooms in this house it would really work, and baffle anyone but an expert detective. Below, of course, are the knives, but the top is inlaid with real parquet. The grave is so sensitive – you saw just now how it seemed to grope – that it can feel the ridges, and adjust itself perfectly to the pattern of the parquet. But of course I agree with you. It's not an indoor game, really: it's a field sport. You go on, will you, and leave me to clear up this mess. I'll join you in a moment.'

Valentine followed Bettisher down into the library. He was very much subdued.

'Well, that was the funniest scene,' remarked Bettisher, chuckling.

'Do you mean just now? I confess it gave me the creeps.'

'Oh no, not that: when you and Dick were talking at cross-purposes.'

'I'm afraid I made a fool of myself,' said Valentine dejectedly. 'I can't quite remember what we said. I know there was something I wanted to ask you.'

'Ask away, but I can't promise to answer.'

Valentine pondered a moment.

'Now I remember what it was.'

'Spit it out.'

'To tell you the truth, I hardly like to. It was something Dick said. I hardly noticed at the time. I expect he was just playing up to me.'

'Well?'

'About these coffins. Are they real?'

'How do you mean "real"?'

'I mean, could they be used as—'

'My dear chap, they have been.'

Valentine smiled, rather mirthlessly.

'Are they full-size – life-size, as it were?'

'The two things aren't quite the same,' said Bettisher with a grin. 'But there's no harm in telling you this: Dick's like all collectors. He prefers rarities, odd shapes, dwarfs, and that sort of thing. Of course any anatomical peculiarity has to have allowance made for it in the coffin. On the whole his specimens tend to be smaller than the general run – shorter, anyhow. Is that what you wanted to know?'

'You've told me a lot,' said Valentine. 'But there was another thing.'

'Out with it.'

'When I imagined we were talking about perambulators—'

'Yes, yes.'

'I said something about their being empty. Do you remember?'

'I think so.'

'Then I said something about them having mannequins inside, and he seemed to agree.'

'Oh, yes.'

'Well, he couldn't have meant that. It would be too – too realistic.'

'Well, then, any sort of dummy.'

'There are dummies and dummies. A skeleton isn't very talkative.'

Valentine stared.

'He's been away,' Bettisher said hastily. 'I don't know what his latest idea is. But here's the man himself.'

Munt came into the room.

'Children,' he called out, 'have you observed the time? It's nearly seven o'clock. And do you remember that we have another guest coming? He must be almost due.'

'Who is he?' asked Bettisher.

'A friend of Valentine's. Valentine, you must be responsible for him. I asked him partly to please you. I scarcely know him. What shall we do to entertain him?'

'What sort of man is he?' Bettisher inquired.

'Describe him, Valentine. Is he tall or short? I don't remember.'

'Medium.'

'Dark or fair?'

'Mouse-coloured.'

'Old or young?'

'About thirty-five.'

'Married or single?'

'Single.'

'What, has he no ties? No one to take an interest in him or bother what becomes of him?'

'He has no near relations.'

'Do you mean to say that very likely nobody knows he is coming to spend Sunday here?'

'Probably not. He has rooms in London, and he wouldn't trouble to leave his address.'

'Extraordinary the casual way some people live. Is he brave or timid?'

'Oh, come, what a question! About as brave as I am.'

'Is he clever or stupid?'

'All my friends are clever,' said Valentine, with a flicker of his old spirit. 'He's not intellectual: he'd be afraid of difficult parlour games or brilliant conversation.'

'He ought not to have come here. Does he play bridge?'

'I don't think he has much head for cards.'

'Could Tony induce him to play chess?'

'Oh, no, chess needs too much concentration.'

'Is he given to wool-gathering, then?' Munt asked. 'Does he forget to look where he's going?'

'He's the sort of man,' said Valentine, 'who expects to find everything just so. He likes to be led by the hand. He is perfectly tame and confiding, like a nicely brought up child.'

'In that case,' said Munt, 'we must find some childish pastime that won't tax him too much. Would he like Musical Chairs?'

'I think that would embarrass him,' said Valentine. He began to feel a tenderness for his absent friend, and a wish to stick up for him. 'I should leave him to look after himself. He's rather shy. If you try to make him come out of his shell, you'll scare him. He'd rather take the initiative himself. He doesn't like being pursued, but in a mild way he likes to pursue.'

'A child with hunting instincts,' said Munt pensively. 'How can we accommodate him? I have it! Let's play "Hide-and-Seek". We shall hide and he shall seek. Then he can't feel that we are forcing ourselves upon him. It will be the height of tact. He will be here in a few minutes. Let's go and hide now.'

'But he doesn't know his way about the house.'

'That will be all the more fun for him, since he likes to make discoveries on his own account.'

'He might fall and hurt himself.'

'Children never do. Now you run away and hide while I talk to Franklin,' Munt continued quietly, 'and mind you play fair, Valentine – don't let your natural affections lead you astray. Don't give yourself up because you're hungry for your dinner.'

The motor that met Hugh Curtis was shiny and smart and glittered in the rays of the setting sun. The chauffeur was like an extension of it, and so quick in his movements that in the matter of stowing Hugh's luggage, putting him in and tucking the rug round him, he seemed to steal a march on time. Hugh regretted this precipitancy, this interference with the rhythm of his thoughts. It was a foretaste of the effort of adaptability he would soon have to make; the violent mental readjustment that every visit, and specially every visit among strangers, entails: a surrender of the personality, the fanciful might call it a little death.

The car slowed down, left the main road, passed through white gateposts and followed for two or three minutes a gravel drive shadowed by trees. In the dusk Hugh could not see how far to right and left these extended. But the house, when it appeared, was plain enough: a large, regular, early nineteenth-century building, encased in cream-coloured stucco and pierced at generous intervals by large windows, some round-headed, some rectangular. It looked dignified and quiet, and in the twilight seemed to shine with a soft radiance of its own. Hugh's spirits began to rise. In his mind's ear he already heard the welcoming buzz of voices from a distant part of the house. He smiled at the man who opened the door. But the man didn't return his smile, and no sound came through the gloom that spread out behind him.

'Mr Munt and his friends are playing "Hide-and-Seek" in the house, sir,' the man said, with a gravity that checked Hugh's impulse to laugh. 'I was to tell you that the library is home, and you were to be "He", or I think he said, "It", sir. Mr Munt did not want the lights turned on till the game was over.'

'Am I to start now?' asked Hugh, stumbling a little as he followed his guide, – 'or can I go to my room first?'

The butler stopped and opened a door. 'This is the library,' he said. 'I think it was Mr Munt's wish that the game should begin immediately upon your arrival, sir.'

A faint coo-ee sounded through the house.

'Mr Munt said you could go anywhere you liked,' the man added as he went away.

Valentine's emotions were complex. The harmless frivolity of his mind had been thrown out of gear by its encounter with the harsher frivolity of his friend. Munt, he felt sure, had a heart of gold which he chose to hide beneath a slightly sinister exterior. With his travelling graves and charnel-talk he had hoped to get a rise out of his guest, and he had succeeded. Valentine still felt slightly unwell. But his nature was remarkably resilient, and the charming innocence of the pastime on which they were now engaged soothed and restored his spirits, gradually reaffirming his first impression of Munt as a man of fine mind and keen perceptions, a dilettante with the personal force of a man of action, a character with a vein of implacability, to be respected but not to be feared. He was conscious also of a growing desire to see Curtis; he wanted to see Curtis and Munt together, confident that two people he liked could not fail to like each other. He pictured the pleasant encounter after the mimic warfare of Hide-and-Seek – the captor and the caught laughing a little breathlessly over the diverting circumstances of their reintroduction. With every passing moment his mood grew more sanguine.

Only one misgiving remained to trouble it. He felt he wanted to confide in Curtis, tell him something of what had happened during the day; and this he could not do without being disloyal to his host. Try as he would to make light of Munt's behaviour about his collection, it was clear he wouldn't have given the secret away if it had not been surprised out of him. And Hugh would find his friend's bald statement of the facts difficult to swallow.

But what was he up to, letting his thoughts run on like this? He must hide, and quickly too. His acquaintance with the lie of the house, the fruits of two visits, was scanty, and the darkness did not help him. The house was long and symmetrical; its principal bedrooms lay on the first floor. Above were servants' rooms, attics, boxrooms, probably – plenty of natural hiding-places. The second storey was the obvious refuge.

He had been there only once, with Munt that afternoon, and he did not specially want to revisit it; but he must enter into the spirit of the game. He found the staircase and went up, then paused: there was really no light at all.

'This is absurd,' thought Valentine. 'I must cheat.' He entered the first room to the left, and turned down the switch. Nothing happened: the current had been cut off at the main. But by the light of a match he made out that he was in a combined bed-and-bathroom. In one corner was a bed, and in the other a large rectangular object with a lid over it, obviously a bath. The bath was close to the door.

As he stood debating he heard footsteps coming along the corridor. It would never do to be caught like this, without a run for his money. Quick as thought he raised the lid of the bath, which was not heavy, and slipped inside, cautiously lowering the lid.

It was narrower than the outside suggested, and it did not feel like a bath, but Valentine's inquiries into the nature of his hiding-place were suddenly cut short. He heard voices in the room, so muffled that he did not at first know whose they were. But they were evidently in disagreement.

Valentine lifted the lid. There was no light, so he lifted it farther. Now he could hear clearly enough.

'But I don't know what you really want, Dick,' Bettisher was saying. 'With the safety-catch it would be pointless, and without it would be damned dangerous. Why not wait a bit?'

'I shall never have a better opportunity than this,' said Munt, but in a voice so unfamiliar that Valentine scarcely recognized it.

'Opportunity for what?' said Bettisher.

'To prove whether the Travelling Grave can do what Madrali claimed for it.'

'You mean whether it can disappear? We know it can.'

'I mean whether it can effect somebody else's disappearance.'

There was a pause. Then Bettisher said: 'Give it up. That's my advice.'

'But he wouldn't leave a trace,' said Munt, half petulant, half pleading, like a thwarted child. 'He has no relations. Nobody knows he's here. Perhaps he isn't here. We can tell Valentine he never turned up.'

'We discussed all that,' said Bettisher decisively, 'and it won't wash.'

There was another silence, disturbed by the distant hum of a motor-car.

'We must go,' said Bettisher.

But Munt appeared to detain him. Half imploring, half whining, he said:

'Anyhow, you don't mind me having put it there with the safety-catch down.'

'Where?'

'By the china-cabinet. He's certain to run into it.'

Bettisher's voice sounded impatiently from the passage:

'Well, if it pleases you. But it's quite pointless.'

Munt lingered a moment, chanting to himself in a high voice, greedy with anticipation: 'I wonder which is up and which is down.'

When he had repeated this three times he scampered away, calling out peevishly: 'You might have helped me, Tony. It's so heavy for me to manage.'

It was heavy indeed. Valentine, when he had fought down the hysteria that came upon him, had only one thought: to take the deadly object and put it somewhere out of Hugh Curtis's way. If he could drop it from a window, so much the better. In the darkness the vague outline of its bulk, placed just where one had to turn to avoid the china-cabinet, was dreadfully familiar. He tried to recollect the way it worked. Only one thing stuck in his mind. 'The ends are dangerous, the sides are safe.' Or should it be, 'The sides are dangerous, the ends are safe'? While the two sentences were getting mixed up in his mind he heard the sound of 'coo-ee', coming first from one part of the house, then from another. He could also hear footsteps in the hall below him.

Then he made up his mind, and with a confidence that surprised him put his arms round the wooden cube and lifted it into the air. He hardly noticed its weight as he ran with it down the corridor. Suddenly he realized that he must have passed through an open door. A ray of moonlight showed him that he was in a bedroom, standing directly in front of an old-fashioned wardrobe, a towering, majestic piece of furniture with three doors, the middle one holding a mirror. Dimly he saw himself reflected there, his burden in his arms. He deposited it on the parquet without making a sound; but on the way out he tripped over a footstool and nearly fell. He was relieved at making so much clatter, and the grating of the key, as he turned it in the lock, was music to his ears.

Automatically he put it in his pocket. But he paid the penalty for his clumsiness. He had not gone a step when a hand caught him by the elbow.

'Why, it's Valentine!' Hugh Curtis cried. 'Now come quietly, and take me to my host. I must have a drink.'

'I should like one, too,' said Valentine, who was trembling all over. 'Why can't we have some light?'

'Turn it on, idiot,' commanded his friend.

'I can't – it's cut off at the main. We must wait till Richard gives the word.'

'Where is he?'

'I except he's tucked away somewhere. Richard!' Valentine called out, 'Dick!' He was too self-conscious to be able to give a good shout. 'Bettisher! I'm caught! The game's over!'

There was silence a moment, then steps could be heard descending the stairs.

'Is that you, Dick?' asked Valentine of the darkness.

'No, Bettisher.' The gaiety of the voice did not ring quite true.

'I've been caught,' said Valentine again, almost as Atalanta might have done, and as though it was a wonderful achievement reflecting great credit upon everybody. 'Allow me to present you to my captor. No, this is me. We've been introduced already.'

It was a moment or two before the mistake was corrected, the two hands groping vainly for each other in the darkness.

'I expect it will be a disappointment when you see me,' said Hugh Curtis in the pleasant voice that made many people like him.

'I want to see you,' declared Bettisher. 'I will, too. Let's have some light.'

'I suppose it's no good asking you if you've seen Dick?' inquired Valentine facetiously. 'He said we weren't to have any light till the game was finished. He's so strict with his servants; they have to obey him to the letter. I daren't even ask for a candle. But *you* know the faithful Franklin well enough.'

'Dick will be here in a moment surely,' Bettisher said, for the first time that day appearing undecided.

They all stood listening.

'Perhaps he's gone to dress,' Curtis suggested. 'It's past eight o'clock.'

'How can he dress in the dark?' asked Bettisher.

Another pause.

'Oh, I'm tired of this,' said Bettisher. 'Franklin! Franklin!' His voice boomed through the house and a reply came almost at once from the hall, directly below them. 'We think Mr Munt must have gone to dress,' said Bettisher. 'Will you please turn on the light?'

'Certainly, sir, but I don't think Mr Munt is in his room.'

'Well, anyhow—'

'Very good, sir.'

At once the corridor was flooded with light, and to all of them, in greater or less degree according to their familiarity with their surroundings, it seemed amazing that they should have had so much difficulty, half an hour before, in finding their way about. Even Valentine's harassed emotions experienced a moment's relaxation. They chaffed Hugh Curtis a little about the false impression his darkling voice had given them. Valentine, as always the more loquacious, swore it seemed to proceed from a large gaunt man with a hare-lip. They were beginning to move towards their rooms, Valentine had almost reached his, when Hugh Curtis called after them:

'I say, may I be taken to my room?'

'Of course,' said Bettisher, turning back. 'Franklin! Franklin! Franklin, show Mr Curtis where his room is. I don't know myself.' He disappeared and the butler came slowly up the stairs.

'It's quite near, sir, at the end of the corridor,' he said. 'I'm sorry, with having no light we haven't got your things put out. But it'll only take a moment.'

The door did not open when he turned the handle.

'Odd! It's stuck,' he remarked: but it did not yield to the pressure of his knee and shoulder. 'I've never known it to be locked before,' he muttered, thinking aloud, obviously put out by this flaw in the harmony of the domestic arrangements. 'If you'll excuse me, sir, I'll go and fetch my key.'

In a minute or two he was back with it. So gingerly did he turn the key in the lock he evidently expected another rebuff; but it gave a satisfactory click and the door swung open with the best will in the world.

'Now I'll go and fetch your suitcase,' he said as Hugh Curtis entered.

'No, it's absurd to stay,' soliloquized Valentine, fumbling feverishly with his front stud, 'after all these warnings, it would be insane. It's what they do in a "shocker", linger on and on, disregarding revolvers and other palpable hints, while one by one the villain picks them off, all except the hero, who is generally the stupidest of all, but the luckiest. No doubt by staying I should qualify to be the hero: I should survive; but what about Hugh, and Bettisher, that close-mouthed rat-trap?' He studied his face in the glass: it looked flushed. 'I've had an alarming increase in blood-pressure: I am seriously unwell: I must go away at once to a nursing home, and Hugh must accompany me.' He gazed round wretchedly at the charmingly appointed room, with its chintz and polished furniture, so comfortable, safe, and unsensational. And for the hundredth time his thoughts veered round and blew from the opposite quarter. It would equally be madness to run away at a moment's notice, scared by what was no doubt only an elaborate practical joke. Munt, though not exactly a jovial man, would have his joke, as witness the game of Hide-and-Seek. No doubt the Travelling Grave itself was just a take-in, a test of his and Bettisher's credulity. Munt was not popular, he had few friends, but that did not make him a potential murderer. Valentine had always liked him, and no one, to his knowledge, had ever spoken a word against him. What sort of figure would he, Valentine, cut, after this nocturnal flitting? He would lose at least two friends, Munt and Bettisher, and cover Hugh Curtis and himself with ridicule.

Poor Valentine! So perplexed was he that he changed his mind five times on the way down to the library. He kept repeating to himself the sentence, 'I'm so sorry, Dick, I find my blood-pressure rather high, and I think I ought to go into a nursing home tonight – Hugh will see me safely there' – until it became meaningless, even its absurdity disappeared.

Hugh was in the library alone. It was now or never; but Valentine's opening words were swept aside by his friend, who came running across the room to him.

'Oh, Valentine, the funniest thing has happened.'

'Funny? Where? What?' Valentine asked.

'No, no, not funny in the sinister sense, it's not in the least serious. Only it's so *odd*. This is a house of surprises. I'm glad I came.'

'Tell me quickly.'

'Don't look so alarmed. It's only very amusing. But I must show it you, or you'll miss the funny side of it. Come on up to my room; we've got five minutes.'

But before they crossed the threshold Valentine pulled up with a start.

'Is *this* your room?'

'Oh, yes. Don't look as if you had seen a ghost. It's a perfectly ordinary room, I tell you, except for one thing. No, stop a moment; wait here while I arrange the scene.'

He darted in, and after a moment summoned Valentine to follow.

'Now, do you notice anything strange?'

'I see the usual evidences of untidiness.'

A coat was lying on the floor and various articles of clothing were scattered about.

'You do? Well then – no deceit, gentlemen.' With a gesture he snatched the coat up from the floor. 'Now what do you see?'

'I see a further proof of slovenly habits – a pair of shoes where the coat was.'

'Look well at those shoes. There's nothing about them that strikes you as peculiar?'

Valentine studied them. They were ordinary brown shoes, lying side by side, the soles uppermost, a short pace from the wardrobe. They looked as though someone had taken them off and forgotten to put them away, or taken them out, and forgotten to put them on.

'Well,' pronounced Valentine at last, 'I don't usually leave my shoes upside-down like that, but you might.'

'Ah,' said Hugh triumphantly, 'your surmise is incorrect. They're *not* my shoes.'

'Not yours? Then they were left here by mistake. Franklin should have taken them away.'

'Yes, but that's where the coat comes in. I'm reconstructing the scene, you see, hoping to impress you. While he was downstairs fetching my bag, to save time I began to undress; I took my coat off and hurled it down there. After he had gone I picked it up. So he never saw the shoes.'

'Well, why make such a fuss? They won't be wanted till morning. Or would you rather ring for Franklin and tell him to take them away?'

'Ah!' cried Hugh, delighted by this. 'At last you've come to the heart of the matter. He *couldn't* take them away.'

'Why couldn't he?'

'Because they're fixed to the floor!'

'Oh, rubbish!' said Valentine. 'You must be dreaming.'

He bent down, took hold of the shoes by the welts, and gave a little tug. They did not move.

'There you are!' cried Hugh. 'Apologize. Own that it is unusual to find in one's room a strange pair of shoes adhering to the floor.'

Valentine's reply was to give another heave. Still the shoes did not budge.

'No good,' commented his friend. 'They're nailed down, or gummed down, or something. The dinner-bell hasn't rung; we'll get Franklin to clear up the mystery.'

The butler when he came looked uneasy, and surprised them by speaking first.

'Was it Mr Munt you were wanting, sir?' he said to Valentine. 'I don't know where he is. I've looked everywhere and can't find him.'

'Are these his shoes by any chance?' asked Valentine.

They couldn't deny themselves the mild entertainment of watching Franklin stoop down to pick up the shoes, and recoil in perplexity when he found them fast in the floor.

'These should be Mr Munt's, sir,' he said doubtfully – 'these should. But what's happened to them that they won't leave the floor?'

The two friends laughed gaily.

'That's what *we* want to know,' Hugh Curtis chuckled. 'That's why we called you: we thought you could help us.'

'They're Mr Munt's right enough,' muttered the butler. 'They must have got something heavy inside.'

'Damned heavy,' said Valentine, playfully grim.

Fascinated, the three men stared at the upturned soles, so close together that there was no room between for two thumbs set side by side.

Rather gingerly the butler stooped again, and tried to feel the uppers. This was not as easy as it seemed, for the shoes were flattened against the floor, as if a weight had pressed them down.

His face was white as he stood up.

'There *is* something in them,' he said in a frightened voice.

'And his shoes were full of feet,' carolled Valentine flippantly. 'Trees, perhaps.'

'It was not as hard as wood,' said the butler. 'You can squeeze it a bit if you try.'

They looked at each other, and a tension made itself felt in the room.

'There's only one way to find out,' declared Hugh Curtis suddenly, in a determined tone one could never have expected from him.

'How?'

'Take them off.'

'Take what off?'

'His shoes off, you idiot.'

'Off what?'

'That's what I don't know yet, you bloody fool!' Curtis almost screamed; and kneeling down, he tore apart the laces and began tugging and wrenching at one of the shoes.

'It's coming, it's coming,' he cried. 'Valentine, put your arms around me and pull, that's a good fellow. It's the heel that's giving the trouble.'

Suddenly the shoe slipped off.

'Why, it's only a sock,' whispered Valentine; 'it's so thin.'

'Yes, but the foot's inside it all right,' cried Curtis in a loud strange voice, speaking very rapidly. 'And here's the ankle, see, and here's where it begins to go down into the floor, see; he must have been a very small man; you see I never saw him, but it's all so crushed—'

The sound of a heavy fall made them turn.
Franklin had fainted.

FEET FOREMOST

The house-warming at Low Threshold Hall was not an event that affected many people. The local newspaper, however, had half a column about it, and one or two daily papers supplemented the usual August dearth of topics with pictures of the house. They were all taken from the same angle, and showed a long, low building in the Queen Anne style flowing away from a square tower on the left which was castellated and obviously of much earlier date, the whole structure giving somewhat the impression to a casual glance of a domesticated church, or even of a small railway train that had stopped dead on finding itself in a park. Beneath the photograph was written something like 'Suffolk Manor House re-occupied after a hundred and fifty years,' and, in one instance, 'Inset, (L.) Mr Charles Ampleforth, owner of Low Threshold Hall; (R.) Sir George Willings, the architect responsible for the restoration of this interesting mediaeval relic.' Mr Ampleforth's handsome, slightly Disraelian head, nearly spiked on his own flagpole, smiled congratulations at the grey hair and rounded features of Sir George Willings who, suspended like a bubble above the Queen Anne wing, discreetly smiled back.

To judge from the photograph, time had dealt gently with Low Threshold Hall. Only a trained observer could have told how much of the original fabric had been renewed. The tower looked particularly convincing. While as for the gardens sloping down to the stream which bounded the foreground of the picture – they had that old-world air which gardens so quickly acquire. To see those lush lawns and borders as a meadow, that mellow brickwork under scaffolding, needed a strong effort of the imagination.

But the guests assembled in Mr Ampleforth's drawing-room after dinner and listening to their host as, not for the first time, he enlarged upon the obstacles faced and overcome in the work of restoration, found it just as hard to believe that the house was old. Most of them had been taken to see it, at one time or another, in process of reconstruction; yet even within a few days of its completion, how unfinished a house looks! Its habitability seems determined in the last few hours. Magdalen Winthrop, whose beautiful, expressive face still (to her hostess' sentimental eye) bore traces of the slight disappointment she had suffered earlier in the evening, felt as if she were in an Aladdin's palace. Her glance wandered appreciatively from the Samarcand rugs to the pale green walls, and dwelt with pleasure on the high shallow arch, flanked by slender columns, the delicate lines of which were emphasized by the darkness of the hall behind them. It all seemed so perfect and so new; not only every sign of decay but the very sense of age had been banished. How absurd not to be able to find a single grey hair, so to speak, in a house that had stood empty for a hundred and fifty years! Her eyes, still puzzled, came to rest on the company, ranged in an irregular circle round the open fireplace.

'What's the matter, Maggie?' said a man at her side, obviously glad to turn the conversation away from bricks and mortar. 'Looking for something?'

Mrs Ampleforth, whose still lovely skin under the abundant white hair made her face look like a rose in snow, bent forward over the cream-coloured satin bedspread she was embroidering and smiled. 'I was only thinking,' said Maggie, turning to her host whose recital had paused but not died upon his lips, 'how surprised the owls and bats would be if they could come in and see the change in their old home.'

'Oh, I do hope they won't,' cried a high female voice from the depths of a chair whose generous proportions obscured the speaker.

'Don't be such a baby, Eileen,' said Maggie's neighbour in tones that only a husband could have used. 'Wait till you see the family ghost.'

'Ronald, please! Have pity on my poor nerves!' The upper half of a tiny, childish, imploring face peered like a crescent moon over the rim of the chair.

'If there is a ghost,' said Maggie, afraid that her original remark might be construed as a criticism, 'I envy him his beautiful surroundings. I would willingly take his place.'

'Hear, hear,' agreed Ronald. 'A very happy haunting-ground. Is there a ghost, Charles?'

There was a pause. They all looked at their host.

'Well,' said Mr Ampleforth, who rarely spoke except after a

pause and never without a slight impressiveness of manner, 'there is and there isn't.'

The silence grew even more respectful.

'The ghost of Low Threshold Hall,' Mr Ampleforth continued, 'is no ordinary ghost.'

'It wouldn't be,' muttered Ronald in an aside Maggie feared might be audible.

'It is, for one thing,' Mr Ampleforth pursued, 'exceedingly considerate.'

'Oh, how?' exclaimed two or three voices.

'It only comes by invitation.'

'Can anyone invite it?'

'Yes, anyone.'

There was nothing Mr Ampleforth liked better than answering questions; he was evidently enjoying himself now.

'How is the invitation delivered?' Ronald asked. 'Does one telephone, or does one send a card: "Mrs Ampleforth requests the pleasure of Mr Ghost's company on – well – what is tomorrow? – the eighteenth August, Moaning and Groaning and Chain Rattling. R.S.V.P."?'

'That would be a sad solecism,' said Mr Ampleforth. 'The ghost of Low Threshold Hall is a lady.'

'Oh,' cried Eileen's affected little voice. 'I'm so thankful. I should be less frightened of a female phantom.'

'She hasn't attained years of discretion,' Mr Ampleforth said. 'She was only sixteen when—'

'Then she's not "out"?'

'Not in the sense you mean. I hope she's not "out" in any sense,' said Mr Ampleforth, with grim facetiousness.

There was a general shudder.

'Well, I'm glad we can't ask her to an evening party,' observed Ronald. 'A ghost at tea-time is much less alarming. Is she what is called a "popular girl"?'

'I'm afraid not.'

'Then why do people invite her?'

'They don't realize what they're doing.'

'A kind of pig in a poke business, what? But you haven't told us yet how we're to get hold of the little lady.'

'That's quite simple,' said Mr Ampleforth readily. 'She comes to the door.'

The drawing-room clock began to strike eleven, and no one spoke till it had finished.

'She comes to the door,' said Ronald with an air of deliberation, 'and then – don't interrupt, Eileen, I'm in charge of the cross-examination – she – she hangs about—'

'She waits to be asked inside.'

'I suppose there is a time-honoured formula of invitation: "Sweet Ermyntrude, in the name of the master of the house I bid thee welcome to Low Threshold Hall. There's no step, so you can walk straight in." Charles, much as I admire your house, I do think it's incomplete without a doorstep. A ghost could just sail in.'

'There you make a mistake,' said Mr Ampleforth impressively. 'Our ghost cannot enter the house unless she is lifted across the threshold.'

'Like a bride,' exclaimed Magdalen.

'Yes,' said Mr Ampleforth. 'Because she came as a bride.' He looked round at his guests with an enigmatic smile.

They did not disappoint him. 'Now, Charlie, don't be so mysterious! Do tell us! Tell us the whole story.'

Mr Ampleforth settled himself into his chair. 'There's very little to tell,' he said, with the reassuring manner of someone who intends to tell a great deal, 'but this is the tale. In the time of the Wars of the Roses the owner of Low Threshold Hall (I need not tell you his name was not Ampleforth) married *en troisièmes noces* the daughter of a neighbouring baron much less powerful than he. Lady Elinor Stortford was sixteen when she came and she did not live to see her seventeenth birthday. Her husband was a bad hat (I'm sorry to have to say so of a predecessor of mine), a very bad hat. He ill-treated her, drove her mad with terror, and finally killed her.'

The narrator paused dramatically but the guests felt slightly disappointed. They had heard so many stories of that kind.

'Poor thing,' said Magdalen, feeling that some comment was necessary, however flat. 'So now she haunts the place. I suppose it's the nature of ghosts to linger where they've suffered, but it seems illogical to me. I should want to go somewhere else.'

'The Lady Elinor would agree with you. The first thing she does when she gets into the house is make plans for getting out. Her visits, as far as I can gather, have generally been brief.'

'Then why does she come?' asked Eileen.

'She comes for vengeance,' Mr Ampleforth's voice dropped at

the word. 'And apparently she gets it. Within a short time of her appearance, someone in the house always dies.'

'Nasty spiteful little girl,' said Ronald, concealing a yawn. 'Then how long is she in residence?'

'Until her object is accomplished.'

'Does she make a dramatic departure – in a thunderstorm or something?'

'No, she is just carried out.'

'Who carries her this time?'

'The undertaker's men. She goes out with the corpse. Though some say—'

'Oh, Charlie, do stop!' Mrs Ampleforth interrupted, bending down to gather up the corners of her bedspread. 'Eileen will never sleep. Let's go to bed.'

'No! No!' shouted Ronald. 'He can't leave off like that. I must hear the rest. My flesh was just beginning to creep.'

Mr Ampleforth looked at his wife.

'I've had my orders.'

'Well, well,' said Ronald, resigned. 'Anyhow, remember what I said. A decent fall of rain, and you'll have a foot of water under the tower there, unless you put in a doorstep.'

Mr Ampleforth looked grave. 'Oh no, I couldn't do that. That would be to invite er – er – trouble. The absence of a step was a precaution. That's how the house got its name.'

'A precaution against what?'

'Against Lady Elinor.'

'But how? I should have thought a draw-bridge would have been more effective.'

'Lord Deadham's immediate heirs thought the same. According to the story they put every material obstacle they could to bar the lady's path. You can still see in the tower the grooves which contained the portcullis. And there was a flight of stairs so steep and dangerous they couldn't be used without risk to life and limb. But that only made it easier for Lady Elinor.'

'How did it?'

'Why, don't you see, everyone who came to the house, friends and strangers alike, had to be helped over the threshold! There was no way of distinguishing between them. At last when so many members of the family had been killed off that it was threatened with extinction, someone conceived a brilliant idea. Can you guess what it was, Maggie?'

'They removed all the barriers and levelled the threshold, so that any stranger who came to the door and asked to be helped into the house was refused admittance.'

'Exactly. And the plan seems to have worked remarkably well.'

'But the family did die out in the end,' observed Maggie.

'Yes,' said Mr Ampleforth, 'soon after the middle of the eighteenth century. The best human plans are fallible, and Lady Elinor was very persistent.'

He held the company with his glittering raconteur's eye.

But Mrs Ampleforth was standing up. 'Now, now,' she said, 'I gave you twenty minutes' grace. It will soon be midnight. Come along, Maggie, you must be tired after your journey. Let me light you a candle.' She took the girl's arm and piloted her into the comparative darkness of the hall. 'I think they must be on this table,' she said, her fingers groping; 'I don't know the house myself yet. We ought to have had a light put here. But it's one of Charlie's little economies to have as few lights as possible. I'll tell him about it. But it takes so long to get anything done in this out-of-the-way spot. My dear, nearly three miles to the nearest clergyman, four to the nearest doctor! Ah, here we are, I'll light some for the others. Charlie is still holding forth about Lady Elinor. You didn't mind that long recital?' she added, as, accompanied by their shadows, they walked up the stairs. 'Charlie does so love an audience. And you don't feel uncomfortable or anything? I am always so sorry for Lady Elinor, poor soul, if she ever existed. Oh, and I wanted to say we were so disappointed about Antony. I feel we got you down today on false pretences. Something at the office kept him. But he's coming tomorrow. When is the wedding to be, dearest?'

'In the middle of September.'

'Quite soon now. I can't tell you how excited I am about it. I think he's such a dear. You both are. Now which is your way, left, right, or middle? I'm ashamed to say I've forgotten.'

Maggie considered. 'I remember; it's to the left.'

'In that black abyss? Oh, darling, I forgot; do you feel equal to going on the picnic tomorrow? We shan't get back till five. It'll be a long day: I'll stay at home with you if you like – I'm tired of ruins.'

'I'd love to go.'

'Good-night, then.'

'Good-night.'

In the space of ten minutes the two men, left to themselves, had succeeded in transforming the elegant Queen Anne drawing-room into something that looked and smelt like a bar-parlour.

'Well,' observed Ronald who, more than his host, had been responsible for the room's deterioration, 'time to turn in. I have a rendezvous with Lady Elinor. By the way, Charles,' he went on, 'have you given the servants instructions in anti-Elinor technique – told them only to admit visitors who can enter the house under their own steam, so to speak?'

'Mildred thought it wisest, and I agree with her,' said Mr Ampleforth, 'to tell the servants nothing at all. It might unsettle them, and we shall have hard work to keep them as it is.'

'Perhaps you're right,' said Ronald. 'Anyhow it's no part of their duty to show the poor lady out. Charles, what were you going to say that wasn't fit for ears polite when Mildred stopped you?'

Mr Ampleforth reflected. 'I wasn't aware—'

'Oh, yes, she nipped your smoking-room story in the bud. I asked "Who carries Lady Elinor out?" and you said "The undertaker's men; she goes out with the corpse," and you were going to say something else when you were called to order.'

'Oh, I remember,' said Mr Ampleforth. 'It was such a small point, I couldn't imagine why Mildred objected. According to one story, she doesn't go out *with* the corpse, she goes out in it.'

Ronald pondered. 'Don't see much difference, do you?'

'I can't honestly say I do.'

'Women are odd creatures,' Ronald said. 'So long.'

The cat stood by the library door, miaowing. Its intention was perfectly plain. First it had wanted to go out; then it strolled up and down outside the window, demanding to come in; now it wanted to go out again. For the third time in half an hour Antony Fairfield rose from his comfortable chair to do its bidding. He opened the door gently – all his movements were gentle; but the cat scuttled ignominiously out, as though he had kicked it. Antony looked round. How could he defend himself from disturbance without curtailing the cat's liberty of movement? He might leave the window and the door open, to give the animal freedom of exit and entrance; though he hated sitting in a room with the door open, he was prepared to make the sacrifice. But he couldn't leave the window open because the rain would come in and spoil Mrs Ampleforth's beautiful silk cushions. Heavens, how it rained! Too bad for the farmers, thought Antony, whose mind was always busying itself with other people's misfortunes. The crops had been looking so well as he drove in the sunshine from the station, and now this sudden storm would beat everything down. He arranged his chair so that he could see the window and not keep the cat waiting if she felt like paying him another visit. The pattering of the rain soothed him. Half an hour and they would be back – Maggie would be back. He tried to visualize their faces, all so well known to him: but the experiment was not successful. Maggie's image kept ousting the others; it even appeared, somewhat grotesquely, on the top of Ronald's well-tailored shoulders. They mustn't find me asleep, thought Antony; I should look too middle-aged. So he picked up the newspaper from the floor and turned to the cross-word puzzle. 'Nine points of the law' in nine-ten letters. That was a very easy one: 'Possession'. Possession, thought Antony; I must put that down. But as he had no pencil and was too sleepy to get one, he repeated the word over and over again: Possession, Possession. It worked like a charm. He fell asleep and dreamed.

In his dream he was still in the library, but it was night and somehow his chair had got turned around so that he no longer faced the window, but he knew that the cat was there, asking to come in; only someone – Maggie – was trying to persuade him not to let it in. 'It's not a cat at all,' she kept saying; 'it's a Possession. I can see its nine points, and they're very sharp.' But he knew that she was mistaken, and really meant nine lives, which all cats have: so he thrust her aside and ran to the window and opened it. It was too dark to see so he put out his hand where he thought the cat's body would be, expecting to feel the warm fur; but what met his hand was not warm, nor was it fur . . . He woke with a start to see the butler standing in front of him. The room was flooded with sunshine.

'Oh, Rundle,' he cried, 'I was asleep. Are they back?'

The butler smiled.

'No, sir, but I expect them every minute now.'

'But you wanted me?'

'Well, sir, there's a young lady called, and I said the master was out, but she said could she speak to the gentleman in the library? She must have seen you, sir, as she passed the window.'

'How very odd. Does she know me?'

'That was what she said, sir. She talks rather funny.'

'All right, I'll come.'

Antony followed the butler down the long corridor. When they reached the tower their footsteps rang on the paved floor. A considerable pool of water, the result of the recent heavy shower, had formed on the flagstones near the doorway. The door stood open, letting in a flood of light; but of the caller there was no sign.

'She was here a moment ago,' the butler said.

'Ah, I see her,' cried Antony. 'At least, isn't that her reflected in the water? She must be leaning against the door-post.'

'That's right,' said Rundle. 'Mind the puddle, sir. Let me give you a hand. I'll have this all cleared up before they come back.'

Five minutes later two cars, closely following each other, pulled up at the door, and the picnic party tumbled out.

'Dear me, how wet!' cried Mrs Ampleforth, standing in the doorway. 'What has happened, Rundle? Has there been a flood?'

'It was much worse before you arrived, madam,' said the butler, disappointed that his exertions with mop, floor-cloth, scrubbing-brush and pail were being so scantily recognized. 'You could have sailed a boat on it. Mr Antony, he—'

'Oh, has he arrived? Antony's here, isn't that splendid?'

'Antony!' they all shouted. 'Come out! Come down! Where are you?'

'I bet he's asleep, the lazy devil,' remarked Ronald.

'No, sir,' said the butler, at last able to make himself heard. 'Mr Antony's in the drawing-room with a lady.'

Mrs Ampleforth's voice broke the silence that succeeded this announcement.

'With a lady, Rundle? Are you sure?'

'Well, madam, she's hardly more than a girl.'

'I always thought Antony was that sort of man,' observed Ronald. 'Maggie, you'd better—'

'It's too odd,' interposed Mrs Ampleforth hastily. 'Who in the world can she be?'

'I don't see there's anything odd in someone calling on us,' said Mr Ampleworth. 'What her name, Rundle?'

'She didn't give a name, sir.'

'That is rather extraordinary. Antony is so impulsive and kind-hearted. I hope – ah, here he is.'

Antony came towards them along the passage, smiling and

waving his hands. When the welcoming and hand-shaking were over:

'We were told you had a visitor,' said Mrs Ampleforth.

'Yes,' said Ronald. 'I'm afraid we arrived at the wrong moment.'

Antony laughed and then looked puzzled. 'Believe me you didn't,' he said. 'You almost saved my life. She speaks such a queer dialect when she speaks at all, and I had reached the end of my small talk. But she's rather interesting. Do come along and see her: I left her in the library.' They followed Antony down the passage. When they reached the door he said to Mrs Ampleforth: 'Shall I go in first? She may be shy at meeting so many people.'

He went in. A moment later they heard his voice raised in excitement.

'Mildred! I can't find her! She's gone!'

Tea had been cleared away, but Antony's strange visitor was still the topic of conversation. 'I can't understand it,' he was saying, not for the first time. 'The windows were shut, and if she'd gone by the door we must have seen her.'

'Now, Antony,' said Ronald severely, 'let's hear the whole story again. Remember, you are accused of smuggling into the house a female of doubtful reputation. Furthermore the prosecution alleges that when you heard us call (we were shouting ourselves hoarse, but he didn't come at once, you remember) you popped her out of that window and came out to meet us, smiling sheepishly, and feebly gesticulating. What do you say?'

'I've told you everything,' said Antony. 'I went to the door and found her leaning against the stonework. Her eyes were shut. She didn't move and I thought she must be ill. So I said, "Is anything the matter?" and she looked up and said, "My leg hurts." Then I saw by the way she was standing that her hip must have been broken once and never properly set. I asked her where she lived, and she didn't seem to understand me; so I changed the form of the question, as one does on the telephone, and asked where she came from, and she said, 'A little further down,' meaning down the hill, I suppose.'

'Probably from one of the men's cottages,' said Mr Ampleforth.

'I asked if it was far, and she said "No," which was obvious, otherwise her clothes would have been wet and they weren't, only a little muddy. She even had some mud on her mediaeval bridesmaid's head-dress (I can't describe her clothes again, Mildred; you know how bad I am at that). So I asked if she'd had a fall, and she said, 'No, she got dirty coming up,' or so I understood her. It wasn't easy to understand her; I suppose she talked the dialect of these parts. I concluded (you all say you would have known long before) that she was a little mad, but I didn't like to leave her looking so rotten, so I said, "Won't you come in and rest a minute?" Then I wished I hadn't.'

'Because she looked so pleased?'

'Oh, much more than pleased. And she said, "I hope you won't live to regret it," rather as though she hoped I should. And then I only meant just to take her hand, because of the water, you know, and she was lame—'

'And instead she flung herself into the poor fellow's arms—'

'Well, it amounted to that. I had no option! So I carried her across and put her down and she followed me here, walking better than I expected. A minute later you arrived. I asked her to wait and she didn't. That's all.'

'I should like to have seen Antony doing the St Christopher act!' said Ronald. 'Was she heavy, old boy?'

Antony shifted in his chair. 'Oh no,' he said, 'not at all. Not at all heavy.' Unconsciously he stretched his arms out in front of him, as though testing an imaginary weight. 'I see my hands are grubby,' he said with an expression of distaste. 'I must go and wash them. I won't be a moment, Maggie.'

That night, after dinner, there was some animated conversation in the servants' hall.

'Did you hear any more, Mr Rundle?' asked a house-maid of the butler, who had returned from performing his final office at the dinner-table.

'I did,' said Rundle, 'but I don't know that I ought to tell you.'

'It won't make any difference, Mr Rundle, whether you do or don't. I'm going to give in my notice tomorrow. I won't stay in a haunted house. We've been lured here. We ought to have been warned.'

'They certainly meant to keep it from us,' said Rundle. 'I myself had put two and two together after seeing Lady Elinor; what Wilkins said when he came in for his tea only confirmed my suspicions. No gardener can ever keep a still tongue in his head. It's a pity.'

'Wouldn't you have told us yourself, Mr Rundle?' asked the cook.

'I should have used my discretion,' the butler replied. 'When I informed Mr Ampleforth that I was no longer in ignorance, he said, "I rely on you, Rundle, not to say anything which might alarm the staff".'

'Mean, I call it,' exclaimed the kitchen-maid indignantly. 'They want to have all the fun and leave us to die like rats in a trap.'

Rundle ignored the interruption.

'I told Mr Ampleforth that Wilkins had been tale-bearing and would he excuse it in an outdoor servant, but unfortunately we were now in possession of the facts.'

'That's why they talked about it at dinner,' said the maid who helped Rundle to wait.

'They didn't really throw the mask off till after you'd gone, Lizzie,' said the butler. 'Then I began to take part in the conversation.'

He paused for a moment.

'Mr Ampleforth asked me whether anything was missing from the house, and I was able to reply, "No, everything was in order."'

'What else did you say?' inquired the cook.

'I made the remark that the library window wasn't fastened, as they thought, but only closed, and Mrs Turnbull laughed and said, "Perhaps it's only a thief, after all," but the others didn't think she could have got through the window anyhow, unless her lameness was all put on. And then I told them what the police had said about looking out for a suspicious character.'

'Did they seem frightened?' asked the cook.

'Not noticeably,' replied the butler. 'Mrs Turnbull said she hoped the gentlemen wouldn't stay long over their port. Mr Ampleforth said, "No, they had had a full day, and would be glad to go to bed." Mrs Ampleforth asked Miss Winthrop if she wanted to change her bedroom, but she said she didn't. Then Mr Fairfield asked if he could have some iodine for his hand, and Miss Winthrop said she would fetch him some. She wanted to bring it after dinner, but he said, "Oh, tomorrow morning will do, darling." He seemed rather quiet.'

'What's he done to his hand?'

'I saw the mark when he took his coffee. It was like a burn.'

'They didn't say they were going to shut the house up, or anything?'

'Oh, Lord, no. There's going to be a party next week. They'll all have to stay for that.'

'I never knew such people,' said the kitchen-maid. 'They'd rather die, and us too, than miss their pleasures. I wouldn't stay another day if I wasn't forced. When you think she may be here in this very room, listening to us!' She shuddered.

'Don't you worry, my girl,' said Rundle, rising from his chair with a gesture of dismissal. 'She won't waste her time listening to you.'

'We really might be described as a set of crocks,' said Mr Ampleforth to Maggie after luncheon the following day. 'You, poor dear, with your headache; Eileen with her nerves; I with – well – a touch of rheumatism; Antony with his bad arm.'

Maggie looked troubled.

'My headache is nothing, but I'm afraid Antony isn't very well.'

'He's gone to lie down, hasn't he?'

'Yes.'

'The best thing. I telephoned for the doctor to come this evening. He can have a look at all of us, ha! ha! Meanwhile, where will you spend the afternoon? I think the library's the coolest place on a stuffy day like this; and I want you to see my collection of books about Low Threshold – my Thresholdiana, I call them.'

Maggie followed him into the library.

'Here they are. Most of them are nineteenth-century books, publications of the Society of Antiquaries, and so on; but some are older. I got a little man in Charing Cross Road to hunt them out for me; I haven't had time to read them all myself.'

Maggie took a book at random from the shelves.

'Now I'll leave you,' said her host. 'And later in the afternoon I know that Eileen would appreciate a little visit. Ronald says it's nothing, just a little nervous upset, stomach trouble. Between ourselves, I fear Lady Elinor is to blame.'

Maggie opened the book. It was called *An Enquiry into the Recent Tragicall Happening at Low Threshold Hall in the County of Suffolk, with some Animadversions on the Barbarous Customs of our Ancestors*. It opened with a rather tedious account of the semi-mythical origins of the Deadham family. Maggie longed to skip this, but she might have to discuss the book with Mr Ampleforth, so she ploughed on. Her persistence was rewarded by a highly coloured picture of Lady Elinor's husband and an account of the cruelties he practised on her. The story would have been too painful to read had not the author (Maggie felt) so obviously drawn upon a very vivid imagination. But suddenly her eyes narrowed. What was this? 'Once in a Drunken Fitt he so mishandled her that her thigh was broken near the hip, and her screames were so loud they were heard by the servants through three closed doors; and yet he would not summon a Chirurgeon, for (quoth he)' – Lord Deadham's reason was coarse in the extreme; Maggie hastened on.

'And in consequence of these Barbarities her nature which was soft and yielding at the first was greatly changed, and those who sawe her now (but Pitie seal'd their lips) would have said she had a Bad Hearte.'

No wonder, thought Maggie, reading with new and painful interest how the murdered woman avenged herself on various descendants, direct and collateral, of her persecutor. 'And it hath been generally supposed by the vulgar that her vengeance was directed only against members of that family from which she taken so many Causeless Hurtes; and the depraved, defective, counterfeit records of those times have lent colour to this Opinion. Whereas the truth is as I now state it, having had access to those death-bed and testamentary depositions which, preserved in ink however faint, do greater service to verity than the relations of Pot-House Historians, enlarged by Memory and confused by Ale. Yet it is on such Testimonies that rash and sceptical Heads rely when they assert that the Lady Elinor had no hand in the late Horrid Occurrence at Low Threshold Hall, which I shall presently describe, thinking that a meer visitor and no blood relation could not be the object of her vengeance, notwithstanding the evidence of two serving-maids, one at the door and one craning her neck from an upper casement, who saw him beare her in: The truth being that she maketh no distinction between persons, but whoso admits her, on him doth her vengeance fall. Seven times she hath brought death to Low Threshold Hall; Three, it is true, being members of the family, but the remaining four indifferent Persons and not connected with them, having in common only this piece of folie, that they, likewise, let her in. And in each case she hath used the same manner of attack, as those who have beheld her first a room's length, then no further than a Lovers Embrace, from her victim have *in articulo mortis* delivered. And the moment when she is no longer seen, which to the watchers seems the Clarion and Reveille of their hopes, is in reality the knell; for she hath not withdrawn further, but approached nearer, she hath not gone out but entered in: and from her dreadful Citadel within the body rejoyces, doubtless, to see the tears and hear the groanes, of those who with Comfortable Faces (albeit with sinking Hearts), would soothe the passage of the parting Soul. Their lacrimatory Effusions are balm to her wicked Minde; the sad gale and ventilation of their sighs a pleasing Zephyre to her vindictive spirit.'

Maggie put down the book for a moment and stared in front of her. Then she began again to read.

'Once only hath she been cheated of her Prey, and it happened thus. His Bodie was already swollen with the malignant Humours she had stirred up in him and his life despaired of when a kitchen-wench was taken with an Imposthume that bled inwardly. She being of small account and but lately arrived they did only lay her in the Strawe, charging the Physician (and he nothing loth, expecting no Glory or Profit from attendance on such a Wretched creature) not to Divide his Efforts but use all his skill to save their Cousin (afterwards the twelfth Lord). Notwithstanding which precaution he did hourly get worse until sodainely a change came and he began to amend. Whereat was such rejoicing (including an Ox roasted whole) that the night was spent before they heard that the serving-maid was dead. In their Revels they gave small heed to this Event, not realizing that they owed His life to Hers; for a fellow-servant who tended the maid (out of charity) declared that her death and the cousin's recovery followed as quickly as a clock striking Two. And the Physician said it was well, for she would have died in any case.

'Whereby we must conclude that the Lady Elinor, like other Apparitions, is subject to certain Lawes. One, to abandon her Victim and seeking another tenement to transfer her vengeance, should its path be crossed by a Body yet nearer Dissolution: and another is, she cannot possess or haunt the corpse after it has received Christian Buriall. As witness the fact that the day after the Interment of the tenth Lord she again appeared at the Doore and being recognized by her inability to make the Transit was turned away and pelted. And another thing I myself believe but have no proof of is: That her power is circumscribed by the walls of the House; those victims of her Malignitie could have been saved but for the dreadful swiftnesse of the disease and the doctor's unwillingness to move a Sicke man; otherwise how could the Termes of her Curse that she pronounced be fulfilled: "They shall be carried out Feet Foremost"?'

Maggie read no more. She walked out of the library with the book under her arm. Before going to see how Antony was she would put it in her bedroom where no one could find it. Troubled and oppressed she paused at the head of the stairs. Her way lay straight ahead, but her glance automatically travelled to the right where, at the far end of the passage, Antony's bedroom lay. She looked again; the door, which she could only just see, was shut now. But she could swear it had closed upon a woman. There was nothing odd in that; Mildred might have gone in, or Muriel, or a servant. But all the same she could not rest. Hurriedly she changed her dress and went to Antony's room. Pausing at the door she listened and distinctly heard his voice, speaking rapidly and in a low tone; but no one seemed to reply. She got no answer to her knock, so, mustering her courage, she walked in.

The blind was down and the room half dark, and the talking continued, which increased her uneasiness. Then, as her eyes got used to the darkness, she realized, with a sense of relief, that he was talking in his sleep. She pulled up the blind a little, so that she might see his hand. The brown mark had spread, she thought, and looked rather puffy as though coffee had been injected under the skin. She felt concerned for him. He would never have gone properly to bed like that, in his pyjamas, if he hadn't felt ill, and he tossed about restlessly. Maggie bent over him. Perhaps he had been eating a biscuit: there was some gritty stuff on the pillow. She tried to scoop it up but it eluded her. She could make no sense of his mutterings, but the word 'light' came in a good deal. Perhaps he was only half asleep and wanted the blind down. At last her ears caught the sentence that was running on his lips: 'She was so light.' Light? A light woman? Browning. The words conveyed nothing to her, and not wishing to wake him she tiptoed from the room.

'The doctor doesn't seem to think seriously of any of us, Maggie, you'll be glad to hear,' said Mr Ampleforth, coming into the drawing-room about six o'clock. 'Eileen's coming down to dinner. I am to drink less port – I didn't need a doctor, alas! to tell me that. Antony's the only casualty: he's got a slight temperature, and had better stay where he is until tomorrow. The doctor thinks it is one of those damnable horse-flies: his arm is a bit swollen, that's all.'

'Has he gone?' asked Maggie quickly.

'Who, Antony?'

'No, no, the doctor.'

'Oh, I'd forgotten your poor head. No, you'll just catch him. His car's on the terrace.'

The doctor, a kindly, harassed middle-aged man, listened patiently to Maggie's questions.

'The brown mark? Oh, that's partly the inflammation, partly the iodine – he's been applying it pretty liberally, you know; amateur physicians are all alike; feel they can't have too much of a good thing.'

'You don't think the water here's responsible? I wondered if he ought to go away.'

'The water? Oh no. No, it's a bite all right, though I confess I can't see the place where the devil got his beak in. I'll come tomorrow, if you like, but there's really no need.'

The next morning, returning from his bath, Ronald marched into Antony's room. The blind went up with a whizz and a smack, and Antony opened his eyes.

'Good morning, old man,' said Ronald cheerfully. 'Thought I'd look in and see you. How goes the blood-poisoning? Better?'

Antony drew up his sleeve and hastily replaced it. The arm beneath was chocolate-coloured to the elbow.

'I feel pretty rotten,' he said.

'I say, that's bad luck. What's this?' added Ronald, coming nearer. 'Have you been sleeping in both beds?'

'Not to my knowledge,' murmured Antony.

'You have, though,' said Ronald. 'If this bed hasn't been slept in, it's been slept on, or lain on. That I can swear. Only a head, my boy, could have put that dent in the pillow, and only a pair of muddy – hullo! The pillow's got it, too.'

'Got what?' asked Antony drowsily.

'Well, if you ask me, it's common garden mould.'

'I'm not surprised. I feel pretty mouldy, too.'

'Well, Antony; to save your good name with the servants, I'll remove the traces.'

With characteristic vigour Ronald swept and smoothed the bed.

'Now you'll be able to look Rundle in the face.'

There was a knock on the door.

'If this is Maggie,' said Ronald, 'I'm going.'

It was, and he suited the action to the word.

'You needn't trouble to tell me, dearest,' she said, 'that you are feeling much better, because I can see that you aren't.'

Antony moved his head uneasily on the pillow.

'I don't feel very flourishing, to tell you the honest truth.'

'Listen' – Maggie tried to make her voice sound casual – 'I don't believe this is a very healthy place. Don't laugh, Antony; we're all of us more or less under the weather. I think you ought to go away.'

'My dear, don't be hysterical. One often feels rotten when one wakes up. I shall be all right in a day or two.'

'Of course you will. But all the same if you were in Sussex Square you could call in Fosbrook – and, well, I should be more comfortable.'

'But you'd be here!'

'I could stay at Pamela's.'

'But, darling, that would break up the party. I couldn't do it; and it wouldn't be fair to Mildred.'

'My angel, you're no good to the party, lying here in bed. And as long as you're here, let me warn you they won't see much of me.'

A look of irritation Maggie had never noticed before came into his face as he said, almost spitefully:

'Supposing the doctor won't allow you to come in? It may be catching, you know.'

Maggie concealed the hurt she felt.

'All the more reason for you to be out of the house.'

He pulled up the bedclothes with a gesture of annoyance and turned away.

'Oh, Maggie, don't keep nagging at me. You ought to be called Naggie, not Maggie.'

This was an allusion to an incident in Maggie's childhood. Her too great solicitude for a younger brother's safety had provoked the gibe. It had always wounded her, but never so much as coming from Antony's lips. She rose to go.

'Do put the bed straight,' said Antony, still with face averted. 'Otherwise they'll think you've been sleeping here.'

'What?'

'Well, Ronald said something about it.'

Maggie closed the door softly behind her. Antony was ill, of course, she must remember that. But he had been ill before, and was always an angelic patient. She went down to breakfast feeling miserable.

After breakfast, at which everyone else had been unusually cheerful, she thought of a plan. It did not prove so easy of execution as she hoped.

'But, dearest Maggie,' said Mildred, 'the village is nearly three miles away. And there's nothing to see there.'

'I love country post-offices,' said Maggie; 'they always have such amusing things.'

'There is a post-office,' admitted Mildred. 'But are you sure it isn't something we could do from here? Telephone, telegraph?'

'Perhaps there'd be a picture-postcard of the house,' said Maggie feebly.

'Oh, but Charlie has such nice ones,' Mildred protested. 'He's so house-proud, you could trust him for that. Don't leave us for two hours just to get postcards. We shall miss you so much, and think of poor Antony left alone all morning.'

Maggie had been thinking of him.

'He'll get on all right without me,' she said lightly.

'Well, wait till the afternoon when the chauffeur or Ronald can run you over in a car. He and Charlie have gone into Norwich and won't be back till lunch.'

'I think I'll walk,' said Maggie. 'It'll do me good.'

'I managed that very clumsily,' she thought, 'so how shall I persuade Antony to tell me the address of his firm?'

To her surprise his room was empty. He must have gone away in the middle of writing a letter, for there were sheets lying about on the writing-table and, what luck! an envelope addressed to Higgins & Stukeley, 312 Paternoster Row. A glance was all she really needed to memorize the address; but her eyes wandered to the litter on the table. What a mess! There were several pages of notepaper covered with figures. Antony had been making calculations and, as his habit was, decorating them with marginal illustrations. He was good at drawing faces, and he had a gift for catching a likeness. Maggie had often seen, and been gratified to see, slips of paper embellished with portraits of herself — full-face, side-face, three-quarter-face. But this face that looked out from among the figures and seemed to avoid her glance, was not hers. It was the face of a woman she had never seen before but whom she felt she would recognize anywhere, so consistent and vivid were the likenesses. Scattered among the loose leaves were the contents of Antony's pocket-book. She knew he always carried her photograph. Where was it? Seized by an impulse, she began to rummage among the papers. Ah, here it was. But it was no longer hers! With a few strokes Antony had transformed her oval face, unlined and soft of feature, into a totally different one, a pinched face with high cheekbones, hollow cheeks, and bright hard eyes, from whose corners a sheaf of fine wrinkles spreads like a fan: a face with which she was already too familiar.

Unable to look at it she turned away and saw Antony standing behind her. He seemed to have come from the bath for he carried a towel and was wearing his dressing-gown.

'Well,' he said. 'Do you think it's an improvement?'

She could not answer him, but walked over to the washstand and took up the thermometer that was lying on it.

'Ought you to be walking about like that,' she said at last, 'with a temperature of a hundred?'

'Perhaps not,' he replied, making two or three goat-like skips towards the bed. 'But I feel rather full of beans this morning.'

Maggie edged away from his smile towards the door.

'There isn't anything I can do for you?'

'Not today, my darling.'

The term of endearment struck her like a blow.

Maggie sent off her telegram and turned into the village street. The fact of being able to do something had relieved her mind: already in imagination she saw Antony being packed into the Ampleforths' Daimler with rugs and hot-water bottles, and herself, perhaps, seated by the driver. They were endlessly kind, and would make no bones about motoring him to London. But though her spirits were rising her body felt tired; the day was sultry, and she had hurried. Another bad night like last night, she thought, and I shall be a wreck. There was a chemist's shop over the way, and she walked in.

'Can I have some sal volatile?'

'Certainly, madam.'

She drank it and felt better.

'Oh, and have you anything in the way of a sleeping draught?'

'We have some allodanol tablets, madam.'

'I'll take them.'
'Have you a doctor's prescription?'
'No.'
'Then I'm afraid you'll have to sign the poison book. Just a matter of form.'

Maggie recorded her name, idly wondering what J. Bates, her predecessor on the list, meant to do with his cyanide of potassium.

'We must try not to worry,' said Mrs Ampleforth, handing Maggie her tea, 'but I must say I'm glad the doctor has come. It relieves one of responsibility, doesn't it? Not that I feel disturbed about Antony — he was quite bright when I went to see him just before lunch. And he's been sleeping since. But I quite see what Maggie means. He doesn't seem himself. Perhaps it would be a good plan, as she suggests, to send him to London. He would have better advice there.'

Rundle came in.

'A telegram for Mr Fairfield, madam.'

'It's been telephoned: "Your presence urgently required Tuesday morning — Higgins & Stukeley." Tuesday, that's tomorrow. Everything seems to point to his going, doesn't it, Charles?'

Maggie was delighted, but a little surprised, that Mrs Ampleforth had fallen in so quickly with the plan of sending Antony home.

'Could he go today?' she asked.

'Tomorrow would be too late, wouldn't it?' said Mr Ampleforth drily. 'The car's at his disposal: he can go whenever he likes.'

Through her relief Maggie felt a little stab of pain that they were both so ready to see the last of Antony. He was generally such a popular guest.

'I could go with him,' she said.

Instantly they were up in arms, Ronald the most vehement of all. 'I'm sure Antony wouldn't want you to. You know what I mean, Maggie, it's such a long drive, in a closed car on a stuffy evening. Charlie says he'll send a man, if necessary.'

Mr Ampleforth nodded.

'But if he were ill!' cried Maggie.

The entrance of the doctor cut her short. He looked rather grave.

'I wish I could say I was satisfied with Mr Fairfield's progress,' he said, 'but I can't. The inflammation has spread up the arm as far as the shoulder, and there's some fever. His manner is odd, too, excitable and apathetic by turns.' He paused. 'I should like a second opinion.'

Mr Ampleforth glanced at his wife.

'In that case wouldn't it be better to send him to London? As a matter of fact, his firm has telegraphed for him. He could go quite comfortably in the car.'

The doctor answered immediately:

'I wouldn't advise such a course. I think it would be most unwise to move him. His firm – you must excuse me – will have to do without him for a day or two.'

'Perhaps,' suggested Maggie trembling, 'it's a matter that could be arranged at his house. They could send over someone from the office. I know they make a fuss about having him on the spot,' she concluded lamely.

'Or, doctor,' said Mr Ampleforth, 'could you do us a very great kindness and go with him? We could telephone to his doctor to meet you, and the car would get you home by midnight.'

The doctor squared his shoulders: he was clearly one of those men whose resolution stiffens under opposition.

'I consider it would be the height of folly,' he said, 'to move him out of the house. I dare not do it on my responsibility. I will get a colleague over from Ipswich tomorrow morning. In the meantime, with your permission, I will arrange for a trained nurse to be sent tonight.'

Amid a subdued murmur of final instructions, the doctor left.

As Maggie, rather late, was walking upstairs to dress for dinner she met Rundle. He looked anxious.

'Excuse me, miss,' he said, 'but have you seen Mr Fairfield? I've asked everyone else, and they haven't. I took him up his supper half an hour ago, and he wasn't in his room. He got his dress clothes out, but they were all on the bed except the stiff shirt.'

'Have you been to look since?' asked Maggie.

'No, miss.'

'I'll go and see.'

She tiptoed along the passage to Antony's door. A medley of sounds, footsteps, drawers being opened and shut, met her ears.

She walked back to Rundle. 'He's in there all right,' she said. 'Now I must make haste and dress.'

A few minutes later a bell rang in the kitchen.
'Who's that?'
'Miss Winthrop's room,' said the cook. 'Hurry up, Lettice, or you'll have Rundle on your track – he'll be back in a minute.'
'I don't want to go,' said Lettice. 'I tell you I feel that nervous—'
'Nonsense, child,' said the cook. 'Run along with you.'
No sooner had the maid gone than Rundle appeared.
'I've had a bit of trouble with Master Antony,' he said. 'He's got it into his head that he wants to come down to dinner. "Rundle," he said to me, confidentially, "do you think it would matter us being seven? I want them to meet my new friend." "What friend, Mr Fairfield?" I said. "Oh," he said, "haven't you seen her? She's always about with me now." Poor chap, he used to be the pick of the bunch, and now I'm afraid he's going potty.'

'Do you think he'll really come down to dinner?' asked the cook, but before Rundle could answer Lettice rushed into the room.

'Oh,' she cried, 'I knew it would be something horrid! I knew it would be! And now she wants a floor-cloth and a pail! She says they mustn't know anything about it! But I won't go again – I won't bring it down, I won't even touch it!'

'What won't you touch?'
'That waste-paper basket.'
'Why, what's the matter with it?'
'It's . . . it's all bloody!'

When the word was out she grew calmer, and even seemed anxious to relate her experience.

'I went upstairs directly she rang' ('That's an untruth to start with,' said the cook) 'and she opened the door a little way and said, "Oh, Lettice, I've been so scared!" And I said, "What's the matter, miss?" And she said, "There's a cat in here." Well, I didn't think that was much to be frightened of, so I said, "Shall I come in and catch him, miss?" and she said (deceitful-like, as it turned out), "I should be so grateful." Then I went in but I couldn't see the cat anywhere, so I said, "Where is he?" At which she pointed to the waste-paper basket away by the dressing-table, and said, "In that waste-paper basket." I said, "Why, that makes it easier, miss, if he'll stay there." She said, "Oh, he'll stay there all right."

Of course I took her meaning in a moment, because I know cats do choose queer, out-of-the-way places to die in, so I said, "You mean the poor creature's dead, miss?" and I was just going across to get him because ordinarily I don't mind the body of an animal when she said (I will do her that justice), "Stop a minute, Lettice, he isn't dead; he's been murdered." I saw she was all trembling, and that made me tremble, too. And when I looked in the basket—well—'

She paused, partly perhaps to enjoy the dramatic effect of her announcement. 'Well, if it wasn't Thomas! Only you couldn't have recognized him, poor beast, his head was bashed in that cruel.'

'Thomas!' said the cook. 'Why, he was here only an hour ago.'

'That's what I said to Miss Winthrop. "Why, he was in the kitchen only an hour ago," and then I came over funny, and when she asked me to help her clean the mess up I couldn't, not if my life depended on it. But I don't feel like that now,' she ended inconsequently. 'I'll go back and do it!' She collected her traps and departed.

'Thomas!' muttered Rundle. 'Who could have wished the poor beast any harm? Now I remember. Mr Fairfield did ask me to get him out a clean shirt . . . I'd better go up and ask him.'

He found Antony in evening dress seated at the writing-table. He had stripped it of writing materials and the light from two candles gleamed on its polished surface. Opposite to him on the other side of the table was an empty chair. He was sitting with his back to the room; his face, when he turned it at Rundle's entrance, was blotchy and looked terribly tired.

'I decided to dine here after all, Rundle,' he said. Rundle saw that the Bovril was still untouched in his cup.

'Why, your supper'll get cold, Mr Fairfield,' he said.

'Mind your own business,' said Antony. 'I'm waiting.'

The Empire clock on the drawing-room chimney-piece began to strike, breaking into a conversation which neither at dinner nor afterwards had been more than desultory.

'Eleven,' said Mr Ampleforth. 'The nurse will be here any time now. She ought to be grateful to you, Ronald, for getting him into bed.'

'I didn't enjoy treating Antony like that,' said Ronald.

There was a silence.

'What was that?' asked Maggie suddenly.

'It sounded like the motor.'

'Might have been,' said Mr Ampleforth. 'You can't tell from here.'

'They strained their ears, but the rushing sound had already died away. 'Eileen's gone to bed, Maggie,' said Mrs Ampleforth. 'Why don't you? We'll wait up for the nurse, and tell you when she comes.'

Rather reluctantly Maggie agreed to go.

She had been in her bedroom about ten minutes, and was feeling too tired to take her clothes off, when there came a knock at the door. It was Eileen.

'Maggie,' she said, 'the nurse has arrived. I thought you'd like to know.'

'Oh, how kind of you,' said Maggie. 'They were going to tell me, but I expect they forgot. Where is she?'

'In Antony's room. I was coming from the bath and his door was open.'

'Did she look nice?'

'I only saw her back.'

'I think I'll go along and speak to her,' said Maggie.

'Yes, do. I don't think I'll go with you.'

As she walked along the passage Maggie wondered what she would say to the nurse. She didn't mean to offer her professional advice. But even nurses are human, and Maggie didn't want this stranger to imagine that Antony was, well, always like that – the spoilt, tiresome, unreasonable creature of the last few hours. She could find no harsher epithets for him, even after all his deliberate unkindness. The woman would probably have heard that Maggie was his fianceé; Maggie would try to show her that she was proud of the relationship and felt it an honour.

The door was still open so she knocked and walked in. But the figure that uncoiled itself from Antony's pillow and darted at her a look of malevolent triumph was not a nurse, nor was her face strange to Maggie; Maggie could see, so intense was her vision at that moment, just what strokes Antony had used to transform her own portrait into Lady Elinor's. She was terrified, but she could not bear to see Antony's rather long hair nearly touching the floor nor the creature's thin hand on his labouring throat. She advanced, resolved at whatever cost to break up this dreadful tableau. She approached near enough to realize that what seemed a stranglehold was probably a caress, when Antony's eyes rolled up at her and words, frothy and toneless like a chain of bursting bubbles, came popping from the corner of his swollen mouth: 'Get out, damn you!' At the same moment she heard the stir of presences behind her and a voice saying, 'Here is the patient, nurse; I'm afraid he's half out of bed, and here's Maggie, too. What *have* you been doing to him, Maggie?' Dazed, she turned about. 'Can't you see?' she cried; but she might have asked the question of herself, for when she looked back she could only see the tumbled bed, the vacant pillow and Antony's hair trailing the floor.

The nurse was a sensible woman. Fortified by tea, she soon bundled everybody out of the room. A deeper quiet than night ordinarily brings invaded the house. The reign of illness had begun.

A special embargo was laid on Maggie's visits. The nurse said she had noticed that Miss Winthrop's presence agitated the patient. But Maggie extracted a promise that she should be called if Antony got worse. She was too tired and worried to sleep, even if she had tried to, so she sat up fully dressed in a chair, every now and then trying to allay her anxiety by furtive visits to Antony's bedroom door.

The hours passed on leaden feet. She tried to distract herself by reading the light literature with which her hostess had provided her. Though she could not keep her attention on the books, she continued to turn their pages, for only so could she keep at bay the conviction that had long been forming at the back of her mind and that now threatened to engulf her whole consciousness: the conviction that the legend about Low Threshold was true. She was neither hysterical nor superstitious, and for a moment she had managed to persuade herself that what she had seen in Antony's room was an hallucination. The passing hours robbed her of that solace. Antony was the victim of Lady Elinor's vengeance. Everything pointed to it: the circumstances of her appearance, the nature of Antony's illness, the horrible deterioration in his character – to say nothing of the drawings, and the cat.

There were only two ways of saving him. One was to get him out of the house; she had tried that and failed; if she tried again she would fail more signally than before. But there remained the other way.

The old book about *The Tragicall Happenings at Low Threshold Hall* still reposed in a drawer; for the sake of her peace of mind Maggie had vowed not to take it out, and till now she kept her vow. But as the sky began to pale with the promise of dawn and her conviction of Antony's mortal danger grew apace, her resolution broke down.

'Whereby we must conclude,' she read, 'that the Lady Elinor, like other Apparitions, is subject to certain Lawes. One, to abandon her Victims and seeking another tenement enter into it and transfer her vengeance, should its path be crossed by a Body yet nearer Dissolution . . .'

A knock, that had been twice repeated, startled her out of her reverie.

'Come in!'

'Miss Winthrop,' said the nurse, 'I'm sorry to tell you the patient is weaker. I think the doctor had better be telephoned for.'

'I'll go and get someone,' said Maggie. 'Is he much worse?'

'Very much, I'm afraid.'

Maggie had no difficulty in finding Rundle; he was already up.

'What time is it, Rundle?' she asked. 'I've lost count.'

'Half-past four, miss.' He looked very sorry for her.

'When will the doctor be here?'

'In about an hour, miss, not more.'

Suddenly she had an idea. 'I'm so tired, Rundle, I think I shall try to get some sleep. Tell them not to call me unless . . . unless . . .'

'Yes, miss,' said Rundle. 'You look altogether done up.'

About an hour! So she had plenty of time. She took up the book again. 'Transfer her vengeance . . . seeking another tenement . . . a Body nearer Dissolution.' Her idle thoughts turned with compassion to the poor servant girl whose death had spelt recovery to Lord Deadham's cousin but been so little regarded: 'the night was spent' before they heard that she was dead. Well, this night was spent already. Maggie shivered. 'I shall die in my sleep,' she thought. 'But shall I feel her come?' Her tired body sickened with nausea at the idea of such a loathsome violation. But the thought still nagged at her. 'Shall I realize even for a moment that I'm changing into . . . into?' Her mind refused to frame the possibility. 'Should I have time to do anyone an injury?' she wondered. 'I could tie my feet together with a handkerchief; that would prevent me from walking.' Walking . . . walking . . . The word let loose on her mind a new flood of terrors. She could not do it! She could not lay herself open for ever to this horrible occupation! Her tormented imagination began to busy itself with the details of her funeral; she saw mourners following her coffin into the church. But Antony was not amongst them; he was better but too ill to be there. He could not understand why she had killed herself, for the note she had left gave no hint of the real reason, referred only to continual sleeplessness and nervous depression. So she would not have his company when her body was committed to the ground. But that was a mistake; it would not be her body, it would belong to that other woman and be hers to return to by the right of possession.

All at once the screen which had recorded such vivid images to her mind's eye went blank; and her physical eye, released, roamed wildly about the room. It rested on the book she was still holding. 'She cannot possess or haunt the corpse,' she read, 'after it has received Christian Buriall.' Here was a ray of comfort. But (her fears warned her) being a suicide she might not be allowed Christian burial. How then? Instead of the churchyard she saw a cross-roads, with a slanting signpost on which the words could no longer be read; only two or three people were there; they kept looking furtively about them and the grave-digger had thrown his spade aside and was holding a stake . . .

She pulled herself together with a jerk. 'These are all fancies,' she thought. 'It wasn't fancy when I signed the poison book.' She took up the little glass cylinder; there were eighteen tablets and the dose was one or two. Daylight was broadening apace; she must hurry. She took some notepaper and wrote for five minutes. She had reached the words 'No one is to blame' when suddenly her ears were assailed by a tremendous tearing, whirring sound: it grew louder and louder until the whole room vibrated. In the midst of the deafening din something flashed past the window, for a fraction of a second blotting out the daylight. Then there was a crash such as she had never heard in her life.

All else forgotten, Maggie ran to the window. An indescribable scene of wreckage met her eyes. The aeroplane had been travelling at a terrific pace: it was smashed to atoms. To right and left the lawn was littered with fragments, some of which had made great gashes in the grass, exposing the earth. The pilot had been flung clear; she could just see his legs sticking out from a flower-bed under the wall of the house. They did not move and she thought he must be dead.

While she was wondering what to do she heard voices underneath the window.

'We don't seem to be very lucky here just now, Rundle,' said Mr Ampleforth.

'No, sir.'

There was a pause. Then Mr Ampleforth spoke again.

'He's still breathing, I think.'

'Yes, sir, he is, just.'

'You take his head and I'll take his feet, and we'll get him into the house.'

Something began to stir in Maggie's mind. Rundle replied:

'If you'll pardon my saying so, sir, I don't think we ought to move him. I was told once by a doctor that if a man's had a fall or anything it's best to leave him lying.'

'I don't think it'll matter if we're careful.'

'Really, sir, if you'll take my advice—'

There was a note of obstinacy in Rundle's voice. Maggie, almost beside herself with agitation, longed to fling open the window and cry 'Bring him in! Bring him in!' But her hand seemed paralysed and her throat could not form the words.

Presently Mr Ampleforth said:

'You know we can't let him stay here. It's beginning to rain.'

(Bring him in! Bring him in!)

'Well, sir, it's your responsibility . . . '

Maggie's heart almost stopped beating.

'Naturally I don't want to do anything to hurt the poor chap.'

(Oh, bring him in! Bring him in!)

The rain began to patter on the pane.

'Look here, Rundle, we must get him under cover.'

'I'll fetch that bit of wing, sir, and put over him.'

(Bring him in! Bring him in!)

Maggie heard Rundle pulling something that grated on the gravel path. The sound ceased and Mr Ampleforth said:

'The very thing for a stretcher, Rundle! The earth's so soft, we can slide it under him. Careful, careful!' Both men were breathing hard. 'Have you got your end? Right.' Their heavy, measured footfalls grew fainter and fainter.

The next thing Maggie heard was the motor-car returning with the doctor. Not daring to go out, and unable to sit down, she stood, how long she did not know, holding her bedroom door ajar. At last she saw the nurse coming towards her.

'The patient's a little better, Miss Winthrop. The doctor thinks he'll pull through now.'

'Which patient?'
'Oh, there was never any hope for the other poor fellow.'
Maggie closed her eyes.
'Can I see Antony?' she said at last.
'Well, you may just peep at him.'
Antony smiled at her feebly from the bed.

THE COTILLON

'But,' protested Marion Lane, 'you don't mean that we've all got to dance the cotillon in masks? Won't that be terribly hot?'

'My dear,' Jane Manning, her friend and hostess, reminded her, 'this is December, not July. Look!' She pointed to the window, their only protection against a soft bombardment of snowflakes.

Marion moved across from the fireplace where they were sitting and looked out. The seasonable snow had just begun to fall, as though in confirmation of Mrs Manning's words. Here and there the gravel still showed black under its powdery coating, and on the wing of the house which faced east the shiny foliage of the magnolia, pitted with pockets of snow, seemed nearly black too. The trees of the park which yesterday, when Marion arrived, were so distinct against the afternoon sky that you could see their twigs, were almost invisible now, agitated shapes dim in the slanting snow. She turned back to the room.

'I think the cotillon's a good idea, and I don't want to make difficulties,' she said. 'I'm not an obstructionist by nature, am I? Tell me if I am.'

'My dear, of course you're not.'

'Well, I was thinking, wouldn't half the fun of the cotillon be gone if you didn't know who was who? I mean, in those figures when the women powder the men's faces, and rub their reflections off the looking-glass, and so on. There doesn't seem much point in powdering a mask.'

'My darling Marion, the mask's only a bit of black silk that covers the top part of one's face; you don't imagine we shan't recognize each other?'

'You may', said Marion, 'find it difficult to recognize the largest, barest face. I often cut my best friends in the street. They needn't put on a disguise for me not to know them.'

'But you can tell them by their voices.'

'Supposing they won't speak?'

'Then you must ask questions.'

'But I shan't know half the people here.'

'You'll know all of us in the house,' her friend said; 'that's sixteen to start with. And you know the Grays and the Fosters and the Boltons. We shall only be about eighty, if as many.'

'Counting gate-crashers?'

'There won't be any.'

'But how will you be able to tell, if they wear masks?'

'I shall know the exact numbers, for one thing, and for another, at midnight, when the cotillon stops, everyone can take their masks off – must, in fact.'

'I see.'

The room was suddenly filled with light. A servant had come in to draw the curtains. They sat in silence until he had finished the last of the windows; there were five of them in a row.

'I had forgotten how long this room was,' Marion said. 'You'll have the cotillon here, I suppose?'

'It's the only possible place. I wish it were a little longer, then we could have a cushion race. But I'm afraid we shall have to forgo that. It would be over as soon as it began.'

The servant arranged the tea-table in front of them and went away.

'Darling,' said Jane suddenly, 'before Jack comes in from shooting with his tired but noisy friends, I want to say what a joy it is to have you here. I'm glad the others aren't coming till Christmas Eve. You'll have time to tell me all about yourself.'

'Myself?' repeated Marion. She stirred in her chair. 'There's nothing to tell.'

'Dearest, I can't believe it! There must be, after all these months. My life is dull, you know – no, not dull, quiet. And yours is always so *mouvementée*.'

'It used to be,' admitted Marion. 'It used to be; but now I—'

There was a sound of footsteps and laughter at the door, and a voice cried 'Jenny, Jenny, have you some tea for us?'

'You shall have it in a moment,' Mrs Manning called back. Sighing, she turned to her friend.

'We must postpone our little séance.'

Five days had gone by – it was the evening of the twenty-seventh, the night of the ball. Marion went up to her room to rest. Dinner was at half-past eight, so she had nearly two hours' respite. She lay down on the bed and turned out all the lights except the one near her head. She felt very tired. She had talked so much during the past few days that even her thoughts had become articulate; they would not stay in her mind; they rose automatically to her lips, or it seemed to her that they did. 'I am glad I did not tell Jenny,' she soliloquized; 'it would only have made her think worse of me, and done no good. What a wretched business.' She extinguished the light, but the gramophone within her went on more persistently than ever. It was a familiar record; she knew every word of it: it might have been called *The Witness for the Defence*. 'He had no reason to take me so seriously,' announced the machine in self-excusatory accents. 'I only wanted to amuse him. It was Hugh Travers who introduced us: he knows what I am like; he must have told Harry; men always talk these things over among themselves. Hugh had a grievance against me, too, once; but he got over it; I have never known a man who didn't.' For a moment Marion's thoughts broke free from their bondage to the turning wheel and hovered over her past life. Yes, more or less, they had all got over it. 'I never made him any promise,' pursued the record, inexorably taking up its tale: 'what right had he to think he could coerce me? Hugh ought not to have let us meet, knowing the kind of man he was – and – and the kind of woman I was. I was very fond of him, of course; but he would have been so exacting, he *was* so exacting. All the same,' continued the record – sliding a moment into the major key only to relapse into the minor – 'left to myself I could have managed it all right, as I always have. It was pure bad luck that he found me that night with the other Harry. That was a dreadful affair.' At this point the record, as always, wobbled and scratched: Marion had to improvise something less painful to bridge over the gap. Her thoughts flew to the other Harry and dwelt on him tenderly; he had been so sweet to her afterwards. 'It was just bad luck,' the record resumed; 'I didn't want to blast his happiness and wreck his life, or whatever he says I did.'

What had he actually said? There was an ominous movement in Marion's mind. The mechanism was being wound up, was going through the whole dreary performance again. Anything rather than that! She turned on the light, jumped off the bed, and searched among her letters. The moment she had it in her hand, she realized that she knew it by heart.

DEAR MARION,

After what has happened I don't suppose you will want to see me again, and though I want to see you, I think it better for us both that I shouldn't. I know it sounds melodramatic to say it, but you have spoilt my life, you have killed something inside me. I never much valued Truth for its own sake, and I am grateful to Chance for affording me that peep behind the scenes last night. I am more grateful to you for keeping up the disguise as long as you did. But though you have taken away so much, you have left me one flicker of curiosity: before I die (or after, it doesn't much matter!) I should like to see you (forgive the expression) unmasked, so that for a moment I can compare the reality with the illusion I used to cherish. Perhaps I shall. Meanwhile goodbye.

Yours once, and in a sense still yours,

HENRY CHICHESTER.

Marion's eyes slid from the letter to the chair beside her where lay mask and domino, ready to put on. She did not feel the irony of their presence; she did not think about them; she was experiencing an immense relief – a relief that always came after reading Harry's letter. When she thought about it it appalled her; when she read it it seemed much less hostile, flattering almost; a testimonial from a wounded and disappointed but still adoring man. She lay down again, and in a moment was asleep.

Soon after ten o'clock the gentlemen followed the ladies into the long drawing-room; it looked unfamiliar even to Jack Manning, stripped of furniture except for a thin lining of gilt chairs. So far everything had gone off splendidly; dinner, augmented by the presence of half a dozen neighbours, had been a great success; but now everyone, including the host and hostess, was a little uncertain what to do next. The zero hour was approaching; the cotillon was supposed to start at eleven and go on till twelve, when the serious dancing would begin; but guests motoring from a distance might arrive at any time. It would spoil the fun of the thing to let the masked and the unmasked meet before the cotillon started; but how could they be kept apart? To preserve the illusion of secrecy Mrs Manning had asked them to announce themselves at the head of the staircase, in tones sufficiently discreet to be heard by her alone. Knowing how fallible are human plans, she had left in the cloakroom a small supply of masks for those men who, she knew, would forget to bring them. She thought her arrangements were proof against mischance, but she was by no means sure; and as she looked about the room and saw the members of the dinner-party stealing furtive glances at the clock, or plunging into frantic and short-lived conversations, she began to share their uneasiness.

'I think,' she said, after one or two unsuccessful efforts to gain the ear of the company, 'I think you had all better go and disguise yourselves, before anyone comes and finds you in your natural state.' The guests tittered nervously at this pleasantry, then with signs of relief upon their faces they began to file out, some by one door, some by the other, according as the direction of their own rooms took them. The long gallery (as it was sometimes magniloquently described) stood empty and expectant.

'There,' breathed Mrs Manning, 'would you have recognized that parlour bandit as Sir Joseph Dickinson?'

'No,' said her husband, 'I wouldn't have believed a mask and a domino could make such a difference. Except for a few of the men, I hardly recognized anyone.'

'You're like Marion; she told me she often cuts her best friends in the street.'

'I dare say that's a gift she's grateful for.'

'Jack! You really mustn't. Didn't she look lovely tonight! What a pity she has to wear a mask, even for an hour!'

Her husband grunted.

'I told Colin Chillingworth she was to be here: you know he's always wanted to see her. He is such a nice old man, so considerate – the manners of the older generation.'

'Why, because he wants to see Marion?'

'No, idiot! But he had asked me if he might bring a guest—'

'Who?'

'I don't remember the man's name, but he has a bilious attack or something, and can't come, and Colin apologized profusely for not letting us know: his telephone is out of order, he said.'

'Very civil of him. How many are we then, all told?'

'Seventy-eight; we should have been seventy-nine.'

'Anyone else to come?'

'I'll just ask Jackson.'

The butler was standing half-way down the stairs. He confirmed Mrs Manning's estimate. 'That's right, Madam; there were twenty-two at dinner and fifty-six have come in since.'

'Good staff-work,' said her husband. 'Now we must dash off and put on our little masks.'

They were hurrying away when Mrs Manning called over her shoulder: 'You'll see that the fires are kept up, Jackson?'

'Oh, yes, Madam,' he replied. 'It's very warm in there.'

It was. Marion, coming into the ballroom about eleven o'clock, was met by a wave of heat, comforting and sustaining. She moved about among the throng, slightly dazed, it is true, but self-confident and elated. As she expected, she could not put a name to many of the people who kept crossing her restricted line of vision, but she was intensely aware of their eyes – dark, watchful but otherwise expressionless eyes, framed in black. She welcomed their direct regard. On all sides she heard conversation and laughter, especially laughter; little trills and screams of delight at identities disclosed; voices expressing bewilderment and polite despair – 'I'm very stupid, I really cannot imagine who you are,' gruff rumbling voices, and high falsetto squeaks, obviously disguised. Marion found herself a little impatient of this childishness. When people recognized her, as they often did (her mask was as much a decoration as a concealment) she smiled with her lips but did not try to identify them in return. She felt faintly scornful of the women who were only interesting provided you did not know who they were. She looked forward to the moment when the real business of the evening would begin.

But now the band in the alcove between the two doors had struck up, and a touch on her arm warned her that she was wanted for a figure. Her partner was a raw youth, nice enough in his way, eager, good-natured and jaunty, like a terrier dog. He was not a type she cared for, and she longed to give him the slip.

The opportunity came. Standing on a chair, rather like the Statue of Liberty in New York Harbour, she held aloft a lighted candle. Below her seethed a small group of masked males, leaping like salmon, for the first to blow the candle out would have the privilege of dancing with the torch-bearer. Among them was her partner; he jumped higher than the rest, as she feared he would; but each time she saw his Triton-like mouth soaring up she forestalled his agility and moved the candle out of his reach. Her arm began to tire; and the pack, foiled so often, began to relax their efforts. She must do something quickly. Espying her host among the competitors, she shamefacedly brought the candle down to the level of his mouth.

'Nice of you,' he said, when, having danced a few turns,

they were sitting side by side. 'I was glad of that bit of exercise.'

'Why, do you feel cold?'

'A little. Don't you?'

Marion considered. 'Perhaps I do.'

'Funny thing,' said her host, 'fires seem to be blazing away all right, and it was too hot ten minutes ago.'

Their eyes travelled inquiringly round the room. 'Why,' exclaimed Manning, 'no wonder we're cold; there's a window open.'

As he spoke, a gust of wind blew the heavy curtains inwards, and a drift of snow came after them.

'Excuse me a moment,' he said. 'I'll soon stop that.'

She heard the sash slam, and in a few moments he was back at her side.

'Now who on earth can have done it?' he demanded, still gasping from contact with the cold air. 'The window was wide open!'

'Wide enough to let anyone in?'

'Quite.'

'How many of us ought there to be?' asked Marion. 'I'm sure you don't know.'

'I do – there are—'

'Don't tell me, let's count. I'll race you.'

They were both so absorbed in their calculations that the leaders of the cotillon, coming round armed with favours for the next figure, dropped into their laps a fan and a pocket-book and passed on unnoticed.

'Well, what do you make it?' they cried almost in unison.

'Seventy-nine,' said Marion. 'And you?'

'Seventy-nine, too.'

'And how many ought there to be?'

'Seventy-eight.'

'That's a rum go,' said Manning. 'We can't both be mistaken. I suppose someone came in afterwards. When I get a chance I'll talk to Jackson.'

'It can't be a burglar,' said Marion, 'a burglar wouldn't have chosen that way of getting in.'

'Besides, we should have seen him. No, a hundred to one it was just somebody who was feeling the heat and needed air. I don't blame them, but they needn't have blown us away. Anyhow, if there is a stranger among us he'll soon have to show up, for in half an hour's time we can take off these confounded masks. I wouldn't say it of everyone, but I like you better without yours.'

'Do you?' smiled Marion.

'Meanwhile, we must do something about these favours. The next figure's beginning. I say, a fur rug would be more suitable, but may I give this fan to you?'

'And will you accept this useful pocket-book?'

They smiled and began to dance.

Ten minutes passed; the fires were heaped up, but the rubbing of hands and hunching of shoulders which had followed the inrush of cold air did not cease. Marion, awaiting her turn to hold the looking-glass, shivered slightly. She watched her predecessor on the chair. Armed with a handkerchief, she was gazing intently into the mirror while each in his turn the men stole up behind her, filling the glass with their successive reflections; one after another she rubbed the images out. Marion was wondering idly whether she would wait too long and find the candidates exhausted when she jumped up from her chair, handed the looking-glass to the leader of the cotillon, and danced away with the man of her choice. Marion took the mirror and sat down. A feeling of unreality oppressed her. How was she to choose between these grotesque faces? One after another they loomed up, dream-like, in the glass, their intense, almost hypnotic eyes searching hers. She could not tell whether they were smiling, they gave so little indication of expression. She remembered how the other women had paused, peered into the glass, and seemed to consider; rubbing away this one at sight, with affected horror, lingering over that one as though sorely tempted, only erasing him after a show of reluctance. She had fancied that some of the men looked piqued when they were rejected; they walked off with a toss of the head; others had seemed frankly pleased to be chosen. She was not indifferent to the mimic drama of the figure, but she couldn't contribute to it. The chill she still felt numbed her mind, and made it drowsy; her gestures seemed automatic, outside the control of her will. Mechanically she rubbed away the reflection of the first candidate, of the second, of the third. But when the fourth presented himself, and hung over her chair till his mask was within a few inches of her hair, the onlookers saw her pause; the hand with the handkerchief lay motionless in her lap, her eyes were fixed upon the mirror. So she sat for a full minute, while the man at the back, never shifting his position, drooped over her like an earring.

'She's taking a good look this time,' said a bystander at last, and the remark seemed to pierce her reverie – she turned round slowly and then gave a tremendous start; she was on her feet in a moment. 'I'm so sorry,' someone heard her say as she gave the man her hand, 'I never saw you. I had no idea that anyone was there.'

A few minutes later Jane Manning, who had taken as much share in the proceedings as a hostess can, felt a touch upon her arm. It was Marion.

'Well, my dear,' she said. 'Are you enjoying yourself?'

Marion's voice shook a little. 'Marvellously!' She added in an amused tone:

'Queer fellow I got hold of just now.'

'Queer-looking, do you mean?'

'Really I don't know; he was wearing a sort of death-mask that covered him almost completely, and he was made up as well, I thought, with French chalk.'

'What else was queer about him?'

'He didn't talk. I couldn't get a word out of him.'

'Perhaps he was deaf.'

'That occurred to me. But he heard the music all right; he danced beautifully.'

'Show him to me.'

Marion's eyes hovered round the room without catching sight of her late partner.

'He doesn't seem to be here.'

'Perhaps he's our uninvited guest,' said Jane, laughing. 'Jack told me there was an extra person who couldn't be accounted for. Now, darling, you mustn't miss this figure: it's the most amusing of them all. After that, there are some favours to be given, and then supper. I long for it.'

'But don't we take off our masks first?'

'Yes, of course, I'd forgotten that.'

The figure described by Mrs Manning as being the most amusing of all would have been much more amusing, Marion thought, if they had played it without masks. If the dancers did not recognize each other, it lost a great deal of its point. Its success depended on surprise. A space had been cleared in the middle of the room, an oblong space like a badminton court, divided into two, not by a net but by a large white sheet supported at either end by the leaders of the cotillon, and held nearly at arm's length above their heads. On one side were grouped the men, on the other the women, theoretically invisible to each other; but Marion noticed that they moved about and took furtive peeps at each other round the sides, a form of cheating which, in the interludes, the leaders tried to forestall by rushing the sheet across to intercept the view. But most of the time these stolen glimpses went on unchecked, to the accompaniment of a good deal of laughter; for while the figure was in progress the leaders were perforce stationary. One by one the men came up from behind and clasped the top edge of the sheet, so that their gloved fingers, and nothing else, were visible the farther side. With becoming hesitation a woman would advance and take these anonymous fingers in her own; then the sheet was suddenly lowered and the dancers stood face to face, or rather mask to mask. Sometimes there were cries of recognition, sometimes silence, the masks were as impenetrable as the sheet had been.

It was Marion's turn. As she walked forward she saw that the gloved hands were not resting on the sheet like the rest; they were clutching it so tightly that the linen was caught up in creases between the fingers and crumpled round their tips. For a moment they did not respond to her touch, then they gripped with surprising force. Down went the leader's arms, down went the corners of the sheet. But Marion's unknown partner did not take his cue. He forgot to release the sheet, and she remained with her arms held immovably aloft, the sheet falling in folds about her and almost covering her head. 'An unrehearsed effect, jolly good, I call it,' said somebody. At last, in response to playful tugs and twitches from the leaders, the man let the sheet go and discovered himself to the humiliated Marion. It was her partner of the previous figure, that uncommunicative man. His hands, that still held hers, felt cold through their kid covering.

'Oh,' she cried, 'I can't understand it — I feel so cold. Let's dance.'

They danced for a little and then sat down. Marion felt chillier than ever, and she heard her neighbours on either side complaining of the temperature. Suddenly she made a decision and rose to her feet.

'Do take me somewhere where it's warmer,' she said. 'I'm perished here.'

The man led the way out of the ballroom, through the

anteroom at the end where one or two couples were sitting, across the corridor into a little room where a good fire was burning, throwing every now and then a ruddy gleam on china ornaments and silver photograph frames. It was Mrs Manning's sitting-room.

'We don't need a light, do we?' said her companion. 'Let's sit as we are.'

It was the first time he had volunteered a remark. His voice was somehow familiar to Marion, yet she couldn't place it; it had an alien quality that made it unrecognizable, like one's own dress worn by someone else.

'With pleasure,' she said. 'But we mustn't stay long, must we? It's only a few minutes to twelve. Can we hear the music from here?'

They sat in silence, listening. There was no sound.

'Don't think me fussy,' Marion said. 'I'm enjoying this tremendously, but Jenny would be disappointed if we missed the last figure. If you don't mind opening the door, we should hear the music begin.'

As he did not offer to move, she got up to open it herself, but before she reached the door she heard her name called.

'Marion!'

'Who said that, you?' she cried, suddenly very nervous.

'Don't you know who I am?'

'Harry!'

Her voice shook and she sank back into her chair, trembling violently.

'How was it I didn't recognize you? I'm – I'm so glad to see you.'

'You haven't seen me yet,' said he. It was like him to say that, playfully grim. His words reassured her, but his tone left her still in doubt. She did not know how to start the conversation, what effect to aim at, what note to strike; so much depended on divining his mood and playing up to it. If she could have seen his face, if she could have even have caught a glimpse of the poise of his head, it would have given her a cue; in the dark like this, hardly certain of his whereabouts in the room, she felt hopelessly at a disadvantage.

'It was nice of you to come and see me – if you did come to see me,' she ventured at last.

'I heard you were to be here.' Again that non-committal tone! Trying to probe him she said:

'Would you have come otherwise? It's rather a childish entertainment, isn't it?'

'I should have come,' he answered, 'but it would have been in – in a different spirit.'

She could make nothing of this.

'I didn't know the Mannings were friends of yours,' she told him. 'He's rather a dear, married to a dull woman, if I must be really truthful.'

'I don't know them,' said he.

'Then you gate-crashed?'

'I suppose I did.'

'I take that as a compliment,' said Marion after a pause. 'But – forgive me – I must be very slow – I don't understand. You said you were coming in any case.'

'Some friends of mine called Chillingworth offered to bring me.'

'How lucky I was! So you came with them?'

'Not with them, after them.'

'How odd. Wasn't there room for you in their car? How did you get here so quickly?'

'The dead travel fast.'

His irony baffled her. But her thoughts flew to his letter, in which he accused her of having killed something in him; he must be referring to that.

'Darling Hal,' she said. 'Believe me, I'm sorry to have hurt you. What can I do to – to—'

There was a sound of voices calling, and her attention thus awakened caught the strains of music, muffled and remote.

'They want us for the next figure. We must go,' she cried, thankful that the difficult interview was nearly over. She was colder than ever, and could hardly keep her teeth from chattering audibly.

'What is the next figure?' he asked, without appearing to move.

'Oh, you know – we've had it before – we give each other favours, then we unmask ourselves. Hal, we really ought to go! Listen! Isn't that midnight beginning to strike?'

Unable to control her agitation, aggravated by the strain of the encounter, the deadly sensation of cold within her, and a presentiment of disaster for which she could not account, she rushed towards the door and her oustretched left hand, finding the switch, flooded the room with light. Mechanically she turned her head to the room; it was empty. Bewildered she looked back over her left shoulder, and there, within a foot of her, stood Harry Chichester, his arms stretched across the door.

'Harry,' she cried, 'don't be silly! Come out or let me out!'

'You must give me a favour first,' he said sombrely.

'Of course I will, but I haven't got one here.'

'I thought you always had favours to give away.'

'Harry, what do you mean?'

'You came unprovided?'

She was silent.

'*I* did not. I have something here to give you – a small token. Only I must have a *quid pro quo*.'

He's mad, thought Marion. I must humour him as far as I can.

'Very well,' she said, looking around the room. Jenny would forgive her – it was an emergency. 'May I give you this silver pencil?'

He shook his head.

'Or this little vase?'

Still he refused.

'Or this calendar?'

'The flight of time doesn't interest me.'

'Then what can I tempt you with?'

'Something that is really your own – a kiss.'

'My dear,' said Marion, trembling, 'you needn't have asked for it.'

'Thank you,' he said. 'And to prove I don't want something for nothing, here is your favour.'

He felt in his pocket. Marion saw a dark silvery gleam; she held her hand out for the gift.

It was a revolver.

'What am I to do with this?' she asked.

'You are the best judge of that,' he replied. 'Only one cartridge has been used.'

Without taking her eyes from his face she laid down the revolver among the bric-à-brac on the table by her side.

'And now your gift to me.'

'But what about our masks?' said Marion.

'Take yours off,' he commanded.

'Mine doesn't matter,' said Marion, removing as she spoke the silken visor. 'But you are wearing an entirely false face.'

'Do you know why?' he asked, gazing at her fixedly through the slits in the mask.

She didn't answer.

'I was always an empty-headed fellow,' he went on, tapping the waxed covering with his gloved forefinger, so that it gave out a wooden hollow sound – 'there's nothing much behind this. No brains to speak of, I mean. Less than I used to have, in fact.'

Marion stared at him in horror.

'Would you like to see? Would you like to look right into my mind?'

'No! No!' she cried wildly.

'But I think you ought to,' he said, coming a step nearer and raising his hands to his head.

'Have you seen Marion?' said Jane Manning to her husband. 'I've a notion she hasn't been enjoying herself. This was in a sense her party, you know. We made a mistake to give her Tommy Cardew as a partner; he doesn't carry heavy enough guns for her.'

'Why, does she want shooting?' inquired her husband.

'Idiot! But I could see they didn't get on. I wonder where she's got to – I'm afraid she may be bored.'

'Perhaps she's having a quiet talk with a howitzer,' her husband suggested.

Jane ignored him. 'Darling, it's nearly twelve. Run into the ante-room and fetch her; I don't want her to miss the final figure.'

In a few seconds he returned. 'Not there,' he said. 'Not there, my child. Sunk by a twelve-inch shell, probably.'

'She may be sitting out in the corridor.'

'Hardly, after a direct hit.'

'Well, look.'

They went away and returned with blank faces. The guests were standing about talking; the members of the band, their hands ready on their instruments, looked up inquiringly.

'We shall have to begin without her,' Mrs Manning reluctantly decided. 'We shan't have time to finish as it is.'

The hands of the clock showed five minutes to twelve.

The band played as though inspired, and many said afterwards that the cotillon never got really going, properly warmed up, till those last five minutes. All the fun of the evening seemed to come to a head, as though the spirit of the dance, mistrustful of its latter-day devotees, had withheld its benison till the final moments. Everyone was too excited to notice, as they whirled past that the butler was standing in one of the doorways with a white and anxious face. Even Mrs Manning, when at last she saw him, called out cheerfully, almost without pausing for an answer:

'Well, Jackson, everything all right, I hope?'

'Can I speak to you a moment, Madam?' he said. 'Or perhaps Mr Manning would be better.'

Mrs Manning's heart sank. Did he want to leave?

'Oh, I expect I shall do, shan't I? I hope it's nothing serious.'

'I'm afraid it is, Madam, very serious.'

'All right, I'll come.' She followed him on to the landing.

A minute later her husband saw her threading her way towards him.

'Jack! Just a moment.'

He was dancing and affected not to hear. His partner's eyes looked surprised and almost resentful, Mrs Manning thought; but she persisted none the less.

'I know I'm a bore and I'm sorry, but I really can't help myself.'

This brought them to a stand.

'Why, Jane, has the boiler burst?'

'No, it's more serious than that, Jack,' she said, as he disengaged himself from his partner with an apology. 'There's been a dreadful accident or something at the Chillingworths'. That guest of theirs, do you remember, whom they were to have brought and didn't—'

'Yes, he stayed behind with a headache – rotten excuse—'

'Well, he's shot himself.'

'Good God! When?'

'They found him half an hour ago, apparently, but they couldn't telephone because the machine was out of order, and had to send.'

'Is he dead?'

'Yes, he blew his brains out.'

'Do you remember his name?'

'The man told me. He was called Chichester.'

They were standing at the side of the room, partly to avoid the dancers, partly to be out of earshot. The latter consideration need not have troubled them, however. The band, which for some time past had been playing nineteenth-century waltzes, now burst into the strains of *John Peel*. There was a tremendous sense of excitement and climax. The dancers galloped by at break-neck speed; the band played fortissimo; the volume of sound was terrific. But above the din – the music, the laughter and the thud of feet – they could just hear the clock striking twelve.

Jack Manning looked doubtfully at his wife. 'Should I go and tell Chillingworth now? What do you think?'

'Perhaps you'd better – it seems so heartless not to. Break it to him as gently as you can, and don't let the others know if you can help it.'

Jack Manning's task was neither easy nor agreeable, and he was a born bungler. Despairing of making himself heard, he raised his hand and cried out, 'Wait a moment!' Some of the company stood still and, imagining it was a signal to take off their masks, began to do so; others went on dancing; others stopped and stared. He was the centre of attention; and before he had got his message fairly delivered, it had reached other ears than those for which it was intended. An excited whispering went round the room: 'What is it? What is it?' Men and women stood about with their masks in their hands, and faces blanker than before they were uncovered. Others looked terrified and incredulous. A woman came up to Jane Manning and said:

'What a dreadful thing for Marion Lane.'

'Why?' Jane asked.

'Didn't you know? She and Harry Chichester were the greatest friends. At one time it was thought—'

'I live out of the world, I had no idea,' said Jane quickly. Even in the presence of calamity, she felt a pang that her friend had not confided in her.

Her interlocutor persisted: 'It was talked about a great deal. Some people said – you know how they chatter – that she didn't treat him quite fairly. I hate to make myself a busybody, Mrs Manning, but I do think you ought to tell her; she ought to be prepared.'

'But I don't know where she is!' cried Jane, from whose mind all thought of her friend had been banished. 'Have you seen her?'

'Not since the sheet incident.'

'Nor have I.'

Nor, it seemed, had anyone. Disturbed by this new misadventure far more than its trivial nature seemed to warrant, Jane hastened in turn to such of her guests as might be able to enlighten her as to Marion's whereabouts. Some of them greeted her inquiry with a lift of the eyebrows but none of them could help her in her quest. Nor could she persuade them to take much interest in it. They seemed to have forgotten that they were at a party, and owed a duty of responsiveness to their hostess. Their eyes did not light up when she came near. One and all they were discussing the suicide, and suggesting its possible motive. The room rustled with their whispering, with the soft hissing sound of 'Chichester' and the succeeding 'Hush!' which was meant to stifle but only multiplied and prolonged it. Jane felt that she must scream.

All at once there was silence. Had she screamed? No, for the noise they had all heard came from somewhere inside the house. The room seemed to hold its breath. There it was again, and coming closer; a cry, a shriek, the shrill tones of terror alternating in a dreadful rhythm with a throaty, choking sound like whooping-cough. No one could have recognized it as Marion Lane's voice, and few could have told for Marion Lane the dishevelled figure, mask in hand, that lurched through the ballroom doorway and with quick stumbling steps, before which the onlookers fell back, zigzagged into the middle of the room.

'Stop him!' she gasped. 'Don't let him do it!' Jane Manning ran to her.

'Dearest, what is it?'

'It's Harry Chichester,' sobbed Marion, her head rolling about on her shoulders as if it had come loose. 'He's in there. He wants to take his mask off, but I can't bear it! It would be awful! Oh, do take him away!'

'Where is he?' someone asked.

'Oh, I don't know! In Jane's sitting-room, I think. He wouldn't let me go. He's so cold, so dreadfully cold.'

'Look after her, Jane,' said Jack Manning. 'Get her out of here. Anyone coming with me?' he asked, looking round. 'I'm going to investigate.'

Marion caught the last words. 'Don't go,' she implored. 'He'll hurt you.' But her voice was drowned in the scurry and stampede of feet. The whole company was following their host. In a few moments the ballroom was empty.

Five minutes later there were voices in the ante-room. It was Manning leading back his troops. 'Barring, of course, the revolver,' he was saying, 'and the few things that had been knocked over, and those scratches on the door, there wasn't a trace. Hullo!' he added, crossing the threshold, 'what's this?'

The ballroom window was open again; the curtains fluttered wildly inwards; on the boards lay a patch of nearly melted snow.

Jack Manning walked up to it. Just within the further edge, near the window, was a kind of smear, darker than the toffee-coloured mess around it, and roughly oval in shape.

'Do you think that's a footmark?' he asked of the company in general.

No one could say.

A CHANGE OF OWNERSHIP

The motor-car felt its way cautiously up the little street that opened upon a field on one side, and somehow looked less suburban by night than it did by day.

'Here?' asked the driver, peering into the semi-rural darkness.

'Just a little farther, if you don't mind,' said his friend. 'Where you can see that black patch in the wall: that's the gate.'

The car crept on.

'Cold?' demanded the man at the wheel. 'These October nights *are* cold. Stuffy place, the theatre.'

'Did I sound cold?' asked his companion, the faint quiver renewing itself in his voice. 'Oh, I can't be, it's such a little way. Feel that,' he added, holding out his hand.

The driver applied his cheek to it and the car wobbled, bumping against the kerb.

'Feels warm enough to me,' he said, 'hot, in fact. Whoa! Whoa! good horse. This it?' he added, turning the car's head round.

'Yes, but don't bother to come in, Hubert. The road is so twisty and there may be a branch down. I'm always expecting them to fall, and I've had a lot of them wired. You never know with these elm-trees.'

'Jumpy kind of devil, aren't you?' muttered Hubert, extricating himself from the car and standing on the pavement. In the feeble moonlight he looked enormous; Ernest, fiddling with the door on his side, wondered where his friend went to when he tucked himself under the wheel. It must dig into him, he thought.

'It's a bit stiff, but you're turning it the wrong way,' said Hubert, coming round to Ernest's side. 'Easy does it. There you are.' He held the door open; Ernest stumbled out, missed his footing and was for a moment lost to sight between the more important shadows of his friend and his friend's car.

'Hold up, hold up,' Hubert enjoined him. 'The road doesn't need rolling.' He set Ernest on his feet and the two figures, so unequal in size, gazed mutely into the black square framed by the gateway. Through the trees, which seemed still to bear their complement of boughs, they could just see the outlines of the house, which repeated by their rectangularity the lines of the gateway. It looked like a large black hat-box, crowned at one corner by a smaller hat-box that was, in fact, a tower. There was a tiny light in the tower, otherwise the house was dark, the windows being visible as patches of intense black, like eyeless sockets in a negro's face.

'You said you were alone in the house,' remarked Hubert, breaking the silence.

'Yes,' his friend replied. 'In a sense I am.' He went on standing where he was, with the motor between him and the gateway.

'In what sense?' persisted his friend. 'Queer devil you are, Ernest; you must either be alone or not alone. Do I scent a romance? In that room with the light in it, for instance—'

'Oh, no,' Ernest protested, fidgeting with his feet. 'That's only the gas in the box-room. I don't know how it comes to be alight. It ought not to be. The least thing blows it out. Sometimes I get up in the night and go and see to it. Once I went four times, because it's so difficult with gas to make sure it's properly turned off. If you turn it off with your thumb you may easily turn it on again with your little finger, and never notice.'

'Well, a little puff of gas wouldn't hurt you,' observed Hubert, walking to the front of the car and looking at it as though in a moment he would make it do something it didn't like. 'Make you sleep better. How's the insomnia?'

'Oh, so-so.'

'Don't want anyone to hold your hand?'

'My dear Hubert, of course not.'

Ernest dashingly kicked a pebble which gyrated noisily on the metal surface. When it stopped all sound seemed to cease with it.

'Tell me about this shadowy companion, Ernest,' said Hubert, giving one of the tyres such a pinch that Ernest thought the car would scream out.

'Companion?' echoed Ernest, puzzled. 'I – I have no companion.'

'What did you mean, then, by saying you were only alone "in a sense"?' demanded Hubert. 'In what sense? Think that out, my boy.' He took a spanner, adjusted it, and gave a savage heave. The car shuddered through its whole length and subsided with a sigh.

'I only meant—' began Ernest.

'Please teacher, I only meant,' mocked Hubert grimly.

'I only meant,' said Ernest, 'that there is a charwoman coming tomorrow at half-past six.'

'And what time is it now?'

'A quarter to twelve.'

As Ernest spoke a distant clock chimed the three-quarters – a curious unsatisfied chime that ended on a note of interrogation.

'How the devil did you know that?' asked Hubert, his voice rising in protest as if such knowledge were not quite nice.

'During the night,' replied Ernest, a hint of self-assertion making itself heard for the first time in his voice, 'I am very sensitive to the passage of time.'

'You ought to loan yourself to our dining-room clock,' observed Hubert. 'It hasn't gone these fifteen months. But where are your servants, Ernest? Where's the pretty parlourmaid? Tell me she's there and I'd come and stop the night with you.'

'She isn't,' said Ernest. 'They're away, all three of them. I came home earlier than I meant. But would you really stay, Hubert? You've got a long way to go – eighteen miles, isn't it?'

'Afraid I can't, old man. Got some business to do early tomorrow.'

'What a pity,' said Ernest. 'If I'd asked you sooner perhaps you could have stayed.'

His voice expressed dejection and Hubert, who was making ready to get into the motor, turned round, holding the door half open.

'Look here, Ernest, I'll stay if it's any consolation to you.'

Ernest seemed to be revolving something in his mind.

'You really think you could?'

'You've only to say the word.'

Again Ernest hesitated.

'I don't think there's a bed aired.'

'Give me a shake-down in that room with the leaky light.'

Ernest turned aside so that his friend might not see the struggle in his face.

'Thank you a thousand times, Hubert. But really there's no need. Truly there isn't. Though it was most kind of you to suggest it.' He spoke as though he was trying to soothe an apprehensive child. 'I couldn't ask you to.'

'Well,' said Hubert, setting his foot on the self-starter, 'on your own head be it. On your tombstone they'll write "Here lieth one who turned a friend into the street at midnight".'

'Oh, no,' said Ernest, like a child.

'Won't they? Damn this self-starter.'

'Isn't it going to work?' asked Ernest hopefully.

'Just you wait a moment and I'll give it hell,' declared Hubert. He got out and wrung the starting-handle furiously. Still the car refused.

'It doesn't seem to want to go,' said Ernest. 'You'd much better stay here.'

'What, *now*?' Hubert exclaimed, as if the car must be taught a lesson, at whatever cost to himself. And then, as though it knew it had met its match, the engine began to throb.

'Good-night, Ernest. Pleasant dreams!'

'Good-night, Hubert, and thank you so much. And, oh ... Hubert!'

The motor began to slow down as Hubert heard Ernest's cry, and his footsteps pattering down the street.

'I only wanted to ask what your telephone number was.'

'Don't I wish I knew! Number double o double o infinity. The thing's been coming every day for six weeks.'

'It's not likely to have been put in today while you were away?'

'No, old boy: more likely when I'm there. Good-night, and don't let yourself get blown up.'

In a few seconds all sound of the motor died away. The god had departed in his car.

'Shall I shut the gates?' thought Ernest. 'No, someone might want to come in. People don't usually drive up to a house in the dead of night, but you can't be sure: there are always accidents, petrol runs out; or it might be an old friend, turned up from abroad. Stranded after leaving the boat-train. "London was so full I couldn't get in anywhere, so I came on here, Ernest, to throw myself on your mercy." "You were quite right, Reggie; wait a moment, and I'll have you fixed up." How easy it would have been to say that to Hubert. But I was quite right, really, to let him go: I mustn't give way to myself, I must learn to live alone, like other people. How nice to be some poor person, a street-arab, for instance, just left school, who had come into some money and naturally bought this house. He's spent a jolly evening with a friend, been to a theatre and comes home quite late, well, almost at midnight.' And no sooner had the word crossed Ernest's mind than he heard, almost with a sense of private complicity, almost as though he had uttered them himself, the first notes of the midnight chime. He could not think against them; and looking round a little dazed he saw he had come only a very few steps into the garden. But already the house seemed larger; he could make out the front door, plumb in the middle of the building, sunk in its neo-Gothic ogee arch. He was standing on a closely clipped lawn; but to his right, across the carriageway, he knew there was that odd flat tract in the long grass. It always looked as if something large had trampled upon it, lain upon it, really: it was like the form of an enormous hare, and each blade of grass was broken-backed and sallow, as though the juice had been squeezed out of it.

But the new householder doesn't mind that, not he. His mind is full of the play. He only thinks, 'Polkin will have some trouble when he comes to mow *that* bit.' And of course he likes the trees; he doesn't notice that the branches are black and dead at the tips, as though the life of the tree were ebbing, dropping back into its trunk, like a failing fountain. He hasn't taken a ladder to peer into that moist channel where the branches fork; it oozes a kind of bright sticky froth, and if you could bring yourself to do it, you could shove your arm in up to the elbow, the wood is so rotten. 'Well, Polkin, if the tree's as far gone as you say, by all means cut it down: I don't myself consider it dangerous, but have it your own way. Get in a couple of Curtis's men, and fell it tomorrow.' So the new owner of Stithies hadn't really liked the tree? Oh, it's not that; he's a practical man; he yields to circumstances. 'Well, the old chap will keep us warm in the winter evenings, Polkin.' 'Yes, sir, and I do hope you'll have some company. You must be that lonely all by yourself, if I may say so, sir.' 'Company, my good Polkin, I should think so! I'm going to give a couple of dances, to start off with.'

How reassuring, how reanimating, the glimpse into the life of the New Proprietor!

More insistently than ever, as the house drew near, did Ernest crave the loan of this imaginary person's sturdy thoughts. He had lived always in cramped, uncomfortable rooms; perhaps shared a bedroom with three or four others, perhaps even a bed! What fun for him, after these constricted years, to come home to a big house of his own, where he has three or four sitting-rooms to choose from, each of which he may occupy by himself! What a pleasure it is for him, in the long evenings, to sit perfectly still in the dining-room, with time hanging on his hands, hearing the clock tick.

How he laughs when suddenly, from under the table or anyhow from some part of the floor, one doesn't quite know where, there comes that strange loud thump, as though someone, lying on his back, had grown restive and given the boards a terrific kick! In an old house like this, of course, the floor-boards do contract and expand; they have seen a great deal; they have something to say, and they want to get it off their chests.

Ernest paused. His reverie had brought him to the edge of the lawn, only a few yards from his front door. On either side the house stretched away, reaching out with its flanks into the night. Well, so would the new proprietor pause, to take a last look at the domain he so dearly loved – the symbol of his escape from an existence which had been one long round of irritating chores, always at somebody's beck and call, always having to think about something outside himself, never alone with his own thoughts! How he had longed for the kind of self-knowledge that only comes with solitude. And now, just before tasting this ecstasy of loneliness at its purest, he pauses. In a moment he will stride to the door which he hasn't troubled to lock, turn the handle and walk in. The hall is dark, but he finds a chair and mounting it lights the gas. Then he goes his nightly round. With that sense of possession, what luxury of ownership, does he feel the catches of the windows. Just a flick to make sure it's fast. As he picks his way through the furniture to the glimmering panes he congratulates himself that now he can look out on a view – as far as the sulky moonlight admits a view – of trees, shrubs, shadows; no vociferous callboys, no youthful blades returning singing after a wet night. Nothing but darkness and silence, within and without. What balm to the spirit! What a vivid sensation of security and repose! Down he goes into the cellar where the gas meter ticks. The window-sash is a flimsy thing – wouldn't keep out a determined man, perhaps; the new proprietor just settles it in its socket, and passes on into the wine-cellar. But no, the sort of man we are considering wouldn't bother to lock up the wine-cellar: such a small window could only let in cats and hedgehogs. It had let in both, and they were discovered afterwards, starved and dead: but that was before the occupancy of the new proprietor. Then upstairs, and the same ceremonial, so rapid and efficient, a formality, really, hardly taking a quarter of an hour: just the eight bedrooms, and the maids' rooms, since they were away. These might take longer. Last of all the box-room, with its unsatisfactory by-pass. It would be dealt with firmly and definitely and never revisited, like a sick person, during the watches of the night. And then, pleasantly tired and ready for bed, the new proprietor would turn to his friend Hubert, whom he had brought back from the play, and bid him good-night.

So absorbed was Ernest in the evocation of this pleasant bedtime scene that, with the gesture of someone retiring to rest, he half held out his hand. But no one took it; and he realized, with a sinking of the heart, that the new proprietor had let him down, was a craven like himself. He walked unsteadily to the door and turned the handle. Nothing happened. He turned it the other way. Still the door resisted him. Suddenly he remembered how once, returning home late at night from taking some letters to the post, the door of the stable, where he kept his bicycle, had been similarly recalcitrant. But when he pushed harder the door yielded a little, as though someone stronger than he was holding it against him and meant to let him in slowly before doing him an injury. He had exerted all his strength. Suddenly the door gave. It was only a tennis-ball that had got wedged between the door and the cobblestone: but he never forgot the episode. For a moment he sat down on the stone step before renewing his attack. He must have managed it clumsily. The door needed drawing towards him or else pushing away from him. He recalled his failure to negotiate the catch of Hubert's car. But his second attempt was as vain as the first. The door wouldn't open, couldn't: it must have been locked on the inside.

Ernest knew, as well as he knew anything, that he had left it unfastened. The lock was of an old-fashioned pattern; it had no tricks of its own. You could be quite certain it was locked, the key turned so stiffly: it had never given Ernest a moment's uneasiness nor demanded nocturnal forfeits from his nervous apprehension. It was locked all right; but who had locked it?

Supposing there was a man who disliked his house, thought Ernest, hated it, dreaded it, with what emotions of relief would he discover, when he returned from a dull play at the witching hour, that the house was locked against him? Supposing this man, from a child, had been so ill at ease in his own home that the most familiar objects, a linen-press or a waste-paper basket, had been full of menace for him: wouldn't he rejoice to be relieved, by Fate, of the horrible necessity of spending the night alone in such a house? And wouldn't he rather welcome than otherwise the burglar or whoever it might be who had so providentially taken possession – the New Proprietor? The man was an abject funk; could scarcely bear to sit in a room alone; spent the greater part of the night prowling about the house torn between two fears – the fear of staying in bed and brooding over neglected windows and gas jets, and the fear of getting up and meeting those windows and gas jets in the dark. Lucky chap to lose, through no fault of his own, all his fears and all his responsibilities. What a weight off his mind! The streets were open to him, the nice noisy streets, even at night-time half full of policemen and strayed revellers, in whose company he could gaily pass what few hours remained till dawn.

But somehow the Old Expropriated had less success, as an imaginative lure, than the New Proprietor. 'I must get in,' thought Ernest. 'It's perfectly simple. There are one, two, three windows I can get in by if I try: four counting the window of the box-room. But first I'll ring the bell.' He rang and a wild peal followed which might have come from the hall instead of the kitchen, it seemed so near. He waited, while at ever-increasing intervals of time the clangour renewed itself, like an expiring hiccough. 'I'll give him another minute,' thought Ernest, taking out his watch. The minute passed but no one came.

When a policeman has tried the handle of the door and found it shut, he often, if he is a true guardian of the law, proceeds to examine the windows. 'Hullo, there, hullo! hullo!' And a handful of gravel, maybe, rattles against the window-panes. Leaping or creeping out of bed, according to his temperament, the startled householder goes to the window. 'What's the matter?' 'Nothing's the matter, only your window's unfastened. There are queer people about tonight – gypsies. You had better come down and fasten it unless you want your silver stolen.' 'Thank you very much, officer; good-night.' And down patters paterfamilias in his warm slippers and his dressing-gown, while the constable patrols the garden with comfortable tread. No one dare molest him, not even if he is ever so wicked. And whoever heard of a wicked policeman? thought Ernest, reconnoitring, at some distance, the dining-room window. He tramps through the shrubberies, cats fly before him, his bull's-eye lantern turns night into day, he could walk through the spinney where the mound is and never turn a hair. And this is how he would open the dining-room window.

It was a sash-window, hanging loose in its grooves. Ernest

inserted his pocket-knife in the crevice and started to prise it open. To his delight and dismay the sash began to move. Half an inch higher and he would be able to get his fingers under it. He was using the haft of the knife now, not the blade. The sash began to move more easily. He curled his fingers under and round it. His face, twisted with exertion, stared blankly upon the cream-coloured blind inside. The blind stirred. He must have let in a current of air. He redoubled his exertions. The sash slid up six inches, and then stuck fast. And he could see why. A hand, pressed flat along the bottom of the sash, was holding it down.

Ernest let go with a cry, and the window was slowly and smoothly closed. He had an impulse to run but he resisted it, and forced himself to walk back to the window. The hand was gone.

Imagine you were a window-cleaner and wanted to open a window and some playful member of the family — a great overgrown lout of a boy, for instance — took it into his head to play a prank like that on you. You know what boys are; they have no mercy; there is a bully embedded in all of them, and pretty near the surface in most. That being so, what would you make of the young gentleman's interference? What line would you take? Clearly he won't hurt you, and he can't, besides, be everywhere at once. Perhaps somebody calls him, or he finds the cat and pulls its tail or blows tobacco-smoke into the spaniel's eyes. For such a lad as that there are a hundred distractions; and while you are quietly going on with your job at the drawing-room window he will be making an apple-pie bed for his small sister in the nursery: too engrossed, my dear Ernest, to remember your existence, certainly too much occupied to follow you about.

And it did seem that Ernest the window-cleaner was likely to be more successful than Ernest the policeman. Crouching like an animal, his hands hanging down in front of him, keeping close to the wall, brushing himself against creepers, scratched by thorns and blackened by soot, at last he reached the drawing-room window and flung himself on his face beneath the sill. The sill was a low one. Half kneeling, half supporting himself on his elbows, he raised himself till his eyes were level with the glass. The fitful moonlight played on this side of the house; a treacherous light, but it served to show him that the Puck of Stithies was occupied elsewhere. With extreme caution, holding his breath, he negotiated the difficult preliminaries; then he stood up straight, and heaved with all his might. The window rushed up a foot and then stuck. Involuntarily he glanced down: yes, there was the hand, flattened on the frame: there was another hand, holding back the blind, and there was a face, not very distinct, but certainly a face.

It was the hand that Ernest, cowering under the thick umbrage of the drooping-ash, remembered best. The face was anybody's face, not really unlike Hubert's: a ruddy, capable face: not exactly angry, but stern, official-looking. But the odd thing about the hand was that it didn't seem like the hand of another person. It was larger than Ernest's, yet he had felt, for the moment that it was presented before his eyes, that it would respond to his volition, move as he wanted it to move. He had been too frightened, at the moment, to act upon this fantastic notion; but couldn't he act upon it next time? Next time. But why not? Imagine a man of average capabilities, physically none too robust, but with a good headpiece on him. He can afford to spare himself; even when he takes on a job that is strange to him he will find out the easiest way, will know just the right moment to bring to bear what little strength he has. Many a slenderly built chap, at the bidding of necessity, had transformed himself into a passable coal-heaver. But to carry a sack of coal or a sack of anything one needs a knack: it's no good taking the load into your arms, you must hoist it on to your back. And when you've carried a sack or two like that, who knows that your luck mayn't change? Many a man who carried a sack in his time, in later life has supped with princes.

Ernest scrambled up the slates, slithered down a gully and grasped the balustrade of the battlement. He had found his way instinctively, or did he remember it? If he hadn't been familiar with the lie of the roofs, even to the point of knowing what slates were loose and would crack or, worse, creak when you trod, how could he have avoided a sprained ankle or a serious fall? Yes, certainly he knew his way about the leads and slates; who wouldn't, if they had lived in a house from childhood, and loved it, though it frightened them, and wanted to have it, and meant to have it, and what went with it, though by a slip of the pen it belonged to someone else?

The window of the Blue Room was just round the corner. Imagine yourself a steeplejack. How delicious to know, while you went about your work with a crowbar or a hammer or whatever heavy, unwieldy instrument it might be, that there was a railing of stone and mortar, two feet high and six inches thick, between you and the ground! The steeplejack would feel he wasn't earning his pay when his life was safeguarded like that. Well, here's a foolproof job! Like putting a grown man in a child's cot, with a high brass *chevaux-de-frise* round it. But nevertheless, rounding the bend, Ernest was overtaken by nausea and lay for some moments stretched out upon the leaden gully, twitching.

But supposing a man was kept out by force from his possessions, or what should have been his? Who would blame him, who would not applaud him, if he went to any reasonable length to recover his property? Should he consult his own safety, or anyone's safety, when he was engaged upon such an undertaking?

Ernest dragged himself to the window. His head was level with the upper sash which was fast in the wall, and looked as if it was fixed there. But the lower sash was about six inches open, with the fold of a blue blind projecting from it.

Up went the sash a long, long way as it seemed, much farther than the others. But as he lifted it there was a whirring sound; the tegument of the blind vanished. The new proprietor was standing there. Ernest stared at him. Was it the face of the poor man who had come into money and acquired Stithies? Or of the coward who owned it? Or of the policeman who protected it, or of the man who cleaned its windows? Or of the coal-heaver or of the steeplejack or of the man who wouldn't let anything stand in his way? It seemed in turn to be all these, yet its essential character never changed. Dazed as he was, Ernest remembered to drop his hands. The apparition dropped his; the window was unguarded. Slowly Ernest lowered and advanced his head. But he had not reckoned on his enemy's faculty for imitation. The simulacrum bowed, leant forward, pressed its face to within three inches of Ernest's. And as it hung there the last expression faded out of it, and was replaced by a featureless oval, dimly phosphorescent. Yet something began to take shape in that mobile, almost fluid tract. Ernest did not wait for it to declare itself, this new visage whose lines he could almost see graven in the air before they settled and bit deep into the flesh.

He was on the dripstone of the tower now, clinging with his fingers to the sham machicolations. Suppose a man meant to commit a murder, did he shrink from risking his own life? Wasn't anything easy to him, in the presence of such a determination? Hadn't it been easy to him, Ernest, when he stood, some ten years ago, on this same dizzy ledge and found, after three failures, the one vulnerable point of Stithies, the box-room window?

Sweating and gasping he reached the window and clung to the stanchion, his back, weak with exhaustion, bending outwards like a bow. But his prescient tormentor had outstripped him. This time the face did not alter. It was Ernest's own face, a hateful face, and the face of a murderer.

Punctually at half-past six, in the gathering light, Mrs Playward passed through the open gateway into the garden of Stithies Court. 'Bless me,' she thought. 'What with the maids away and the young gentleman in bed I shan't be able to get in.' The suspicion that she had made the journey for nothing weighed heavily on Mrs Playward. 'It's not as if I am as young as I was,' she told herself. But, having come so far, it was worth while to make sure that none of the doors was unlocked. The front door seemed to open of itself, such was her amazement at finding it unfastened. 'Well, I never,' she declared. 'And he always said to be so fidgety about robbers.' She heaved a sigh. 'Best to get it over,' she muttered. 'If there's one step there's eighty.' Having collected the machinery of her profession she mounted the spiral staircase that led to the box-room. Her eyesight was defective, a fact to which, when reproached for apparent negligence, she often drew the attention of her clients. The staircase was lighted by a couple of slit windows, set deep in the wall. At the second of them she paused, partly to recover her breath, partly to relieve her eyes from the strain of peering into the gloom. By leaning forward she could just see the road below. 'Well, I declare,' she muttered, 'if Polkin hasn't been and left his overcoat out on the path all night. That good black one he told me he was promised by Mr Ernest. Some men don't know when they're well off.' Breathing heavily she resumed her journey. The condition of this box-room was heart-breaking, trunks, cardboard boxes, gas-rings, fenders, disused furniture all covered with a layer of dust. But she hardly noticed that becasue a stranger sight claimed her attention. The casement window was wide open.

She walked towards it. A huge black trunk with a flat top stood directly under the window, and in the dust which thickly coated it there were four curious marks. Two pairs of each. The farther ones, the marks nearest the window, she made out at once. They were the prints of hands. The fingers, pointing into the room, were splayed out and unnaturally elongated; where the hand joined the wrist there was a long shapeless smear. Opposite them, and within an arm's length, were the other marks. At first they meant nothing to her: two symmetrical black smudges with rounded tops and a thin track of dust between them. The imprint of a man's knees perhaps? Panic descended on Mrs Playward. She fled, screaming 'Mr Ernest, Mr Ernest, something has happened in the box-room!' No one answered her; when she hammered on Mr Ernest's door no one replied, and when she went in, the room was empty.

THE THOUGHT

Henry Greenstream had always looked forward to his afternoon walk. It divided the day for him. In ideal circumstances a siesta preceded it and he awoke to a new morning, a false dawn, it is true, but as pregnant with unexpressed promise as the real one. For some weeks now, however, sleep had deserted his after-luncheon cushion; he could get to the brink of unconsciousness, when thoughts and pictures drifted into his mind independently of his will, but not over.

Still, the walk was the main thing even if he started on it a little tired. It calmed, it satisfied, it released. For an hour and twenty-five minutes he enjoyed the freedom of the birds of the air. Impressions and sensations offered themselves to him in an unending flow, never outstaying their welcome, never demanding more from his attention than a moment's recognition. Lovely and pleasant voices that tonelessly proclaimed the harmony between him, Henry Greenstream, and the spirit of all created things.

Or they had proclaimed it till lately. Lately the rhythm of his thoughts had been disturbed by an interloper, yes, an interloper, but an interloper from within. Like a cuckoo that soon ceased to be a visitor, the stranger had entered his mind and now dwelt there, snatching at the nourishment meant for its legitimate neighbours. They pined, they grew sickly while Henry Greenstream suckled the parasite.

He knew what it was and whence it came. It was an infection from his conscience which had taken offence at an act so trivial that surely no other conscience would have noticed it. Indeed, he had himself almost forgotten what it originated in – something about a breach of confidence that (reason assured him a thousand times) could have harmed nobody. And when it stirred inside him it was not to remind him of his fault and recall the circumstances of his lapse, but simply to hurt him; to prick the tender tegument which, unpierced, assures comfort to the mind.

If it did not spoil his life it fretted him, reducing his capacity for enjoyment; and most of all did it make its presence felt when he took his afternoon exercise. The aery shapes that then haunted his imagination could not suppress it, nor was the scenery through which he passed such as to distract him from himself. Town gave way to suburb; surburb to ribbon development; only when it was time to turn back did he emerge into the unspoilt countryside. Motors rushed by; an occasional tramp asked for a match; dogs idled on the pavement. All this was uninspiring but at the same time it fostered his mood; even the ugly little houses, with their curtains drawn aside to reveal a plant or a pretentious piece of china, invited pleasing speculations. Confidently he looked forward to his reunion with these humble landmarks. But they had lost their power to draw him out, and lately he had invented a new and less satisfying form of mental pastime. Much less satisfying; for it consisted of counting the minutes that elapsed between one visitation of the Thought and the next. Even so might a Chinese malefactor seek to beguile himself while under the water-torture by calculating the incidence of the drops.

Where the signpost pointed to Aston Highchurch Mr Greenstream paused. He had been walking half an hour and the Thought had recurred twenty-two times; that was an average of nearly once a minute, a higher average than yesterday, when he had got off with fourteen repetitions. It was in fact a record: a bad record. What could he do to banish this tedious symptom? Stop counting, perhaps? Make his mind a blank? He wandered on with uncertain footsteps unlike his ordinary purposeful stride. Ahead of him the October sun was turning down the sky; behind, the grass (for the fields now began to outnumber the houses) took on a golden hue; above, the clouds seemed too lazy to obey what little wind there was. It was a lovely moment that gathered to itself all the harmony of which the restless earth was capable. Mr Greenstream opened his heart to the solace of the hour and was already feeling refreshed when ping! the Thought stung him again.

'I must do something about this,' thought Mr Greenstream, 'or I shall go mad.'

He looked round. To his left, in the hedge beyond the grass verge, was a wicket-gate, and from it a path ran diagonally over the shoulder of a little hill, a shabby asphalt path that gleamed in the sunlight and disappeared, tantalizingly, into the horizon. Mr Greenstream knew where it led, to Aston Highchurch; but so conservative was he that in all these years of tramping down the main road he had never taken it. He did so now. In a few minutes he was on the high land in what seemed a different world, incredibly nearer the sky. Turning left along a country lane bordered by trees and less agreeably by chicken runs, he kept catching sight of a church; and at length he came to a path that led straight to it across a stubble field. It lay with its back to him, long and low, with a square tower at the further end that gave it the look of a cat resting on tucked-in legs, perhaps beginning to purr.

Mr Greenstream stopped at the churchyard gate and stared up at the tower to make out what the objects were which, hanging rather crazily at the corners below the parapet, had looked in the distance like whiskers, and completed the feline impression made by the church. A whiskered church! The idea amused Mr Greenstream until his watchful tormentor, ever jealous of his carefree moments, prodded him again. With a sigh he entered the porch and listened. No sound. The door opened stiffly to confront him with a pair of doors, green baize this time. He went back and shut the outer door, then the inner ones, and felt he had shut out the world. The church was empty; he had it to himself.

It was years since Mr Greenstream had been inside a church except on ceremonial occasions or as a sightseer, and he did not quite know what to do. This was a Perpendicular church, light, airy and spacious, under rather than over furnished. The seats were chairs made of wood so pale as to be almost white: they were lashed together with spars, and the whole group, with its criss-cross of vertical and horizontal lines, made an effect that was gay and pretty and, in so far as it suggested rigging, faintly nautical.

Mr Greenstream wandered up to the nave but felt a reluctance, for which he could not quite account, to mount the chancel steps: in any case there was little of note there and the east window was evidently modern. Straying back along the north aisle wall he read the monumental inscriptions, black lettering on white marble or white lettering on black marble. Then he came face to face with the stove, an impressive cylinder from which issued a faint crackling. His tour seemed to be over; but he was aware of a feeling of expectancy, as if the church were waiting for him to do something.

'After all, why not?' he thought, sinking to his knees. But he could not pray at once – he had lost the habit, he did not know how to begin. Moreover he felt ashamed of coming to claim the benefits of religion when for many years he had ignored its obligations. Such a prayer would be worse than useless; it was an insult; it would put God against him. Then the Thought came with its needle-jab and he waited no longer but prayed vehemently and incoherently for deliverance. But a morbid fear assailed him that it was not enough to think the words, for some of them, perhaps the most operative, might be left out, telescoped or elided by the uncontrollable hurry of his mind, so he repeated his petition out loud. Until he had ceased to speak he did not notice how strange his voice sounded in the empty church, almost as if it did not belong to him. Rising shakily to his feet he blinked, dazzled by the daylight, and stumbled out of the church without a backward look.

Not once on the homeward journey to his narrow house in Midgate was Mr Greenstream troubled by the Thought. His relief and gratitude were inexpressible; but it was not till the next day that he realized that the visit to Aston Highchurch had been a turning point in his life. Doctors told him that his great enemy was his morbid sense of guilt. Now, so long as St Cuthbert's, Aston Highchurch, stood, he need not fear it.

Fearful yet eager he began to peer down a future in which, thanks to the efficacy of prayer, the desires of his heart would meet with no lasting opposition from the voice of his conscience. He could indulge them to the full. Whatever they were, however bad they were, he need not be afraid that they would haunt him afterwards. The Power whose presence he had felt in church would see to that.

It was a summer evening and the youth of Aston Highchurch would normally have been playing cricket on the village green, but the game fell through because a handful of the regulars had failed to turn up. There was murmuring among the disappointed remnant, and inquiry as to what superior attraction had lured away the defaulters.

'I know,' said a snub-nosed urchin, 'because I heard them talking about it.'

'Well, tell us, Tom Wignall.'

'They said I wasn't to.'

'Come on, you tell us or . . .'

According to their code a small but appreciable amount of physical torture released the sufferer from further loyalty to his plighted word. After a brief but strident martyrdom the lad, nothing loth, yielded to the importunity of his fellows.

'It's about that praying chap.'

'What, old Greenpants?'

'Yes. They've gone to watch him at it.'

'Where?'

'In the tower gallery. Fred Buckland pinched the key when the old man wasn't looking.'

'Coo, they'll cop it if they're caught.'

'Why, they aren't doing no harm. You can't trespass in a church.'

'That's all you know. They haven't gone there just to watch, neither.'

'Why, what are they going to do?'

'Well,' said Tom Wignall importantly, 'they're going to give him a fright. Do you know what he does?'

'He prays, doesn't he?'

'Yes, but he don't pray to himself. He prays out loud, and he shouts sometimes, and rocks himself about. And he doesn't pray for his father and mother—'

'He hasn't got any, so I've heard,' said an older boy, who, to judge from his caustic tone, seemed to be listening with some impatience to Tom Wignall's revelations. 'He's an orphan.'

'Anyhow,' the speaker resumed unabashed, 'he doesn't pray for his kind or his country, or to be made good or anything like that. He confesses his sins.'

'Do you mean he's done a murder?'

'Fred Buckland couldn't hear what it was, but it must have been something bad or he wouldn't have come all this way to confess it.'

This reasoning impressed the audience.

'Must have been murder,' they assured each other, 'or forgery anyhow.'

'But that isn't all,' continued the speaker, intoxicated by the attention he was receiving. 'He prays for what he didn't ought.'

'Why, you can pray for anything you like,' opined one of the listeners.

'That you can't. There's heaps of things you mustn't pray for. You mustn't pray to get rich, for one thing, and' (he lowered his voice) 'you mustn't pray for anyone to die.'

'Did he do that?'

'Fred Buckland said that's what it sounded like.'

There was a pause.

'I think the poor chap's barmy if you ask me,' said the older boy. 'I bet his prayers don't do no one any harm nor him any good either.'

'That's where you make a mistake,' said the spokesman of the party. 'That's where you're wrong. Fred Buckland says he got a car and a chauffeur and all. Fred Buckland says he wouldn't be surprised if he's a millionaire.'

'You bet he is,' scoffed the older boy. 'You bet that when he prayed somebody dropped down dead and left him a million. Sounds likely, doesn't it?'

The circle of listeners stirred. All the faces broadened with scepticism and one boy took up his bat and played an imaginary forward stroke. Tom Wignall felt that he was losing ground. He was like a bridge-player who has held up his ace too long.

'Anyhow,' he said defiantly, 'Fred Buckland says that church is no place for the likes of him who've got rich by praying in a way they ought to be ashamed of. And I tell you, he's going to give old Greenpants a fright. He's going to holler down at him from the tower in a terrible voice, and Greenpants'll think it's God answering him from Heaven, or perhaps the Devil, and he'll get such a fright he'll never set foot in Aston again. And good riddance, I say.'

Tom's own voice rose as he forced into it all the dramatic intensity he could muster. But he had missed his moment. One or two of his companions looked serious and nodded, but the rest, with the unerring instinct of boys for a change of leadership, a shifting of moral ascendancy, threw doubtful glances towards their senior. They were wavering. They would take their cue from him.

'Lousy young bastards,' he said, 'leaving us all standing about like fools on a fine evening like this. I should like to tan their hides.'

There was a murmur of sympathetic indignation, and he added, 'What makes them think the chap's coming today to pray, anyhow?'

Tom Wignall answered sullenly: 'He comes most days now . . . And if you want to know, Jim Chantry passed him on his motorbike the other side of Friar's Bridge. He didn't half jump when Jim honked in his ear,' Tom concluded with unrepentant relish. 'He'll be here any time now.'

'Well,' said the older boy stretching himself luxuriously, 'You chaps can go and blank yourselves. There's nothing else for you to do. I'm off.' He sauntered away, grandly, alone, towards the main road. Those silly mutts need a lesson. I'll spoil their little game for them, he thought.

The tower gallery at St Cuthbert's, Aston Highchurch, was a feature most unusual in parish churches. But the tower was rather unusual too. Its lower storey, which rose fifty or more feet to the belfry floor, was open to the main body of the building; only an arch divided it from the nave. The gallery, a stone passage running along the tower wall just above the west window, was considerably higher than the apex of the arch. It was only visible from the western end of the church, and itself commanded a correspondingly restricted view – a view that was further impeded by the lightly swaying bell-ropes. But Fred Buckland and his four conspirators could see, through the flattened arc of the arch, a portion of the last six rows of chairs. The sunlight coming through the window below them fell on the chairs, picking them out in gold and making a bright patch like the stage of a theatre.

'He ought to be here by now, didn't he?' one urchin whispered.

'Shut up!' hissed the ringleader. 'It'll spoil everything if he hears us.'

They waited, three of them with their backs pressed against the wall, their faces turned this way and that as in a frieze, looking very innocent and naughty. Fred, who had more than once sung carols from this lofty perch, embraced a baluster and let his feet dangle over the edge.

Five minutes passed, ten, a quarter of an hour. The sinking sun no longer lay so brightly on the foreground; shadows began to creep in from the sides. The boys even began to see each other less plainly.

'I'm frightened,' whispered a voice. 'I wish we hadn't come. I want to go home.'

'Shut up, can't you?'

More minutes passed and the church grew darker.

'I say, Fred,' a second voice whispered, 'what time does your old man come to shut the church up?'

'Seven o'clock these evenings. It still wants a quarter to.'

They waited; then one whispered in a tense voice, 'I believe that's him.'

'Who?'

'Old Greenpants, of course.'

'Did you hear anything?'

'No, but I thought I saw something move.'

'You're barmy. That's the shadow of the bell-rope.'

They strained their eyes.

'I don't think it was, Fred. It moves when the bell-rope doesn't.'

'Funny if somebody else should be spying on old Greenpants.'

'Maybe it's him who's spying on us.'

'What, old Greenpants?'

'Of course. Who else could it be?'

'I wish I could see what that was moving,' the boy said again. 'There, close by the stove.'

'I suppose it couldn't get up to us?'

'Not unless it came by the bell-rope,' said Fred decisively. 'I've locked the door of the stairs and the only other key my dad has. You're in a funk, that's your trouble. Only the Devil could shin up one of them ropes.'

'They wouldn't let him come into church, would they?'

'He might slip in if the north door was open.'

Almost as he spoke a puff or wind blew up in their faces and the six bell-ropes swayed in all directions lashing each other and casting fantastic shadows.

'That's him,' Fred hissed. 'Don't you hear his footsteps? I bet that's him. Just wait till he gets settled down. Now, all together: "God is going to punish thee, Henry Greenstream, thou wicked man".'

In creditable unison, their voices quavered through the church. What result they expected they hardly knew themselves, nor did they have time to find out; for the sacristan, appearing with a clatter of boots at the gallery door, had them all like rats in a trap. Fear of committing sacrilege by blasphemy for a moment took away his powers of speech; then he burst out, 'Come on, you little blackguards! Get down out of here! Oh, you'll be sore before I've finished with you!'

A spectator, had there been one, would have noticed that the sounds of snivelling and scuffling were momentarily stilled as the staircase swallowed them up. A minute later they broke out again, with louder clamour; for though Fred got most of the blows the others quickly lost their morale, seeing how completely their leader had lost his.

'I'll take a strap to you when I get you home,' thundered the sacristan, 'trying to disturb a poor gentleman at his devotions.'

'But, Dad, he wasn't in the church!' protested Fred between his sobs.

'It wasn't your fault if he wasn't,' returned his father grimly.

For some months after being warned Henry Greenstream came no more to St Cuthbert's, Aston Highchurch. Perhaps he found another sanctuary, for certainly there was no lack of them in the district. Perhaps, since he had a motor, he found it more convenient to drive out into the country where (supposing he needed them) were churches in sparsely populated areas, untenanted by rude little boys. He had never been a man to advertise his movements, and latterly his face had worn a closed look, as if he had been concealing them from himself. But he had to tell the chauffeur where to go, and the man was immensely surprised when, one December afternoon, he received an order to drive to Aston Highchurch. 'We hadn't taken that road for an age,' he afterwards explained.

'Stop when I tap the window,' Mr Greenstream said, 'and then I shall want you to do something for me.'

At the point where the footpath leads across the fields Mr Greenstream tapped and got out of the car.

'I'm going on to the church now,' he said, 'but I want you to call at the Rectory, and ask the Reverend Mr Ripley if he would step across to the church and ... and hear my confession. Say it's rather urgent. I don't know how long I shall be gone.'

The chauffeur, for various reasons, had not found Mr Greenstream's service congenial; he had in fact handed his notice in that morning. But something in his employer's tremulous manner touched him, and surprising himself, he said:

'You wouldn't like me to go with you as far as the church, sir?'

'Oh, no, thank you, Williams. I think I can get that far.'

'I only thought you didn't look very fit, sir.'

'Is that why you decided to leave me?' asked Mr Greenstream, and the man bit his lip and was silent.

Mr Greenstream walked slowly towards the church, absently and unsuccessfully trying to avoid the many puddles left by last night's storm. It had been a violent storm, and now though the wind was gone, the sky, still burning streakily as with the embers of its own ill-temper, had a wild, sullen look.

Mr Greenstream reached the porch but didn't go in. Instead he walked round the church, stumbling among the graves, for some were unmarked by headstones; and on the north side, where no one ever went, the ground was untended and uneven.

It took him some minutes to make the circuit, but when he had completed it he started again. It was on his second tour that he discovered – literally stumbled against – the gargoyle, which, of course, has been replaced now. The storm had split it but the odd thing was that the two halves, instead of being splintered and separated by their fall, lay intact on the sodden grass within a few inches of each other. Mr Greenstream could not have believed the grinning mask was so big. It had split where the spout passed through it: one half retained the chin, the other was mostly eye and cheek and ear. Mr Greenstream could see the naked spout hanging out far above him, long and bent and shining like a black snake. The comfortless sight may have added to the burden of his thoughts, for he walked on more slowly. This time, however, he did not turn aside at the porch, but went straight in, carefully shutting the inner and outer doors behind him.

It was past four o'clock and the church was nearly dark, the windows being only visible as patches of semi-opaque brightness. But there *was* a light which shone with a dull red glow, a burning circle hanging in the air a foot or two from the ground. It looked like a drum that had caught fire within, but it was not truly luminous; it seemed to attract the darkness rather than repel it. For a moment Mr Greenstream could not make out what the strange light was. But when he took a step or two towards it and felt the heat on his face and hands he knew at once. It was the stove. The zealous sacristan, mindful of the chilly day, had stoked it up until it was red hot.

Mr Greenstream was grateful for the warmth, for his hands were cold and his teeth chattering. He would have liked to approach the stove and bend over it. But the heat was too fierce for that, it beat him back. So he withdrew to the outer radius of its influence. Soon he was kneeling, and soon – the effect of the warmth on a tired mind and a tired body, asleep.

It must have been the cold that woke him, cold, piercing cold, that seemed solid, like a slab of ice pressing against his back. The stove still glared red in front of him, but it had no more power to warm him physically than has a friendly look or a smiling face. Whence did it come, this deadly chill? Ah! He looked over his left shoulder and saw that the doors, which he remembered shutting, were now open to the sky and the north wind. To shut them again was the work of a moment. But why were they open? he wondered, turning back into the church. Why, of course, of course, the clergyman had opened them, the Rector of Aston Highchurch, who was coming at his request to hear his confession. But where was he, and why did he not speak? And what was the reddish outline that moved towards him in the darkness? For a moment his fancy confused it with the stove, or it might be the stove's reflection, thrown on one of the pillars. But on it came, bearing before it that icy breath he now knew had nothing to do with the north wind.

'Mr Ripley, Mr Ripley,' he murmured, falling back into the warmth of the stove, feeling upon his neck its fierce assault. Then he heard a voice like no voice he had ever heard, as if the darkness spoke with the volume of a thousand tongues.

'I am your confessor. What have you to say?'

'My death must be my answer,' he replied, the consciousness of annihilation on him.

When Mr Greenstream's chauffeur learned that the Rector was not at home he left a message and then returned to the car, for he knew from experience that his master's unaccountable church-going often kept him a long time. But when an hour had gone by he felt vaguely anxious and decided to see if anything was the matter. To his surprise he found the church door open, and noticed a smell coming from it which he had never associated with a church. Moving gingerly in the dark, he advanced towards where a sound of hissing made itself heard. Then he struck a match, and what he saw caused him to turn and run in terror for the door. On the threshold he almost collided with Mr Ripley, hastening from the Rectory on his errand of mercy. Together they overcame the repugnance which either of them would have felt singly, lifted Mr Greenstream's body from the stove across which it hung and laid it reverently on the pavement.

The newspapers at first gave out that Mr Greenstream had been burned to death, but the medical authorities took a different view.

'In my opinion,' one doctor said, 'he was dead before he even touched the stove, and paradoxical as it may seem, the physical signs indicate that he was frozen, not burned to death.

'He was perhaps trying to warm himself – why, we shall never know.'

CONRAD AND THE DRAGON

Once upon a time there was a boy who lived with his mother and father in a country five days' journey beyond the boundaries of Europe. As he was only twelve years old when this story begins, he did not have to work for his living, but played about in the woods in which his house was, generally by himself. But sometimes he would stand and watch his two brothers felling trees and sawing them up, for, like his father, they were foresters, and every now and then they would let him ride home astride a tree-trunk, jogging up and down above the horses. This he enjoyed, when once he got over the fear of falling off, and he would have joined them oftener, but he was afraid lest Leo might say, 'Now, Conrad, it's your turn to do something; just mind those horses for ten minutes,' or 'Conrad, come here and lean your heavy weight against this sapling, so that I can get the axe to it.' Then Conrad would have to go; unless Rudolph chimed in with, 'Oh, let the boy alone, Leo, he's more hindrance than help.' Conrad would be half glad and half sorry at Rudolph's intervention; he wanted to lend a hand, but he was afraid the horse might tread on his toes, or the sapling spring up and hit him. He was very fond of his brothers, especially the younger, Rudolph, and he admired them, they were so strong and capable; he did not believe he would ever be able to do what they did, even when he grew up. 'I am not meant to be a forester,' he told himself.

It so happened that one afternoon Leo put the axe in his hands, and tried more persistently than ever to teach him how to use it. Conrad had been only half attending; he swung the axe clumsily, and it glanced off the tree on to his foot, making a deep gash in his boot. Leo spoke sharply to him for his awkwardness, and Conrad, without waiting to hear what Rudolph might say in his defence, dropped the axe and ran away, crying, nor did he pause for breath until the sounds that came from the clearing had ceased altogether.

Here the forest was very thick and silent, and though there

seemed to be plenty of little paths going hither and thither, a stranger to the wood would have found that they led nowhere in particular, to an abandoned clearing, perhaps, or just into the undergrowth. But Conrad, who knew this part of the wood by heart, was not at all alarmed. He was feeling too hurt and angry with his brothers to be sorry that he had damaged his boot, though it would mean his father buying another pair; what he dreaded was that the axe might have cut his foot, in which case he would have to swallow his pride and go back to his brothers to beg a ride, for he was a long way from home.

He examined the gash as well as the dim light permitted, but there was no sign of blood; and when he took off his boot to look closer he found that the stocking was lightly cut, but the skin below it was unharmed. What a lucky escape! It must be magic, Conrad thought, white magic, much rarer than the black kind which he had been warned against, and which was all too common in this part of the world. How nice if he could meet, in some dell or coppice, the good fairy who, at the critical moment, had turned the axe's edge! He peered about; he kissed the air, hoping to attract her; but if she was there she remained invisible. But Conrad, encouraged by the discovery that he was unhurt, felt twice the boy he was; so far from running back to his brothers, he would prove to them that he did not need their protection; he would press on through the forest further than he had ever gone before, and would not be home till nightfall. He had some food in his satchel and, as it was early autumn, there were plenty of berries on the trees. He started off.

Soon the wood changed its character. Instead of being flat, it turned into a succession of narrow valleys which Conrad always seemed to have to cross at their deepest point, scrambling up and down as best he could, for path there was none. He began to feel tired, and the sharp, hard leather of his damaged boot stuck into him and hurt him. He kept on meaning to turn back, but whenever he reached the crest of a ridge, it looked such a little way to the next that he always decided to cross just one more valley. They were long and empty, lit up their whole length by the sun which, away on Conrad's right, was now so low that he could see it without lifting his eyes. It would soon be night. Suddenly he lost heart and made up his mind to stop at the next hilltop. It was only a few yards' climb.

But once there, what a sight met his eyes – worth the whole

journey, worth far, far more than all the efforts he had made. An immense valley, like the others, only larger, and flooded with orange light, stretched away to the left; and blocking the end a huge square rock, almost a mountain, with a castle built into its summit, so cunningly you could not tell where rock ended and stone began. Conrad strained his eyes. In the clear air of that country, of course, it was possible to see an immense distance; the castle might be five miles away, might be ten, might be twenty. But there was a picture of it in the kitchen at home, and he recognized it at once. It was the royal castle, the palace of the King.

Clearly there was a ceremony in progress, for the castle was gaily decorated with large and little flags; bright-coloured rugs and tapestries hung from the windows, and scarlet streamers attached to the pinnacles flapped and floated in the breeze. Where the valley narrowed to a gorge in front of the castle was a huge black mass, divided by a white road; this mass Conrad presently made out to be a crowd of people ranged on either side of the highway; soldiers on horseback posted at the corners and at regular intervals along the track were keeping the road clear, while along it in fours marched heralds blowing trumpets, and moving so slowly they scarcely seemed to move at all.

All at once the trumpeters halted, turned, stepped back and lined the road, their trumpets still extended. There was a pause in which nothing seemed to move; the breeze held its breath, the flags, hanging straight down, looked little thicker than their poles. Then, in the mouth of the long white channel appeared four men on horseback, followed at some distance by a single horseman, whose uniform glittered as though with jewels and on whose helmet was a great white plume. His head was slightly bent, whether in pride or humility, Conrad could not tell; perhaps he was acknowledging the cheers of the spectators, who had broken into frenzied movement, waving their arms and flinging their hats into the air.

So, in the heart of a welcome he could never have known before, he proceeded, until the whole crowd, and Conrad with it, had stared their fill at him, and the first flight of steps seemed only a few yards away. Exactly what happened then Conrad never remembered. There was a movement in the face of the living rock, a wrinkling and crumbling, and a drift of powdery smoke flung up into the air. A hole appeared in the hillside, and out of it came a head – a snake-like head, blacker than the hole it issued from, solid as ebony, large as the shadow of a cloud. It writhed this way and that on its thick round neck, then suddenly darted forward. The crowd gave way on either hand, leaving in the centre a bulging space like an egg. Conrad saw the plumed horseman look back over his shoulder. That way lay safety; but he preferred not to save himself. Conrad did not wait to see him ride to his death; his last impression of the scene, before he took to his heels, was of a sudden hurricane that caught the face of the castle and stripped it bare of every flag, carpet and tapestry that emblazoned it.

Ill news travels fast, and thus it was that when night fell, Conrad's absence from home was scarcely noticed. 'What can have happened to the boy?' his mother asked more than once, but nobody took the matter up, they were too busy, the brothers and their friends, discussing the awful fate that had overtaken Princess Hermione's suitor. As they all talked at once, I had better give the substance of what they said. The Princess was to have been bethrothed that day to the heir of a neighbouring monarch. He was a handsome man, gallant and brave, an excellent match in every way.

'Had the Princess ever seen him?' asked Conrad's mother.

'How does that affect the matter?' exclaimed her husband. 'The alliance would have made us the strongest nation upon earth. Who will want to marry her now?'

'There will be plenty,' said Leo promptly. 'The Princess is but seventeen, and the most beautiful woman in the world.'

Nobody denied this, for it was known to be true. The Princess's beauty was so great it had already become a proverb. The men of other countries, when they wanted to describe a beautiful woman, said she was as lovely as a rose, or as the day, or as a star; but the people of this country, if they wanted to praise something, said it was as beautiful as Princess Hermione. She was so beautiful that anything she did, even speaking, made her less lovely, ruffled her beauty, as it were; so she did little and spoke seldom. Also she rarely went out in public, it was unfair to people, they couldn't help falling in love with her. So retiring was her nature that ordinary folk like Conrad and his brothers knew little about her except that she was lovely.

'Of course,' said Leo, 'someone will have to go properly armed to fight this dragon. That poor fellow didn't have a chance in his fine clothes. The king may call out the militia; or perhaps they'll just stop its hole up and starve it out.'

'I'm afraid it will be a great shock to the Princess,' their mother said.

Thereupon they fell to arguing as to where the Princess could have been when the Dragon burst out from the cliff and devoured her luckless suitor. One said she had been seen at a window; another that she was praying in the chapel. Of course it was all hearsay, but they defended their versions with great vigour. At last their father, tired of the fruitless argument, observed:

'I don't suppose she was anywhere in particular.'

'Why, she must have been somewhere,' they protested.

'Well, I've told you what I think,' said he; and at that moment Conrad came in.

He expected a beating for being in so late, and at any other time he might have got it. But tonight, so great was the excitement, his tardy arrival was treated as something of a joke. To turn their attention away from his lateness he meant to tell them, at once, the story of what he had seen in the wood – he had got it by heart. But no sooner had he begun, partly from exhaustion but more from sickness as the details came up before his mind, he turned faint and had to stop. His brothers laughed at him, and returned to their own pet theories of what happened at the castle. Conrad felt disappointed. Though coming home had taken him twice as long as going, it had all been a marvellous adventure, which he thought his parents and brothers would clamour to hear about! Whereas Leo hardly took any interest in his story, and even Rudolph said that from such a position he couldn't have seen anything with certainty. Just because they were grown up they did not believe his experiences could matter to anyone. They went on discussing how many people besides the Prince the Dragon had eaten, and what had happened to the torrent of black blood it was supposed to have emitted – things they knew nothing about. What a tame ending to an exciting day!

Of course, the court went into mourning, and a general fast was proclaimed, for it was rightly decided to neglect nothing that might lead to the Dragon's destruction. But from the first the Prince's would-be avengers were faced by an almost insuperable obstacle. The Dragon had utterly disappeared, leaving no trace; even the hole by which it came out had closed up; and professional mountaineers tied to ropes searched the face of the rock with pickaxes and even microscopes, to find an opening, without success. The very wall-flowers that the Princess was reported to be so fond of, bloomed there just as before; and popular opinion became irritated against the experts who, it said, were looking in the wrong place and deliberately prolonging their job. Short of blasting the rock, which would have endangered the castle, every means was tried to make the Dragon come out. A herald was sent, quaking with fright, to ask it to state its terms; because those learned in dragonology declared that in the past dragons had been appeased by an annual sacrifice of men and maidens. When the Dragon made no reply the herald was instructed to play upon its vanity, and issue a formal challenge on behalf of one or other of the most redoubtable champions in the country: let it name the day and settle the matter by single combat. Still the Dragon made no sign, and the herald, embolded by this display of cowardice, said that since it was such a poor spirited thing he was ready to fight it himself, or get his little brother to do so. But the Dragon took no notice at all.

As the weeks lengthened into months without any demonstration by the Dragon, public confidence grew apace. One circumstance especially fostered this. It was feared that the neighbouring monarch who had so unluckily lost his eldest son would demand compensation, possibly with threats. But his attitude proved unexpectedly conciliatory. He absolved them of all negligence, he said; no one could be forearmed against a Dragon; and his son had met a gallant death on behalf (as it were) of the most beautiful lady in the world. After this handsome declaration it was hoped that he himself might come forward as a candidate for Princess Hermione's hand, for he was a widower. But he did not.

Suitors were not lacking, however; indeed, since the appearance of the dragon they had multiplied enormously. The fame of that event went abroad carrying the Princess's name into remote countries where even the rumour of her beauty had failed to penetrate. Now she was not only beautiful, she was unfortunate: the Dragon, some said, was the price she paid for her beauty. All this, combined with the secrecy which made her way of life a matter of speculation, invested the Princess with an extraordinary glamour. Everyone in the land, even the humblest, wanted to do something for her, they knew not what. Daily she received sackfuls of letters, all telling the same tale: that she was the most wonderful of women, that the writer adored her and wished that he, not the Prince, had had the honour of dying for her. A few even expressed the hope that the Dragon would reappear, so that they might put their devotion to the test.

But of course no one believed that it really would. Some who had not been eyewitnesses declared that the Dragon was an hallucination; that the Prince had just died of joy upon finding himself at last so near the Princess, and that the spectators, drunk with excitement, had imagined the rest. The majority felt confident for a different reason. Dragons, like comets and earthquakes, were things of rare occurrence. We know little about them, they argued, but at any rate we can be sure of this: if we have seen *one* dragon in our lives, we are not likely to see another. Many carried this argument a step further, and maintained that the kingdom had never been so safe from visitation by dragons as it was now; it had got the Dragon over, so to speak.

Before eighteen months were up the Dragon had passed into a joke. In effigy it was dragged round at fairs and processions, and made to perform laughable antics. Writers in the newspapers, when they wanted to describe a groundless fear, or a blessing in disguise, referred to it as 'Princess Hermione's Dragon'. Such as gave the monster serious thought congratulated themselves that it had come and gone without doing them any personal harm. Factories sprang up and business flourished, and in the tide of national prosperity, a decent period having elapsed, another suitor presented himself for the honour of winning Princess Hermione's hand.

He came of a royal house scarcely less distinguished (the newspapers said more distinguished) than his predecessor's. Preparations for his reception were made on a grander scale than before, to illustrate the growing resources of the country, and they were made on a completely different plan, so that there might be no question of comparison with the former ceremony. One alteration was this: at the instance of the Minister of War, who said it would stimulate recruiting, a detachment of machine-gunners, armed with a new type of gun and carrying many rounds of blank ammunition, was posted on a convenient ledge commanding the spot where the Dragon had broken out. And there was to be one further change. The Princess's first suitor, when he realized his danger and turned to face the Dragon, had cried out 'Dearest Hermione!' or something to that effect, some protestation of loyalty and love; he had not time to say much, but nobody could recollect his exact words. The new pretendant proposed, and his idea was universally applauded, that he should kneel at the foot of the steps and make a little speech, half a prayer, amplifying the sentiments of adoration and devotion that imminent death had wrung from the lips of his predecessor.

And so, when the day came, the people assembled to enjoy the spectacle in greater numbers than before. They were in the highest spirits, for the ceremony had a double appeal: it was to celebrate the betrothal of their beloved Princess, and her deliverance from the Dragon. Salvoes from the machine-gun emplacements above their heads, mingling with the strains of martial music and the caterwauling of private instruments, raised their excitement to frenzy. The silence in which the Prince knelt down to do homage to his bride-to-be was painful in its intensity. But no sooner had the last words passed his lips than there came a rumbling roar, a convulsion in the cliff, and the poor wretch was whirled aloft between the Dragon's jaws, to disappear into the mysterious recesses of the hillside.

The scene that followed was indescribable, and for a week, throughout the length and breadth of the kingdom, panic reigned. Frantic efforts were made to explain the causes of the calamity in the wickedness of individuals or in the mismanagement of the country. Impostors appeared and won a short hour of notoriety and influence by declaring that so-and-so was the culprit; and many innocent persons whose only fault was that they were uglier or richer or somehow different from the rest, perished at the hands of the mob. The government, more composed, arranged a few judicial executions, among the sufferers being the officers who had served the machine-gunners with blank ammunition. Even the King was covertly censured, and not allowed to contribute to the enormous indemnity which the Prime Minister, in the name of the country, handed over to the dead Prince's father: a sum so large that it had to be raised by a wholesale increase of taxation.

Only the Princess escaped blame. As before, she was alone, no one knew exactly where, at the precise moment of the catastrophe; but when she was found, a few minutes later, half-swooning in her room, her courage impressed everyone. She was soon able to write with her own hand a letter of condolence to the man who had so nearly been her father-in-law; when published in the newspapers, its eloquent phrases touched all hearts. Most miserable of women, she said, she had been the means of bringing death to two brave men – the second perhaps even more promising than the first. But what raised such a fury of protest was her concluding sentence – that she thought she must retire from the world. From all quarters of the country came letters begging her not to, so numerous that special mail-trains had to be run.

There was no difficulty in finding fresh champions for the Princess; her fame had increased with her misfortunes. She had never been so popular. Public confidence was reinvigorated by the verdict of military experts, who asserted that the disaster could not have happened if the machine-gunners had been properly armed. 'Give it a few rounds rapid,' they said, 'and we shan't be troubled by it any more.' The populace believed them. There had been too much muddling along; preparations for the Princess's coming betrothal must be put in the hands of the military. The commander-in-chief announced that no member of the general public would be admitted to the ceremony, for the Dragon, though its days were now numbered, was still not to be trifled with. The Prince's escort (he had already been chosen) was to be formed exclusively of picked troops, drilled to perfection and armed with the latest weapons. As they marched along the valley to take up their positions, the sun shone down on thousands of steel helmets: they looked invincible.

Alas, alas. The Prince had no sooner voiced his passionate plea than the hillside quaked and the Dragon darted out. It was warmly welcomed. Ten thousand soft-nosed rifle bullets must have struck it, and volleys of machine-gun fire, but in vain. The cruel eyes never even blinked. One satisfaction it missed, however. The firing continued long after the Prince was in mid-air. He must have been riddled with bullets, stone-dead, before the Dragon got him into his lair. He had been killed by his own defenders, a possibility that had never entered into the calculation of the military authorities.

To chronicle the events of the next two years is a grievous task, and one that the historian would gladly skip. The country went through a miserable time. The supply of eligible Princes would not last for ever, so it was decided to accept the offers of champions who, though of good birth, were more remarkable for valour than for rank. Supposing it did not fall to the spear of the first, seven different warriors were to engage the Dragon on seven successive days. If it survived these encounters, it would at any rate be tired, and in no fit state to engage the Prince of royal blood, though of no great personal prowess, who was to attempt it on the eighth day. But the Dragon was not exhausted at all; it seemed to have profited from practice, and found the Royal Prince as easy a prey as his seven predecessors.

So ended the first phase. The country's nobility shed its blood in gallons and still volunteers pressed forward, drawn from its thinning ranks. But then began an agitation, founded partly on democratic feeling, partly on the devotion which every man in the country worthy of the name, aye, and many outside it, cherished for the Princess Hermione: why should the glory of her rescue be confined to a privileged class? The King gave his consent; the Chamberlain's office was nearly stampeded; and at last a blacksmith, a redoubtable fellow, was selected as the People's Champion against the Dragon.

Of course there was no thought of his marrying her, nor did he presume to such an honour. As he stood at the foot of the steps accompanied only by a handful of friends who came at their own risk (the public had long since been excluded) he would gladly have allayed his nervousness by saying a few words, if not of love to the Princess at least of defiance to the Dragon. But he was not allowed to speak; and this, much as he resented it at the time, undoubtedly saved his life; for the Dragon did not condescend to appear.

No, its hate, rage, and lust of blood were clearly reserved for those who really loved the Princess and were in a position to marry her. The Dragon was not the enemy of the people, but the enemy of the Princess.

As soon as this was realized, there was obviously only one thing to do, and the King gave his consent to it, though sorely against his will. Anyone, of whatever station in life, who could kill the Dragon, should marry the Princess and have half the kingdom as well.

As always when a last desperate step is taken, hope surged up to greet the new proposal. It was obviously the right solution; why had no one thought of it before, and saved all this bloodshed? Enthusiasm ran high; combats were of almost daily occurrence; and in each one, though the upshot was always the same, the newspapers (seeing that they ran no risk, the public was again admitted to the scene) found some encouraging circumstance: the Dragon had lost a tooth, or its inky crest was streaked with grey, or it was a second late in appearing, or it was fat and slow with good living, or it had grinned and looked almost benevolent. The unfortunate heroes had displayed this one a neat piece of footwork, that, a shrewd thrust which might have pierced the side of a ship: while they were all commended for some original phrase, some prettily-turned compliment to the address of the Princess.

Not the least part of the whole ordeal was the framing of this preliminary speech; it was the only way by which the competitors could measure their skill against each other, since their performances against the Dragon hardly differed at all. There was no doubt that the Dragon disliked hearing the Princess praised; the more ardent and graceful the language in which she was wooed, the more vigorous was its onslaught.

Leo, Conrad's brother, was one of the first to volunteer, but his actual encounter with the Dragon tarried because he lacked scholarship to put into words the love that burned in him. But his production, to judge from the zest with which the monster gobbled him up, must have had some literary merit. Conrad missed his fiery, impatient brother. Little had his parents realized that the Dragon, which had seemed an affair for Kings and Queens and Governments, would take its toll from them. But their pride in their son's sacrifice upheld them, and lessened their grief.

Conrad, however, grew more despondent daily. He dreaded lest Rudolph, his favourite brother, should take it into his head to challenge the Dragon. Rudolph was less hot-headed than Leo and – surely a great safeguard – he was engaged to be married. Married men were prohibited (or, as Conrad put it to himself, exempted) from Dragon-baiting – though more than one, concealing his true condition, had gone out to meet a bachelor's death.

Conrad lost no opportunity of urging the charms of Charlotte, his brother's sweetheart; in and out of season he proclaimed them and begged Rudolph to marry her. In his anxiety for his brother's safety he more than once let drop a disparaging remark about the Princess, comparing her unfavourably to Charlotte. Rudolph told him to shut up or he would get himself into trouble: a madman who had spoken disrespectfully of the Princess had been torn to pieces by the mob.

'Of course the Princess is beautiful,' Conrad admitted, 'but she is fair: you told me you only admired dark women. Promise me you will marry Charlotte before the month is out.'

'How can I,' asked Rudolph, 'when I've no money and no home to take her to?'

Conrad knew that this was not strictly true; his brother was a gay young man, but he had some money laid by. Conrad, though he earned little, spent nothing at all.

'If you marry her a fortnight from today,' he begged, 'you shall have all my savings, and I will be a forester instead of going to the University.'

It cost him something to say this, but Rudolph answered with his light laugh:

'Keep your money, my dear Conrad, you will want it when your turn comes to fight the Dragon.'

This was not very encouraging, and Conrad began to ask himself was there no other way of keeping Rudolph out of harm's reach. The King had offered an enormous prize to anyone who could suggest a solution to the Dragon problem, and many women, cripples, elderly men and confirmed husbands had sent in suggestions. One was that the intending suitor should visit the castle in disguise. This was turned down because, even if the man got safely in, the Dragon would still be at large. Another proposed that the Royal Magician should give place to one more competent. To this the Home Secretary replied that it was a bad plan to change horses in mid-stream; the Magician had a world-wide reputation; he had performed many noteworthy feats in the past, he knew the lay-out of the castle as no one else did, and he was a close friend of Princess Hermione: it would be cruel to deprive her of his presence.

Most of the proposals, though meant helpfully, only put the authorities' backs up, implying as they did some dissatisfaction with the way things were being handled. One malcontent even dared to remark that at this rate the Princess would never get married. The newspapers made fun of him and he lost his job.

'If only I could get *inside* the castle,' thought Conrad, 'I might be able to do something. But I shall have to be very tactful.'

He began to write, but the pen would not answer to his thoughts. It seemed to have a will of its own, which was struggling against his. Instead of the valuable suggestion he wanted to make, a message of very different import kept appearing on the paper, in broken phrases like, 'my life to your service', 'no better death than this'. Tired of trying to control it, he let the pen run on; when it stopped, he found he had written a little love-address to the

Princess, very like those printed between heavy black lines (almost every day now) in the memorial columns in the newspapers. Puzzled, he threw the thing aside and applied himself to his task. Now it went better; he signed it, wrote 'The Princess Hermione' on the envelope and took it to the post. It would be some days before it reached her, if it ever did; she must have so many letters to deal with.

When he got home he found Rudolph in the room. He was standing by the table holding something in his hand.

'Ha, ha!' said he, 'I've found you out.'

Conrad could not imagine what he meant.

'Yes,' went on Rudolph, putting his hands behind his back. 'You've been deceiving me. You're in love with the Princess. You've been trying to persuade me not to fight the Dragon because you want the glory of killing it yourself.'

Rudolph was laughing, but Conrad cried out in agitation, 'No, no, you don't understand.'

'Well, listen then,' said Rudolph, and he began to read Conrad's declaration of love to the Princess; mockingly at first, then more seriously, and finally with a break in his voice and tears standing in his eyes.

They were silent for a moment, then Conrad held out his hand for the paper. But Rudolph would not part with it.

'Don't be silly,' Conrad pleaded. 'Give it to me.'

'What do you want it for?' asked Rudolph.

'I want to burn it!' cried Conrad recklessly.

'No, no!' said Rudolph, half laughing and gently pushing his brother away. 'I must have it – it may come in useful – who knows.'

He went out, taking the paper with him. Conrad felt uncomfortable; somehow he guessed he had done a silly thing.

He had. Two days later Rudolph casually announced that he had sent in his name as a candidate for the privilege of freeing Princess Hermione from her tormentor and that his application had been accepted.

'It's fixed for Thursday,' he remarked gaily. 'Poor old Dragon.'

His mother burst into tears, his father left the room and did not come back for an hour; but Conrad sat in his chair, without noticing what was going on round him. At last he said:

'What about Charlotte?'

'Oh,' said Rudolph airily, 'she's anxious for me to go. She's not like you pretend to be. She's sorry for the Princess. "I expected you'd want to go," she said to me. "I shall be waiting for you when you come back."'

'Was that all?' asked Conrad.

'Oh, she gave me her blessing.'

Conrad pondered. 'Did you tell her you were in love with the Princess?' he asked at length.

Rudolph hesitated. 'I couldn't very well tell her that, could I? It wouldn't have been kind. Besides, I'm not really in love with the Princess, of course: that's the difficulty. It was that speech you wrote – you know' (Conrad nodded) 'made me feel I was. I shall just try to be in love with her as long as the combat lasts. If I wasn't, you know, the Dragon wouldn't come out and I should miss my chance. But,' he added more cheerfully, 'I shall recite your address, and that will deceive it.'

'And then?'

'Oh, then I shall just come back and marry Charlotte. She understands that. You can give us some of your money if you like. I won't take it all. I'm not greedy.'

He went off whistling. Conrad's heart sank. He knew his brother's moods, this careless manner betokened that his mind was made up.

Who the first founder of the royal castle was, and when he built it, no one precisely knew. The common people ascribed its origin to the whim of some god or hero; and professional historians, though they scoffed at this idea, had no definite theory to put in its place – at least none they all agreed upon. But the castle had been many times rebuilt, at the bidding of changing fashions, and of the present edifice it was doubtful whether any part was more than a thousand years old. Its position on the solitary rock, defended by precipices on all sides save one, gave it so much natural strength that it was generally considered impregnable. According to common report, there were more rooms hollowed out of the rock than built of stones and mortar. Later architects, taking advantage of this, had concentrated their efforts on giving a grace and elegance to the exterior that no other fortress could boast, adorning it with turrets and balconies of an aery delicacy and windows embellished with the richest tracery their imaginations could devise. Windows that generously admitted the sun into wide, spacious rooms, the damasks and brocades of which, thus exposed to the noon-day glare, had need of constant renewal.

But the Princess Hermione had chosen for her favourite sitting-room a chamber in another part of the castle, so deeply embedded in the rock that the light of day reached it only by an ingenious system of reflectors. Nor could you tell what the season was, for a fire burned there all the year round. The room was not easy of access, nor did the Princess mean it to be. There was one known way into it, by a narrow, winding stair; but if report could be believed, there were several ways out – dark passages leading probably to bolt-holes in the rock. For years no one had troubled to explore them, but they had a fascination for the Princess, who knew them by heart and sometimes surprised her parents by appearing suddenly before them, apparently from nowhere.

She was sitting by the fireside, deep in a chair, and looking at some papers, which neither the firelight nor the twilight reflected down from above quite allowed her to read. Suddenly a shadow fell across the page and she could see nothing. The Princess looked up: a man was standing in front of her, shutting out the firelight; she knew no more than you or I how he had got there, but she was not surprised to see him.

'Well,' said the magician, for it was he. 'Are you still unsatisfied?'

The Princess turned her head, hidden by the chair-back, invisible to us; but the shadow of her features started up on the wall, a shadow so beautiful that (report said) it would not disappear when the Princess turned again, but clung on with a life of its own, until dissolved by the magician.

'Yesterday, at any rate, was a success,' the Princess murmured.

'Will you read me what he said?' asked the magician.

'Give me some light,' she commanded, and the room began to fill with radiance.

The Princess turned over the papers in her lap.

'Rudolph, Rudolph,' she muttered. 'Here he is – Do you really want to hear what the poor oaf says?'

'Is it like the others?'

'Exactly the same, only a particularly fine specimen.'

Though she tried to make her voice sound unconcerned, the Princess spoke with a certain relish; and her silhouette, stretched upon the wall, trembled and changed and became less pleasing. She turned and noticed it.

'Oh, there's that thing at its tricks again,' she sighed irritably. 'Take it away.'

The shadow faded.

'Well,' she said, settling herself again in the depths of her chair. 'Here it is.'

Her voice, slightly mimicking the peasants' burr, was delicious to hear.

'Most Gracious Princess: Men have been known to pity the past and dread the future, never, it seems to me, with much reason until now. But now I say, in the past there was no Princess Hermione; in the future, in the far future, dearest angel (may you live for ever), there will be none; none to die for. Therefore I say, Wretched Past! Miserable Future! And I bless this present hour in which Life and Death are one, one act in your service, one poem in your honour!'

The Princess paused: then spoke in her own voice.

'Didn't he deserve eating?'

'Your Highness, he did.'

'But now,' she continued in a brisker tone, 'I've got something different to read to you. Altogether different. In fact I've never received anything like it before.'

The shadow, which, like a dog that dreads reproof but cannot bear its banishment, had stolen back to the wall, registered a tiny frown on the Princess's forehead.

For the letter was certainly an odd one. The writer admitted frankly that he was not brave, nor strong, nor skilled in arms. He was afraid of a mouse, so what could he do against a dragon? The Princess was a lady of high intelligence, she would be the first to see the futility of such a sacrifice. She was always in his thoughts, and he longed to do some tiny service for her. He could not bear to think of her awaiting alone the issue of the combat between her champion and the Dragon. The strain must be terrible. He would count himself ever honoured if she would allow him to bear her company, even behind a screen, even outside the door, during those agonizing moments.

'What a pity I can't grant his request!' said the Princess, when she had finished. 'I like him, I like him for not wanting to offer up his life for me. I like him for thinking that women have other interests than watching men gratify their vanity by running into danger. I like him because he credits me with intelligence. I like him because he considers my feelings, and longs to be near me when there is no glory to be gained by it. I like him because he would study my moods and find out what I needed, and care for me all the day long, even when I was in no particular danger. I like him because he would love me without a whole population of terrified half-wits egging him on! I like him for a thousand things – I think I love him.'

'Your Highness! Your Highness!' said the magician, stirring uneasily. 'Remember the terms of the spell.'

'Repeat them: I have forgotten.'

> If he loves you
>   And you love not,
> Your suitor's life's
>   Not worth a jot,

sang the magician cheerfully.

'That's all we need to know,' sighed the Princess, who really recollected the spell perfectly. 'It always happens that way, and always will. But go on.'

> If he loves you
>   And you love him,
> I cannot tell
>   What Chance may bring,

chanted the magician in a lower tone.

'But if "he" were Conrad,' said the Princess teasingly, 'surely you could make a guess? And now for the last condition.'

The magician's voice sank to a whisper:

> If you love him
>   And he reject you,
> A thousand spells
>   Will not protect you.

'Ha! Ha!' cried the Princess, rocking with laughter so that the shadow on the wall flickered like a butterfly over a flower, 'all the same I love this Conrad!'

'He's but a lad, your Highness, barely turned seventeen.'

'The best age – I love him.'

'He's a slothful sort, his letter shows; a dreamer, not a man.'

'I love him.'

'While you were reading, I summoned his likeness here – he is ill-favoured – has lost a front tooth.'

'Regular features are my abhorrence – I love him.'

'He is sandy-haired and freckled and untidy in his dress.'

'Never mind, I love him.'

'He is self-willed and obstinate; his parents can do nothing with him.'

'I could: I love him.'

'He likes insects and crawling things: his pockets are full of spiders and centipedes.'

'I shall love them for his sake.'

'He cares for waterfalls and flowers and distant views.'

'I love him more than ever.'

'But,' said the magician, suddenly grave, 'I'm not sure that he loves you.'

'Ah!' cried the Princess, jubilation in her voice. 'I love him most of all for that!'

There was a pause. The shadow on the wall swooned from the oppression of its beauty, and slid to the floor.

'But of course he loves me,' the Princess murmured to herself. 'Everyone does, and so must he.'

She looked up at the magician for confirmation; but he had gone. Then she saw that something was missing.

'Magician! Magician!' she cried. 'You've taken my Conrad's letter. I want it back!'

But the magician, if he heard her, did not answer.

Conrad's suggestion, when published in the papers, produced a disagreeable impression. It was called mawkish and unmanly and insulting to the dignity of the Princess. *Forester's Son Wants To Be Male Nurse*, ran the headline. However, the letter was so inept, it could not be taken seriously. Conrad was evidently a little weak in the head. The Princess had all the virtues, but especially two: courage and unselfishness. Naturally she would have liked company in the hour of trial – and many were ready to offer it, from the King downwards: she had no need of the services of a woodman's unlicked cub. But she preferred to spare her friends the sight of her mental and physical anguish. It was the best she could do, she said in her gracious, winning way, to soften the burden a miserable fate had cast, through her, upon her country-men. So she retired and encountered her dark destiny alone, with the aid of such courage as she could summon. Conrad, the article concluded charitably, was no doubt too thick in the head to understand such delicacy of feeling; but surely his parents might have stopped him from making a fool of himself in public: the noble example of his brothers might have stopped him.

Conrad was too miserable after Rudolph's death to mind cutting a sorry figure in the public eye. Fortunately for him he had few acquaintances and spent much time in the woods alone; so at first he was scarcely aware of his unpopularity. But the neighbours were quick to point out to his parents what a dishonour their son had brought on the district; it has sent the whole province by the ears, they said, and started a government inquiry as to why our part of the world has been so backward in sending volunteers to fight the Dragon. This touched to the quick many people who had never heard of Conrad, and who now realized they might be called on to display their heroism in front of the castle, whether they would or no; for it was whispered that there might be an official round-up of likely young men.

His father and mother did their best to keep all this from Conrad. They were hurt and puzzled by his action, but they knew what a blow his brother's death had been, and did not want to distress him needlessly. But as he walked about the woods, especially at night-time, he would hear a stone go whizzing by him, or see a stick break at his feet; and demanding the cause of these attentions from one of the culprits, a lad rather smaller than himself, he was told very fully and in words that hurt. His foolish letter had got the place a bad name and he himself was this, that, and the other.

Conrad tried to take no notice and go his own way. But after five years in increasing calamity, the temper of the people had changed. True, the Princess found champions enthusiastic as ever; but they were men of a different kidney, always discovering good reasons why others should go out to battle and they themselves remain at home. These busybodies could not let Conrad alone, and Conrad, who was enjoying life far less than five years ago had seemed possible, saw there was only one thing to do. He must challenge the Dragon himself.

He did not go into training, as his brothers had done, with walks before breakfast and nourishing, unappetising food; he did not, if he chanced to spy fantastic-looking bush, set spurs to his horse and with a wild cry aim at it with his axe. Had he made the experiment he would have fallen off, for his horsemanship had not improved. Nor did he spend his savings on the purchase of costly weapons, and a military equipment of plume, breastplate, and golden epaulette, to charm the spectator's eye. His preparations were quite simple and only one of them cost him thought. This was the speech he would have to make at the foot of the steps.

He knew that it must be a declaration of love, or the Dragon would ignore it. But since Rudolph's death, his indifference to the Princess had deepened into positive dislike, almost hatred. He could not bring himself to say he loved her, even without meaning it. So he set himself to devise a form of words which would sound to the greedy, stupid Dragon sufficiently like praise, but to him, the speaker, would mean something quite different. When this was done, there still remained one thing: to leave his savings to Charlotte, his brother's fiancée. These last few weeks, when no one had a kind word for him, and even his parents seemed neutral, she had gone out of her way to be nice to him.

A letter came written on parchment under a great red seal, calling him by flattering and endearing terms, and fixing three o'clock as the hour for the contest. Conrad started early, before the November morning was well astir. He was riding the horse his father had lent him: the Dragon did not fancy horsemeat. Conrad would have felt safer on foot, but besides his luncheon he had an axe to carry, and the castle was seventeen miles away. He was wearing his old suit, as it seemed a pity to spoil his best one. As he went along, mostly walking, but occasionally trotting if the horse stumbled, people stopped work or came out of their houses to look at him. They knew why he was there and though they did not cheer or clap, they did not insult or ridicule him, which was some comfort.

But when six hours later the portals of the ravine opened before him, the castle burst into view, and the whole scene branded so long on his memory renewed itself, and at such dreadfully close quarters, his heart sank. He had not been able to eat his luncheon and still carried it (having been taught not to throw food away) in a satchel hung round his neck. This embarrassed him, for he thought the onlookers would laugh. But at present there were very few onlookers; the spectacle had become so common, it hardly awakened any interest.

Soon he was near enough to the flight of stairs to be able to distinguish the separate steps, and the crowd began to thicken somewhat. A little boy blew a sudden blast on a tin trumpet in the very ear of Conrad's horse. It pranced about in alarm, and Conrad, clutching wildly at its man and neck, was ignominiously

CONRAD AND THE DRAGON

thrown. He was rather shaken, but not too much shaken to hear the crowd laugh and ask each other what sort of champion was this, who couldn't sit on his horse properly.

Conrad dared not remount his horse for fear of falling off; and a good-natured man offered to lead it for him, a few paces in the rear, so that he could get on if he liked. He was glad to be rid of it on such easy terms. But he was aware of cutting an awkward figure on foot, in dusty clothes, trailing an axe which he tried to use as a walking-stick. The crowd, who liked its champions gay, reckless, and handsome, received him coldly. He felt they grudged their admiration and withheld their good-will. Once at school, through hard work and industry, he had won a prize. To receive it he had to pass through a long line of his schoolfellows. They applauded for the moment – it was the rule – and then fell to staring at him critically and resentfully. He remembered the scene.

But in the castle the Princess Hermione, her face pressed against the window-pane, watched every inch of his progress. 'It's he, it's Conrad. I knew it was!' she cried. 'You must let me wait another moment, Magician. Just one more moment!'

Conrad was trying to distract his mind by repeating over and over the address he meant to deliver to the Princess. When he was nervous his memory always betrayed him. He had a copy of the speech in his cap, to read if his mind became a blank. He wished he could do something to propitiate the spectators, besides smiling nervously at them; he knew that his tactics with the Dragon would shock them, for he carried in his pocket a phial of chloroform, wrapped in a handkerchief; he meant to break and wave this in the Dragon's face before using the steel. Suddenly he was aware that the horse was no longer following. The man had drawn it to one side and was standing in front of it, his hands over his eyes. The crowd had fallen back. Conrad had reached the steps. The castle clock struck three.

He knelt down, took off his cap, and said:

'Most Wonderful Princess,

'This is a moment I have long looked forward to, with what feelings you best may guess. The many who had knelt before me have been eloquent in your praise; who am I to add a syllable to their tribute? But I know it is not the words you value, most discerning Princess, but the heart that inspires them.'

At this moment the rock heaved, the Dragon came forth and hung over Conrad with lolling tongue. He could feel its hot breath on his cheek. The words died on his lips, he stared wildly round, then remembered the cue in his cap, and went on without looking up.

'All have loved you well, but some (dare I say it?) have voiced their love less happily than others. They said: "This my love, though great, is but an acorn that will grow with years into an oak." But when I remember what you have done for me: rescued me from the dull round of woodland life; raised me from obscurity into fame; transformed me from a dreamer into a warrior, an idler into a hunter of Dragons; deigned to make yourself the limit of my hopes and the end of my endeavours – I have no words to thank you, and cannot love you more than I do now!'

The more sensitive in the crowd had already turned away. The hardier spirits, with eyes glued to the scene, saw an unfamiliar thing. The Dragon swayed, dipped, hesitated. Its tongue licked the dust at Conrad's feet. He, who had hitherto done nothing to defend himself, drew out the handkerchief and threw it awkwardly but with a lucky aim, right into the Dragon's scarlet mouth. The beast roared, snorted, coughed, whimpered, and in a moment looked less terrible. Conrad, taking heart, lifted the axe and struck at the scaly neck towering above him. It was a clumsy blow, unworthy of a woodman, but it found its mark. A torrent of green blood gushed out, evaporating before it reached the ground. The Dragon's claws lost their hold on the rock, and it sprawled outwards, exposing a long black tubular body no one had seen till now. The neck dropped to within easy reach of Conrad's axe, and encouraged by the frenzied cheering behind him, he hacked at it again and again. Its balance lost, the Dragon seemed bewildered and helpless; a child could have tackled it, it was as passive under the axe as a felled tree. Conrad seemed to be having matters all his own way, when suddenly the Dragon made a convulsive movement and wriggled backwards into the rock, which closed over it. Conrad was left in possession of the field.

The crowd stopped cheering; no one quite knew what to do, least of all Conrad, who was still standing by the steps, half-dazed. That the Dragon had retired wounded and discomfited was plain to all; but perhaps it was only biding its time, gathering its strength for a fresh attack. It had so long seemed invincible; they could not believe it was dead.

But when seconds passed and nothing happened, they began to

surge round Conrad, weeping and laughing and trying to take his hand. From the castle, too, came signs of rejoicing, a faint cheering and fluttering of handkerchiefs, then a full-throated roar and flags waved from every window. A little throng began to form at the top of the steps, the King in the centre, his sceptre in his hand and his crown on his head. They were all laughing and talking together; it was clear they had never expected Conrad to win, they had made no plans for his reception, and were all rather enjoying the informal meeting. They called and beckoned to Conrad to come up; but he did not understand, so the crowd came behind and pushed him. As he moved up, the King came down, alone; they met in midstair, the King kissed Conrad and embraced him, and they walked up to the castle arm-in-arm.

'And now I must present you to my daughter,' the King was saying as they reached the top, and the members of the Court were pressing forward with shining eyes to congratulate the victor of the Dragon. 'Where is she? She's away somewhere, she'll come in a minute. Silly child, she's missed all the fun.'

'Hermione! Your Royal Highness!' called the ladies of the Court, in their light, eager voices, peering into the hall, staring up at the windows. And the crowd, nearly ninety feet below, took up the cry, 'Hermione! We want Princess Hermione!' It was an immense crowd now, for all the town was running to the spot, and the volume of sound was terrific. Everyone was delighted with the noise that he or she was making; even the group by the castle door winked and nudged and poked each other in the ribs, while they cried 'Hermione!' at the top of their voices. Only Conrad did not join in the cry.

But still she delayed. The crowd shouted itself hoarse; the ladies of the Court coughed and wrinkled up their faces and looked appealingly at each other; the King frowned slightly, for he felt she ought to be here now; but still the Princess did not come.

Then they all burst out excitedly. 'Where can she be? Let's go and look for her,' while others said, 'No, no, the shock would harm her, we must break it to her gradually.' There was quite a little confusion and uproar of voices arguing this way and that, stirring the general gaiety to an even higher pitch. They flocked into the castle dividing hither and thither, their silvery laughter lost among the corridors and colonnades.

Conrad had been torn from the King's side and hurried into the building before he knew what he was doing. Several people promised to show him the way, but when they had gone a little distance, they forgot about him, and flew off, with shouts of laughter, to join their own friends. Conrad seemed to be alone in the long dark corridor, but when he looked round, there was a man standing at the far end of it. Conrad walked towards him, calling out to him to wait; but the fellow hurried on, though how he could go like that, his face looking backwards all the time, Conrad did not understand.

Through doors, along passages, down steps they went, always with the same distance between them, always getting lower and lower; Conrad felt the cold on his cheeks and hands. At last a door, indistinguishable from the surrounding masonry, opened, showing him a room. Conrad followed his guide in, then lost sight of him.

On a couch by the wall lay the Princess, her head turned away, and in the whiteness of her neck a gash dreadful to behold. On the wall above her hung the shadow to which her indescribable beauty had lent a kind of life: it could not long survive her, and just as Conrad took in the perfection of its loveliness, it faded.

He fell on his knees by the couch. How long he knelt, he could not tell, but when he looked up, the room was full of people.

'You have killed her,' someone said.

Conrad rose and faced them.

'I did not kill her: I killed the Dragon.'

'Look,' said another voice. 'She has the same wound in her neck.'

'That wound I gave the Dragon.'

'And what is this?' asked a third, pointing to a ball of linen, tightly grasped in the Princess Hermione's outstretched hand. He took it and shook it out: the smell of chloroform filled the air. A cluster of eyes read the name in the corner of the handkerchief: it was Conrad's.

'And you poisoned her as well!' they gasped.

'That poison,' said Conrad, 'I gave to the Dragon.'

One or two nodded their heads; but the rest shouted:

'But you *must* have killed her! How else did she die?'

Conrad passed his hand across his face.

'Why should I kill her? I love her,' he said in a broken voice. 'It was the Dragon I killed.'

Then, as they all gazed at him fascinated, he added:

'But the Dragon was the Princess!'

Immediately there was a terrible hubbub, and to shouts of 'Liar', 'Murderer', 'Traitor', Conrad was hustled from the room and lodged in a neighbouring dungeon. He was released almost immediately and never brought up for trial, though a section of the Press demanded it.

A story was put about that the Princess had somehow met her death defending Conrad from the Dragon; and Conrad, when asked if this was so, would not altogether deny it. His hour of popularity as slayer of the Dragon soon passed, and in its place he incurred the lasting odium of having been somehow concerned in the Princess's death. 'He ought never to have used that chloroform,' was a criticism repeated with growing indignation from mouth to mouth. 'No sportsman would have.' It was a mark of patriotism to make light of the Dragon's misdeeds, for their long continuance redounded little to the country's credit and capacity. They were speedily forgotten, while the fame of Princess Hermione, a national treasure, went mounting ever higher in the hearts of her countrymen. Before the year was out, Conrad had heard a man in the street say to his friend:

'What does it matter if the Princess did change herself into a dragon? She only did it for a lark.'

Conrad went back to his home, but he soon received an official intimation that in his own and the common interest, he ought to leave the country. The government would find him a passport and pay his fare. This was all the reward he got for killing the Dragon, but he went gladly enough – the more gladly that Charlotte consented to go with him. She stipulated, however, that they should make their home in a Republic. There they were married and lived happily ever after.

THE ISLAND

How well I remembered the summer aspect of Mrs Santander's island, and the gratefully deciduous trees among the pines of that countryside coming down to the water's edge and over it! How their foliage, sloping to a shallow dome, sucked in the sunlight, giving it back all grey and green! The sea, tossing and glancing, refracted the light from a million spumy points; the tawny sand glared, a monochrome unmitigated by shades; and the cliffs, always bare, seemed to have achieved an unparalleled nudity, every speck on their brown flanks clamouring for recognition.

Now every detail was blurred or lost. In the insufficient, ill-distributed November twilight the island itself was invisible. Forms and outlines survive but indistinctly in the memory; it was hard to believe that the spit of shingle on which I stood was the last bulwark of that huge discursive land-locked harbour, within whose meagre mouth Mrs Santander's sea-borne territory seemed to ride at anchor. In the summer I pictured it as some crustacean, swallowed by an ill-turned starfish, but unassimilated. How easy it had been to reach it in Mrs Santander's gay plunging motorboat! And how inaccessible it seemed now, with the motor-boat fallen, as she had written to tell me, into war-time disuse, with a sea running high and so dark that, save for the transparent but scarcely luminous wave-tips, it looked like an agitated solid. The howling of the wind, and the oilskins in which he was encased, made it hard to attract the ferryman's attention. I shouted to him: 'Can you take me over to the island?'

'No, I can't,' said the ferryman, and pointed to the tumultuous waves in the harbour.

'What are you here for?' I bawled. 'I tell you I must get across; I have to go back to France tomorrow.'

In such circumstances it was impossible to argue without heat. The ferryman turned, relenting a little. He asked querulously in the tone of one who must raise a difficulty at any cost: 'What if we both get drowned?'

What a fantastic objection! 'Nonsense,' I said. 'There's no sea to speak of; anyhow, I'll make it worth your while.'

The ferryman grunted at my unintentional pleasantry. Then, as the landing stage was submerged by the exceptionally high tide, he carried me on his back to the boat, my feet trailing in the water. The man lurched at every step, for I was considerably heavier than he; but at last, waist-deep in water, he reached the boat and turned sideways for me to embark. How uncomfortable the whole business was. Why couldn't Mrs Santander spend November in London like other people? Why was I so infatuated as to follow her here on the last night of my leave when I might have been lolling in the stalls of a theatre? The craft was behaving oddly, rolling so much that at every other stroke one of the boatman's attenuated seafaring oars would be left high and dry. Once, when we happened to be level with each other, I asked him the reason of Mrs Santander's seclusion. At the top of his voice he replied; 'Why, they do say she be lovesick. Look out!' he added, for we had reached the end of our short passage and were 'standing by' in the succession of breakers. But the ferryman misjudged it. Just as the keel touched the steep shingle bank, a wave caught the boat, twisted it round and half over, and I lost my seat and rolled about in the bottom of the boat, getting very wet.

How dark it was among the trees. Acute physical discomfort had almost made me forget Mrs Santander. But as I stumbled up the grassy slope I longed to see her.

She was not in the hall to welcome me. The butler, discreetly noticing my condition, said: 'We will see about your things, sir.' I was thankful to take them off, and I flung them about the floor of my bedroom – that huge apartment that would have been square but for the bow-window built on to the end. The wind tore at this window, threatening to drive it in; but not a curtain moved. Soundlessness, I remembered, was characteristic of the house. Indeed, I believe you might have screamed yourself hoarse in that room and not have been heard in the adjoining bathroom. Thither I hastened and wallowed long and luxuriously in the marble bath; deliberately I splashed the water over the side, simply to see it collected and marshalled away down the little grooves that unerringly received it. When I emerged, swathed in hot towels, I found my clothes already dried and pressed. Wonderful household. A feeling of unspeakable well-being descended upon me as, five minutes before dinner-time, I entered the drawing-room. It was empty. What pains Mrs Santander must be bestowing on her toilette! Was it becoming her chief asset? I wondered. Perish the thought! She had a hundred charms of movement, voice and expression, and yet she defied analysis. She was simply irresistible! How Santander, her impossible husband, could have retired to South America to nurse an injured pride, or as he doubtless called it, an injured honour, passed my comprehension. She had an art to make the most commonplace subject engaging. I remembered having once admired the lighting of the house. I had an odd fancy that it had a quality not found elsewhere, a kind of whiteness, a power of suggesting silence. It helped to give her house its peculiar hush. 'Yes,' she had said, 'and it's all so simple; the sea makes it, just by going in and out!' A silly phrase, but her intonation made it linger in the memory like a charm.

I sat at the piano and played. There were some songs on the music rest – Wolf, full of strange chords and accidentals so that I couldn't be sure I was right. But they interested me; and I felt so happy that I failed to notice how the time was drawing on – eight o'clock, and dinner should have been at a quarter to. Growing a little restless, I rose and walked up and down the room. One corner of it was in shadow, so I turned on all the lights. I had found it irritating to watch the regular expansion and shrinkage of my shadow. Now I could see everything; but I still felt constrained, sealed up in that admirable room. It was always a shortcoming of mine not to be able to wait patiently. So I wandered into the dining-room and almost thought – such is the power of overstrung anticipation – that I saw Mrs Santander sitting at the head of the oval table. But it was only an effect of the candlelight. The two places were laid, hers and mine; the glasses with twisty stems were there, such a number of glasses for the two of us! Suddenly I remembered I was smoking and, taking an almond, I left the room to its four candles. I peeped inside the library; it was in darkness, and I realized, as I fumbled for the switch without being able to find it, that I was growing nervous. How ridiculous! Of course, Mrs Santander wouldn't be in the library and in the dark. Abandoning the search for the switch, I returned to the drawing-room.

I vaguely expected to find it altered, and yet I had ceased to expect to see Mrs Santander appear at any moment. That always happens when one waits for a person who doesn't come. But there *was* an alteration – in me. I couldn't find any satisfaction in struggling with Wolf; the music had lost its hold. So I drew a chair up to the china-cabinet; it had always charmed me with its figures of Chinamen, those white figures, conventional and stiff, but so smooth and significant. I found myself wondering, as often before, whether the ferocious pleasure in their expressions was really the Oriental artist's conception of unqualified good humour, or whether they were not, after all, rather cruel people. And this disquieting topic aroused others that I had tried successfully to repress: the exact connotation of my staying in the house as Mrs Santander's guest, an unsporting little mouse playing when the cat was so undeniably, so effectually away. To ease myself of these obstinate questionings, I leant forward to open the door of the cabinet, intending to distract myself by taking one of the figures into my hands. Suddenly I heard a sound and looked up. A man was standing in the middle of the room.

'I'm afraid the cabinet's locked,' he said.

In spite of my bewilderment, something in his appearance struck me as odd: he was wearing a hat. It was a grey felt hat, and he had an overcoat that was grey too.

'I hope you don't take me for a burglar,' I said, trying to laugh.

'Oh no,' he replied, 'not that.' I thought his eyes were smiling, but his mouth was shadowed by a dark moustache. He was a handsome man. Something in his face struck me as familiar; but it was not an unusual type and I might easily have been mistaken.

In the hurry of getting up I knocked over a set of fire-irons – the cabinet flanked the fireplace – and there was a tremendous clatter. It alarmed and then revived me. But I had a curious feeling of defencelessness as I stooped down to pick the fire-irons up, and it was difficult to fix them into their absurd sockets. The man in grey watched my operations without moving. I began to resent his presence. Presently he moved and stood with his back to the fire, stretching out his fingers to the warmth.

'We haven't been introduced,' I said.

'No,' he replied, 'we haven't.'

Then, while I was growing troubled and exasperated by his behaviour, he offered an explanation. 'I'm the engineer Mrs Santander calls in now and then to superintend her electric plant. That's how I know my way about. She's so inventive, and she doesn't like to take risks.' He volunteered this. 'And I came in here in case any of the fittings needed adjustment. I see they don't.'

'No,' I said, secretly reassured by the stranger's account of himself; 'but I wish – of course, I speak without Mrs Santander's authority – I wish you'd have a look at the switches in the library. They're damned inconvenient.' I was so pleased with myself for having compassed the expletive that I scarcely noticed how the engineer's fingers, still avid of warmth, suddenly became rigid.

'Oh, you've been in the library, have you?' he said.

I replied that I had got no further than the door. 'But if you can wait,' I added politely to this superior mechanic who liked to style himself an engineer, 'Mrs Santander will be here in a moment.'

'You're expecting her?' asked the mechanic.

'I'm staying in the house,' I replied stiffly. The man was silent for several moments. I noticed the refinement in his face, the good cut of his clothes. I pondered upon the physical disability that made it impossible for him to join the army.

'She makes you comfortable here?' he asked; and a physical disturbance, sneezing or coughing, I supposed, seized him, for he took out his handkerchief and turned from me with all the instinct of good breeding. But I felt that the question was one his station scarcely entitled him to make, and ignored it. He recovered himself.

'I'm afraid I can't wait,' he said. 'I must be going home. The wind is dropping. By the way,' he added, 'we have a connection in London. I think I may say it's a good firm. If ever you want an electric plant installed! – I left a card somewhere.' He searched for it vainly. 'Never mind,' he said, with his hands on the door, 'Mrs Santander will give you all particulars.' Indulgently I waved my hand, and he was gone.

A moment later it seemed to me that he wouldn't be able to cross to the mainland without notifying the ferryman. I rang the bell. The butler appeared. 'Mrs Santander is very late, sir,' he said.

'Yes,' I replied, momentarily dismissing the question. 'But there's a man, a mechanic or something – you probably know.' The butler looked blank. 'Anyhow,' I said, 'a man has been here attending to the lighting; he wants to go home; would you telephone the boatman to come and fetch him away?'

When the butler had gone to execute my order, my former discomfort and unease returned. The adventure with the engineer had diverted my thoughts from Mrs Santander. Why didn't she come? Perhaps she had fallen asleep, dressing. It happened to women when they were having their hair brushed. Gertrude was imperious and difficult; her maid might be afraid to wake her.

Then I remembered her saying in her letter, 'I shall be an awful fright because I've had to give my maid the sack.' It was funny how the colloquialisms jarred when you saw them in black and white; it was different when she was speaking. Ah, just to hear her voice! Of course, the loss of her maid would hinder her, and account for some delay. Lucky maid, I mused confusedly, to have her hair in your hands! Her image was all before me as I walked aimlessly about the room. Half tranced with the delight of that evocation, I stopped in front of a great bowl, ornamented with dragons, that stood on the piano. Half an hour ago I had studied its interior that depicted terra-cotta fish with magenta fins swimming among conventional weeds. My glance idly sought the pattern again. It was partially covered by a little slip of paper. Ah! the engineer's card!' His London connection! Amusedly I turned it over to read the fellow's name.

Mr Maurice Santander.

I started violently, the more that at the same moment there came a knock at the door. It was only the butler; but I was so bewildered I scarcely recognized him. Too well-trained, perhaps, to appear to notice my distress, he delivered himself almost in a speech. 'We can't find any trace of the person you spoke of, sir. The ferryman's come across and he says there's no one at the landing-stage.'

'The gentleman,' I said, 'has left this,' and I thrust the card into the butler's hand.

'Why, that must be Mr Santander!' the servant of Mr Santander's wife at last brought out.

'Yes,' I replied, 'and I think perhaps as it's getting late, we ought to try and find Mrs Santander. The dinner will be quite spoiled.'

Telling the butler to wait and not to alarm the servants, I went alone to Gertrude's room. From the end of a long passage I saw the door standing partly open; I saw, too, that the room was in darkness. There was nothing strange in that, I told myself; but it would be methodical, it would save time, to examine the intervening rooms first. Examine! What a misleading word. I banished it, and 'search' came into my mind. I rejected that too. As I explored the shuttered silences I tried to find a formula that would amuse Gertrude, some facetious understatement of my agitated quest. 'A little tour of inspection' – she would like that. I could almost hear her say: 'So you expected to find me under a sofa!' I wouldn't tell her that I had looked under the sofas, unless to make a joke of it: something about dust left by the housemaid. I rose to my knees, spreading my hands out in the white glow. Not a speck. But wasn't conversation – conversation with Gertrude – made up of little half-truths, small forays into fiction? With my hand on the door – it was of the last room and led on to the landing – I rehearsed the pleasantry aloud: 'During the course of a little tour of inspection, Gertrude, I went from one dust-heap to another, from dust unto dust I might almost say . . . ' This time I must overcome my unaccountable reluctance to enter her room. Screwing up my courage, I stepped into the passage, but for all my resolution I got no further.

The door still stood as I had first seen it – half open; but there was a light in the room – a rather subdued light, possibly from the standard lamp by the bed. I knocked and called 'Gertrude!' and when there was no reply I pushed open the door. It moved from right to left so as not to expose the bulk of the room, which lay on the left side. It seemed a long time before I was fairly in.

I saw the embers of the fire, the pale troubled lights of the mirror, and, vivid in the pool of light by the bed, a note. It said: 'Forgive me dearest, I have had to go. I can't explain why, but we shall meet some time. All my love, G.' There was no envelope, no direction, but the handwriting was hers and the informality characteristic of her. It was odd that the characters, shaky as they were, did not seem to have been written in haste. I was trying to account for this, trying to stem, by an act of concentration, the tide of disappointment that was sweeping over me, when a sudden metallic whirr sounded in my ear. It was the telephone – the small subsidiary telephone that communicated with the servants' quarters. 'It will save their steps,' she had said, when I urged her to have it put in; and I remembered my pleasure in this evidence of consideration, for my own motives had been founded in convenience and even in prudence. Now I loathed the black shiny thing that buzzed so raucously and never moved. And what could the servants have to say to me except that Mr Santander had – well, gone. What else was there for him to do? The instrument rang again and I took up the receiver.

'Yes?'

'Please, sir, dinner is served.'

'Dinner!' I echoed. It was nearly ten, but I had forgotten about that much-postponed meal.

'Yes, sir. Didn't you give orders to have it ready immediately? For two, I think you said, sir.' The voice sounded matter-of-fact enough, but in my bewilderment I nearly lost all sense of what I was doing. At last I managed to murmur in a voice that might have been anybody's: 'Yes, of course, for two.'

On second thoughts, I left the telephone disconnected. I felt just then that I couldn't bear another summons. And, though my course was clear, I did not know what to do next; my will had nothing but confusion to work with. In the dark, perhaps, I might collect myself. But it didn't occur to me to turn out the light; instead, I parted the heavy curtains that shut off the huge bow-window and drew them behind me. The rain was driving furiously against the double casements, but not a sound vouched for its energy. A moon shone at intervals, and by the light of one gleam, brighter than the rest, I saw a scrap of paper, crushed up, lying in a corner. I smoothed it out, glad to have employment for my fingers, but darkness descended on the alcove again and I had to return to the room. In spite of its crumpled condition I made out the note – easily, indeed, for it was a copy of the one I had just read. Or perhaps the original; but why should the same words have been written twice and even three times, not more plainly, for Gertrude never tried to write plainly, but with a deliberate illegibility?

There was only one other person besides Gertrude, I thought, while I stuffed the cartridges into my revolver, who could have written that note, and he was waiting for me downstairs. How would he look, how would he explain himself? This question occupied me to the exclusion of a more natural curiosity as to *my* appearance, *my* explanation. They would have to be of the abruptest. Perhaps, indeed, they wouldn't be needed. There were a dozen corners, a dozen points of vantage all well known to Mr Santander between me and the dining-room door. It came to me inconsequently that the crack of a shot in that house would make no more noise than the splintering of a tooth-glass on my washing-stand. And Mr Santander, well versed no doubt in South American revolutions, affrays, and shootings-up, would be an adept in the guerilla warfare to which military service hadn't accustomed me. Wouldn't it be wiser, I thought, irresolutely contemplating the absurd bulge in my dinner jacket, to leave him to his undisputed mastery of the situation, and not put it to the proof? It was not like cutting an ordinary engagement. A knock on the door interrupted my confused consideration of social solecisms.

'Mr Santander told me to tell you he is quite ready,' the butler said. Through his manifest uneasiness I detected a hint of disapproval. He looked at me askance; he had gone over. But couldn't he be put to some use? I had an idea.

'Perhaps you would announce me,' I said. He couldn't very well refuse, and piloted by him I should have a better chance in the passages and an entry valuably disconcerting. 'I'm not personally known to Mr Santander,' I explained. 'It would save some little awkwardness.'

Close upon the heels of my human shield I threaded the passages. Their bright emptiness reassured me; it was inconceivable, I felt, after several negotiated turns, that anything sinister could lurk behind those politely rounded corners – Gertrude had had their angularities smoothed into curves; it would be so terrible, she said, if going to bed one stumbled (one easily might) and fell against an *edge*! But innocuous as they were I preferred to avoid them. The short cut through the library would thus serve a double purpose, for it would let us in from an unexpected quarter, from that end of the library, in fact, where the large window, so perilous-looking – really so solid on its struts and stays – perched over the roaring sea.

'This is the quickest way,' I said to the butler, pointing to the library door. He turned the handle. 'It's locked, sir.'

'Oh, well.'

We had reached the dining-room at last. The butler paused with his hand on the knob as though by the mere sense of touch he could tell whether he were to be again denied admittance. Or perhaps he was listening or just thinking. The next thing I knew was that he had called out my name and I was standing in the room. Then I heard Mr Santander's voice. 'You can go, Collins.' The door shut.

My host didn't turn round at once. All I could make out, in the big room lighted only by its four candles and the discreet footlights of dusky pictures, was his back, and – reflected in the mirror over the mantelpiece – his eyes and forehead. The same mirror showed my face too, low down on the right-hand side, curiously unrelated. His arms were stretched along the mantelpiece and he was stirring the fire with his foot. Suddenly he turned and faced me.

'Oh, you're there,' he said. 'I'm so sorry.'

We moved to the table and sat down. There was nothing to eat.

I fell to studying his appearance. Every line of his dinner-jacket, every fold in his soft shirt, I knew by heart; I seemed always to have known them.

'What are you waiting for?' he suddenly demanded rather loudly. 'Collins!' he called. 'Collins!' His voice reverberated through the room, but no one came. 'How stupid of me,' he muttered; 'of course, I must ring.' Oddly enough he seemed to look to me for confirmation. I nodded. Collins appeared, and the meal began.

Its regular sequence soothed him, for presently he said: 'You must forgive my being so distrait. I've had rather a tiring journey – come from a distance, as they say. South America, in fact.' He drank some wine reflectively. 'I had one or two things to settle before . . . before joining the Army. Now I don't think it will be necessary.'

'Necessary to settle them?' I said.

'No,' he replied. 'I have settled them.'

'You mean that you will claim exemption as an American citizen?'

Again Mr Santander shook his head. 'It would be a reason, wouldn't it? But I hadn't thought of that.'

Instinct urged me to let so delicate a topic drop; but my nerves were fearful of a return to silence. There seemed so little, of all that we had in common, to draw upon for conversation.

'You suffer from bad health, perhaps?' I suggested. But he demurred again.

'Even Gertrude didn't complain of my health,' he said, adding quickly, as though to smother the sound of her name: 'But you're not drinking.'

'I don't think I will,' I stammered. I had meant to say I was a teetotaller.

My host seemed surprised. 'And yet Gertrude had a long bill at her wine merchant's,' he commented, half to himself.

I echoed it involuntarily: 'Had?'

'Oh,' he said, 'it's been paid. That's partly,' he explained, 'why I came home – to pay.'

I felt I couldn't let this pass.

'Mr Santander,' I said, 'there's a great deal in your behaviour that I don't begin (is that good American?) to understand.'

'No?' he murmured, looking straight in front of him.

'But,' I proceeded, as truculently as I could, 'I want you to realize—'

He cut me short. 'Don't suppose,' he said, 'that I attribute all my wife's expenditure to you.'

I found myself trying to defend her. 'Of course,' I said, 'she has the house to keep up; it's not run for a mere song, a house like this.' And with my arm I tried to indicate to Mr Santander the costly immensity of his domain. 'You wouldn't like her to live in a pigsty, would you? And there's the sea to keep out – why, a night like this must do pounds' worth of damage!'

'You are right,' he said, with a strange look; 'you even underestimate the damage it has done.'

Of course, I couldn't fail to catch his meaning. He meant the havoc wrought in his affections. They had been strong, report said – strong enough for her neglect of them to make him leave the country. They weren't expressed in half-measures, I thought, looking at him with a new sensation. He must have behaved with a high hand, when he arrived. How he must have steeled himself to drive her out of the house, that stormy night, ignoring her piteous protestations, her turns and twists which I had never been able to ignore! She was never so alluring, never so fertile in emotional appeals, as when she knew she was in for a scolding. I could hear her say, 'But, Maurice, however much you hate me, you couldn't really want me to get *wet*!' and his reply: 'Get out of this house, and don't come back till I send for you. As for your lover, leave me to look after him.' He was looking after me, and soon, no doubt, he would send for her. And for her sake, since he had really returned to take part in her life, I couldn't desire this estrangement. Couldn't I even bridge it over, bring it to a close? *Beati pacifici*. Well, I would be a peace-maker too.

Confident that my noble impulses must have communicated themselves to my host, I looked up from my plate and searched his face for signs of abating rigour. I was disappointed. But should I forgo or even postpone my atonement because he was stiff-necked? Only it was difficult to begin. At last I ventured.

'Gertrude is really very fond of you, you know.'

Dessert had been reached, and I, in token of amity and goodwill, had helped myself to a glass of port wine.

For answer he fairly glared at me. 'Fond of me!' he shouted.

I was determined not to be browbeaten out of my kind offices.

'That's what I said; she has a great heart.'

'If you mean,' he replied, returning to his former tone, 'that it has ample accommodation! – but your recommendations come too late; I have delegated her affections.'

'To me?' I asked, involuntarily.

He shook his head. 'And in any case, why to you?'

'Because I—'

'Oh, no,' he exclaimed passionately. 'Did she deceive you – has she deceived you into believing *that* – that *you* are the alternative to *me*? You aren't unique – you have your reduplications, scores of them!'

My head swam, but he went on, enjoying his triumph. 'Why, no one ever told me about you! She herself only mentioned you once. You are the least – the least of all her lovers!' His voice dropped. 'Otherwise you wouldn't be here.'

'Where should I be?' I fatuously asked. But he went on without regarding me.

'But I remember this house when its silence, its comfort, its isolation, its uniqueness were for us, Gertrude and me and . . . and for the people we invited. But we didn't ask many – we preferred to be alone. And I thought at first she was alone,' he wound up, 'when I found her this evening.'

'Then why,' I asked, 'did you send her away and not me?'

'Ah,' he replied with an accent of finality, 'I wanted you.'

While he spoke he was cracking a nut with his fingers and it must have had sharp edges, for he stopped, wincing, and held the finger to his mouth.

'I've hurt my nail,' he said. 'See?'

He pushed his hand towards me over the polished table. I watched it, fascinated, thinking it would stop; but still it came on, his body following, until if I hadn't drawn back, it would have touched me, while his chin dropped to within an inch of the table, and one side of his face was pillowed against his upper arm.

'It's a handicap, isn't it?' he said, watching me from under his brows.

'Indeed it is,' I replied; for the fine acorn-shaped nail was terribly torn, a jagged rent revealing the quick, moist and gelatinous. 'How did you manage to do that?' I went on, trying not to look at the mutilation which he still held before my eyes.

'Do you really want to know how I did it?' he asked. He hadn't moved, and his question, in its awkward irregular delivery, seemed to reflect the sprawled unnatural position of his body.

'Do tell me,' I said, and added, nervously jocular, 'but first let me guess. Perhaps you met with an accident in the course of your professional activities, when you were mending the lights, I mean, in the library.'

At that he jumped to his feet. 'You're very warm,' he said, 'you almost burn. But come into the library with me, and I'll tell you.'

I prepared to follow him.

But unaccountably he lingered, walked up and down a little, went to the fireplace and again (it was evidently a favourite relaxation) gently kicked the coals. Then he went to the library door, meaning apparently to open it, but he changed his mind and instead turned on the big lights of the dining-room. 'Let's see what it's really like,' he said. 'I hate this half-light.' The sudden illumination laid bare that great rich still room, so secure, so assured, so content. My host stood looking at it. He was fidgeting with his dinner jacket and had so little self-control that, at every brush of the material with his damaged finger, he whimpered like a child. His face, now that I saw it fairly again, was twisted and disfigured with misery. There wasn't one imaginable quality that he shared with his sumptuous possessions.

In the library darkness was absolute. My host preceded me, and in a moment I had lost all sense of even our relative positions. I backed against the wall, and by luck my groping fingers felt the switch. But its futile click only emphasized the darkness. I began to feel frightened, with an acute immediate alarm very different from my earlier apprehensions and forebodings. To add to my uneasiness my ears began to detect a sound, a small irregular sound; it might have been water dripping, yet it seemed too definitely consonantal for that; it was more like an inhuman whisper. 'Speak up,' I cried, 'if you're talking to me!' But it had no more effect, my petulant outcry, than if it had fallen on the ears of the dead. The disquieting noise persisted, but another note had crept into it – a soft labial sound, like the licking of lips. It wasn't intelligible, it wasn't even articulate, yet I felt that if I listened longer it would become both. I couldn't bear the secret colloquy; and though it seemed to be taking place all round me, I made a rush into what I took to be the middle of the room. I didn't get very far, however. A chair sent me sprawling, and when I picked myself up it was to the accompaniment of a more familiar sound. The curtains were being drawn apart and the moonlight, struggling in, showed me shapes of furniture and my own position, a few feet from the door. It showed me something else, too.

How could my host be drawing the curtains when I could see him lounging, relaxed and careless, in an armchair that, from its position by the wall, missed the moon's directer ray? I strained my eyes. Very relaxed, very careless he must be, after what had passed between us, to stare at me so composedly over his shoulder, no, more than that, over his very back! He faced me, though his shoulder, oddly enough, was turned away. Perhaps he had practised it – a contortionist's trick to bewilder his friends. Suddenly I heard his voice, not from the armchair at all but from the window.

'Do you know now?'

'What?' I said.

'How I hurt my finger?'

'No,' I cried untruthfully, for that very moment all my fears told me.

'I did it strangling my wife!'

I rushed towards the window, only to be driven back by what seemed a solid body of mingled sleet and wind. I heard the creak of the great casement before it whirled outwards, crashing against the mullion and shattering the glass. But though I fought my way to the opening I wasn't quick enough. Sixty feet below the eroding sea sucked, spouted and roared. Out of it jags of rock seemed to rise, float for a moment and then be dragged under the foam. Time after time great arcs of spray sprang hissing from the sea, lifted themselves to the window as though impelled by an insatiable curiosity, condensed and fell away. The drops were bitter on my lips. Soaked to the skin and stiff with cold, I turned to the room. The heavy brocade curtains flapped madly or rose and streamed level with the ceiling, and through the general uproar I could distinguish separate sounds, the clattering fall of small objects and the banging and scraping of pictures against the walls. The whole weather-proof, sound-proof house seemed to be ruining in, to be given up to darkness and furies . . . and to me. But not wholly, not unreservedly, to me. Mrs Santander was still at her place in the easy chair.

NIGHT FEARS

The coke-brazier was elegant enough but the night-watchman was not, consciously at any rate, sensitive to beauty of form. No; he valued the brazier primarily for its warmth. He could not make up his mind whether he liked its light. Two days ago, when he first took on the job, he was inclined to suspect the light; it dazzled him, made a target of him, increased his helplessness; it emphasized the darkness. But tonight he was feeling reconciled to it; and aided by its dark, clear rays, he explored his domain – a long narrow rectangle, fenced off from the road by poles round and thick as flag-posts and lashed loosely at the ends. By day they seemed simply an obstacle to be straddled over; but at night they were boundaries, defences almost. At their junctions, where the warning red lanterns dully gleamed, they bristled like a barricade. The night-watchman felt himself in charge of a fortress.

He took a turn up and down, musing. Now that the strangeness of the position had worn off he could think with less effort. The first night he had vaguely wished that the 'No Thoroughfare' board had faced him instead of staring uselessly up the street: it would have given his thoughts a rallying-point. Now he scarcely noticed its blankness. His thoughts were few but pleasant to dwell on, and in the solitude they had the intensity of sensations. He arranged them in cycles, the rotation coming at the end of ten paces or so when he turned to go back over his tracks. He enjoyed the thought that held his mind for the moment, but always with some agreeable impatience for the next. If he surmised there would be a fresh development in it, he would deliberately refrain from calling it up, leave it fermenting and ripening, as it were, in a luxury of expectation.

The night-watchman was a domesticated man with a wife and two children, both babies. One was beginning to talk. Since he took on his job wages had risen, and everything at home seemed gilt-edged. It made a difference to his wife. When he got home she would say, as she had done on the preceding mornings, 'Well, you do look a wreck. This night work doesn't suit you, I'm sure.' The night-watchman liked being addressed in that way and hearing his job described as night work; it showed an easy competent familiarity with a man's occupation. He would tell her, with the air of one who had seen much, about the incidents of his vigil, and what he hadn't seen he would invent, just for the pleasure of hearing her say: 'Well, I never! You do have some experiences, and no mistake.' He was very fond of his wife. Why, hadn't she promised to patch up the old blue-paper blinds, used once for the air-raids, but somewhat out of repair as a consequence of their being employed as a quarry for paper to wrap up parcels? He hadn't slept well, couldn't get accustomed to sleeping by day, the room was so light; but these blinds would be just the thing, and it would be nice to see them and feel that the war was over and there was no need for them, really.

The night-watchman yawned as for the twentieth time perhaps he came up sharp against the boundary of his walk. Loss of sleep, no doubt. He would sit in his shelter and rest a bit. As he turned and saw the narrowing gleams that transformed the separating poles into thin lines of fire, he noticed that nearly at the end, just opposite the brazier in fact and only a foot or two from the door of his hut, the left line was broken. Someone was sitting on the barrier, his back turned on the night-watchman's little compound. 'Strange I never heard him come,' thought the man, brought back with a jerk from his world of thoughts to the real world of darkness and the deserted street – well, no, not exactly deserted, for here was someone who might be inclined to talk for half an hour or so. The stranger paid no attention to the watchman's slowly advancing tread. A little disconcerting. He stopped. Drunk, I expect, he thought. This would be a real adventure to tell his wife. 'I told him I wasn't going to stand any rot from him. "Now, my fine fellow, you go home to bed; that's the best place for you," I said.' He had heard drunk men addressed in that way, and wondered doubtfully whether he would be able to catch the tone; it was more important than the words, he reflected. At last, pulling himself together, he walked up to the brazier and coughed loudly, and feeling ill-at-ease, set about warming his hands with such energy he nearly burned them.

As the stranger took no notice, but continued to sit wrapped in thought, the night-watchman hazarded a remark to his bent back.

'A fine night,' he said rather loudly, though it was ridiculous to raise one's voice in an empty street. The stranger did not turn round.

'Yes,' he replied, 'but cold; it will be colder before morning.' The night-watchman looked at his brazier, and it struck him that the coke was not lasting so well as on the previous nights. I'll put some more on, he thought, picking up a shovel; but instead of the little heap he had expected to see, there was nothing but dust and a few bits of grit – his night's supply had been somehow overlooked. 'Won't you turn round and warm your hands?' he said to the person sitting on the barrier. 'The fire isn't very good, but I can't make it up, for they forgot to give me any extra, unless somebody pinched it when my back was turned.' The night-watchman was talking for effect; he did not really believe that anyone had taken the coke. The stranger might have made a movement somewhere about the shoulders.

'Thank you,' he said, 'but I prefer to warm my back.'

Funny idea that, thought the watchman.

'Have you noticed,' proceeded the stranger, 'how easily men forget? This coke of yours, I mean; it looks as if they didn't care about you very much, leaving you in the cold like this.' It had certainly grown colder, but the man replied cheerfully: 'Oh, it wasn't that. They forgot it. Hurrying to get home, you know.' Still, they might have remembered, he thought. It was Bill Jackson's turn to fetch it – Old Bill, as the fellows call him. He doesn't like me very much. The chaps are a bit stand-offish. They'll be all right when I know them better.

His visitor had not stirred. How I would like to push him off, the night-watchman thought, irritated and somehow troubled. The stranger's voice broke in upon his reflections.

'Don't you like this job?'

'Oh, not so bad,' said the man carelessly; 'good money, you know.'

'Good money,' repeated the stranger scornfully. 'How much do you get?'

The night-watchman named the sum.

'Are you married, and have you got any children?' the stranger persisted.

The night-watchman said 'Yes,' without enthusiasm.

'Well, that won't go very far when the children are a bit older,' declared the stranger. 'Have you any prospect of a rise?' The man said no, he had just had one.

'Prices going up, too,' the stranger commented.

A change came over the night-watchman's outlook. The feeling of hostility and unrest increased. He couldn't deny all this. He longed to say, 'What do you think you're getting at?' and rehearsed the phrase under his breath, but couldn't get himself to utter it aloud; his visitor had created his present state of mind and was lord of it. Another picture floated before him, less rosy than the first: an existence drab-coloured and with the dust of conflict, but relieved by the faithful support of his wife and children at home. After all, that's the life for a man, he thought; but he did not cherish the idea, did not walk up and down hugging it, as he cherished and hugged the other.

'Do you find it easy to sleep in the daytime?' asked the stranger presently.

'Not very,' the night-watchman admitted.

'Ah,' said the stranger, 'dreadful thing, insomnia.'

'When you can't go to sleep, you mean,' interpreted the night-watchman, not without a secret pride.

'Yes,' came the answer. 'Makes a man ill, mad sometimes. People have done themselves in sooner than stand the torture.'

It was on the tip of the night-watchman's tongue to mention that panacea, the blue blinds. But he thought it would sound foolish, and wondered whether they would prove such a sovereign remedy after all.

'What about your children? You won't see much of them,' remarked the stranger, 'while you are on this job. Why, they'll grow up without knowing you! Up when their papa's in bed, and in bed when he's up! Not that you miss them much, I dare say. Still, if children don't get fond of their father while they're young, they never will.'

Why didn't the night-watchman take him up warmly, assuring him they were splendid kids; the eldest called him daddy, and the younger, his wife declared, already recognized him. She knew by its smile, she said. He couldn't have forgotten all that; half an hour ago it had been one of his chief thoughts. He was silent.

'I should try and find another job if I were you,' observed the stranger. 'Otherwise you won't be able to make both ends meet. What will your wife say then?'

The man considered; at least he thought he was facing the question, but his mind was somehow too deeply disturbed, and circled wearily and blindly in its misery. 'I was never brought up to a trade,' he said hesitatingly; 'father's fault.' It struck him that he had never confessed that before; had sworn not to give his father away. What am I coming to? he thought. Then he made an effort. 'My wife's all right, she'll stick to me.' He waited, positively dreading the stranger's next attack. Though the fire was burning low, almost obscured under the coke ashes that always seem more lifeless than any others, he felt drops of perspiration on his forehead, and his clothes, he knew, were soaked. I shall get a chill, that'll be the next thing, he thought; but it was involuntary: such an idea hadn't occurred to him since he was a child, supposedly delicate.

'Yes, your wife,' said the stranger at last, in tones so cold and clear that they seemed to fill the universe; to admit of no contradiction; to be graven with a fine unerring instrument out of the hard rock of truth itself. 'You won't see much of her either. You leave her pretty much to herself, don't you? Now with these women, you know, that's a *risk*.' The last word rang like a challenge; but the night-watchman had taken the offensive, shot his one little bolt, and the effort had left him more helpless than ever.

'When the eye doth not see,' continued the stranger, 'the heart doth not grieve; on the contrary, it makes merry.' He laughed, as the night-watchman could see from the movement of his shoulders. 'I've known cases very similar to yours. When the cat's away, you know! It's a pity you're under contract to finish this job' (the night-watchman had not mentioned a contract), 'but as you are, take my advice and get a friend to keep an eye on your house. Of course, he won't be able to stay the night – of course not; but tell him to keep his eyes open.'

The stranger seemed to have said his say, his head drooped a little more; he might even be dropping off to sleep. Apparently he did not feel the cold. But the night-watchman was breathing hard and could scarcely stand. He tottered a little way down his territory, wondering absurdly why the place looked so tidy; but what a travesty of his former progress. And what a confusion in his thoughts, and what a thumping in his temples. Slowly from the writhing, tearing mass in his mind a resolve shaped itself; like a cuckoo it displaced all others. He loosened the red handkerchief that was knotted round his neck, without remembering whose fingers had tied it a few hours before, or that it had been promoted (not without washing) to the status of a garment from the menial function of carrying his lunch. It had been an extravagance, that tin carrier, much debated over, and justified finally by the rise in the night-watchman's wages. He let the handkerchief drop as he fumbled for the knife in his pocket, but the blade, which was stiff, he got out with little difficulty. Wondering vaguely if he would be able to do it, whether the right movement would come to him, why he hadn't practised it, he took a step towards the brazier. It was the one friendly object in the street . . .

Later in the night the stranger, without putting his hands on the pole to steady himself, turned round for the first time and regarded the body of the night-watchman. He even stepped over into the little compound and, remembering perhaps the dead man's invitation, stretched out his hands over the still warm ashes in the brazier. Then he climbed back and, crossing the street, entered a blind alley opposite, leaving a track of dark, irregular footprints; and since he did not return it is probable that he lived there.

THE KILLING BOTTLE

Unlike the majority of men, Jimmy Rintoul enjoyed the hour or so's interval between being called and having breakfast; for it was the only part of the day upon which he imposed an order. From nine-fifteen onwards the day imposed its order upon him. The bus, the office, the hasty city luncheon; then the office, the bus, and the unsatisfactory interval before dinner: such a promising time and yet, do what he would with it, it always seemed to be wasted. If he was going to dine alone at his club, he felt disappointed and neglected; if, as seldom happened, in company, he felt vaguely apprehensive. He expected a good deal from his life, and he never went to bed without the sense of having missed it. Truth to tell, he needed a stimulus, the stimulus of outside interest and appreciation, to get the best out of himself. In a competitive society, with rewards dangled before his eyes, his nature fulfilled itself and throve. How well he had done at school, and even afterwards, while his parents lived to applaud his efforts. Now he was thirty-three; his parents were dead; there was no one close enough to him to care whether he made a success of his life or not. Nor did life hand out to grown-up men incontestable signs of merit and excellence, volumes bound in vellum or silver cups standing proudly on ebony pedestals. No, its awards were far less tangible, and Jimmy, from the shelter of his solicitors' office, sometimes felt glad that its more sensational prizes were passing out of his reach – that he need no longer feel obliged, as he had once felt, to climb the Matterhorn, play the *Moonlight Sonata*, master the Spanish language, and read the *Critique of Pure Reason* before he died. His ambition was sensibly on the ebb.

But not in the mornings. The early mornings were still untouched by the torpors of middle-age. Dressing was for Jimmy a ritual, and like all rituals it looked forward to a culmination. Act followed act in a recognized sequence, each stage contributing its peculiar thrill, opening his mind to a train of stimulating and agreeable thoughts, releasing it, encouraging it. And the culmination: what was it? Only his morning's letters and the newspaper! Not very exciting. But the newspaper might contain one of those helpful, sympathetic articles about marriage, articles that warned the reader not to rush into matrimony, but to await the wisdom that came with the early and still more with the late thirties; articles which, with a few tricks of emphasis, of skipping here and reading between the lines there, demonstrated that Jimmy Rintoul's career, without any effort of his own, was shaping itself on sound, safe lines. The newspaper, then, for reassurance; the letters for surprise! And this morning an interesting letter would be particularly welcome. It would distract his mind from a vexing topic that even the routine of dressing had not quite banished − the question of his holiday, due in a fortnight's time.

Must it be Swannick Fen again? Partly for lack of finding others to take their place, he had cherished the interests of his boyhood, of which butterfly-collecting was the chief. He was solitary and competitive, and the hobby ministered to both these traits. But alas! he had not the patience of the true collector; his interest fell short of the lesser breeds, the irritating varieties of Wainscots and Footmen and whatnots. It embraced only the more sensational insects − the large, the beautiful, and the rare. His desire had fastened itself on the Swallow-tail butterfly as representing all these qualities. So he went to Swannick, found the butterfly, bred it, and presently had a whole hutch-full of splendid green caterpillars. Their mere number, the question of what to do with them when they came out, whether to keep them all in their satiating similarity, to give them away, or to sell them; to let them go free so that the species might multiply, to the benefit of all collectors; to kill all but a few, thus enhancing the value of his own − these problems vexed his youthful, ambitious, conscientious mind. Finally he killed them all. But the sight of four setting-boards plastered with forty identical insects destroyed by a surfeit his passion for the Swallow-tail butterfly. He had coaxed it with other baits: the Pine Hawk moth, the Clifden Nonpareil; but it would not respond, would accept no substitute, being, like many passions, monogamous and constant. Every year, in piety, in conservatism, in hope, he still went to Swannick Fen; but with each visit the emotional satisfaction diminished. Soon it would be gone.

However, there on his dressing-table (for some reason) stood the killing bottle — mutely demanding prey. Almost without thinking he released the stopper and snuffed up the almond-breathing fumes. A safe, pleasant smell; he could never understand how anything died of it, or why cyanide of potassium should figure in the chemists' book of poisons. But it did; he had had to put his name against it. Now, since the stuff was reputed to be so deadly, he must add a frail attic to the edifice of dressing and once more wash his hands. In a fortnight's time, he thought, I shall be doing this a dozen times a day.

On the breakfast-table lay a large, shiny blue envelope. He did not recognize the handwriting, nor, when he examined the postmark, did it convey anything to him. The flap, gummed to the top and very strong, resisted his fingers. He opened it with a knife and read:

VERDEW CASTLE.

MY DEAR RINTOUL,

How did you feel after our little dinner on Saturday? None the worse, I hope. However, I'm not writing to inquire about your health, which seems pretty good, but about your happiness, or what I should like to think would be your happiness. Didn't I hear you mutter (the second time we met, I think it was, at Smallhouse's) something about going for a holiday in the near future? Well, then, couldn't you spend it here with us, at Verdew? Us being my brother Randolph, my wife, and your humble servant. I'm afraid there won't be a party for you; but we could get through the day somehow, and play bridge in the evenings. Randolph and you would make perfect partners, you would be so kind to each other. And didn't you say you collected bugs? Then by all means bring your butterfly-net and your killing bottle and your other engines of destruction and park them here; there are myriads of green-flies, bluebottle-flies, may-flies, dragon-flies, and kindred pests which would be all the better for your attentions. Now don't say no. It would be a pleasure to us, and I'm sure it would amuse you to see ye olde castle and us living in our medieval seclusion. I await the favour of a favourable reply, and will then tell you the best way of reaching the Schloss, as we sometimes call it in our German fashion.

Yours,
ROLLO VERDEW.

Jimmy stared at this facetious epistle until its purport faded from his mind, leaving only a blurred impression of redundant loops and twirls. Verdew's handwriting was like himself, bold and dashing and unruly. At least, this was the estimate Jimmy had formed of him, on the strength of three meetings. He had been rather taken by the man's bluff, hearty manner, but he did not expect Verdew to like him: they were birds of a different feather. He hadn't felt very well after the dinner, having drunk more than was good for him in the effort to fall in with his host's mood; but apparently he had succeeded better than he thought. Perhaps swashbucklers like Verdew welcomed mildness in others. If not, why the invitation? He considered it. The district might be entomologically rich. Where exactly was Verdew Castle? He had, of course, a general idea of its locality, correct to three counties; he knew it was somewhere near the coast. Further than that, nothing; and directly he began to sift his knowledge he found it to be even less helpful than he imagined. The notepaper gave a choice of stations: wayside stations they must be, they were both unknown to him. The postal, telegraphic, and telephonic addresses all confidently cited different towns – Kirton Tracy, Shrivecross, and Pawlingham – names which seemed to stir memories but never fully awakened recollection. Still, what did it matter? Verdew had promised to tell him the best route, and it was only a question of getting there, after all. He could find his own way back.

Soon his thoughts, exploring the future, encountered an obstacle and stopped short. He was looking ahead as though he had made up his mind to go. Well, hadn't he? The invitation solved his immediate difficulty: the uncertainty as to where he should take his holiday. The charm of Swannick had failed to hold him. And yet, perversely enough, his old hunting-ground chose this very moment to trouble him with its lures: its willows, its alders, the silent clumps of grey rushes with the black water in between. The conservatism of his nature, an almost superstitious loyalty to the preferences of his early life, protested against the abandonment of Swannick – Swannick, where he had always done exactly as he liked, where bridge never intruded, and the politenesses of society were unknown. For Jimmy's mind had run forward again, and envisaged existence at Verdew Castle as divided between holding open the door for Mrs Rollo Verdew and exchanging compliments and forbearances and commiseration with Rollo's elder (or perhaps younger, he hadn't said) brother Randolph across the bridge-table, with a lot of spare time that wasn't really spare and a lot of being left to himself that really meant being left to everybody.

Jimmy looked at the clock: it was time to go. If it amused his imagination to fashion a mythical Verdew Castle, he neither authorized nor forbade it. He still thought himself free to choose. But when he reached his office his first act was to write his friend a letter of acceptance.

Four days later a second blue envelope appeared on his breakfast-table. It was evidently a two-days' post to Verdew Castle, for Rollo explained that he had that moment received Jimmy's welcome communication. There followed a few references, neccessarily brief, to matters of interest to them both. The letter closed with the promised itinerary:

> So we shall hope to see you in ten days' time, complete with lethal chamber and big-game apparatus. I forget whether you have a car; but if you have, I strongly advise you to leave it at home. The road bridge across the estuary has been dicky for a long time. They may close it any day now, since it was felt to wobble the last time the Lord-Lieutenant crossed by it. You would be in a mess if you found it shut and had to go trailing thirty miles to Amplesford (a hellish road, since it's no one's interest to keep it up). If the bridge carried the Lord-Lieutenant it would probably bear you, but I shouldn't like to have your blood on my head! Come, then, by train to Verdew Grove. I recommend the four o'clock; it doesn't get here till after dark, but you can dine on it, and it's almost express part of the way. The morning train is too bloody for anything: you would die of boredom before you arrived, and I should hate that to happen to any of my guests. I'm sorry to present you with such ghastly alternatives, but the Castle was built here to be out of everyone's reach, and by Heaven, it is! Come prepared for a long stay. You must. I'm sure the old office can get on very well without you. You're lucky to be able to go away as a matter of course, like a gentleman. Let us have a line and we'll send to meet you, not my little tin kettle but Randolph's majestic Daimler. Good-bye.
>
> Yours,
> ROLLO.

It was indeed a troublesome, tedious journey, involving changes of train and even of station. More than once the train, having entered a terminus head first, steamed out tail first, with the result that Rintoul lost his sense of direction and had a slight sensation of vertigo whenever, in thought, he tried to recapture it. It was half-past nine and the sun was setting when they crossed the estuary. As always in such places the tide was low, and the sun's level beams illuminated the too rotund and luscious curves of a series of mud-flats. The railway-line approached the estuary from its marshy side, by a steep embankment. Near by, and considerably below, ran the road bridge – an antiquated affair of many arches, but apparently still in use, though there seemed to be no traffic on it. The line curved inwards, and by straining his neck Rintoul could see the train bent like a bow, and the engine approaching a hole, from which a few wisps of smoke still issued, in the ledge of rock that crowned the farther shore. The hole rushed upon him; Rintoul pulled in his head and was at once in darkness. The world never seemed to get light again. After the long tunnel they were among hills that shut out the light that would have come in, and stifled the little that was left behind. It was by the help of the station lantern that he read the name, Verdew Grove, and when they were putting his luggage on the motor he could scarcely distinguish between the porter and the chauffeur. One of them said:

'Did you say it was a rabbit?'

And the other: 'Well, there was a bit of fur stuck to the wheel.'

'You'd better not let the boss see it,' said the first speaker.

'Not likely.' And so saying, the chauffeur, who seemed to be referring to an accident, climbed into the car. As Rollo had said, it was a very comfortable one. Jimmy gave up counting the turns and trying to catch glimpses of the sky over the high hedges, and abandoned himself to drowsiness. He must have dozed, for he did not know whether it was five minutes or fifty before the opening door let in a gust of cool air and warned him that he had arrived.

For a moment he had the hall to himself. It did not seem very large, but to gauge its true extent was difficult, because of the arches and the shadows. Shaded lamps on the tables gave a diffused but very subdued glow; while a few unshaded lights, stuck about in the groining of the vault, consuming their energy in small patches of great brilliancy, dazzled rather than assisted the eye. The fact that the spaces between the vaulting-ribs were white-washed seemed to increase the glare. It was curious and not altogether happy, the contrast between the brilliance above and the murk below. No trophies of the chase adorned the walls; no stags' heads or antlers, no rifles, javelins, tomahawks, assegais, or krisses. Clearly the Verdews were not a family of sportsmen. In what did Randolph Verdew's interests lie? Rintoul wondered, and he was walking across to the open grate, in whose large recess a log-fire flickered, when the sound of a footfall startled him. It came close, then died away completely, then still in the same rhythm began again. It was Rollo.

Rollo with his black moustaches, his swaggering gait, his large expansive air, his noisy benevolence. He grasped Jimmy's hand.

But before he could say more than 'Damned glad', a footman appeared. He came so close to Jimmy and Rollo that the flow of the latter's eloquence was checked.

'Mr Rintoul is in the Pink Room,' announced the footman.

Rollo put his little finger in his mouth and gently bit it.

'Oh, but I thought I said—'

'Yes, sir,' interrupted the footman. 'But Mr Verdew thought he might disturb Mr Rintoul in the Onyx Room, because sometimes when he lies awake at night he has to move about, as you know, sir. And he thought the Pink Room had a better view. So he gave orders for him to be put there, sir.'

The footman finished on a tranquil note and turned to go. But Rollo flushed faintly and seemed put out.

'I thought it would have been company for you having my brother next door,' he said. 'But he's arranged otherwise, so it can't be helped. Shall I take you to the room now, or will you have a drink first? That is, if I can find it,' he muttered. 'They have a monstrous habit of sometimes taking the drinks away when Randolph has gone to bed. And by the way, he asked me to make his excuses to you. He was feeling rather tired. My wife's gone, too. She always turns in early here; she says there's nothing to do at Verdew. But, my God, there's a lot that wants doing, as I often tell her. This way.'

Though they found the whisky and soda in the drawing-room, Rollo still seemed a little crestfallen and depressed; but Jimmy's spirits, which sometimes suffered from the excessive buoyancy of his neighbour's, began to rise. The chair was comfortable; the room, though glimpses of stone showed alongside the tapestries, was more habitable and less ecclesiastical than the hall. In front of him was an uncurtained window through which he could see, swaying their heads as though bent on some ghostly conference, a cluster of white roses. I'm going to enjoy myself here, he thought.

Whatever the charms of the Onyx Room, whatever virtue resided in the proximity of Mr Randolph Verdew, one thing was certain: the Pink Room had a splendid view. Leaning out of his window the next morning Jimmy feasted his eyes on it. Directly below him was the moat, clear and apparently deep. Below that again was the steep conical hill on which the castle stood, its side intersected by corkscrew paths and level terraces. Below and beyond, undulating ground led the eye onwards and upwards to where, almost on the horizon, glittered and shone the silver of the estuary. Of the castle were visible only the round wall of Jimmy's tower, and a wing of the Tudor period, the gables of which rose to the level of his bedroom window. It was half-past eight and he dressed quickly, meaning to make a little tour of the castle precincts before his hosts appeared.

His intention, however, was only partially fulfilled, for on arriving in the hall he found the great door still shut, and fastened with a variety of locks and bolts, of antique design and as hard to open, it seemed, from within as from without. He had better fortune with a smaller door, and found himself on a level oblong stretch of grass, an island of green, bounded by the moat on the east and on the other side by the castle walls. There was a fountain in the middle. The sun shone down through the open end of the quadrangle, making the whole place a cave of light, flushing the warm stone of the Elizabethan wing to orange, and gilding the cold, pale, mediaeval stonework of the rest. Jimmy walked to the moat and tried to find, to right or left, a path leading to other parts of the building. But there was none. He turned round and saw Rollo standing in the doorway.

'Good-morning,' called his host. 'Already thinking out a plan of escape?'

Jimmy coloured slightly. The thought had been present in his mind, though not in the sense that Rollo seemed to mean it.

'You wouldn't find it very easy from here,' remarked Rollo, whose cheerful humour the night seemed to have restored. 'Because even if you swam the moat you couldn't get up the bank: it's too steep and too high.'

Jimmy examined the farther strand and realized that this was true.

'It would be prettier,' Rollo continued, 'and less canal-like, if the water came up to the top; but Randolph prefers it as it used to be. He likes to imagine we're living in a state of siege.'

'He doesn't seem to keep any weapons for our defence,' commented Jimmy. 'No arquebuses or bows and arrows; no vats of molten lead.'

'Oh, he wouldn't hurt anyone for the world,' said Rollo. 'That's one of his little fads. But it amuses him to look across to the river like one of the first Verdews and feel that no one can get in without his leave.'

'Or out either, I suppose,' suggested Jimmy.

'Well,' remarked Rollo, 'some day I'll show you a way of getting out. But now come along and look at the view from the other side; we have to go through the house to see it.'

They walked across the hall, where the servants were laying the breakfast-table, to a door at the end of a long narrow passage. But it was locked. 'Hodgson!' shouted Rollo.

A footman came up.

'Will you open this door, please?' said Rollo. Jimmy expected him to be angry, but there was only a muffled irritation in his voice. At his leisure the footman produced the key and let them through.

'That's what comes of living in someone else's house,' fumed Rollo, once they were out of earshot. 'These lazy devils want waking up. Randolph's a damned sight too easy-going.'

'Shall I see him at breakfast?' Jimmy inquired.

'I doubt it.' Rollo picked up a stone, looked round, for some reason, at the castle, and threw the pebble at a thrush, narrowly missing it. 'He doesn't usually appear till lunchtime. He's interested in all sorts of philanthropical societies. He's always helping them to prevent something. He hasn't prevented you, though, you naughty fellow,' he went on, stooping down and picking up from a stone several fragments of snails' shells. 'This seems to be the thrushes' Tower Hill.'

'He's fond, of animals, then?' asked Jimmy.

'Fond, my boy?' repeated Rollo. 'Fond is not the word. But we aren't vegetarians. Some day I'll explain all that. Come and have some bacon and eggs.'

That evening, in his bath, a large wooden structure like a giant's coffin, Jimmy reviewed the day, a delightful day. In the morning he had been taken round the castle; it was not so large as it seemed from outside – it had to be smaller, the walls were so thick. And there were, of course, a great many rooms he wasn't shown, attics, cellars, and dungeons. One dungeon he had seen: but he felt sure that in a fortress of such pretensions there must be more than one. He couldn't quite get the 'lie' of the place at present; he had his own way of finding his room, but he knew it wasn't the shortest way. The hall, which was like a Clapham Junction to the castle's topographical system, still confused him. He knew the way out, because there was only one way, across a modernized draw-bridge, and that made it simpler. He had crossed it to get at the woods below the castle, where he had spent the afternoon, hunting for caterpillars. 'They' had really left him alone – even severely alone! Neither of Rollo's wife nor of his brother was there yet any sign. But I shall see them at dinner, he thought, wrapping himself in an immense bath-towel.

The moment he saw Randolph Verdew, standing pensive in the drawing-room, he knew he would like him. He was an etherealized version of Rollo, taller and slighter. His hair was sprinkled with grey and he stooped a little. His cloudy blue eyes met Jimmy's with extraordinary frankness as he held out his hand and apologized for his previous non-appearance.

'It is delightful to have you here,' he added. 'You are a naturalist, I believe?'

His manner was formal but charming, infinitely reassuring.

'I am an entomologist,' said Jimmy, smiling.

'Ah, I love to watch the butterflies fluttering about the flowers – and the moths, too, those big heavy fellows that come in of an evening and knock themselves about against the lights. I have often had to put as many as ten out of the windows, and back they come – the deluded creatures. What a pity that their larvae are harmful and in some cases have to be destroyed! But I expect you prefer to observe the rarer insects?'

'If I can find them,' said Jimmy.

'I'm sure I hope you will,' said Randolph, with much feeling. 'You must get Rollo to help you.'

'Oh,' said Jimmy, 'Rollo—'

'I hope you don't think Rollo indifferent to nature?' asked his brother, with distress in his voice and an engaging simplicity of manner. 'He has had rather a difficult life, as I expect you know. His affairs have kept him a great deal in towns, and he has had little leisure – very little leisure.'

'He must find it restful here,' remarked Jimmy, again with the sense of being more tactful than truthful.

'I'm sure I hope he does. Rollo is a dear fellow; I wish he came here oftener. Unfortunately his wife does not care for the country, and Rollo himself is very much tied by his new employment – the motor business.'

'Hasn't he been with Scorcher and Speedwell long?'

'Oh no: poor Rollo, he is always trying his hand at something new. He ought to have been born a rich man instead of me.' Randolph spread his hands out with a gesture of helplessness. 'He could have done so much, whereas I – ah, here he comes. We were talking about you, Rollo.'

'No scandal, I hope; no hitting a man when he's down?'

'Indeed no. We were saying we hoped you would soon come into a fortune.'

'Where do you think it's coming from?' demanded Rollo, screwing up his eyes as though the smoke from his cigarette had made them smart.

'Perhaps Vera could tell us,' rejoined Randolph mildly, making his way to the table, though his brother's cigarette was still unfinished. 'How is she, Rollo? I hoped she would feel sufficiently restored to make a fourth with us this evening.'

'Still moping,' said her husband. 'Don't waste your pity on her. She'll be all right tomorrow.'

They sat down to dinner.

The next day, or it might have been the day after, Jimmy was coming home to tea from the woods below the castle. On either side of the path was a hayfield. They were mowing the hay. The mower was a new one, painted bright blue; the horse tossed its head up and down; the placid afternoon air was alive with country sounds, whirring, shouts, and clumping footfalls. The scene was full of an energy and gentleness that refreshed the heart. Jimmy reached the white iron fence that divided the plain from the castle mound, and, with a sigh, set his feet upon the zigzag path. For though the hill was only a couple of hundred feet high at most, the climb called for an effort he was never quite prepared to make. He was tramping with lowered head, conscious of each step, when a voice hailed him.

'Mr Rintoul!'

It was a foreign voice, the i's pronounced like e's. He looked up and saw a woman, rather short and dark, watching him from the path above.

'You see I have come down to meet you,' she said, advancing, with short, brisk, but careful and unpractised steps. And she added, as he still continued to stare at her: 'Don't you know? I am Mrs Verdew.'

By this time she was at his side.

'How could I know?' he asked, laughing and shaking the hand

she was already holding out to him. All her gestures seemed to be quick and unpremeditated.

'Let us sit here,' she said, and almost before she had spoken she was sitting, and had made him sit, on the wooden bench beside them. 'I am tired from walking downhill; you will be tired by walking uphill; therefore we both need a rest.'

She decided it all so quickly that Jimmy, whose nature had a streak of obstinacy, wondered if he was really so tired after all.

'And who should I have been, who could I have been, but Mrs Verdew?' she demanded challengingly.

Jimmy saw that an answer was expected, but couldn't think of anyone who Mrs Verdew might have been.

'I don't know,' he said feebly.

'Of course you don't, silly,' said Mrs Verdew. 'How long have you been here?'

'I can't remember. Two or three days, I think,' said Jimmy, who disliked being nailed down to a definite fact.

'Two or three days? Listen to the man, how vague he is!' commented Mrs Verdew, with a gesture of impatience apostrophizing the horizon. 'Well, whether it's three days or only two, you must have learnt one thing – that no one enters these premises without leave.'

'Premises?' murmured Jimmy.

'Hillside, garden, grounds, premises,' repeated Mrs Verdew. 'How slow you are! But so are all Englishmen.'

'I don't think Rollo is slow,' remarked Jimmy, hoping to carry the war into her country.

'Sometimes too slow, sometimes too fast, never the right pace,' pronounced his wife. 'Rollo misdirects his life.'

'He married you,' said Jimmy gently.

Mrs Verdew gave him a quick look. 'That was partly because I wanted him to. But only just now, for instance, he has been foolish.'

'Do you mean he was foolish to come here?'

'I didn't mean that. Though I hate the place, and he does no good here.'

'What good could he do?' asked Jimmy, who was staring vacantly at the sky. 'Except, perhaps, help his brother to look after – to look after—'

'That's just it,' said Mrs Verdew. 'Randolph doesn't need any help, and if he did he wouldn't let Rollo help him. He wouldn't even have him made a director of the coal-mine!'

'What coal-mine?' Jimmy asked.

'Randolph's. You don't mean to say you didn't know he had a coal-mine? One has to tell you everything!'

'I like you to tell me things!' protested Jimmy.

'As you don't seem to find out anything for yourself, I suppose I must. Well, then: Randolph has a coal-mine, he is very rich, and he spends his money on nothing but charitable societies for contradicting the laws of nature. And he won't give Rollo a penny – not a penny though he is his only brother, his one near relation in the world! He won't even help him to get a job!'

'I thought he had a job,' said Jimmy, in perplexity.

'You thought that! You'd think anything,' exclaimed Mrs Verdew, her voice rising in exasperation.

'No, but he told me he came here for a holiday,' said Jimmy pacifically.

'Holiday, indeed! A long holiday. I can't think why Rollo told you that. Nor can I think why I bore you with all our private troubles. A man can talk to a woman about anything; but a woman can only talk to a man about what interests him.'

'But who is to decide that?'

'The woman, of course; and I see you're getting restless.'

'No, no. I was so interested. Please go on.'

'Certainly not. I am a Russian, and I often know when a man is bored sooner than he knows himself. Come along,' pulling him from the bench much as a gardener uproots a weed; 'and I will tell you something very interesting. Ah, how fast you walk! Don't you know it's less fatiguing to walk uphill slowly – and you with all those fishing-nets and pill-boxes. And what on earth is that great bottle for?'

'I try to catch butterflies in these,' Jimmy explained. 'And this is my killing bottle.'

'What a horrible name. What is it for?'

'I'm afraid I kill the butterflies with it.'

'Ah, what a barbarian! Give it to me a moment. Yes, there are their corpses, poor darlings. Is that Randolph coming towards us? No, don't take it away. I can carry it quite easily under my shawl. What was I going to tell you when you interrupted me? I remember – it was about the terrace. When I first came here I used to feel frightfully depressed – it was winter and the sun set so early, sometimes before lunch! In the afternoons I used to go down the mound, where I met you, and wait for the sun to dip below that bare hill on the left. And I would begin to walk quite slowly towards the castle, and all the while the sun was balanced on the hilltop like a ball! And the shadow covered the valley and kept lapping my feet, like the oncoming tide! And I would wait till it reached my ankles, and then run up into the light, and be safe for a moment. It was such fun, but I don't expect you'd enjoy it, you're too sophisticated. Ah, here's Randolph. Randolph, I've been showing Mr Rintoul the way home; he didn't know it – he doesn't know anything! Do you know what he does with this amusing net? He uses it to catch tiny little moths, like the ones that get into your furs. He puts it over them and looks at them, and they're so frightened, they think they can't get out; then they notice the little holes, and out they creep and fly away! Isn't it charming?'

'Charming,' said Randolph, glancing away from the net and towards the ground.

'Now we must go on. We want our tea terribly!' And Mrs Verdew swept Jimmy up the hill.

With good fortune the morning newspaper arrived at Verdew Castle in time for tea, already a little out of date. Jimmy accorded it, as a rule, the tepid interest with which, when abroad, one contemplates the English journals of two days ago. They seem to emphasize one's remoteness, not lessen it. Never did Jimmy seem farther from London, indeed, farther from civilization, than when he picked up the familiar sheet of *The Times*. It was like a faint rumour of the world that had somehow found its way down hundreds of miles of railway, changed trains and stations, rumbled across the estuary, and threaded the labyrinth of lanes and turnings between Verdew Grove and the castle. Each day its news seemed to grow less important, or at any rate less important to Jimmy. He began to turn over the leaves. Mrs Verdew had gone to her room, absent-mindedly taking the killing bottle with her. He was alone; there was no sound save the crackle of the sheets. Unusually insipid the news seemed. He turned more rapidly. What was this? In the middle of page fourteen, a hole? No, not a mere hole: a deliberate excision, the result of an operation performed with scissors. What item of news could anyone have found worth reading, much less worth cutting out? To Jimmy's idle mind, the centre of page fourteen assumed a tremendous importance, it became the sun of his curiosity's universe. He rose;

with quick cautious fingers he searched about, shifting papers, delving under blotters, even fumbling in the more public-looking pigeon-holes.

Suddenly he heard the click of a door opening, and with a bound he was in the middle of the room. It was only Rollo, whom business of some kind had kept all day away from home.

'Enter the tired bread-winner,' he remarked. 'Like to see the paper? I haven't had time to read it.' He threw something at Jimmy and walked off.

It was *The Times*. With feverish haste Jimmy turned to page fourteen and seemed to have read the paragraph even before he set eyes on it. It was headed: *Mysterious Outbreak at Verdew*.

'The sequestered, little-known village of Verdew-le-Dale has again been the scene of a mysterious outrage, recalling the murders of John Didwell and Thomas Presland in 1910 and 1912, and the occasional killing of animals which has occurred since. In this instance, as in the others, the perpetrator of the crime seems to have been actuated by some vague motive of retributive justice. The victim was a shepherd dog, the property of Mr J. R. Cross. The dog, which was known to worry cats, had lately killed two belonging to an old woman of the parish. The Bench, of which Mr Randolph Verdew is chairman, fined Cross and told him to keep the dog under proper control, but did not order its destruction. Two days ago the animal was found dead in a ditch, with its throat cut. The police have no doubt that the wound was made by the same weapon that killed Didwell and Presland, who, it will be remembered, had both been prosecuted by the RSPCA for cruelty and negligence resulting in the deaths of domestic animals. At present no evidence has come to light that might lead to the detection of the criminal, though the police are still making investigations.'

'And I don't imagine it will ever come to light,' Jimmy muttered.

'What do you suppose won't come to light?' inquired a voice at his elbow. He looked up. Randolph Verdew was standing by his chair and looking over his shoulder at the newspaper.

Jimmy pointed to the paragraph.

'Any clue to the identity of the man who did this?'

'No,' said Randolph after a perceptible pause. 'I don't suppose there will be.' He hesitated a moment and then added:

'But it would interest me much to know how that paragraph found its way back into the paper.'

Jimmy explained.

'You see,' observed Randolph, 'I always cut out, and paste into a book, any item of news that concerns the neighbourhood, and especially Verdew. In this way I have made an interesting collection.'

'There seem to have been similar occurrences here before,' remarked Jimmy.

'There have, there have,' Randolph Verdew said.

'It's very strange that no one has even been suspected.'

Randolph Verdew answered obliquely:

'Blood calls for blood. The workings of justice are secret and incalculable.'

'Then you sympathize a little with the murderer?' Jimmy inquired.

'I?' muttered Randolph. 'I think I hate cruelty more than anything in the world.'

'But wasn't the murderer cruel?' persisted Jimmy.

'No,' said Randolph Verdew with great decision. 'At least,' he added in a different tone, 'the victims appear to have died with the minimum of suffering. But here comes Vera. We must find a more cheerful topic of conversation. Vera, my dear, you won't disappoint us of our bridge tonight?'

Several days elapsed, days rendered slightly unsatisfactory for Jimmy from a trivial cause. He could not get back his killing bottle from Mrs Verdew. She had promised it, she had even gone upstairs to fetch it; but she never brought it down. Meanwhile, several fine specimens (in particular a large female Emperor moth) languished in match-boxes and other narrow receptacles, damaging their wings and even having to be set at liberty. It was very trying. He began to feel that the retention of the killing bottle was deliberate. In questions of conduct he was often at sea. But in the domain of manners, though he sometimes went astray, he considered that he knew very well which road to take, and the knowledge was a matter of pride to him. The thought of asking Mrs Verdew a third time to restore his property irked him exceedingly. At last he screwed up his courage. They were walking down the hill together after tea.

'Mrs Verdew,' he began.

'Don't go on,' she exclaimed. 'I know exactly what you're going to say. Poor darling, he wants to have his killing bottle back. Well, you can't. I need it myself for those horrible hairy moths that come in at night.'

'But Mrs Verdew—!' he protested.

'And please don't call me Mrs Verdew. How long have we known each other? Ten days! And soon you've got to go! Surely you could call me Vera!'

Jimmy flushed. He knew that he must go soon, but didn't realize that a term had been set to his stay.

'Listen,' she continued, beginning to lead him down the hill. 'When you're in London I hope you'll often come to see us.'

'I certainly will,' said he.

'Well, then, let's make a date. Will you dine with us on the tenth? That's tomorrow week.'

'I'm not quite sure—' began Jimmy unhappily, looking down on to the rolling plain and feeling that he loved it.

'How long you're going to stay?' broke in Mrs Verdew, who seemed to be able to read his thoughts. 'Why do you want to stay? There's nothing to do here: think what fun we might have in London. You can't like this place and I don't believe it's good for you; you don't look half as well as you did when you came.'

'But you didn't see me when I came, and I feel very well,' said Jimmy.

'Feeling is nothing,' said Mrs Verdew. 'Look at me. Do I look well?' She turned up to him her face: it was too large, he thought, and dull and pallid with powder; the features were too marked; but undeniably it had beauty. 'I suppose I do: I feel well. But in this place I believe my life might stop any moment of its own accord! Do you never feel that?'

'No,' said Jimmy, smiling.

'Sit down,' she said suddenly, taking him to a seat as she had done on the occasion of their first meeting, 'and let me have your hand – not because I love you, but because I'm happier holding something, and it's a pretty hand.' Jimmy did not resist: he was slightly stupefied, but somehow not surprised by her behaviour. She held up his drooping hand by the wrist, level with her eyes, and surveyed it with a smile, then she laid it, palm upward, in her lap. The smile vanished from her face: she knitted her brows.

'I don't like it,' she said, a sudden energy in her voice.

'I thought you said it was a pretty hand,' murmured Jimmy.

'I did, you know I don't mean that. It is pretty: but you don't deserve to have it, not your eyes, nor your hair; you are idle and complacent and unresponsive and ease-loving – you only think of your butterflies and your killing bottle!' She looked at him fondly; and Jimmy for some reason was rather pleased to hear all this. 'No, I meant that I see danger in your hand, in the lines.'

'Danger to me?'

'Ah, the conceit of men! Yes, to you.'

'What sort of danger – physical danger?' inquired Jimmy, only moderately interested.

'*Danger de mort*,' pronounced Mrs Verdew.

'Come, come,' said Jimmy, bending forward and looking into Mrs Verdew's face to see if she was pretending to be serious. 'When does the danger threaten?'

'Now,' said Mrs Verdew.

Oh, thought Jimmy, what a tiresome woman! So you think I'm in danger, do you, Mrs Verdew, of losing my head at this moment? God, the conceit of women! He stole a glance at her; she was looking straight ahead, her lips pursed up and trembling a little, as though she wanted him to kiss her. Shall I? he thought, for compliance was in his blood and he always wanted to do what was expected of him. But at that very moment a wave of irritability flooded his mind and changed it: she had taken his killing bottle, spoilt and stultified several precious days, and all to gratify her caprice. He turned away.

'Oh, I'm tougher than you think,' he said.

'Tougher?' she said. 'Do you mean your skin? All Englishmen have thick skins.' She spoke resentfully; then her voice softened. 'I was going to tell you—' She uttered the words with difficulty, and as though against her will. But Jimmy, not noticing her changed tone and still ridden by his irritation, interrupted her.

'That you'd restore my killing bottle?'

'No, no,' she cried in exasperation, leaping to her feet. 'How you do harp on that wretched old poison bottle! I wish I'd broken it!' She caught her breath, and Jimmy rose too, facing her with distress and contrition in his eyes. But she was too angry to heed his change of mood. 'It was something I wanted you to know – but you make things so difficult for me! I'll fetch you your bottle,' she continued wildly, 'since you're such a child as to want it! No, don't follow me; I'll have it sent to your room.'

He looked up; she was gone, but a faint sound of sobbing disturbed the air behind her.

It was evening, several days later, and they were sitting at dinner. How Jimmy would miss these meals when he got back to London! For a night or two, after the scene with Mrs Verdew, he had been uneasy under the enforced proximity which the dining-table brought; she looked at him reproachfully, spoke little, and when he sought occasions to apologize to her, she eluded them. She had never been alone with him since. She had, he knew, little control over her emotions, and perhaps her pride suffered. But her pique, or whatever it was, now seemed to have passed away. She looked lovely tonight, and he realized he would miss her. Rollo's voice, when he began to speak, was like a commentary on his thoughts.

'Jimmy says he's got to leave us, Randolph,' he said. 'Back to the jolly old office.'

'That is a great pity,' said Randolph in his soft voice. 'We shall miss him, shan't we, Vera?'

Mrs Verdew said they would.

'All the same, these unpleasant facts have to be faced,' remarked Rollo. 'That's why we were born. I'm afraid you've had a dull time, Jimmy, though you must have made the local flora and fauna sit up. Have you annexed any prize specimens from your raids upon the countryside?'

'I have got one or two good ones,' said Jimmy with a reluctance that he attributed partially to modesty.

'By the way,' said Rollo, pouring himself out a glass of port, for the servants had left the room, 'I would like you to show Randolph that infernal machine of yours, Jimmy. Anything on the lines of a humane killer bucks the old chap up no ends.' He looked across at his brother, the ferocious cast of his features softened into an expression of fraternal solicitude.

After a moment's pause Randolph said: 'I should be much interested to be shown Mr Rintoul's invention.'

'Oh, it's not my invention,' said Jimmy a little awkwardly.

'You'll forgive me disagreeing with you, Rollo,' Mrs Verdew, who had not spoken for some minutes, suddenly remarked, 'I don't think it's worth Randolph's while looking at it. I don't think it would interest him a bit.'

'How often have I told you, my darling,' said Rollo, leaning across the corner of the table towards his wife, 'not to contradict me? I keep a record of the times you agree with me: December, 1919, was the last.'

'Sometimes I think that was a mistake,' said Mrs Verdew, rising in evident agitation, 'for it was then I promised to marry you.' She reached the door before Jimmy could open it for her.

'Ah, these ladies!' moralized Rollo, leaning back and closing his eyes. 'What a dance the dear things lead us, with their temperaments.' And he proceeded to enumerate examples of feminine caprice, until his brother proposed that they should adjourn to the bridge-table.

The next morning, Jimmy was surprised to find a note accompany his early morning tea.

> Dear Mr Rintoul (it began), since I mustn't say 'Dear Jimmy'. ('I never said she mustn't' Jimmy thought.) I know it isn't easy for any man, most of all an Englishman, to understand moods, but I do beg you to forgive my foolish outburst of a few days ago. I think it must have been the air or the lime in the water that made me *un po' nervosa*, as the Italians say. I know you prefer a life utterly flat and dull and even – it would kill me, but there! I am sorry. You can't expect me to change, *à mon âge*! But anyhow try to forgive me.
>
> Yours,
> VERA VERDEW.
>
> P.S. – I wouldn't trouble to show that bottle to Randolph. He has quite enough silly ideas in his head as it is.

What a nice letter, thought Jimmy drowsily. He had forgotten the killing bottle. I won't show it to Randolph, Jimmy thought, unless he asks me.

But soon after breakfast a footman brought him a message: Mr Verdew was in his room and would be glad to see the invention (the man's voice seemed to put the word into inverted commas) at Mr Rintoul's convenience. 'Well,' reflected Jimmy, 'if he's to see it working it must have something to work on.' Aimlessly he strolled over the drawbridge and made his way, past blocks of crumbling wall, past grassy hummocks and hollows, to the terraces. They were gay with flowers; and looked at from above, the lateral stripes and bunches of colour, succeeding each other to the bottom of the hill, had a peculiarly brilliant effect. What should he catch? A dozen white butterflies presented themselves for the honour of exhibiting their death-agony to Mr Randolph Verdew, but Jimmy passed them by. His collector's pride demanded a nobler sacrifice. After twenty minutes' search he was rewarded; his net fell over a slightly battered but still recognizable specimen of the Large Tortoiseshell butterfly. He put it in a pill-box and bore it away to the house. But as he went he was visited by a reluctance, never experienced by him before, to take the butterfly's life in such a public and coldblooded fashion; it was not a good specimen, one that he could add to his collection; it was just cannon-fodder. The heat of the day, flickering visibly upwards from the turf and flowers, bemused his mind; all around was a buzzing and humming that seemed to liberate his thoughts from contact with the world and give them the intensity of sensations. So vivid was his vision, so flawless the inner quiet from which it sprang, that he came up with a start against his own bedroom door. The substance of his day-dream had been forgotten; but it had left its ambassador behind it – something that whether apprehended by the mind as a colour, a taste, or a local inflammation, spoke with an insistent voice and always to the same purpose: 'Don't show Randolph Verdew the butterfly; let it go, here, out of the window, and send him an apology.'

For a few minutes, such was the force of this inward monitor, Jimmy did contemplate setting the butterfly at liberty. He was prone to sudden irrational scruples and impulses, and if there was nothing definite urging him the other way he often gave in to them. But in this case there was. Manners demanded that he should accede to his host's request; the rules of manners, of all rules in life, were the easiest to recognize and the most satisfactory to act upon. Not to go would be a breach of manners.

'How kind of you,' said Randolph, coming forward and shaking Jimmy's hand, a greeting that, between two members of the same household, struck him as odd. 'You have brought your invention with you?'

Jimmy saw that it was useless to disclaim the honour of its discovery. He unwrapped the bottle and handed it to Randolph.

Randolph carried it straight away to a high window, the sill of which was level with his eyes and above the top of Jimmy's head. He held the bottle up to the light. Oblong in shape and about the size of an ordinary jam jar, it had a deep whitish pavement of plaster, pitted with brown furry holes like an overripe cheese. Resting on the plaster, billowing and coiling up to the glass stopper, stood a fat column of cotton-wool. The most striking thing about the bottle was that word *poison* printed in large, loving characters on a label stuck to the outside.

'May I release the stopper?' asked Randolph at length.

'You may,' said Jimmy, 'but a whiff of the stuff is all you want.'

Randolph stared meditatively into the depths of the bottle. 'A rather agreeable odour,' he said. 'But how small the bottle is. I had figured it to myself as something very much larger.'

'Larger?' echoed Jimmy. 'Oh, no, this is quite big enough for me. I don't need a mausoleum.'

'But I was under the impression,' Randolph Verdew remarked, still fingering the bottle, 'that you used it to destroy pests.'

'If you call butterflies pests,' said Jimmy, smiling.

'I am afraid that some of them must undeniably be included in that category,' pronounced Mr Verdew, his voice edged with a melancholy decisiveness. 'The cabbage butterfly, for instance. And it is, of course, only the admittedly noxious insects that need to be destroyed.'

'All insects are more or less harmful,' Jimmy said.

Randolph Verdew passed his hand over his brow. The shadow of a painful thought crossed his face, and he murmured uncertainly:

'I think that's a quibble. There are categories... I have been at some pains to draw them up ... The list of destructive lepidoptera is large, too large ... That is why I imagined your lethal chamber would be a vessel of considerable extent, possibly large enough to admit a man, and its use attended by some danger to an unpractised exponent.'

'Well,' said Jimmy, 'there's enough poison here to account for half a town. But let me show you how it works.' And he took the pill-box from his pocket. Shabby, battered and cowed, the butterfly stood motionless, its wings closed and upright.

'Now,' said Jimmy, 'you'll see.'

The butterfly was already between the fingers and half-way to the bottle, when he heard, faint but clear, the sound of a cry. It was two syllabled, like the interval of the cuckoo's call inverted, and might have been his own name.

'Listen!' he exclaimed. 'What was that? It sounded like Mrs Verdew's voice.' His swiftly turning head almost collided with his host's chin, so near had the latter drawn to watch the operation, and chased the tail-end of a curious look from Randolph Verdew's face.

'It's nothing,' he said. 'Go on.'

Alas, alas, for the experiment in humane slaughter! The butterfly must have been stronger than it looked; the power of the killing bottle had no doubt declined with frequent usage. Up and down, round and round flew the butterfly; its frantic flutterings could be heard through the thick walls of its glass prison. It clung to the cotton-wool, pressed itself into corners, its straining, delicate tongue coiling and uncoiling in the effort to suck in a breath of living air. Now it was weakening. It fell from the cotton-wool and lay its back on the plaster slab. It jolted itself up and down and, when strength for this movement failed, it clawed the air with its thin legs as though pedalling an imaginary bicycle. Suddenly, with a violent spasm, it gave birth to a thick cluster of yellowish eggs. Its body twitched once or twice and at last lay still.

Jimmy shrugged his shoulders in annoyance and turned to his host. The look of horrified excitement whose vanishing vestige he had seen a moment before, lay full and undisguised upon Randolph Verdew's face. He only said:

'Of what flower or vegetable is that dead butterfly the parasite?'

'Oh, poor thing,' said Jimmy carelessly, 'it's rather a rarity. Its caterpillar may have eaten an elm-leaf or two – nothing more. It's too scarce to be a pest. It's fond of gardens and frequented places, the book says – rather sociable, like a robin.'

'It could not be described as injurious to human life?'

'Oh, no. It's a collector's specimen really. Only this is too damaged to be any good.'

'Thank you for letting me see the invention in operation,' said Randolph Verdew, going to his desk and sitting down. Jimmy found his silence a little embarrassing. He packed up the bottle and made a rather awkward, self-conscious exit.

The four bedroom candles always stood, their silver flashing agreeably, cheek by jowl with the whisky decanter and the hot-water kettle and the soda. Now, the others having retired, there were only two, one of which (somewhat wastefully, for he still had a half-empty glass in his hand) Rollo was lighting.

'My dear fellow,' he was saying to Jimmy, 'I'm sorry you think the new model insecticide fell a bit flat. But Randolph's like that, you know: damned undemonstrative cove, I must say, though he's my own brother.'

'He wasn't exactly undemonstrative,' answered Jimmy, perplexity written on his face.

'No, rather like an iceberg hitting you amidships,' said his friend. 'Doesn't make a fuss, but you feel it all the same. But don't you worry, Jimmy; I happen to know that he enjoyed your show. Fact is, he told me so.' He gulped down some whisky.

'I'm relieved,' said Jimmy, and he obviously spoke the truth. 'I've only one more whole day here, and I should be sorry if I'd hurt his feelings.'

'Yes, and I'm afraid you'll have to spend it with him alone,' said Rollo, compunction colouring his voice. 'I was coming to that. Fact is, Vera and I have unexpectedly got to go away tomorrow for the day.' He paused; a footman entered and began walking uncertainly about the room. 'Now, Jimmy,' he went on, 'be a good chap and stay on a couple of days more. You do keep us from the blues so. That's all right, William, we don't want anything,' he remarked parenthetically to the footman's retreating figure. 'I haven't mentioned it to Randolph, but he'd be absolutely charmed if you'd grave our humble dwelling a little longer. You needn't tell anyone anything: just stay, and we shall be back the day after tomorrow. It's hellish that we've got to go, but you know this bread-winning business: it's the early bird that catches the worm. And talking of that, we have to depart at cockcrow. I may not see you again – that is, unless you stay, as I hope you will. Just send a wire to the old blighter who works with you and tell him to go to blazes.'

'Well,' said Jimmy, delighted by the prospect, 'you certainly do tempt me.'

'Then fall, my lad,' said Rollo, catching him a heavy blow between the shoulder-blades. 'I shan't say good-bye, but "au revoir". Don't go to bed sober; have another drink.'

But Jimmy declined. The flickering candles lighted them across the hall and up the stone stairs.

And it's lucky I have a candle, Jimmy thought, trying in vain the third and last switch, the one on the reading-lamp by the bed. The familiar room seemed to have changed, to be closing hungrily, with a vast black embrace, upon the nimbus of thin clear dusk that shone about the candle. He walked uneasily up and down, drew a curtain and let in a ray of moonlight. But the silver gleam crippled the candlelight without adding any radiance of its own, so he shut it out. This window must be closed, thought Jimmy, that opens on to the parapet, for I really couldn't deal with a stray cat in this localized twilight. He opened instead a window that gave on to the sheer wall. Even after the ritual of tooth-cleaning he was still restless and dissatisfied, so after a turn or two he knelt by the bed and said his prayers – whether from devotion or superstition he couldn't tell: he only knew that he wanted to say them.

'Come in!' he called next morning, in answer to the footman's knock.

'I can't come in, sir,' said a muffled voice. 'The door's locked.'

How on earth had that happened? Then Jimmy remembered. As a child he always locked the door because he didn't like to be surprised saying his prayers. He must have done so last night, unconsciously. How queer! He felt full of self-congratulation – he didn't know why. 'And – oh, William!' he called after the departing footman.

'Yes, sir?'

'The light's fused, or something. It wouldn't go on last night.'

'Very good, sir.'

Jimmy addressed himself to the tea. But what was this? Another note from Mrs Verdew!

> DEAR JIMMY (he read),
> You will forgive this impertinence, for I've got a piece of good news for you. In future, you won't be able to say that women never help a man in his career! (Jimmy was unaware of having said so.) As you know, Rollo and I have to leave tomorrow morning. I don't suppose he told you why, because it's rather private. But he's embarking on a big undertaking that will mean an enormous amount of litigation and lawyer's fees! Think of that! (Though I don't suppose you think of anything else.) I know he wants you to act for him: but to do so you positively *must* leave Verdew tomorrow. Make any excuse to Randolph; send yourself a telegram if you want to be specially polite: but you must catch the night train to London. It's the chance of a life. You can get through to Rollo on the telephone next morning. Perhaps we could lunch together – or dine? *A bientôt*, therefore.
>
> VERA VERDEW.
>
> P.S. – I shall be furious if you don't come.

Jimmy pondered Mrs Verdew's note, trying to read between its lines. One thing was clear: she had fallen in love with him. Jimmy smiled at the ceiling. She wanted to see him again, so soon, so soon! Jimmy smiled once more. She couldn't bear to wait an unnecessary day. How urgent women were! He smiled more indulgently. And, also, how exacting. Here was this cock-and-bull story, all about Rollo's 'undertaking' which would give him, Jimmy, the chance of a lifetime! And because she was so impatient she expected him to believe it! Luncheon, indeed! Dinner! How could they meet for dinner, when Rollo was to be back at Verdew that same evening? In her haste she had not even troubled to make her date credible. And then: 'I shall be furious if you don't come.' What an argument! What confidence in her own powers did not that sentence imply! Let her be furious, then, as furious as she liked.

Her voice, just outside his door, interrupted his meditation.

'Only a moment, Rollo, it will only take me a moment!'

And Rollo's reply, spoken in a tone as urgent as hers, but louder:

'I tell you there isn't time: we shall miss the train.'

He seemed to hustle her away downstairs, poor Vera. She had really been kind to Jimmy, in spite of her preposterous claims on his affection. He was glad he would see her again tomorrow . . . Verdew was so much nicer than London . . . He began to doze.

On the way back from the woods there was a small low church with a square tower and two bells – the lower one both cracked and flat. You could see up into the belfry through the slats in the windows. Close by the church ran a stream, choked with green scum except where the cattle went down to drink, and crossed by a simple bridge of logs set side by side. Jimmy liked to stand on the bridge and listen to the unmelodious chime. No one heeded it, no one came to church, and it had gone sour and out of tune. It gave Jimmy an exquisite, slightly morbid sense of dereliction and decay, which he liked to savour in solitude; but this afternoon a rustic had got there first.

'Good-day,' he said.

'Good-day,' said Jimmy.

'You're from the castle, I'm thinking?' the countryman surmised.

'Yes.'

'And how do you find Mr Verdew?'

'Which Mr Verdew?'

'Why, the squire, of course.'

'I think he's pretty well,' said Jimmy.

'Ah, he may appear to be so,' the labourer observed; 'but them as has eyes to see and ears to hear, knows different.'

'Isn't he a good landlord?' asked Jimmy.

'Yes,' said the old man. 'He's a tolerably good landlord. It isn't that.' He seemed to relish his mysteriousness.

'You like Mr Rollo Verdew better?' suggested Jimmy.

'I wouldn't care to say that, sir. He's a wild one, Mr Rollo.'

'Well, anyhow, Mr Randolph Verdew isn't wild.'

'Don't you be too sure, sir.'

'I've never seen him so.'

'There's not many that have. And those that have – some won't tell what they saw and some can't.'

'Why won't they?'

'Because it's not their interest to.'

'And why can't the others?'

'Because they're dead.'

There was a pause.

'How did they die?' asked Jimmy.

'That's not for me to say,' the old man answered, closing his mouth like a trap. But this gesture, as Jimmy had already learned, was only part of his conversational technique. In a moment he began again:

'Did you ever hear of the Verdew murders?'

'Something.'

'Well, 'twasn't only dogs that was killed.'

'I know.'

'But they were all killed the same way.'

'How?'

'With a knife,' said the old man. 'Like pigs. From ear to ear,' he added, making an explanatory gesture; 'from ear to ear.' His voice became reminiscent. 'Tom Presland was a friend o' mine. I seed him in the evening and he said, he says "That blamed donkey weren't worth a ten-pound fine." And I said, "You're lucky not to be in prison," for in case you don't know, sir, the Bench here don't mind fellows being a bit hasty with their animals, although Mr Verdew is the chairman. I felt nigh killing the beast myself sometimes, it was that obstinate. "But, Bill," he says, "I don't feel altogether comfortable when I remember what happened to Jack Didwell." And sure enough he was found next morning in the ditch with his throat gapin' all white at the edges, just like poor old Jack. And the donkey was a contrary beast, that had stood many a knock before, harder than the one what killed him.'

'And why is Mr Verdew suspected?'

'Why, sir, the servants said he was in the castle all night and must have been, because the bridge was drawed. But how do they know he had to use the bridge? Anyhow, George Wiscombe swears he saw him going through Nape's Spinney the night poor old Tom was done in. And Mr Verdew has always been cruel fond of animals, that's another reason.'

How easy it is, thought Jimmy, to lose one's reputation in the country!

'Tell me,' he said, 'how does Mr Verdew satisfy his conscience when he eats animals and chickens, and when he has slugs and snails killed in the garden?'

'Ah, there you've hit it,' said the old man, not at all nonplussed. 'But they say Mr Rollo Verdew has helped him to make a mighty great list of what may be killed and what mayn't, according as it's useful-like to human beings. And anybody kills anything, they persuade him it's harmful and down it goes on the black list. And if he don't see the thing done with his own eyes, or the chap isn't hauled up before the Bench, he doesn't take on about it. And in a week or less it's all gone from his mind. Jack and Tom were both killed within a few days of what they'd done becoming known; so was the collie dog what was found here a fortnight back.'

'Here?' asked Jimmy.

'Close by where you're standing. Poor beast, it won't chase those b——y cats no more. It was a mess. But, as I said, if what you've done's a week old, you're safe, in a manner of speaking.'

'But why, if he's really dangerous,' said Jimmy, impressed in spite of himself by the old man's tacit assumption of Randolph's guilt, 'doesn't Mr Rollo Verdew get him shut up?' This simple question evoked the longest and most pregnant of his interlocutor's pauses. Surely, thought Jimmy, it will produce a monstrous birth, something to make suspicion itself turn pale.

'Now don't you tell nothing of what I'm saying to you,' said the old man at length. 'But it's my belief that Mr Rollo don't want his brother shut up; no, nor thought to be mad. And why? Because if people know he's mad, and he goes and does another murder, they'll just pop him in the lunatic asylum and all his money will go to government and charity. But if he does a murder like you or me might, and the circumstances are circumstantial, he'll be hanged for it, and all the money and the castle and the coal-mine will go into the pockets of Mr Rollo.'

'I see,' said Jimmy. 'It sounds very simple.'

'I'm not swearing there's anything of the sort in Mr Rollo's mind,' said the old man. 'But that's the way I should look at it if I was him. Now I must be getting along. Good-night, sir.'

'Good-night.'

Of course it wasn't really night, only tea-time, five o'clock; but he and his acquaintance would meet no more that day, so perhaps the man was right to say good-night. Jimmy's thoughts, as he worked his way up the castle mound, were unclear and rather painful. He didn't believe a tithe of what the old man said. It was not even a distortion of the truth; it was ignorant and vulgar slander, and had no relation to the truth except by a kind of contiguity. But it infected his mood and gave a disagreeable direction to his thoughts. He was lonely; Randolph had not appeared at lunch, and he missed Rollo, and even more he missed (though this surprised him) Rollo's wife. He hadn't seen much of them, but suddenly he felt the need of their company. But goodness knows where they are, thought Jimmy; I can't even telephone to them. In the midst of these uneasy reflections he reached his bedroom door. Walking in, he could not for a moment understand why the place looked so strange. The he realized; it was empty. All his things had been cleared out of it.

'Evidently,' thought Jimmy, 'they've mistaken the day I was going away, and packed me!' An extraordinary sensation of relief surged up into his heart. Since his luggage was nowhere to be seen, it must have been stacked in the hall, ready for his departure by the evening train. Picturing himself at the booking-office of Verdew Grove station buying a ticket for London, Jimmy started for the hall.

William cut short his search.

'Were are looking for your things, sir?' he asked, with a slight smile. 'Because they're in the Onyx Room. We've moved you, sir.'

'Oh,' said Jimmy, following in the footman's wake. 'Why?'

'It was Mr Verdew's orders, sir. I told him the light was faulty in your bedroom, so he said to move you into the Onyx Room.'

'The room next his?'

'That's right, sir.'

'Couldn't the fuse be mended?'

'I don't think it was the fuse, sir.'

'Oh, I thought you said it was.'

So this was the Onyx Room – the room, Jimmy suddenly remembered, that Rollo had meant him to have in the beginning. Certainly its colours were dark and lustrous and laid on in layers, but Jimmy didn't care for them. Even the ceiling was parti-coloured. Someone must have been given a free hand here;

perhaps Vera had done the decoration. The most beautiful thing in the room was the Chinese screen masking the door that communicated, he supposed, with Randolph's bedroom. What a clatter it would make if it fell, thought Jimmy, studying the heavy, dark, dully-shining panels of the screen. The door opening would knock it over. He heard the footman's voice.

'Is it for one night or more, sir? I've packed up some of your things.'

'I'm not sure yet,' said Jimmy. 'William, will this screen move?'

The footman took hold of the screen with both hands and telescoped it against his chest. There was revealed an ordinary-looking door covered with green baize. Jimmy could see the point of a key-head, so the door was probably not very thick.

'This used to be the dressing-room,' William volunteered, as though making a contribution to Jimmy's unspoken thoughts.

'Thank you,' said Jimmy, 'and would you mind putting the screen back? . . . And, William!'

The footman stopped.

'There's still time to send a telegram?'

'Oh yes, sir. There's a form here.'

All through his solitary tea Jimmy debated with himself as to whether he should send the telegram — a telegram of recall, of course, it would be. The message presented no difficulty. 'Wire if Croxford case opens Tuesday.' He knew that it did, but his attendance was not at all necessary. He was undoubtedly suffering from a slight attack of nerves; and nowadays one didn't defy nerves, one yielded to them gracefully. 'I know that if I stay I shall have a bad night,' he thought; 'I might as well spend it in the train.' But of course he hadn't meant to go at all; he had even promised Rollo to stay. He had wanted to stay. To leave abruptly tonight would be doubly rude: rude to Randolph, rude to Rollo. Only Vera would be pleased. Vera, whose clumsy attempt to lure him to London he had so easily seen through. Vera, whose 'I shall be furious if you don't come' rankled whenever he thought of it. Every moment added its quota to the incubus of indecision that paralysed his mind. Manners, duty, wishes, fears, all were contradictory, all pulled in different directions. A gust of apprehension sent him hot-foot to the writing-table. The telegram was ready written when, equally strong, an access of self-respect came and made him tear it up. At last he had an idea. At six o'clock he would send the telegram; the office might still be open. There might still be time to get a reply. If, in spite of his twofold obstacle he had an answer, he could take it as the voice of fate, and leave that night . . .

At half-past seven William came in to draw the curtains; he also brought a message. Mr Verdew begged Mr Rintoul to excuse him, but he felt a little unwell, and was dining in his own room. He hoped to see Mr Rintoul tomorrow to say good-bye. 'You are going, then, sir?' added the footman.

Jimmy blindfolded his will, and took an answer at random from among the tablets of his mind.

'Yes. And – William!' he called out.

'Sir?'

'I suppose it's too late now for me to get an answer to my telegram?'

'I'm afraid so, sir.'

For a second Jimmy sunned himself in a warm flow of recovered self-esteem. Luck had saved him from a humiliating flight. Now his one regret was that his nerves had cheated him of those few extra days at Verdew. 'If there had been a bolt on my side of the green door,' he said to himself, 'I should never have sent that telegram.'

How like in some ways, was the last evening to the first. As bedtime approached, he became acutely conscious of his surroundings – of the stone floors, the vaulted passages, the moat, the drawbridge – all those concrete signs which seemed to recall the past and substitute it for the present. He was completely isolated and immured; he could scarcely believe he would be back in the real, living world tomorrow. Another glass of whisky would bring the centuries better into line. It did; and, emboldened by its heady fumes, he inspected, with the aid of his candle (for the ground-floor lights had been turned out) the defences of door and window, and marvelled anew at their parade of clumsy strength. Why all these precautions when the moat remained, a flawless girdle of protection?

But was it flawless? Lying in bed, staring at the painted ceiling, with its squares and triangles and riot of geometrical designs, Jimmy smiled to remember how Rollo had once told him of a secret entrance, known only to him. He had promised to show it to Jimmy, but he had forgotten. A nice fellow Rollo, but he didn't believe they would ever know each other much better. When dissimilar natures come together, the friendship blossoms quickly, and as quickly fades. Rollo and Jimmy just tolerated each other – they didn't share their lives, their secrets, their secret passages . . .

Jimmy was lying on his back, his head sunk on the brightly lit pillow, his mind drowsier than his digestion. To his departing consciousness the ceiling looked like a great five of diamonds spread over his head; the scarlet lozenges moved on hinges, he knew that quite well, and as they moved they gave a glimpse of black and let in a draught. Soon there would be a head poking through them all, instead of through this near corner one, and that would be more symmetrical. But if I stand on the bed I can shut them; they will close with a click. If only this one wasn't such a weight and didn't stick so . . .

Jimmy awoke in a sweat, still staring at the ceiling. It heaved and writhed like a half-dead moth on the setting-board. But the walls stood still, so that there was something more than whisky at the back of it. And yet, when he looked again, the ceiling did not budge.

The dream was right; he could touch the ceiling by standing on the bed. But only with the tips of his fingers. What he needed was a bar of some kind with which to prise it open. He looked round the room, and could see nothing suitable but a towel-horse. But there were plenty of walking-sticks downstairs. To light his candle and put on his dressing-gown and slippers was the work of a moment. He reached the door in less time than it takes to tell. But he got no further, because the door was locked.

Jimmy's heart began to beat violently. Panic bubbled up in him like water in a syphon. He took a wild look around the room, ran to the bed-head, and pressed the bell-button as though he meant to flatten it in its socket. Relief stole in his heart. Already he heard in imagination the quick patter of feet in the corridor, the hurried, whispered explanations, the man's reassuring voice: 'I'll be with you in a moment, sir.' Already he felt slightly ashamed of his precipitate summons, and began to wonder how he should explain it away. The minutes passed, and nothing happened. He need not worry yet; it would take William some time to dress, and no doubt he had a long way to come. But Jimmy's returning anxiety cried out for some distraction, so he left the edge of the bed where he had been sitting, fetched the towel-horse, and, balancing unsteadily on the mattress, began to prod the ceiling. Down came little flakes and pellets of painted plaster; they littered the sheets, and would be very uncomfortable to sleep on... Jimmy stooped to flick them away, and saw from the tail of his eye that since he rang five minutes had gone by. He resumed the muffled tattoo on the ceiling. Suddenly it gave, the red diamond shot upwards and fell back, revealing a patch of black and letting in a rush of cool air.

As, stupefied, Jimmy lowered his eyes, they fell upon the screen. It was moving stealthily outwards, toppling into the room. Already he would see a thin strip of the green door. The screen swayed, paused, seemed to hang by a hair. Then, its leaves collapsing inwards upon each other, it fell with a great crash upon the floor. In the opening stood Randolph, fully dressed; he had a revolver in his right hand, and there was a knife between his teeth. It was curved and shining, and he looked as though he were taking a bite out of the new moon.

The shot missed Jimmy's swaying legs, the knife only grazed his ankle, and he was safe in the darkness of the attic, with the bolt of the trap-door securely shut. He ran trembling in the direction the draught came from, and was rewarded first by a sense of decreasing darkness, and then by a glimpse, through a framed opening in the roof, of the stars and the night sky.

The opening was low down, and to climb out was easy. He found himself in a leaden gully, bounded on one side by a shallow parapet two feet high, and on the other, as it seemed, by the slope of the roof. Finding his way along the gully, he was brought up sharp against an octagonal turret, that clearly marked the end of the building. The moat was directly below him. Turning to the left, he encountered another similar turret, and turning to the left again he found himself up against a wall surmounted by tall chimneys. This wall appeared to be scored with projections and indentations – soot-doors he guessed them to be; he hoped to be able to use them to climb the wall, but they were awkwardly spaced, close to the parapet, and if he missed his footing he ran the risk of falling over its edge.

He now felt a curious lightheartedness, as though he had shuffled off every responsibility: responsibility towards his pyjamas, which were torn and dirty, towards his foot, which was bleeding, towards trains, letters, engagements – all the petty and important demands of life. Cold, but not unhappy, he sat down to await daybreak.

The clock had just chimed three-quarters, which three-quarters he did not know, when he heard a scraping sound that seemed to come from the corresponding parapet across the roof. He listened crouching in the angle between the chimney wall and the battlement. His fears told him that the sound was following the track by which he had come; the shuffling grew indistinct, and then, the first turret passed, began to draw nearer. It could only be Randolph, who clearly had some means of access to the roof other than the trap-door in Jimmy's bedroom. He must have, or he could not have reached it to spy on his victim while he was asleep. Now he was turning the last corner. Jimmy acted quickly and with the courage of desperation. At the corner where he crouched there projected above the battlement three sides of an octagonel turret, repeating the design of the true turrets at the end. Grasping the stone as well as he could, he lowered himself into space. It was a terrible moment, but the cautious shuffle of Randolph's approach deadened his fear. His arms almost at their full stretch, he felt the dripstone underneath his feet. It seemed about six inches wide, with a downward curve, but it sufficed. He changed his grip from the plain stone band of the parapet to the pierced masonry beneath it, which afforded a better purchase, and held his breath. Randolph could not find him unless he leant right over the balustrade. This he did not do. He muttered to himself; he climbed up to the apex of the roof; he examined the flue-doors, or whatever they were. All this Jimmy could clearly see through the quatrefoil to which he was clinging. Randolph muttered, 'I shall find him when the light comes,' and then he disappeared. The clock struck four, four-fifteen, four-thirty, and then a diffused pallor began to show itself in the eastern sky.

The numbness that had taken hold of Jimmy's body began to invade his mind, which grew dull and sleepy under the effort of compelling his tired hands to retain their hold. His back curved outwards, his head sank upon his breast; the changes of which his cramped position admitted were too slight to afford his body relief. So that he could not at once look round when he heard close above his head the sound of an opening door and the sharp rattle of falling mortar. He recognized the figure as it passed him – Rollo's.

Jimmy restrained his impulse to call out. Why had Rollo come back? Why was he swaggering over the roofs of Verdew Castle at daybreak looking as though he owned it? It was not his yet. Rollo turned, and in the same leisurely fashion walked back towards

Jimmy's corner. His face was set and pale, but there was triumph in his eyes, and cruelty, and the marks of many passions which his everyday exterior had concealed. Then his eyebrows went up, his chin quivered, and his under-lip shot out and seemed to stretch across his face. 'Just five minutes more, five minutes more; I'll give him another five minutes,' he kept muttering to himself. He leaned back against the wall. Jimmy could have touched the laces of his shoes, which were untied and dirty. 'Poor old Jimmy, poor old James!' Rollo suddenly chanted, in a voice that was very distinct, but quite unlike his own. To Jimmy's confused mind he seemed to be speaking of two people, neither of whom was connected with himself. 'Never mind, Jimmy,' Rollo added in the conciliatory tone of one who, overcome by his better nature, at last gives up teasing. 'Anyhow, it's ten to one against.' He stumbled down the gully and round the bend.

Jimmy never knew how he summoned strength to climb over the parapet. He found himself sprawling in the gully, panting and faint. But he had caught sight of a gaping hole like a buttery hatch amid the tangle of soot-doors, and he began to crawl towards it. He was trying to bring his stiff knee up to his good one when from close by his left ear he heard a terrible scream. It went shooting up, and seemed to make a glittering arc of sound in the half-lit sky. He also thought he heard the words, 'Oh, God, Randolph, it's me!' but of this he was never certain. But through all the windings of Rollo's bolt hole, until it discharged itself at the base of a ruined newel-staircase among the outbuildings, he still heard the agonized gasping, spasmodic, yet with a horrible rhythm of its own, that followed Rollo's scream. He locked the cracked, paintless door with the key that Rollo had left, and found himself among the lanes.

Late in the evening of the same day a policeman asked to see Mrs Verdew, who was sitting in a bedroom in the King's Head inn at Fremby, a market town ten miles from Verdew Castle. She had been sitting there all day, getting up from time to time to glance at a slip of paper pinned to one of the pillows. It was dated, '7.30 a.m., July 10th,' and said, 'Back in a couple of hours. Have to see a man about a car. Sorry – Rollo.' She wouldn't believe the constable when he said that her husband had met with an accident some time early that morning, probably about five o'clock. 'But look! But look!' she cried. 'See for yourself! It is his own handwriting! He says he went away at half-past seven. Why are all Englishmen so difficult to convince?'

'We have a statement from Mr Randolph Verdew,' said the policeman gently. 'He said that he . . . he . . . he met Mr Rollo at the castle in the early hours of the morning.'

'But how can you be so stupid!' cried Mrs Verdew. 'It wasn't Rollo – it was Mr Rintoul who . . . '

'What name is that?' asked the policeman, taking out his notebook.

SHORT STORY COLLECTIONS IN EVERYMAN

A SELECTION

The Secret Self
Short Stories by Women
'A superb collection' *Guardian* **£4.99**

Selected Short Stories and Poems
THOMAS HARDY
The best of Hardy's Wessex in a unique selection **£4.99**

The Best of Sherlock Holmes
ARTHUR CONAN DOYLE
All the favourite adventures in one volume **£4.99**

Great Tales of Detection
Nineteen Stories
Chosen by Dorothy L. Sayers **£3.99**

Short Stories
KATHERINE MANSFIELD
A selection displaying the remarkable range of Mansfield's writing **£3.99**

Selected Stories
RUDYARD KIPLING
Includes stories chosen to reveal the 'other' Kipling **£4.50**

The Strange Case of Dr Jekyll and Mr Hyde and Other Stories
R. L. STEVENSON
An exciting selection of gripping tales from a master of suspense **£3.99**

Modern Short Stories 2: 1940-1980
Thirty-one stories from the greatest modern writers **£3.50**

The Day of Silence and Other Stories
GEORGE GISSING
Gissing's finest stories, available for the first time in one volume **£4.99**

Selected Tales
HENRY JAMES
Stories portraying the tensions between private life and the outside world **£5.99**

£4.99

£6.99

AVAILABILITY

All books are available from your local bookshop or direct from
Littlehampton Book Services Cash Sales, 14 Eldon Way, LinesideEstate, Littlehampton, West Sussex BN17 7HE. PRICES ARE SUBJECT TO CHANGE.

To order any of the books, please enclose a cheque (in £ sterling) made payable to Littlehampton Book Services, or phone your order through with credit card details (Access, Visa or Mastercard) on 0903 721596 (24 hour answering service) stating card number and expiry date. Please add £1.25 for package and postage to the total value of your order.

CLASSIC NOVELS IN EVERYMAN

A SELECTION

The Way of All Flesh
SAMUEL BUTLER
A savagely funny odyssey from joyless duty to unbridled liberalism £4.99

Born in Exile
GEORGE GISSING
A rationalist's progress towards love and compromise in class-ridden Victorian England £4.99

David Copperfield
CHARLES DICKENS
One of Dickens' best-loved novels, brimming with humour £3.99

The Last Chronicle of Barset
ANTHONY TROLLOPE
Trollope's magnificent conclusion to his Barsetshire novels £4.99

He Knew He Was Right
ANTHONY TROLLOPE
Sexual jealousy, money and women's rights within marriage – a novel ahead of its time £6.99

Tess of the D'Urbervilles
THOMAS HARDY
The powerful, poetic classic of wronged innocence £3.99

Wuthering Heights and Poems
EMILY BRONTE
A powerful work of genius – one of the great masterpieces of literature £3.50

Tom Jones
HENRY FIELDING
The wayward adventures of one of literatures most likable heroes £5.99

The Master of Ballantrae and Weir of Hermiston
R. L. STEVENSON
Together in one volume, two great novels of high adventure and family conflict £4.99

£3.99

£2.99

£3.99

AVAILABILITY

All books are available from your local bookshop or direct from
Littlehampton Book Services Cash Sales, 14 Eldon Way, LinesideEstate, Littlehampton, West Sussex BN17 7HE. PRICES ARE SUBJECT TO CHANGE.

To order any of the books, please enclose a cheque (in £ sterling) made payable to Littlehampton Book Services, or phone your order through with credit card details (Access, Visa or Mastercard) on 0903 721596 (24 hour answering service) stating card number and expiry date. Please add £1.25 for package and postage to the total value of your order.

CLASSIC FICTION IN EVERYMAN

A SELECTION

Frankenstein
MARY SHELLEY
A masterpiece of Gothic terror in its original 1818 version **£3.99**

Dracula
BRAM STOKER
One of the best known horror stories in the world **£3.99**

The Diary of A Nobody
GEORGE AND WEEDON GROSSMITH
A hilarious account of suburban life in Edwardian London **£4.99**

Some Experiences and Further Experiences of an Irish R. M.
SOMERVILLE AND ROSS
Gems of comic exuberance and improvisation **£4.50**

Three Men in a Boat
JEROME K. JEROME
English humour at its best **£2.99**

Twenty Thousand Leagues under the Sea
JULES VERNE
Scientific fact combines with fantasy in this prophetic tale of underwater adventure **£4.99**

The Best of Father Brown
G. K. CHESTERTON
An irresistible selection of crime stories – unique to Everyman **£3.99**

The Collected Raffles
E. W. HORNUNG
Dashing exploits from the most glamorous figure in crime fiction **£4.99**

£2.99

£5.99

£5.99

AVAILABILITY

All books are available from your local bookshop or direct from
Littlehampton Book Services Cash Sales, 14 Eldon Way, LinesideEstate, Littlehampton, West Sussex BN17 7HE. PRICES ARE SUBJECT TO CHANGE.

To order any of the books, please enclose a cheque (in £ sterling) made payable to Littlehampton Book Services, or phone your order through with credit card details (Access, Visa or Mastercard) on 0903 721596 (24 hour answering service) stating card number and expiry date. Please add £1.25 for package and postage to the total value of your order.

WOMEN'S WRITING IN EVERYMAN

A SELECTION

Female Playwrights of the Restoration
FIVE COMEDIES
Rediscovered literary treasures in a unique selection **£5.99**

The Secret Self
SHORT STORIES BY WOMEN
'A superb collection' *Guardian* **£4.99**

Short Stories
KATHERINE MANSFIELD
An excellent selection displaying the remarkable range of Mansfield's talent **£3.99**

Women Romantic Poets 1780-1830: An Anthology
Hidden talent from the Romantic era, rediscovered for the first time **£5.99**

Selected Poems
ELIZABETH BARRETT BROWNING
A major contribution to our appreciation of this inspiring and innovative poet **£5.99**

Frankenstein
MARY SHELLEY
A masterpiece of Gothic terror in its original 1818 version **£3.99**

The Life of Charlotte Brontë
MRS GASKELL
A moving and perceptive tribute by one writer to another **£4.99**

Vindication of the Rights of Woman and The Subjection of Women
MARY WOLLSTONECRAFT
AND J. S. MILL
Two pioneering works of early feminist thought **£4.99**

The Pastor's Wife
ELIZABETH VON ARNIM
A funny and accomplished novel by the author of *Elizabeth and Her German Garden* **£5.99**

£4.99

£2.99

£5.99

AVAILABILITY

All books are available from your local bookshop or direct from
Littlehampton Book Services Cash Sales, 14 Eldon Way, LinesideEstate, Littlehampton, West Sussex BN17 7HE. PRICES ARE SUBJECT TO CHANGE.

To order any of the books, please enclose a cheque (in £ sterling) made payable to Littlehampton Book Services, or phone your order through with credit card details (Access, Visa or Mastercard) on 0903 721596 (24 hour answering service) stating card number and expiry date. Please add £1.25 for package and postage to the total value of your order.

AMERICAN LITERATURE IN EVERYMAN

A SELECTION

Selected Poems
HENRY LONGFELLOW
A new selection spanning the whole of Longfellow's literary career **£7.99**

Typee
HERMAN MELVILLE
Melville's stirring debut, drawing directly on his own adventures in the South Sea **£4.99**

Billy Budd and Other Stories
HERMAN MELVILLE
The compelling parable of innocence destroyed by a fallen world **£4.99**

The Scarlet Letter
NATHANIEL HAWTHORNE
The compelling tale of an independent woman's struggle against a crushing moral code **£3.99**

The Last of The Mohicans
JAMES FENIMORE COOPER
The classic tale of old America, full of romantic adventure **£5.99**

The Red Badge of Courage
STEPHEN CRANE
A vivid portrayal of a young soldier's experience of the American Civil War **£2.99**

Essays and Poems
RALPH WALDO EMERSON
An indispensable edition celebrating one of the most influential American writers **£5.99**

The Federalist
HAMILTON, MADISON, AND JAY
Classics of political science, these essays helped to found the American Constitution **£6.99**

Leaves of Grass and Selected Prose
WALT WHITMAN
The best of Whitman in one volume **£6.99**

£5.99

£4.99

£4.99

AVAILABILITY

All books are available from your local bookshop or direct from
Littlehampton Book Services Cash Sales, 14 Eldon Way, LinesideEstate, Littlehampton, West Sussex BN17 7HE. PRICES ARE SUBJECT TO CHANGE.

To order any of the books, please enclose a cheque (in £ sterling) made payable to Littlehampton Book Services, or phone your order through with credit card details (Access, Visa or Mastercard) on 0903 721596 (24 hour answering service) stating card number and expiry date. Please add £1.25 for package and postage to the total value of your order.

ESSAYS, CRITICISM AND HISTORY IN EVERYMAN

A SELECTION

The Embassy to Constantinople and Other Writings
LIUDPRAND OF CREMONA
An insider's view of political machinations in medieval Europe **£5.99**

The Rights of Man
THOMAS PAINE
One of the great masterpieces of English radicalism **£4.99**

Speeches and Letters
ABRAHAM LINCOLN
A key document of the American Civil War **£4.99**

Essays
FRANCIS BACON
An excellent introduction to Bacon's incisive wit and moral outlook **£3.99**

Puritanism and Liberty: Being the Army Debates (1647-49) from the Clarke Manuscripts
A fascinating revelation of Puritan minds in action **£7.99**

History of His Own Time
BISHOP GILBERT BURNET
A highly readable contemporary account of the Glorious Revolution of 1688 **£7.99**

Biographia Literaria
SAMUEL TAYLOR COLERIDGE
A masterpiece of criticism, marrying the study of literature with philosophy **£4.99**

Essays on Literature and Art
WALTER PATER
Insights on culture and literature from a major voice of the 1890s **£3.99**

Chesterton on Dickens: Criticisms and Appreciations
A landmark in Dickens criticism, rarely surpassed **£4.99**

Essays and Poems
R. L. STEVENSON
Stevenson's hidden treasures in a new selection **£4.99**

£3.99

£4.99

AVAILABILITY

All books are available from your local bookshop or direct from
Littlehampton Book Services Cash Sales, 14 Eldon Way, LinesideEstate, Littlehampton, West Sussex BN17 7HE. PRICES ARE SUBJECT TO CHANGE.

To order any of the books, please enclose a cheque (in £ sterling) made payable to Littlehampton Book Services, or phone your order through with credit card details (Access, Visa or Mastercard) on 0903 721596 (24 hour answering service) stating card number and expiry date. Please add £1.25 for package and postage to the total value of your order.